Blessing's Baron

Seven Unsuitable Sisters
Book 1

BY MAEVE GREYSON

DRAGONBLADE PUBLISHING, INC.

Dragonblade Publishing, Inc. is an imprint of Kathryn Le Veque Novels, Inc.
P.O. Box 23
Moreno Valley, CA 92556
ceo@dragonbladepublishing.com

Produced in the United States of America

First Edition October 2024
Trade Paperback Edition

Additional Dragonblade books by Author Maeve Greyson

Seven Unsuitable Sisters Series
Blessing's Baron (Book 1)

The Sisterhood of Independent Ladies Series
To Steal a Duke (Book 1)
To Steal a Marquess (Book 2)
To Steal an Earl (Book 3)

Once Upon a Scot Series
A Scot of Her Own (Book 1)
A Scot to Have and to Hold (Book 2)
A Scot To Love and Protect (Book 3)

Time to Love a Highlander Series
Loving Her Highland Thief (Book 1)
Taming Her Highland Legend (Book 2)
Winning Her Highland Warrior (Book 3)
Capturing Her Highland Keeper (Book 4)
Saving Her Highland Traitor (Book 5)
Loving Her Lonely Highlander (Book 6)
Delighting Her Highland Devil (Book 7)
When the Midnight Bell Tolls (Novella)

Highland Heroes Series
The Guardian (Book 1)
The Warrior (Book 2)
The Judge (Book 3)
The Dreamer (Book 4)
The Bard (Book 5)
The Ghost (Book 6)
A Yuletide Yearning (Novella)

Love's Charity (Novella)

Also from Maeve Greyson
Guardian of Midnight Manor (Novella)
Once Upon a Haunted Highland Mist (Novella)

Chapter One

Broadmere House
London, England
Late September 1819

L ADY BLESSING ABAROUGH, *Essie* to her siblings and third-born of the eight offspring of the now sorrowfully departed Duke and Duchess of Broadmere, clenched her teeth and held her breath to keep the tears at bay. They had all known Papa would never last long without Mama at his side. He had adored her so, and when the dreadful consumption finally claimed her, he had been inconsolable. Now, a mere six months into the mourning for his precious Cassia, Papa had succumbed to a broken heart and joined his beloved in the great beyond.

Serendipity, Blessing's eldest sister, reached over and squeezed her hand. Blessing's sisters, all six of them, and her brother Chance had always teased that she was Papa's favorite. They didn't do it with malice or mean intent because, in truth, Papa cherished all his children and made them each feel special. But in her heart, Blessing knew without the slightest doubt she had always been closest to their wonderful father.

She cut a sideways glance at her only brother where he sat on the other side of Serendipity. Out of habit, they had seated themselves in birth order when Mr. Granville Sutherland, Papa and Mama's solicitor, gathered them into the parlor for the reading of the will.

Chance was now the fifth Duke of Broadmere at the tender age of two and twenty. While Blessing loved her brother, she harbored some doubt about his ability to take Papa's place as head of the family. As Mama had so often observed, Chance toiled most strenuously when it came to enjoyable activities, but when it came to applying himself to more sober endeavors, he dabbled at them.

Blessing eased out the breath she held, took in another, and held it again while blinking faster to beat back the tears. Her loneliness for Mama had barely become manageable, and now she faced the insurmountable task of grieving for Papa too. She swallowed hard and glanced at her brother again. He stared straight ahead, his powerful jaw locked in place, much as Papa had always done when he was determined to charge through an unpleasant situation. Blessing had no doubt Chance would do his best to care for them, but she wondered if his best would be good enough. In his defense, though, he did seem much older these days and far less carefree and haphazard than before.

Once again behind the gauzy black veil she had recently put away after the appropriate mourning period for Mama, Blessing shifted her attention to the esteemed Mr. Sutherland and his junior partner and son, Mr. Sutherland the younger. Mr. Sutherland the older, as the Abarough brood had taken to calling him after being introduced to his son, would keep Chance—or at least *attempt* to keep her brother—from doing anything foolhardy. She only prayed that Chance would heed the man's advice.

As the solicitor seated himself behind the small table placed in front of their line of chairs, she sat taller, perfecting her posture as Mama had always taught them. The kindly man with his snowy-white hair in barely tamed tufts looked as miserable as each of the eight Abaroughs. Blessing didn't doubt the man's sorrow was genuine. Mama and Papa had considered Mr. Sutherland a dear friend—not just a family solicitor.

He looked up from the papers in his hands and peered over the tops of his spectacles, eyeing each of them in turn before focusing on Chance. "With your permission, Your Grace?"

Chance paused a hairsbreadth longer than necessary, as if suddenly realizing that Mr. Sutherland was addressing him and not Papa. Blessing noticed how her brother flinched before tipping a curt nod. Her heart went out to him, and she prayed Papa had prepared him for what lay ahead.

Mr. Sutherland straightened the sheaf of papers by tapping them on the table until the edges were even. He neatly stacked the pile in front of him, slid his spectacles higher on his nose, and cleared his throat with a long, drawn-out *harrumph*. "I cannot express how much it pains me to be here today under these circumstances." His mournful expression spoke much louder than his words. He squinted at Serendipity, then swept his gaze to Blessing and on down the line of sisters, ending with Merry, the youngest Abarough daughter at the tender age of ten and five. "Your Papa set aside generous dowries as well as ample allotments for each of you, as I understand you well know, since he felt it important you be fully aware of your situations when the time came." He shook his head and gave a disgruntled snort. "Sadly, that time is now at hand, and my old friend knew it would be here before any of us were ready to embrace it."

He settled a worried scowl on Chance. "While Your Grace may not be pleased with the contents of this will, I do hope you bear in mind that your parents thought it best for all concerned. They constructed it as they did in the hopes that each of you would discover the same depths of joy and happiness they knew in their time together."

Chance narrowed his eyes as if sighting a target on the solicitor's forehead. "Pray, get on with it, Mr. Sutherland. Making this day draw out even longer than necessary is a cruelty I do not wish any of us to be forced to endure."

Mr. Sutherland gave the faintest nod, his face tightening with a thoughtful pucker. "Your Grace will not receive the entirety of his inheritance until all your sisters are married. Happily. To gentlemen of their own choosing. For love's sake—as your parents were."

Chance leaned forward, tilting his head as if that would help him hear the edict of the will differently. "I beg your pardon, Mr. Sutherland?"

The solicitor wet his lips, shifted with a deep inhale, then snorted the breath back out. "Your Grace shall receive a monthly stipend. An allowance set by your parents until such time as the conditions of the will are fully met. Your Papa thought the amount ample, but…"

"But?" Chance prompted him.

Mr. Sutherland cleared his throat. "You may find it somewhat *restrictive*, Your Grace."

"Why would my father do such a thing?" Chance demanded.

Blessing gritted her teeth to keep from reacting. Apparently, Papa had shared her doubts about Chance's ability to follow in his footsteps with any degree of success.

"Your parents thought long and thoroughly about the terms they wished to set in this will," Mr. Sutherland said. "They wanted each of you to marry for love, and for you, Your Grace…" He tucked his chin and cleared his throat again. "Your mother and father felt it would help you mature into your role as the fifth Duke of Broadmere with as little risk to the estate as possible."

"But my sisters are wholly unsuitable for the Marriage Mart!" Chance jumped to his feet as though ready to charge into battle. "My parents indulged them. Spoiled them beyond redemption." He flung a hand in the air and swept it down the line to include each of his siblings. "All seven are wild, giddy, opinionated things whom no man in his right mind would ever wish to marry." He jerked his head at Serendipity and Blessing. "And the lion's share of them are entirely too old to retrain and break to the *ton*'s bridle with any hope of success. We might have a chance at changing Merry's behavior, but even at her tender age of ten and five, that is extremely doubtful." He threw both hands in the air, then jabbed a finger at the pile of papers in front of the solicitor. "I want that abomination contested. Immediately."

Blessing and Serendipity rose in unison and turned on him.

"Now see here, Chance!" Serendipity poked him in the chest, backing him up a step. "You will apologize to us at once and stop behaving like an overgrown horse's arse. Do you hear me?"

"See what I mean?" Chance said to Mr. Sutherland before turning back to his sister. "You just proved my point, Seri. What woman speaks in such a manner?"

"A woman defending herself against an overgrown horse's arse." Blessing whipped off her veil and charged toward him. "Mama would box your ears, and Papa would punch you in the nose for saying such things just because you're afraid you won't get to go to the gaming hells or travel to the Continent at the slightest whim, as you've always done before."

"Now, ladies," Mr. Sutherland began, then snapped his mouth shut when both of them turned a silencing glare on him before continuing to advance on their brother.

"Everything I said was true," Chance said, jutting his chin higher. "Serendipity, you with your mother henning won't marry until the rest are married off and happily settled. Blessing, you won't leave that infernal observatory Papa built for you. Fortuity wants nothing but her books. Grace is infatuated with her horses and dogs. Joy gambles worse than I do—"

"I do not!" Joy stood at attention and pointed at him. "I always win my bets. You always lose."

"Be that as it may..." Chance continued, backing away. "The only thing Felicity loves is food, and Merry is too young to be married!"

"That is the first thing you have said that is not cruel." Merry popped up and flitted to her sisters to administer hugs. "And Blessing is right. Mama would box your ears, and Papa would thrash you for being so very mean to us on this terrible day."

"I am not being mean." Chance backed into the wall with a

solid thump. "I am being honest."

"Is this any way to honor your parents?" Mr. Sutherland banged his fist on the table. "Shame on all of you! Your parents loved each of you more than life itself and drew up this will out of that love." He yanked on his sleeves to straighten them, then shook a finger at Chance. "Apologize to your sisters, Your Grace. Even when overwrought or angry, a brother should always protect his sisters. I know your papa taught you better behavior than I have witnessed thus far." Before Chance could speak, Mr. Sutherland continued, "Ladies, you would do well to heed what your brother has so clumsily noted and attempt to rectify your actions or resign yourselves to living under the same roof with him for the remainder of your days." He tugged on his sleeves again. "I ask you—is that what you truly wish for yourselves? A future where you never have homes of your own? No children? A future where you are nothing more than a sibling? I understand that the circumstances of the past few years have trapped you— what with caring for your mother during her illness, mourning her death, and now losing your father." He threw up his hands, then thumped the table again. "Do you not wish to move forward and claim the happy lives you so richly deserve?"

"All I wish is that Mama and Papa were still here," Blessing said, her voice cracking, and the tears she had held at bay finally escaping. Oh, how she ached for her parents and would give anything for another of their hugs.

Mr. Sutherland's shoulders slumped, his son bowed his head, and Chance scrubbed his face with both hands.

"I wish they were still here too, Essie," Chance told her, his tone suddenly hoarse with emotion. He pulled her and Serendipity into a hug and waved for the rest of his sisters to join in. "Forgive me, my precious pets. I was thinking only of myself. Seri and Essie have the right of it. I am a horse's arse."

"An overgrown horse's arse," Serendipity corrected him.

"An enormously overgrown one," Joy added.

"Mama and Papa are probably laughing right now." Blessing

pulled a handkerchief from her sleeve and pressed it to the corners of her eyes. "Remember how they always stood back and let us squabble, laughing all the while unless one of us picked up a weapon?"

"They always wanted us to work it out for ourselves," Chance said. "Work together and negotiate a peace acceptable to all parties involved."

"Without bullying, lying, or cheating." The knot in Blessing's throat loosened just a little. Mama and Papa were together again. That was all that really mattered for now. "Surely, between the eight of us, we can figure this terrible new time of our lives out?"

"As I see it, it is quite easy," Chance said with a subtle wiggle of a blond eyebrow. "All of you simply need to marry as soon as possible."

"Happily marry for love." Blessing cut her eyes over at Mr. Sutherland. "Correct?"

With a hint of relief in his smile, the old solicitor nodded. "Yes, Lady Blessing. Happily marry for love. Not for dowry or duty."

"Heaven help us," Chance groaned. "We shall be trapped together till the grave."

❧

Broadmere House
London, England
April 1820

"You are the eldest sister, Seri. That makes it only proper that your lovely neck be first in the marriage noose." Blessing moved out from behind the telescope and pulled a face at Serendipity, resenting the interruption more than her sibling would ever know. "Besides—if Chance had his way about it, our family would be the talk of the *ton* for having the first wedding in London with seven brides and grooms. This Season, no less." She couldn't resist rolling her eyes. "Wouldn't that confuse our doddering old vicar?"

"Essie!" Serendipity gave her the very same look Mama had always used whenever less than impressed with her children's conversations. She added a heavy sigh. "I shall pray for your soul."

"Pray for your own soul," Blessing advised with a warning tip of her head. "You are as deep in this muddle as the rest of us. More so, really." She couldn't resist a petty smirk. "What with your being the eldest."

"Do you not wish to marry?"

"Of course I wish to marry. Someday off in the future. Under my terms—and the terms of the will. Not to satisfy Chance's whims, nor your intention to parade us through every social gathering available as though we are fruits that must be promptly eaten before we rot." Blessing glared at her sister, daring her to deny it. "And as I said, as eldest, you should be eaten first."

Serendipity's dark sapphire eyes flashed with irritation as she smoothed a stray curl behind her ear, a curl so blonde it was almost as white as a dove's breast. Blessing had always envied her sister for the shade of her eyes. While the color of their hair was the same snowy blonde, and their height and slenderness very much alike, Blessing's eyes were a light, clear blue like that of tinted crystal rather than the deep, regal shade of her sister's.

Marching forward with the tight-lipped expression that warned her usually amiable nature had reached its limit, Serendipity closed the astrological journal with such a resounding pop that the small table on which it rested shuddered. "I cannot in good conscience marry and leave this home until I see each of you happily settled in the love match Mama and Papa envisioned for us all. I promised Mama. Would you have me go back on my word? Word given during Mama's last days?"

Blessing bowed her head. She had pushed her dearest sister too far. "No, Seri. I would never ask you to break your word to Mama. You know that." Then an irksome suspicion filled her, making her slowly lift her head and narrow her eyes. "You already knew the terms of the will. Even before Mama died. Didn't you?"

Serendipity turned aside while setting her chin to a haughty angle. "What a ridiculous thing to say."

"And yet you do not deny it." Blessing waited, knowing her sister to be a miserably poor liar. When they were little and into mischief, Serendipity's inability to lie had gotten them sent to bed without their supper on numerous occasions. "Mama told you what the will said, and you didn't think to warn the rest of us?"

Her sister twitched a shrug. "There was nothing to warn of. It is only natural for all of us to marry someday, and Mama and I may have discussed it a time or two." She aimed a pointed glare at Blessing. "Why do you think Mama insisted we all be presented before she died? Even when Merry and Felicity were entirely too young to come out officially in Society? It brought her great comfort to know we had been to the drawing room, as behooves the daughter of an esteemed peer—especially since it was Queen Charlotte's final drawing room before she passed."

"I am hurt that you did not share this with me." And Blessing *was* hurt. Deeply. As the two eldest and most like-minded, according to Papa, she and Serendipity shared everything from a bedchamber to dresses, slippers, and opinions. Fortuity, the next sister in line, shared their bedchamber as well but always kept her nose buried in her books and papers.

Blessing folded her arms across the front of her favorite morning dress of pale blue edged in lace and fancifully sprinkled with darker blue cornflowers. At a little over six months since Papa's passing, they had only just set aside the black bombazine of mourning. Once more, color filled the Broadmere household, yet the dark cloud of Chance's anxiousness to marry them off added a grayish tint to everything like the swash of a dirty paintbrush across a precious watercolor.

"I have decided not to marry," she announced, meaning it more than she had ever meant anything before.

Serendipity pinched the bridge of her nose as if suffering from the sudden onset of a headache. When she lifted her head, she looked at Blessing with such weariness that it tugged at her sister's heart. "You wish to spend the rest of your days living with Chance? A man capable of becoming even more fractious than a spoiled toddler denied its sweets?"

"Chance never comes to my observatory." Blessing swept a heartfelt gaze around the wondrous room Papa had built for her. A room made for studying the stars. She and Papa had shared many a robust conversation about the mysteries of the universe here. "My dear brother could either remain here at the town-house or move to one of our other residences." Although she very much doubted he would ever give over his place in London without an unpleasant scene. After all, he enjoyed the many amusements the city had to offer.

"Nevertheless, Lady Atterley was a dear friend of Mama's," Serendipity said, changing the subject with her gentle but firm stubbornness. "She is giving this ball to reintroduce us to Society as she knew Mama would have wanted."

"Just because you were Mama's favorite does not afford you the right to use her memory as a weapon to achieve the results you wish." While holding her sister in a hard glare, Blessing reopened the astrological journal with a defiant thump.

"Chance was Mama's favorite, and you very well know it." Serendipity returned a hard glare of her own. "We must attend. All of us. Chance has already accepted." She waved Blessing forward. "Come. We must choose our gowns and then guide the others in their choices."

"Merry is naught but ten and six, and Felicity ten and seven. A bit young to be used as bait to snare Chance's full inheritance, don't you think?" Blessing refused to allow some lecherous old dowry hunter to sink his claws into her youngest sisters.

Serendipity moved to the doorway, glanced up and down the hallway, then lowered her voice. "While I have not addressed that particular fact with our brother, please know that I keep it at the forefront of my thoughts." With a significant arch of her fair eyebrows, she added, "Always."

"Meaning?"

"Meaning I intend to ensure that Merry and Felicity have at least two more years of grace from Chance's edict to fall in love and marry. They will attend the parties to keep up appearances and give Chance a false sense of our honoring his wishes, but I refuse to allow them to be sacrificed like a pair of fatted calves."

"Milk-fed veal," Blessing corrected her, "and at least we agree on that."

"I am not the enemy here," Serendipity countered. She held out her hand. "Now, come. We shall choose our gowns, guide the others in their choices, and then enjoy a nice pot of tea before time to dress."

Thankfully, as they swept up the stairs, they did not encounter their brother. Blessing flexed her fingers, wishing she were a male so she could punch Chance in the nose. A hint of remorse flickered through her at the scandalous thought. Mama and Papa would not approve of such unladylike ideas at all.

As they entered the room, their sister Fortuity, Tutie to those who wished to tease her, never paused or looked up from her writing desk in her corner of the expansive bedchamber the three of them shared. The other four sisters, Grace, Joy, Felicity, and Merry, shared an even larger suite of rooms on the same floor—the two suites connected by a shared sitting room.

"Time to scrub the ink from your fingers, dear sister." Blessing pulled open both doors of her wardrobe and tried to stir at least a modicum of interest in dressing for the evening. "Lady Atterley's ball is tonight. Remember?"

Fortuity lifted her golden blonde head, feigned a cough, then patted her chest. "I fear I am unwell and will not be able to attend." She cleared her throat again before dipping her quill and continuing to scratch across the foolscap in front of her.

"You lie as poorly as Seri," Blessing said with a disgusted shake of her head. "Did it ever occur to you that claiming poor health would be much more convincing if you took to your bed and pinched your cheeks to make them appear flushed?" Honestly, was it any wonder that she and her sisters had never gotten away with the slightest bit of mischief as children?

Fortuity eyed her with a pained frown as though suddenly realizing she had planned her subterfuge poorly. "I felt compelled to finish this chapter."

"Well, you are also compelled to attend Lady Atterley's ball with the rest of us," Serendipity said as she brought forward several choices of gowns. "And I am glad you lie as poorly as I do." She cut a sour look at Blessing. "One should not be proud or accomplished when it comes to the telling of falsehoods."

"One should be if they wish to get away with anything other than sitting in the parlor and discussing the weather," Blessing said under her breath as she dove back into the depths of her wardrobe. What did it matter what she wore, since she in no way wished to attract attention? She chewed on her lip while eyeing her gowns. Nothing too fetching would do, but, then again, anything horrendous would as much as shout her intentions to avoid matrimony at all costs—or at least avoid it until she was ready.

The simple blue satin made somewhat fancy by a diaphanous overlay of even paler blue that started at the empire waist and fluttered gracefully to the floor to give the impression of a breezy blue mist would do. No lace, sparkling glass beads, seed pearls, or delicate embroidery decorated the gown. It was simple, subdued, and the perfect thing to wear when one wished to fade into the background and disappear. She pulled it from the wardrobe and draped it over the chair beside her bed.

"Fortuity?" She understood her sister completely, but this battle they faced had to be played with a great deal more cunning than simply ignoring it or trying to run and hide. "Do work on ridding your fingers of the ink stains. Please? I do not like this any more than you do, but as Seri so coldly pointed out, we have no choice."

"I did not point out anything in a cold manner," Serendipity said, her retort muffled since she was still somewhat buried in Fortuity's wardrobe. She withdrew a gown of the palest yellow and held it high. "This one? Isn't this one of your favorites?"

"Does it really matter?" Fortuity asked with a despondent sigh.

"Of course it matters," Serendipity said with a strained smile that made Blessing arch both her fair brows. "One must always strive to look one's best."

"Must one?" Blessing couldn't resist asking in her most impertinent tone.

"Yes, one must," Serendipity forced through clenched teeth before turning back to Fortuity. "Make the best of it, sister. That is all any of us can do."

"And not fall in love," Blessing advised with a wicked grin. "Remember the requirements of the will. We do not *have* to marry anyone we do not wish to marry."

A thoughtfulness came over Fortuity like the lazy rising of the sun. "That is right. Darling brother cannot marry us off to whomever he wishes if he expects to gain access to the entirety of the Broadmere accounts." She set her quill aside and stoppered her inkwell. "Is the water Meggie brought up still quite warm? Warm works best on these stains." Without waiting for an answer, Fortuity hurried into the dressing room that also served as a place for either bathing in the lovely copper tub at its center or much quicker refreshing at the counter that held three large porcelain bowls with matching pitchers filled with water.

"Do not encourage her defiance," Serendipity whispered to Blessing. "You know how easily sparks can burst into raging infernos between her and Chance."

"Dearest Seri." Blessing shook her head in disbelief as she returned to the blue satin gown she had laid out and tried to remember if she had loaned the matching slippers to one of the other sisters. "Are you so naïve as to believe there will be anything but raging infernos in our foreseeable future?"

"I do so hate conflict."

"I know." Blessing offered her sister a sincere smile. Serendipity had always been the peacekeeper. "But you might as well resign yourself to the fact that our household will be in an uproar for quite a while." She went to the bellpull beside the door and tugged on it. "Gird your loins, sister. We are at war."

Chapter Two

L ORD THORNE KNIGHTWOOD, the baron since his odious father's passing, handed off his hat, gloves, and greatcoat to the Atterley manservant waiting to attend arriving guests in the cloakroom. He kept an eye on his mother as a maid helped her remove her cloak and offered assistance in changing out of the serviceable boots the eccentric lady had insisted on wearing to prevent any soiling of her satin slippers that perfectly matched her gown.

Unfortunately for his mother, the respectful maid kept her head bowed and her chin tucked so tightly to her chest that her mouth was not visible, making it impossible for Lady Roslynn Knightwood to read the girl's lips and understand what she said. Thorne hurried over and directed the young woman while keeping his face turned toward his mother so she might realize what was happening.

Appreciation for his tactfulness gleamed in his dear parent's eyes before she cast a beaming smile upon the young maid. "Thank you ever so much for helping with my slippers. In my excitement to join the festivities, I fear I paid no attention at all to what you were saying."

"Happy to be of help, my lady." The maid offered a polite curtsy, then hurried off to store away Lady Roslynn's things until such time as she called for them.

Thorne arched a dark brow at his mother as he offered his

arm.

"Do not say it," she warned him in a stern whisper. "I refuse to be seen out and about with an ear trumpet."

He settled her hand in the crook of his elbow and gave it a reassuring pat. "I understand, Mother. I shall stay close in case further needs arise." His heart ached for her. She so loved parties and social gatherings now that his cruel father had passed, and she was no longer at risk of his open ridicule of her. But her ability to hear had diminished more and more with each passing Season. Some voices, if they were deep and clear enough, gave her no trouble at all. But higher-pitched voices, especially the soft whisperings of the latest *on dit*, were impossible for her to fully make out. As long as she could see their faces, though, the movement of their lips told her precisely what they said. Thorne thanked the Almighty that his mother's eyesight was still as keen as a falcon's. She could read the tattling of tales even if she sat across the room from the gossiping mouths of the *ton*.

"All these lovely young ladies and you intend to stay at my side?" She chuckled warmly as she snapped open a fan resplendent in a lavender and rose floral print that matched her gown. "Nonsense, my sweet boy. How shall I ever know the joy of grandchildren if you do not mingle and choose a wife? Why, we are well past the midpoint of this Season. Have none of the new young ladies tempted you?"

"Now, Mother." He gave her hand an affectionate yet warning pat.

"It is high time you ceased wasting yourself on those unavailable for marriage," she continued behind the protection of her lace-trimmed fan, her tone no longer lighthearted. "Do not think I am unaware of your clandestine activities. I may be growing deaf, but I am not some bacon-brained fool without resources or informants."

"Dearest Mother—now is neither the time nor the place." He found his parent's awareness of his assignations not only disturbing but confounding. His *clandestine activities*, as she so indelicately put it, demanded the utmost discretion, and he prided himself on being quite accomplished in that area. Or so he had thought. Especially since most of the lovelies inviting him into their beds were married—not happily, but married all the same. While some would consider him quite the rake, he looked at it as more of a service to Polite Society. After all, the fact that he was a mere baron, a lower rung on the Marriage Mart ladder, made him the perfect candidate to provide all the attention and passion those lonely wives and widows who had sworn to never marry again so richly deserved. Quite generous of him, he thought, and the ladies almost always agreed.

Except one in particular.

The exquisite yet somewhat alarmingly possessive Lady Constance Myrtlebourne narrowed her eyes at him from across the ballroom.

"That one appears ready to poison you, dear boy," Lady Roslynn said, still shielding her words with her fan.

"She is...persistent." Thorne refused to discuss his jealous former lover. Especially with his mother. He veered away from Lady Myrtlebourne's baleful glare, turning them in the direction of three ladies he knew his beloved parent would be delighted to join.

As he had known she would, his mother released his arm and flew to her trio of friends like a plump little partridge bedecked in lavender satin and lace. They greeted her with open arms and the happiest of excited tittering. Their reactions made Thorne smile. He liked those ladies.

It angered him to no end that several of the *ton* still turned the other way whenever his mother entered a room—a horrid, lingering effect from the years when his father publicly mocked her for everything from the way she wore her hair to the way she walked and talked.

Thorne's mother was kindness itself, and he adored her for it. Perhaps, because of the cruel treatment she endured from both her husband and the presumptuous wives of his cronies, Lady

Roslynn championed those unjustly targeted by Polite Society's haughtiest and loudest few. A sense of pride made Thorne's chest tighten. Heaven help those whom his mother deemed wicked and petty. As she had advised earlier, she had her resources and, if at all possible, would see that the mean-spirited persons, no matter their rank among the peerage, received proper retribution for their backbiting ways.

He bowed to his mother's friends. "Lady Westerbin. Lady Urnstall. Lady Kettering."

"Lord Knightwood, always a pleasure." Lady Westerbin beamed at him. "We were so hoping to see you and our dearest Roslynn this evening."

"Quite right," Lady Urnstall agreed. "Our Roslynn completes our happy circle."

Lady Kettering shooed him away with a mischievous glint in her eyes. "And we already have much *on dit* to share with her. Off you go now, your lordship. Find a young lovely anxious to marry and give your precious mama some grandchildren to spoil."

"Might I recommend one of the Duke of Broadmere's exquisite sisters?" Lady Westerbin said, sounding unabashedly conspiratorial. "All seven must marry before His Grace can receive the full of his inheritance." She chortled a pleased-with-herself laugh while twitching her fan ever faster. "Or so I hear. You know the family is richer than Croesus. The young ladies' dowries are sure to be quite impressive."

"They are very lovely, my son," his mother said with a tip of her head toward a cluster of fair-haired young ladies who looked like a breathtaking bouquet of delicate flowers ready to be picked apart by the most eligible bachelors of the *ton*. "I currently see only five, but I feel certain the other two are nearby. Well worth checking into, do you not agree?"

"Mother."

"Oh dear." Lady Roslynn rolled her eyes, then shook her head at her friends. "Even I heard the admonishment in that tone."

Moving as one, the four matrons lifted their widespread fans until nothing but the disapproval in their eyes was visible. "Shall we move to the windows, my dears?" Lady Urnstall suggested with a lofty sniff. "The air has become quite close here."

Thorne frowned as his mother and her friends turned as one and hurried away, finding their behavior even more eccentric than usual. The hairs rose on the back of his neck as a familiar scent of rosewater enhanced with what he had once found an alluring hint of clover washed across him. A sudden sensation of a trap about to snap shut on him made him turn.

"Lord Knightwood."

Silently damning the elderly women for their desertion without at least a hint of warning about what was headed his way, Thorne forced a polite smile and bowed. "Lady Myrtlebourne—pleasure."

"Is that a compliment or an offer?" the auburn-haired beauty asked in a sultry tone while moving closer. She leaned in until the voluptuousness of her curves brushed against him.

Thorne eased away until a respectable distance existed between them, then smiled and tipped his head at a rather large gentleman headed their way. "Neither, since your husband is coming to fetch you. Mind yourself, dear Constance. Things ended well between us. Let us keep it that way, shall we?"

As her much older yet obviously quite virile husband reached them, Thorne offered a perfunctory dip of his chin. He didn't like the man. Not because Myrtlebourne outranked him as an earl, but because the rude fellow was a known bully whose birthright had denied him the opportunity to prowl the docks, pummeling unsuspecting fools with his meaty fists—an occupation he would have been well suited for. Thorne forced the closest thing to a smile that he could manage. "Lord Myrtlebourne."

"Knightwood," the brutish man drawled as he took his wife's hand and settled it firmly on his arm. "Come, Constance. I have indulged you long enough. Make your farewells. It is time we take our leave."

"I understand you are weary, my lord, after returning to London only yesterday…" The coldness of Lady Myrtlebourne's tone left no doubt that she didn't give a whit about her husband's comfort. "But did you fail to notice Arabella is here? She and her husband offered to escort me home later when I mentioned you might wish to leave early. Poor dears. They know so very few here and are desperate for me to stay and introduce them." She fluttered her eyelashes and gave the man a provocative pout that didn't fool Thorne for a moment and made him wonder if Lord Myrtlebourne would swallow his wife's lie or insist upon her being obedient and departing with him.

The hulking earl fixed a heavy-lidded gaze on his wife, looking as if he were contemplating ways to make her suffer rather than seduce her. "You may stay, Constance," he said after a lengthy pause. "Be prepared to thank me properly once you arrive home. Understood?"

Even though a bit of the color drained from her face, Lady Myrtlebourne gracefully inclined her head, then offered him a deep curtsy. "Understood, my lord. Many thanks for your generosity."

Without offering Thorne so much as another glance to acknowledge his existence, the earl turned and strode away, plowing through those in his path as if they were an annoyance that could hardly be borne.

As soon as the man exited the grand ballroom, Lady Myrtlebourne rewarded Thorne with a winning smile. "Now we may enjoy our evening, my lord. Shall we repair to the gardens for some air?"

"No thank you, my lady." Thorne dismissed himself with a stiff bow, then turned in search of his mother and her gaggle of nattering yet enjoyable friends. While it might be rude to leave Lady Myrtlebourne unattended to find her way back to wherever she had come from, it was necessary. He had ended their assignation when she had become a mite too clingy for his liking, and he fully intended to keep things ended. Besides—with her husband back from the Continent, the Americas, or wherever the devil the man had been, her time would be better spent with him.

"Knightwood!"

Thank heavens, Thorne thought. He turned and clapped a hand on the shoulder of his oldest and dearest friend, not giving a damn that the exuberant greeting might be considered improper decorum for such a social gathering as Lady Atterley's grand ball of the Season. "Ravenglass! You old devil. It has been an age."

"Indeed, it has," Viscount Matthew Ravenglass agreed with a broad smile. "'Tis good to be back in London."

"How was India?"

"Hot." Ravenglass glanced around the ballroom, then emitted a quiet huff of amusement. "Not as searing as yon lady's angry gaze aimed at you, though. Ousted her from your bed, did you?"

"No." Thorne smoothed a hand over his perfectly tied cravat. "We mutually agreed to part months ago, and for that, I am exceedingly glad. Now she can concentrate on her husband, Lord Myrtlebourne."

"Lord Bull?"

Thorne nodded, deciding the insulting moniker for the earl was quite fitting.

"You always did enjoy a bit of danger," Ravenglass observed. "However, I must mention that the look in that lady's eyes is anything but *mutual agreement.*" He continued scanning the room. His perusal halted again. "I say, where did Lady Atterley find such a bevy of diamonds? And I do not recall seeing any of them before. Foreign ladies, perhaps? I wasn't abroad that long."

"Broadmere daughters." Thorne silently counted the fair-haired lovelies again. "According to Mother and her impeccable resources, there should be seven. Two appear to be missing."

"Broadmere," Ravenglass repeated. "Daughters of the duke who passed a little over six months ago? And didn't their mother pass almost six months to the day before that?"

Thorne eyed his friend, amazed that he kept up with such details. "You would have to ask Mother. She keeps up with such things."

"And the only *things* you keep up with are the whereabouts of husbands. Correct?"

"It indeed pays to do so."

The viscount continued to study the ladies as if unable to get his fill. "Two seem extremely young to be in search of husbands."

"Ah..." Thorne lifted the glass of champagne he'd just accepted from a servant bearing a tray filled with glasses of the sparkling refreshment. "According to Lady Westerbin, all seven of the sisters must marry before their brother, the new duke, can come into the full of his inheritance." He frowned while trying to remember the rest of what Lady Westerbin had said. "Something about the requirements of the will. She also mentioned generous dowries for each of the ladies."

Ravenglass nodded. "Of that, I have no doubt. Old Broadmere was quite plump in the pocket and known to never squander his resources. A fine, upstanding man, from what I remember." He thoughtfully sipped from the glass he had taken from the tray offered by the same smiling servant. "Perhaps we should seek an introduction."

"Why?" Thorne stared at his friend, unable to believe his ears. "They are indeed lovely but are also determined to find husbands. Since when do you aspire to be leg-shackled?"

"I do not." Ravenglass's tone had lowered to a deep hum, a sure sign the man was plotting. Then he shielded his mouth behind his glass. "But might I suggest we do something other than stand here? Your Lady Myrtlebourne is headed this way and appears to be bringing reinforcements in the form of a female companion to pull me away from our conversation."

"She is not my—" Thorne cut himself off. Now was not the time to talk. Now was the time to move. "Remember how I saved you from the odious Miss Treadwell last Season?" He edged them toward the wall of open doors leading into the renowned Atterley Gardens. "How you said you owed me a great debt?"

"I remember," Ravenglass said with a heavy sigh. He squared off to face the pair of women headed their way and widened his stance. "Run, man. I shall delay them as long as possible."

"I am not a coward," Thorne said, more to himself than his friend, although the hasty retreat shamed him. "I simply do not wish to cause a scene that would embarrass Mother."

"Understood." Ravenglass arched a brow. "They are almost here. Run."

"Damn the woman." Thorne charged out the doors with a long, hurried stride. Lady Myrtlebourne needed to accept their liaison had run its course, and her time would now be better spent on her husband. He descended the terrace steps and entered the gardens, guilt-ridden about leaving poor Ravenglass as the last line of defense against the irascible woman and her friend. The maze of shrubbery would do nicely for his purposes. He worked his way deeper into the twists and turns with as little disturbance as possible to more than one brazen couple in search of privacy among the hedges.

After a while, the maze opened into a well-manicured, circular area that struck him as a place intended for solitude and reflection. Far enough from the house's brightly burning lamps and shielded from most of the garden's torchlight by taller hedgerows and a wall of columns reminiscent of ancient Greek ruins, the brilliant spattering of stars across the blue black velvet of the night sky put on a breathtaking show. Without even realizing he did so, Thorne reached up, stretching toward the ethereal diamonds as though intent on plucking them from the sky. They seemed that close and made him feel as insignificant as a mote of dust.

"I stood on display with our sisters for as long as I intend to. Go back inside, Seri. Your time is better spent seeing to the other members of the marriageable Broadmere flock." The musical voice pulling Thorne's attention away from the heavens effervesced with a lyrical note of utter contentment. "Besides, dear sister, I have my stars. What more do I need?"

"Essie—please do not be quarrelsome."

Thorne squinted, searching the shadowy clearing for what appeared to be the two missing Broadmere sisters—at least, he supposed they were, according to what he had just overheard. He finally made out the ladies in question standing not too far across the way. When he took a step to retreat and give them their privacy, loose pebbles of the path crunched beneath his shoes.

"Did you hear that?" said the one Essie had called Seri.

"Show yourself, you eavesdropping coward," Essie demanded, "and do not think we are unable to protect ourselves." The fearless lady gripped her fan as if ready to use it as a club.

"Forgive my intrusion, ladies." Thorne stepped out from the shadows of the hedgerow with his hands held high. "I had no idea anyone was here other than myself—a seeker of solitude and quiet respite from the festivities." He considered the fact he had come across such an entertaining pair of beauties a boon from above, a nudge from Divine Providence.

"Your name, sir?" Essie did not sound at all convinced that he had not followed them and then lain in wait for an opportune moment to pounce.

"Lord Thorne Knightwood," he replied to her with a slight bow. "If you would care to accompany me inside, I would happily introduce you to my mother, Lady Roslynn Knightwood, whom I escorted to this lovely event. She will vouch for my character as will her three dearest friends, Ladies Westerbin, Urnstall, and Kettering. Perhaps you know of them?"

Neither lady answered, so he drew closer still and offered them his friendliest smile. "And forgive me, but I could not help but overhear that you are Lady Essie and Lady Seri?"

"We are most certainly not," declared the one he had clearly heard addressed as Essie. "At least, my lord, to you we are not."

"Forgive my sister, my lord," said the one he knew to be Seri as she gave him a graceful curtsy. "What she means to say is that she is Lady Blessing. *Essie* is a family pet name." She caught Lady Blessing by the arm and must have lightly pinched her, because the irritated young woman jumped, then fixed Seri with a furious scowl.

Thorne bit the inside of his cheek to keep from laughing. Instead, he gave a courteous bow. "Forgive me, Lady Blessing. It is a pleasure to meet you."

She gave a grudging curtsy, then yanked her sister forward. "This is my *eldest* sister, Lady Serendipity. *Seri* is our pet name for her." She lifted her chin to a defiant angle and added, "Among other names that I shall refrain from mentioning here."

With his breath held until he felt certain he would not laugh out loud, Thorne bowed again. "I am honored to meet you, Lady Serendipity."

"Thank you, my lord." Lady Serendipity cast a nervous look back toward the house. "We were just about to head back inside. Weren't we, Blessing?"

"No, we were not," Lady Blessing said with a directness that made her sister gasp and Thorne smile. "But I suppose we will now, so you might enjoy your quiet respite in the solitude you seek, my lord."

"On the contrary, dear ladies." He moved to stand between them and offered each of them an arm. "I would be honored and delighted to escort the two of you back inside to ensure your safe return to the gala." He adopted a low, mysterious tone. "After all, one never knows what might be lurking in the darkness."

"Indeed," Lady Blessing said. That he had failed to impress her resounded unmistakably in that one word, making him yet again struggle not to laugh. This particular Broadmere sister was a delight as well as a beauty.

"That is most kind of you, my lord," Lady Serendipity stressed while leaning forward to shoot a narrow-eyed glare across him to her sister.

While Lady Serendipity appeared to be the more tractable of the pair, Thorne found he preferred the excitement of waiting to hear what unfettered opinion Lady Blessing might choose to share next. Deciding to goad her into divulging even more, he glanced skyward one last time before they took the path back into the maze. *"Your* stars are brilliant tonight, Lady Blessing."

"Thank you," she said without missing a beat. "Since you were eavesdropping—which is very rude, by the way—did you agree with what I said about the constellation that was most visible this evening?"

"Alas," he said, softly chuckling, "I fear I missed that portion of your discourse. Would you care to repeat it?"

"I would not."

"Blessing," Lady Serendipity said through what sounded like tightly clenched teeth. "I beg your forgiveness, my lord. When my sister is feeling unwell, she becomes a bit fractious."

"I am not feeling unwell," Lady Blessing clarified before Thorne could comment. As they stepped into the golden glow of the torches surrounding the broad terrace, she turned to him, the brilliance of her aquamarine eyes flashing. "I would rather be home in my observatory on such a delightful evening for stargazing, and yet my night is wasted here, where I am lined up and put on display for—"

"Blessing! That is quite enough." Lady Serendipity caught hold of her sister's hand and tugged her up the steps while glancing back at Thorne with a forced smile that surely had to make the poor woman's cheeks ache. "It was a pleasure meeting you, Lord Knightwood. Thank you for seeing us safely back to the ball."

Lady Blessing yanked herself free just before they passed through the doors to re-enter the ballroom. Fisting her hands at her sides, she squared her shoulders and marched back inside without her *elder* sister's assistance.

Thorne stood at the bottom of the steps staring after her. A smile crept across his lips, matching the growing burn the enticing lady had ignited deep within him. What fire and wit that Broadmere daughter possessed. While her sisters might be considered diamonds of the first water, Lady Blessing was utterly incomparable.

"I must have a dance with that lady," he informed the torch sputtering beside him. He vaulted up the steps and hurried inside, thankful that his height enabled him to see the span of the room and spot his angry angel, his beautiful astrophile, darting through the crowd to rejoin the rest of her sisters.

"Lord Knightwood!"

He ignored Lady Myrtlebourne's insistent call, maintaining his course with determined steps to the reunited sisters of Broadmere. The first strains of a waltz filled the air, urging him to move faster. A waltz—the perfect first dance with the witty lady who would no doubt do her best to refuse him. But her sister, the staunch observer of decorum, the lovely Lady Serendipity, would surely support his cause and *entice* Lady Blessing to accept his request for a dance.

As he drew near, Lady Blessing turned, met his gaze, then narrowed her eyes as if to dare him to be foolish enough to take a step closer. He almost laughed. The lady didn't realize just how much he loved a dare. He halted in front of her, bowed, then held out his hand. "Might I have the pleasure of this dance, Lady Blessing?"

She opened her mouth to refuse. He saw it in her eyes. But then she stumbled forward and kept herself from falling by catching hold of his hand. "Seri!" she hissed as he swept her into his arms and out onto the floor before she could escape.

"Not *Seri*, my lady. Lord Knightwood, remember?" He couldn't resist teasing her, knowing her sister had bumped her into play without a qualm about doing so.

"I am well aware of your name, my lord." With every turn, she shot an infuriated glare back at her sister, who stood on the edge of the dance floor, smiling and nodding at her.

"For one so determined to avoid this waltz, you are perfection itself, my lady. I do not believe I have ever had the pleasure of such a talented partner."

She snorted and rolled her eyes at his intentionally overdone flummery. "I did not *wish* to waltz." She settled a tight-jawed scowl on him, thrilling him immensely. "I never said I *couldn't*."

"Indeed, you did not." He breathed her in, intoxicated by the delightful combination of sweet lilacs and angry, yet desirable, young woman. "Earlier you mentioned an observatory?" he asked, noting how the tension left her at the mention of it.

"I did."

He almost laughed again but prudently chose not to. It would surely anger her even more. The minx intended to make him work for a conversation that might sway her opinion of him. Admirable, indeed. *"At home in your observatory,"* he said, repeating the memory almost word for word. "Not many are fortunate enough to have access to their own private observatory."

"Papa had it built for me." Her voice had gone soft, filled with emotion, reminding him of her father's recent passing.

"Forgive me, Lady Blessing. I did not mean to stir your sorrow on this lovely evening."

"Think nothing of it, my lord. You had no way of knowing." But the sheen of unshed tears in her lovely blue eyes was unmistakable. She lifted her chin and resettled her hand in his as they twirled across the floor. "You would have been better served had you asked Serendipity to dance," she said after releasing a put-upon sigh. "I am not the one you want, Lord Knightwood."

"On the contrary, Lady Blessing. You are the very one I want."

Her gaze cut to him as if he had just slandered her. "And what is *that* supposed to mean?"

"I meant no insult, my lady."

She narrowed her eyes into a leery squint, then moved to step away from him, but he tightened his hold and kept her close.

"The music has stopped, my lord." She arched a fair brow to a daunting angle that would frighten a lesser man.

With more regret than he had felt in a very long time when leaving a woman's company, he released her, took a step back, and bowed.

With a curtsy so miserly he almost missed it, she turned to leave but paused and turned back. A corner of her mouth, so delectable and tempting, curled up the slightest bit in an unmistakable smile. "Next time," she said, soft and low. "Seek Serendipity for a dance. You would be better served if you did so."

"Nay, my lady," he was quick to answer. "You are the Broadmere sister I want."

Chapter Three

"**B**ROTHER WISHES TO see the flock in the parlor," Merry called from the hallway, then scampered away. The delicate *pat-patting* of her lighthearted skipping faded as she raced off to gather the rest of the sisters, whom Chance so lovingly, and sometimes not so lovingly, referred to as *the flock*.

"Well, the flock is going to be short by one," Blessing said under her breath. "This little goose is staying put." She adjusted the declination on her telescope, then recorded the degree in her journal. Chance could go straight to the devil if he thought she was going to waste another moment of her life reflecting on the ridiculousness of last night. Besides, she felt sure Serendipity could give him a much more accurate, minute-by-minute record of all that had happened, because making lists and remembering every last detail was something at which her sister excelled— annoyingly so.

Merciful heavens, the tedium of Lady Atterley's ball had been excruciating, only relieved when Blessing had escaped outside to admire Ursa Major, Leo, and Leo Minor. The constellations had indeed been glorious last night. But then Serendipity had found her and dragged her back inside.

Blessing straightened and stared down at the entry in her journal. No. Serendipity had not dragged her back inside. The annoying Lord Knightwood had. Well, he hadn't dragged them but escorted them. She allowed herself a thoughtful puckering of her mouth as she stared off into the distance, recalling everything about the man.

One must never pucker, Mama's voice said quite clearly in her mind, interrupting her thoughts. *Puckering mars one's face with dreadful lines.*

The sage advice, in Mama's voice when she had been healthy, made Blessing swallow hard and rub a hand across her mouth to smooth away any wrinkles forming from the pucker. She hoped Mama's sayings never stopped popping into her thoughts. They kept her precious mother close.

She cleared her throat and tapped the graphite tip of her pencil on her journal. Her thoughts took it upon themselves to return to the impertinent Lord Knightwood. The man thought a lot of himself. That was easy enough to tell. If pressed, she might grudgingly admit he was rather nice to look upon. Some might even call him handsome with that coal-black hair of his and those dark eyes flashing with equal parts gallantry and wickedness. Yes, *some* might call him handsome. But that didn't necessarily mean that she would. He also enjoyed teasing a soul even more than Chance did—which lowered her opinion of him even more. He had said his name was Thorne. That made her smile. Thorne was a fitting name for him because he was as annoying as one.

A tall man. While they had waltzed, she'd had to look up to glare at him rather than aim her sourness at his cravat. "Powerful, too," she mused aloud. Even through her gloves, the strength of his hands and the muscular hardness of his broad shoulders had been impossible not to notice—even to someone more interested in stars than dance partners.

Lord Thorne Knightwood, he'd said, but hadn't expounded on his *lordliness.* She wasn't certain if Knightwood was his surname or place name. She'd never heard of the man, so didn't know his rank in the peerage other than he wasn't a duke, because then Serendipity would have *Your Grace'd* the poor man to death. Her sister always knew who was who among the *ton.*

A heartfelt sigh slipped free of Blessing. Serendipity always knew who was who because when their mother had become too ill to leave her bed, she had kept up with all the latest *on dit* and dutifully reported it to Mama to bolster her spirits. If Blessing were to guess, Serendipity probably *still* kept track of all the gossip and relayed it to their parents through her nightly prayers.

Merry rapped her knuckles on the bold brass plate Papa had ordered installed on the door. The plate read: *Blessing's Observatory. Entry by invitation only. You have been warned.* "Chance is growing most impatient, and it is not fair that the rest of us must listen to him gnash his teeth because of you."

Blessing rolled her eyes at her youngest sister. "This is all so ridiculous."

"Ridiculous or not," Merry said, "since Chance can no longer afford the many entertainments to which he is accustomed, and most of his chums have turned out to be the fair-weather sort, it is we who must suffer with keeping him amused until we can be rid of him."

"Perhaps we should all donate to his monthly allotment." Blessing set the heavy glass paperweight on her journal, exited the observatory with Merry, and locked the door. "Then he could still play with his friends and leave us alone."

"I doubt we could afford Chance's amusements." Merry glanced down the hallway behind them, then lowered her voice. "Once, I overheard Papa shouting at him about behaving like a responsible man rather than a spoiled child." She covered her mouth but failed to stifle a giggle. "He also told him it was far past time for Chance to use his head for something other than a hat rack."

Blessing's heart lightened immensely. She could just hear Papa bending Chance's ear about his irresponsible behavior. She caught hold of her sister's hand and gave it a squeeze. "We will get through this. I'm sure Mama and Papa both are watching over us."

"Well, I wish Papa would thump Chance on the back of the head and make him be quiet."

Blessing couldn't hold back an amused snort just as they entered the parlor where the rest of the family was gathered.

"I do hope your dance partner from last night is the reason for your joyous mood, dear sister." Chance beamed at her from where he stood in front of the hearth with the rest of their sisters perched in chairs, facing him as if he were about to read them a sermon. Before she could counter his remark, he swept a disappointed gaze across the others. "From what I observed and from all that Serendipity tells me, last night you were the only one who even attempted to cooperate."

"Attempted to cooperate?" Blessing snorted again before looking at Serendipity. "Have you finally learned how to tell a convincing lie?"

"You danced with Lord Knightwood," Serendipity said. "Brother saw you as well."

"A waltz," Fortuity said while scrubbing at an ink stain on her finger. "We all saw you."

"Before the lot of you scattered," Serendipity growled at them, turning a hard glare on the rest as she took her place beside their brother. "Cowards! Each and every one of you. You knew as soon as Essie took to the floor that others would seek dances with all of you, and you ran."

"Dowry hunters," Fortuity retorted.

"How would you know?" Serendipity asked. "You were too busy sinking into the shadows at the back of the room, writing notes, and stuffing them into your reticule."

"The lion's share of them had *fortune hunting* emblazoned on their foreheads," Gracie said as she leaned over to rub the belly of her favorite hound.

"And you took off to the stables to see the horses with Lady Martha!" Serendipity countered, then pointed at Joy, Felicity, and Merry. "Joy disappeared into an alcove to play cards with her friends, Felicity kept sneaking cakes and hiding behind the draperies, and Merry laughed in the face of every gentleman who spoke to her."

"They were older than Papa!" Merry said before folding her arms and winding up for a proper pout. "Two were certainly older than Grandpapa would have been had he still been alive."

"Ten and six and ten and seven," Blessing said to Serendipity, reminding her sibling of the grace period from marriage they had sworn to give Merry and Felicity as the two youngest sisters.

"What is that supposed to mean?" Chance demanded. He looked from Blessing to Serendipity and back again. "You know how I hate it when any of you speak in your *sister code*."

"Will that be all, brother?" Blessing knew it irritated Chance to no end that he was stuck here in their parlor rather than out with the friends who only kept company with him because he spent money like pouring water from a bucket.

"That will *not* be all, Blessing." He glared at her with eyes such a dark blue that they sometimes hinted at a shade of the deepest purple—especially if he was angry. From their current shade of saturated amethyst, they had sorely tried his temper this afternoon. "When will you see Lord Knightwood again?" he asked.

"How should I know?" Had her brother lost what little sense she had ever given him credit for having? "I spoke with him for the length of a waltz, and then we parted ways." She grinned, then winked at Fortuity. "I hid in the library after that. Tutie, you would have loved it. So many books."

"Oh my," Fortuity groaned. "I was so busy taking down notes on character traits, I completely forgot about the library."

"Did you even suggest to the man that you would welcome callers? Be interested in his attention?" Chance dug his thumbs into his temples and rubbed in slow circles.

"Of course I didn't. I don't even know the man." Blessing shook her head. "Go lie down in a dark room. It will make your head feel better."

"What will make my head feel better is if someone would give me the slightest bit of hope that Lady Atterley's grand ball was not a complete waste of our time!"

"Do not shout at me, brother." She had once shoved him out of a tree when they were children. If necessary, she would find a way to do so again. She noticed Serendipity—the eternal peacemaker—looking far more troubled than the situation warranted. "Speak your mind, sister. You might as well. Your worries are on your face."

Serendipity gave Chance's shoulder a sympathetic pat. "Lord Knightwood might not be the best gentleman caller for our Essie."

"Finally." Blessing dramatically clasped her hands to her chest. "A voice of reason."

Chance scrubbed a hand across his face and slowly lowered himself into a chair. "Knightwood," he repeated with a pained squint as if it hurt to focus his thoughts. After a few moments, he slowly closed his eyes, shook his head, then turned to Serendipity. "Lord *Thorne* Knightwood? Was that the man's name? I saw him but did not recall him at the time."

Serendipity nodded. "Lord Thorne Knightwood. The very one."

"Care to share?" Blessing couldn't help it. Her curiosity was piqued.

"Lord Knightwood. Quite the wealthy baron. He does not marry women," Chance said. "He beds them."

"Chance!" Serendipity cuffed him on the shoulder.

He scowled at her, then pointed at Blessing. "Out of each of you, Essie is the one who could best deal with him." He pointed at her again and added a curt nod. "She can change him. Mama said Papa was once quite the rake—until he met her."

"I am done here." Blessing turned to go, then paused and looked back at her two elder siblings, who appeared entirely too thoughtful for her liking. "Do. Not."

"Do not what?" Serendipity asked with feigned innocence.

"There you are, Lady Blessing," said Walters, the Broadmere butler for the past eternity and a half. "This just came for you, my lady." He held out a silver salver bearing a single envelope.

"Anyone willing to give odds that it's from the rakish Lord Knightwood?" Joy called out with a teasing grin.

Blessing ignored her wagering sibling, picked up the envelope, and eyed the seal that consisted of three trees with a pair of swords across them, the blades crossed as if barring entry to the small forest. It appeared the baron had quite the straightforward emblem. A pair of swords to signify *knight* and a trio of trees for *wood*.

She returned the unopened envelope to the salver. "Tell the messenger my answer is *no*."

Walters blinked as if not quite sure of what she'd just said. "Messenger, my lady?"

"I assume a messenger is waiting for my answer?"

The butler shook his head. "No, my lady. The missive was delivered by a young lad who scampered away as soon as I accepted it."

Chance appeared at her side, snatched up the letter, and pushed it back into her hands. "Read it."

On Blessing's other side, Serendipity bobbed her head while excitedly squeezing her arm. "Yes, do. Read it."

"Oh, good heavens, you two are quite the unbelievable pair." Blessing broke the seal, slid her thumb under the flap, and unfolded the costly white paper she considered far too elaborate for something as simple as an invitation or request that would be refused. The note read:

My dearest Lady Blessing,

I wish to thank you for the pleasure of your company yesterday evening. I cannot remember when last I enjoyed a waltz so very much. In fact, I had intended to seek the pleasure of another joyous dance with you, but you must have already hurried home to gaze at your stars, since the night was so lovely and clear.

I look forward to the next time I may enjoy your delightful company.

Until then, I remain your ever-faithful and adoring serv-

ant—

Thorne Alexander Knightwood

"What a lovely note," Serendipity whispered.

"Well done, indeed," Chance said, nodding his approval.

"Sheer impertinence and flummery." Blessing refolded the paper and wished Walters had remained so she could toss it back on the salver. *"My dearest Lady Blessing.* Indeed." She strode over to the hearth to dispose of the silliness, but the rest of her sisters swarmed her and snatched it out of her hand.

"We want to read it too," Merry said as she darted across the room with it. As the most petite of the flock, she was also the quickest and most agile. Fortuity, Grace, Joy, and Felicity clamored for her to read the note aloud.

Serendipity caught Blessing by the arm, tugged her into the hallway, and pulled her into the much quieter library. "See what could have happened had you not hidden yourself away after the waltz?"

"What do you mean, *what could have happened*? I do not know what you read, but all I read was that the man sought another dance. From what you and Chance said earlier, I am sure he found another partner who was much more accommodating than I."

"And I cannot believe you were going to toss that lovely missive into the fire," her sister said as if Blessing hadn't said a word. "Mama saved all of Papa's letters."

"Mama loved Papa." While yes, the letter had been rather nice in an over-flattering sort of way, Blessing felt sure that Lord Knightwood meant nothing by it. The man probably had them printed *en masse* like the tittle-tattle sheets, and all he had to do was add the unsuspecting lady's name at the top and sign his at the bottom. She suddenly itched to examine it closer to confirm her suspicions but then remembered his mention of *her* stars. That realization made her pucker her mouth with a thoughtful scowl.

"Mama said never to pucker, remember?" Serendipity chided with a knowing smile. "Admit it, Essie. The note was a rather nice touch. He even remembered your love of the stars."

"I admit nothing."

Serendipity laughed. "I am not the only sister incapable of telling a proper lie."

"And what is that supposed to mean?"

"It means that if you would allow yourself to, you might actually enjoy getting to know Lord Knightwood."

"I do not—"

Serendipity stopped her with a lifted hand. "I did not say *marry* or *love*. I merely said you might enjoy getting to know the man. What if he is a fellow star lover?"

"If he is the rake you and Chance said he was, then stars are not what he loves." Blessing couldn't resist a wicked giggle. "Unless he's the one on his back in the meadow at night."

"Blessing Isolde Iris Abarough! Shame on you. What would Mama say?"

"Probably my full name, in exactly the same manner as you just did." Blessing hurried to soothe her sister with a repentant tip of her head and a humble curtsy. "Forgive me. You know I wouldn't say such a thing in front of the others. I only did it because you and Chance are making entirely too much of this."

"Do you truly never wish to marry?" Serendipity sounded so despondent that it touched Blessing's heart and forced her to share a bit of her true feelings.

"I would love to marry for love, but if you tell Chance or the others I admitted to that and truly meant it, I will swear you are lying." She caught Serendipity's hand and gave it a sisterly squeeze. "It's just that everything is happening too soon. Too quickly after..." She paused and swallowed hard to force the interminable knot of stormy emotions that never left her, back down where she constantly fought to keep them. "Papa and Mama have not been gone that long, and I never imagined going through any of this without either of them here to support us or give advice."

"I know, Essie." Serendipity gathered her into a hug. "I wish they were here too."

A light knock on the door was followed by Walters quietly saying, "Lady Blessing?"

"Come in, Walters. It's safe." Blessing bowed her head, rubbed her brow, and wondered how Chance had managed to curse her with his headache.

The ancient butler toddled into the library balancing a silver tray in one hand, and once again it held a single sealed note. "Another missive just arrived, my lady, and begging your pardon, but it bears the same seal as the one from earlier."

"Not an hour has passed since the arrival of the first." Her curiosity piqued, Blessing snatched up the letter and hurried to open it.

> *My dearest Lady Blessing,*
>
> *Since I felt quite certain you would consider my first corre-spondence flummery and toss it into the hearth fire, I simply had to send a second to stress that I meant each and every word I wrote in the first.*
>
> *You are a delight, my lady. I look forward to the time when you find our acquaintance so joyful that you grant me the ultimate pleasure of addressing you as "Essie."*
>
> *As ever, your faithful and adoring servant—*
>
> *Thorne*

Blessing tried not to smile but failed so miserably that she pressed her fingers across her lips as though insulted by Lord Knightwood's even more daring impertinence.

Serendipity arched a brow at her. "His lordship appears to be quite observant."

Refolding the letter and keeping it safely tucked against her while she crossed her arms over her chest, Blessing assumed an air of indifference. "His letters are rakish flirtations intended to get him closer to my *virtues*—which I can assure you are quite safe from whatever he has in mind. He does not *marry*, remember?"

"Perhaps not yet, but he described your reaction as though he had watched you through the window," Serendipity argued. "If Merry hadn't snatched the first letter out of your hand, it would have already been ashes ready to be swept into the bin." With a hearty laugh, she shook a finger, making Blessing seriously consider pinching her. "He even used the word *flummery*! You called it the same. He already knows and understands you, dear sister, whether you wish it or not."

"If you speak of this to Chance, I will fill your bedclothes with frogs—the biggest I can find."

"Essie." Serendipity made a face and clicked her tongue as if scolding a child. "We are both too old for that childhood game, and you know it."

"I am still quite able to catch a bucketful of frogs, I assure you." Blessing tucked Knightwood's note down the front of her dress, securing it behind her corset. "Try me and see."

"Fine. I shan't speak of it to Chance." Serendipity held up a finger. "Unless Lord Knightwood takes further steps to court you." She offered a sympathetic shrug. "With Papa gone, Chance must give his permission should you fall in love with *anyone* and seek to marry."

"I am one and twenty, and do not need my brother's permission." Even though she knew it to be immature and petulant, Blessing stamped her foot. "He is not and never will be Papa."

"But he is the head of the household now," Serendipity quietly reminded her, her earlier levity gone. "As the Duke of Broadmere and according to the will, his signature is required to advise Mr. Sutherland to pay out your dowry. One can only assume that Papa and Mama stipulated that to ease some of the sting of placing him on a rather tight allowance until he learns how to better handle his responsibilities."

Blessing shooed away her sister's words. "Putting the cart

before the horse, are you not, dear sister? I am not concerned about my dowry. I simply do not want Chance encouraged in Lord Knightwood's regard, and have him champing at the bit for the reading of the banns. Once the baron discovers how stubborn I can be about keeping my skirts down where they belong, I am sure he will move on to easier prey and forget all about me."

"We shall see, dear sister." Serendipity opened the library door and looked back as she stepped out into the hallway. "We shall see."

As the library door closed behind her sister, Blessing blew out a disgruntled huff and retreated to the tall front window overlooking St. James's Street. It was best to remain here in the library until the furor that Lord Knightwood's notes had caused calmed down. As she had told Serendipity, life was moving on entirely too fast. Good heavens, they had just come out of mourning in time for Easter, and if it were left up to Chance, they would all be married by May Day.

A lone figure across the street, strolling back and forth at a leisurely yet purposeful pace, caught her attention. When he turned the second time to repeat his circuit, he looked her way, tipped his hat, then drew what appeared to be three more notes from an inner coat pocket and fanned them out like a hand of cards. His smile shone with an entirely improper boldness, sending a shiver through her—not entirely unpleasant, but it made her catch her breath and filled her with renewed determination to remain steadfast and true to herself. Lord Thorne Knightwood's title should be King of Impertinence. How dare he traipse up and down the street in front of her home?

Rather than retreat from the window and look like a coward, she pointed at him and arched a stern brow, a silent order for him to behave himself and trot off in search of some other young woman to prey upon. She felt sure he would understand her meaning with no trouble. After all, had he not eerily known what her reaction would be to his first missive?

His beguiling smile stretched even wider, revealing a pair of dimples she had failed to notice last night. He doffed his hat and gave an elaborate bow that made her remember the ending to both his letters: *your faithful and adoring servant.*

Indeed! She spun away from the window in a huff, then halted midway across the library and looked down. Her hands were clasped to her chest, pressing the second note tightly to her heart. "I am being utterly ridiculous," she announced to the room at large. Only the mantel clock answered with its ever-faithful tick-tock echoing through the quiet.

"Lady Blessing?" Walters quietly called from the partially opened door.

"Do not dare bring another note to me, Walters."

"But my lady—"

"Walters."

The butler cleared his throat and respectfully tipped his head. "Yes, my lady. I shall deliver any correspondence addressed to you to your observatory and then lock the door upon my leaving. Will that do, my lady?"

Blessing pulled in a deep breath and huffed it out. It was not the butler's fault that she had drawn the attention of the annoying Lord Knightwood. "Yes, Walters. That will do."

Chapter Four

"From what Georgina tells me..." Lady Roslynn began, then paused for a sip of her tea.

Thorne held up a hand to prevent his mother from continuing without clarification. "Georgina?" While he trusted her information implicitly, he still preferred knowing its origin, even though it could be said that her sources put hunting hounds to shame when they caught the scent of the latest *on dit*.

Lady Roslynn pulled a face as she leaned forward to help herself to a tomato and cucumber sandwich. "Lady Georgina Westerbin—a most reliable source, dear boy. Remember how much she knew about the Broadmere daughters the other evening?"

"Ah, yes. Lady Westerbin. Carry on."

"Well..." His mother paused for effect, clearly delighting in the conversation. "All the Broadmere daughters were presented at the last drawing room Queen Charlotte held before she passed, and it is said that Her Majesty was duly impressed with all of them."

"But that would have been over two years ago. How is it that they disappeared from Society and are just now seeking husbands? Two of them would have been at an astonishingly young age at that time, but I suppose it would not be unheard of for a future match to be secured." He set aside his tea while fixing a thoughtful frown on his mother.

"Their beloved mother became quite ill." Lady Roslynn sadly shook her head. "Consumption. None of the daughters would leave her bedside to attend any social functions that Season—and later they refused to leave her side because they did not wish her to pass without them gathered around her."

"Then the mourning period," Thorne remarked, remembering what Ravenglass had told him.

"And their father's death and the mourning period after *that*," Lady Roslynn added. "Their parents were a rare love match. I am told their father died because he could not endure life without their mother." The hint of a calculating smile curved her mouth. "Did one of them interest you, my dear boy? Are you finally ready to set aside your unacceptable dabbling?"

"Mother, really." Thorne took up his tea again only to discover it had gone tepid.

She twitched a shrug. "Why else would you inquire about the Broadmere ladies?" She surprised him with the suddenness of a motherly scowl. "You will treat them with respect. Do you hear? I refuse to have it known that my son debauched a daughter of such a fine family. The Broadmeres were much admired by the *ton*, even though they chose to rear their children in a rather unorthodox manner."

"How so?" Now his interest was well and truly piqued, and he also hoped to keep the topic on the Broadmeres and not his pastimes.

"Only a few nannies were retained while the children were extremely young because they are all quite close in age—each of them merely a year apart, I believe. After that, Lady Broadmere attended to her young with great delight, tutoring her son and allowing her daughters to explore their interests, whether such interests were considered standard for young ladies or not. She was a highly educated woman and had her mind set on how her children should be prepared for the world. It is said the duke fully supported her and even saw to it that the children were indulged in whatever educational pursuits they desired."

"Lady Blessing loves the stars," Thorne mused. "Her father built her an observatory."

"Lady Blessing," his mother repeated, squinting as if deep in concentration. "She is the third in birth order, I believe. Or was it the second-born? The current duke is not only the only son but also the firstborn."

"The sister who was with her when I discovered them in the Atterleys' garden was Lady Serendipity." He grinned at the memory. "Lady Blessing made it very clear that her companion was her *older* sister."

His mother chuckled as she placed another sandwich and a sweetmeat biscuit on her plate. "So, the young lady attempted to deflect your advances onto her older sister, did she?" She clicked her tongue and gave him a teasing look. "Were you rude to her, Thorne? Usually the ladies find you quite charming. I've read their whispers after you've returned them to wherever you found them at whatever soirée we are attending." She made an exaggerated clearing of her throat and arched a brow at him. "Or shall I say I've read them when they were ladies *deserving* of your attention?"

"Mother." Damned if the topic hadn't veered back to his habits that his mother despised.

"I do not like the *other* whispers I read about my son," she continued. Displeasure filled her tone, but it was the disappointment in her eyes that cut him to the quick. "You promised me you would never behave like your father." Her soft accusation stung.

"That is why I have never married." When his cruel father wasn't belittling his mother with hateful insults, the man openly flaunted his many mistresses, causing her even more humiliation and pain. Thorne prided himself on discretion and had sworn never to marry to avoid the risk of hurting a woman the way his father had hurt his mother—because his grandfather had been the same. Remaining single would ensure he never became the callous monster his father and grandfather had been.

"If that is your only defense," his mother said with a huff, "then stay away from the Broadmere daughters." She set aside her plate as if her appetite had suddenly left her. "They are all fine ladies, unusual in some ways but fine all the same. And they deserve a marriage where they will be cherished. They deserve better than to be toyed with like a child's bauble, then cast aside when their novelty dulls."

Thorne bowed his head, accepting the scolding advice with humility. Not only because he knew he had earned it, but because he loved and respected his mother. He hated that his behavior had reminded her of painful memories best left buried in the past. "I promise you, I will do nothing to harm any of the Broadmere daughters or lessen your opinion of me even further."

"Do not attempt to heap guilt upon me for speaking my mind," she said quietly. "You know you are my greatest joy and treasure. And I am very proud of you for many things. Always have been. It is your behavior with ladies—and I use that term loosely—that I despise." She rang the small bell on the table beside her. "We are done with our tea now."

"Are you ousting me, Mother?"

"Yes." She lifted her plump chin higher and fixed him with a look that let him know quite clearly she was still not entirely happy with him. "Remember what I said about the Broadmere daughters. Do not disappoint me in that respect."

He rose from his seat, feeling well and thoroughly put in his place. Instead of bowing, he moved to her side and kissed her cheek. "I will not disappoint you, Mother. I promise."

"We shall see." She poured herself another cup of tea, indicating she wasn't finished with her favorite time of day, merely finished with him.

Thorne accepted the dismissal, offered a contrite bow, and quietly left the room. Mother had never before been quite so vocal about his *unacceptable dabbling*, as she had put it. He found it mildly disturbing.

Cadwick, the family butler, came to an abrupt halt as Thorne cut in front of him upon entering the hallway. "Forgive me, my lord."

"Forgive *me*, Cadwick. I nearly broadsided you."

The man accepted the apology with a stoic bow. Ever reticent, the butler rarely showed any emotions whatsoever. "I am sure the fault was mine, my lord. Lord Ravenglass is here. I took the liberty of placing him in the library."

"Thank you, Cadwick. That will be all, since we shan't require tea." Thorne turned and headed that way before allowing himself to smile at Cadwick's choice of words. The butler always sounded as if he considered guests as items that required *placing* somewhere.

When Thorne entered the library, Ravenglass looked up from a book he was paging through as he lounged in the leather wingback chair in front of the desk. "Old Cadwick led me to believe you were having a *private* tea with Lady Roslynn, so I made myself comfortable."

Thorne flinched, not minding that his friend understood the true intent of Mother's tea. "The old devil probably knew Mother wished to inform me that, in her estimation, my behavior leaves a great deal to be desired, and she wishes me to change it."

"Ah." Ravenglass nodded as he closed the book and placed it on the desk. "I fear the lovely Lady Myrtlebourne did not help your cause in that regard. The other night at the Atterleys' ball, she made quite the scene when you escaped her."

"I still owe you for that one."

"Indeed, you do." Ravenglass steepled his fingers and tipped his head to one side. "If you don't mind my asking, how did you placate your mother—about your behavior, that is?"

"I promised to treat the Broadmere daughters with all the respect and decorum due them."

"So, you lied."

"I did not lie." Thorne went to the liquor cabinet and held up a decanter of port. At Ravenglass's nod, he poured a glass for each of them. "I was the perfect gentleman during my waltz with Lady

Blessing."

"And after?"

Thorne shrugged as he handed Ravenglass his drink, then took a sip of his own. "There was no *after*. The lady disappeared."

"From what I observed," Ravenglass said, "they all did. The sisters, that is. The duke remained in the ballroom looking slightly bored and more than a little irritated."

"Yes, well, if memory serves, while his father was alive, young Broadmere never held on to a coin long enough to warm it in his hand. If he has yet to come into the full of his inheritance, as Lady Westerbin reported, perhaps the estate's will reined in his spending—and therefore reined in his amusements."

"Poor chap," Ravenglass said. "He appeared quite without friends at the ball." The viscount winked. "He had plenty of company in the form of marriage-minded mamas and their daughters, but no men at his side to help fend them off."

"I wonder…" Thorne paused, trying to bring the duke to mind but failing.

"What are you plotting?"

"If we befriend the brother, would that not get us closer to the sisters?"

"Asks the man who just swore to his mother that he had no intention of defiling the Broadmere ladies." Ravenglass arched a dark brow. "Or have you decided it high time to marry and produce the next baron?"

"I have not decided to marry." Thorne rolled his shoulders. Even saying the word set him on edge. "I tire of clingy widows and other men's wives. I merely think it might be a welcome change to visit with a young lady who…"

"You cannot finish that sentence." Ravenglass snorted. "If they do not end up in your bed, you have no idea what to do with them."

"And you do?"

"I am not the one obsessed with the Broadmere sisters."

"I am not obsessed." Thorne downed the remainder of his

port and set the glass on the desk. "Merely…interested. If you had spoken to Lady Blessing, you would understand completely. The lady speaks her mind with wittiness and candor and could not care less if anyone likes what she says." He couldn't help but laugh. "She is brutally honest."

Ravenglass joined with his own laughter. "Then perhaps I should endeavor to meet her. She sounds as refreshing as a breath of country air."

"Lady Blessing is mine," Thorne said a little stronger than he intended to. "Pick one of the other six."

The viscount arched his brow again and chuckled. "*Yours*, you say? Powerful words for a man who intends to treat the lady properly yet refuses to marry her. Do you not fear giving her the wrong impression? I wager that would go against what you promised Lady Roslynn as well."

"I promised her I would treat them with the utmost respect and decorum," Thorne said, "not take them to the altar." However, he knew that no matter what he had promised anyone, he would see Lady Blessing again. When she had scowled at him from her window, looking as though she was threatening to set the dogs on him, he had known at that moment that he needed to—no, not just needed to, but absolutely *had* to spend more time in the lovely lady's presence. Even if it was merely to endure her cutting wit and stinging tongue. As Ravenglass had said, she was as refreshing as a breath of country air. "As a matter of fact, I was on my way to call upon her this very day."

"Well then, by all means, do not let me delay you any further. I am off to the club. Just thought I would stop in to see if you wished to join me."

Ravenglass's rakish grin assured Thorne his friend had taken no insult at the not-so-subtle hint that the visit was at an end. In fact, he took the amused speculation in the man's eyes as a dare. "Thank you, old friend. I might stop by later—depending upon my visit with Lady Blessing."

"I shall look forward to hearing the report." The viscount

headed out the library door and nodded at the butler to fetch his hat and gloves. He turned back to Thorne with a wicked grin. "I could drop you off on my way to the club."

"And then have me begging them to hail a carriage for my ride home? Thank you, but no. I shall take the curricle."

"A curricle is not large enough for yourself, the lady, and her chaperone." Ravenglass donned his hat and gloves and headed down the hall toward the front door. Without looking back, he held up a finger and reminded Thorne, "Respect and decorum, Knightwood. Respect and decorum." The man was out the door and gone before Thorne could come up with a proper retort.

As much as he hated to admit it, though, his old friend had made a fair point. If lucky enough to convince the lady to come for a ride in the park, he needed to offer a conveyance that told her he fully expected them to be respectably chaperoned. The phaeton would do, but undoubtedly Lady Blessing and her chaperone would be more comfortable in the landau.

"Cadwick, have Thompson bring the landau 'round, please."

With a nod, the butler went to do as requested.

Thorne glanced at his apparel: dark blue dress coat, matching waistcoat, and cream trousers rather than pantaloons. Quite respectable, and appropriate for calling on Lady Blessing at this hour of the day. The question was: would she receive him? A rueful smile came to him. He doubted that she would—but then again, he had always loved a challenge.

When Cadwick returned, he brought Thorne his hat and gloves, then strode to the front door and pulled it open. "Thompson will be around momentarily, my lord."

"Thank you, Cadwick." Thorne stepped out into the sunshine and pulled in a deep breath. While London's air was not nearly as fresh as that of the country, at least it was quite tolerable, since it was early spring and the fetidness of the town in summer had yet to set in.

The landau rattled into view and halted, and Thorne climbed inside.

"Broadmere House on St. James's," he told his coachman as he settled back against the opulent leather squab.

"Very good, my lord." Thompson urged the stunning pair of Cleveland Bays into motion.

Thorne was proud of his horses with their rich brown coats, black points, and black manes and tails. They perfectly set off the earthy tones of the landau, its exterior a glossy black but its interior a lighter sable that reminded him of the color of tea with a healthy dollop of cream. It was not unknown to him that some called him a vain coxcomb, but little did they know that it had taken him years to repair the damage his father had waged upon the family coffers. He had bloody well earned the right to enjoy the fruits of his labors.

It took no time at all to reach the Broadmere residence. After Thompson brought the carriage to a halt in front of the place, Thorne sat there for a long moment, staring at the door. What the devil was he doing here? He flexed his fingers, opening and closing his hands where they rested atop his thighs. Indeed, he wanted to see Lady Blessing again. Spar with her wit. Learn more about what it took to make the lady smile. But then what? He pulled in a deep breath, held it for a second, then let it ease out, hoping it would ease the disturbingly warm tightness in his chest that made itself known whenever he thought of the spirited woman who had no qualms about telling him exactly what she thought of him. The longer he sat there, the worse the tightness became.

"What the devil am I doing here?" he asked himself a second time.

"My lord?" Thompson twisted around in the driver's seat and arched a brow.

Damned if Thorne could have the man take him away now. Even if he told Thompson to hie to the club, word would spread throughout the household that the master had lost his nerve. Thorne also knew it would be reported to his mother. The staff cherished Lady Roslynn and took great pains to keep her informed. That was probably how Mother knew so much about his *unacceptable dabbling*. Servants knew everything.

He forced himself up out of the seat and stepped down onto the walkway. "I am unsure how long I will be, Thompson. If the lads get restless—well, even if they do not, let them stretch their legs and enjoy the day. The park is close. I am sure Broadmere will allow me a footman to flag you down should you not be here when I am ready to leave."

"I can keep a watch on the place while the lads get a bit of exercise, my lord. Never you fear." Thompson tipped his hat and eased the landau away from the curb.

"Up the steps, Knightwood," Thorne muttered to himself, still struggling with the wisdom of coming here in the first place. What the blazes did he hope to accomplish other than to tease himself with a woman he could never have? Before he turned tail and ran like a coward, he tapped the heavy door knocker on the brass plate.

After what felt like an interminable length of time, the same ancient man who had opened the door for the young messenger the other day eyed him with a watery-eyed squint before intoning, "Good day. May I help you?"

Thorne handed his card to the butler and said, "Lord Knightwood to call upon Lady Blessing." If he endeavored to be proper, he would simply leave his card and call at another time to give the lady the opportunity to warm to the idea. But he could only do so much *proper* in a day. If she chose to refuse him, at least she would have his card. "Lord Knightwood to see Lady Blessing?" he repeated a little louder in case the butler suffered from hearing loss due to his age.

With a perfect nod, the man opened the door wider. "Come in, my lord. I am unsure as to whether the Lady Blessing is receiving today. If you would be so good as to wait here, I shall return momentarily."

Thorne noticed the butler didn't offer to take his hat or gloves before ambling down the hallway. Apparently the man didn't hold out much hope for Thorne's success in being seen by the stargazing Broadmere sister. He ignored the urge to rock forward onto the balls of his feet, then back on his heels. *You are not some inexperienced lad,* he told himself. *Stop acting like one.* How on earth had he reduced himself to such behavior? He was always in control.

The elderly servant reappeared, and much like Cadwick's, the man's face was devoid of emotion, revealing absolutely nothing. "Lady Blessing will see you in her observatory, my lord. Please follow me." He turned, then halted almost as an afterthought, spun back around, and held out his hand. "Forgive me, my lord. May I take your hat and gloves?"

Thorne removed his gloves, then swept off his hat and tossed them inside it. "Here you are, my good man. Thank you."

The butler bowed, turned on his heel, then resumed his slow, hitching pace back down the hallway. Thorne almost swore he heard the elderly servant's joints creaking. But he understood Broadmere's desire to keep the man. After all, loyalty was often difficult to come by.

"Here we are, my lord." The butler halted in front of a closed door that was painted a gleaming white and had a large brass plate bolted to its center panel. The plate read: *Blessing's Observatory. Entry by invitation only. You have been warned.*

Thorne smiled and nervously ran his hand across the folds of his stylishly tied cravat. "I consider myself fortunate indeed to be received in the inner sanctum."

"You have no idea, my lord," the butler said before trundling off—either forgetting or choosing *not* to announce Thorne's arrival.

With a chuckle, Thorne shook his head. He took no offense. After all, he knew well enough how to work a door latch. He opened the door and eased inside, taking care to move slowly as if a trap awaited.

"He forgot again, Essie," a voice sang out from somewhere deeper in the high-ceilinged, cavernous room.

"Leave Walters alone, Tutie. He's old and doing his best." Lady Blessing stepped out from behind the largest and most elaborate telescope Thorne had ever seen. She smoothed an errant curl away from her face, trying but failing to tuck it back in with the others. The stubborn tress, as silky and white as an angel's wing, escaped again and fell alongside the soft curve of her cheek. "Do not be offended by our butler, Lord Knightwood. It is not just you he treats this way, but everyone. He's getting on in years but refuses to take his pension and rest. Chance...I mean...His Grace..."

As she paused and rolled her eyes, Thorne had to hold his breath to keep from laughing. This woman's wit was so refreshing. It filled him with such joy, he would willingly spend the rest of his days laughing with her.

"His Grace," she continued, "doesn't have the heart to forcibly pension him off."

"I find that quite commendable of His Grace," Thorne said. "There are several members of my staff who have been with me so long they are more family than servants."

Both her fair eyebrows rose as though she didn't believe him. But rather than call him a liar, she slightly turned and motioned for the one she had called *Tutie* to come forward. "I don't recall if you met this sister of mine at Lady Atterley's ball, so allow me to introduce her. Lady Fortuity. She is fourth in the pecking order, going from oldest to youngest."

"Lady Fortuity, it is an honor." Thorne offered her a bow, noting how she barely stepped out of the shadows as though wishing she could disappear.

The young woman curtsied, then cut her eyes over at Lady Blessing and waited.

Lady Blessing shrugged. "Don't look at me like that. I have no idea what a chaperone does other than make sure my virtue remains intact. Treat this situation like one of your character studies."

Lady Fortuity appeared to like that idea, because she noticeably relaxed before hurrying over to a table and settling down in front of several pieces of foolscap. She picked up what appeared to be a graphite pencil, eyed Thorne for a brief moment, then started writing.

"Character study?" Thorne asked Lady Blessing while trying to behave as if this unusual visit was something he experienced every day.

"Tutie…" Lady Blessing made a face, then drew in a deep breath and blew it out. *"Lady Fortuity* is a writer. Her stories are delightful, and she hopes to have them published someday."

"How interesting," he said even though he wasn't quite certain he wished to end up in some sort of published story. He had enough trouble avoiding too many appearances in the tittle-tattle sheets. "I trust you write fiction and change the names of all your characters to protect their true identities, Lady Fortuity?"

"Of course," the girl said softly without looking up from her notes.

With a faint smile, Lady Blessing waved him closer to the telescope. After a glance in her sister's direction, she gave an amused shake of her head. "She is lost to us now. The faster she writes, the deeper she delves into her worlds." She squared her shoulders and arched a brow, much like she had done the other day when glaring at him from her window. "What can I do for you, Lord Knightwood?"

"Do for me?" The lady sounded like a merchant ready to wait on him.

"Why are you here?" she said more slowly, as though adjusting her opinion of his intelligence or the lack thereof.

He offered her his most beguiling smile, the one that usually made the ladies swoon at his feet. "Why, I am calling on you, Lady Blessing. I found your company the other evening most charming and wish to know you better." When she didn't react as he'd expected, he pointed at the telescope. "And I wished to learn more about your observatory."

"I see." She puckered her mouth, then seemed to jerk as

though startled and smoothed her fingers across her lips as if trying to wipe the pucker away. "Are you a student of astronomy?"

Common sense bade him answer honestly, or she'd call him out on the lie. "Nothing so educated or formal, my lady. I merely find that a sense of peace settles across me when I gaze at the night sky and lose myself in its grandeur."

She almost smiled but managed to catch herself and stop it in time. But her eyes betrayed her. She heartily approved of his answer. It made him even more determined to coax her smile free.

With an acknowledging twitch of a brow, she moved to one side, then pointedly nodded at the telescope's eyepiece. "Would you care to look? I just adjusted it for more accuracy in one of Fortuity's stories. Her research, you might say."

"But it's daylight," he gently reminded her, not wishing to deter or insult her.

Both her fair brows, darker than her gleaming white hair but still quite blonde, rose once again until they nearly reached the short, wispy tendrils framing her forehead. "I am well aware of the time," she said, her tone slightly mocking. She nodded at the eyepiece again. "Have a look, my lord. You might be surprised at what you see."

Deciding to humor her, he peered into the eyepiece, then straightened and frowned.

No. That was not possible.

He bent and looked again.

"What do you see, my lord?"

"The moon," he breathed with reverence. "Every blessed circle, shadow, and dimple of it."

"Craters, mountains, and ridges," she corrected him, a hint of merriment in her voice. "And yet if you step out onto the balcony and peer up into the sky, all you might see is the faintest white outline of the moon's edge, since it's early afternoon."

"Amazing." The image was so crisp and clear, he felt as

though he could reach out and touch it. He straightened again and met her lively aquamarine gaze that made everything else pale in comparison. "Now I better understand your wish to be here on the clear night of Lady Atterley's ball. Who knows what stunning things you could have seen?"

"Thank you." The delighted look she gave him made the warm tightness in the center of his chest burn even hotter and radiate through him.

He swallowed hard and fought the urge to reach out and touch her cheek—or, heaven forbid, sample the sweetness of her perfectly pink lips. No. No matter how badly he longed for the feel of her in his arms, Lady Blessing was not to be trifled with.

"You are quite welcome, Lady Blessing," he managed to say. "Glad to be of service." But something in her eyes gave him pause. Was that a bit of longing he saw in them? Might she be attracted to him too?

Perhaps some fresh air was in order. It would do them both good. "I brought the landau," he announced with perhaps a tad too much energy. What the blazes was his bloody problem today? He was not an inexperienced cub. "Would you and Lady Fortuity care to join me for a ride in the park? As I am sure you already know the day is quite lovely for an outing."

Her delight disappeared as though it had never existed, immediately replaced with calm indifference. "No, thank you, Lord Knightwood." She made her way to the door and opened it wide, clearly dismissing him. "But I have enjoyed our visit. Thank you so much for calling today."

He eyed her but then decided against attempting to change her mind. No, that simply wouldn't do. Something about the lady told him she would set her stance and hold fast like the stubbornest of mules. He bowed to Lady Fortuity, who gave him the barest dip of her chin before returning her attention to her papers. "Good day, Lady Fortuity."

"Good day, Lord Knightwood," she said without looking up again.

He went to Lady Blessing and bowed again. "Thank you so much for your time today, my lady. You are indeed a treasure."

"Good day, Lord Knightwood," she said with the slightest curtsy, but he didn't miss the look in her eyes or the heightened blush across her cheeks. The lady liked him. He almost danced his way down the hallway, already planning the next move to impress the lovely Lady Blessing and find a way to draw her expression of delight back out into the open.

Chapter Five

"HE SEEMS TO like you very much."

Blessing eyed her sister, trying to decide how to keep Fortuity quiet or convince her to report Lord Knightwood's visit in such a manner as to stanch their brother's marriage-minded aspirations. Fortuity couldn't lie to save her soul—much like Serendipity. Not that Blessing could lie either, but at least she possessed the ability to dance around a subject with at least a modicum of artfulness. "You heard what Chance and Seri said about the man."

"That he is a rake?"

"Exactly. Beds them. Doesn't wed them."

"Then why did he visit and behave like the perfect gentleman?" Fortuity adjusted the flame on the lamp beside her, then scribbled another note in the margins of a sheet so full she would soon have to start a fresh one.

"I have no idea." And that filled Blessing with a heady mixture of fascination and dread. If the man had no interest in marriage, then his calls were tantamount to an insult, to his saying he considered her a lightskirt and easy prey. In that case, how dare he! But rather than make her angry, if she was honest, it made her somewhat sad. Well, maybe not sad—but unhappily wistful?

She shook her head to rid herself of the thought. Good heavens, Chance had contaminated her thinking—making her view the subject of matrimony with an overt amount of seriousness. She snorted the silliness right out of her head.

"You like him." Fortuity sat there staring at her while thoughtfully chewing on the end of her pencil.

"I do not know the man." Blessing busied herself at the telescope even though she had researched and written every detail she could about the moon without actually going there.

"You know him well enough to know whether or not you like him."

"I met the man in the garden at a ball, danced a waltz with him, and spoke with him today for *perhaps* a quarter of an hour. I daresay that is not knowing someone well enough to know whether or not you like them."

"Intuition and heart," Fortuity countered. "Remember what Mama said about Papa? How she knew within moments of meeting him that he was the one for her?" She patted her chest. "Mama said a woman's heart and intuition are their very best compasses for navigating life's path." After pausing to make another note on her parchment, she tapped on it, then gave Blessing a meaningful look. "What does your intuition and heart tell you?"

"That I do not know him well enough." Blessing was not about to confide in Fortuity, because not only could her younger sister not tell a passable lie, but she was also incapable of keeping a secret. Serendipity was the only safe confidante, and in this matter, even she was questionable.

A light thump on the bottom of the observatory door, as though someone had gently kicked it, interrupted them. Without opening it, Walters called out in a strained voice, "A delivery has arrived for you, my lady."

Blessing frowned at Fortuity, who responded with a curious shrug and shooed her to hurry and open it. Blessing crossed the room, opened the door, and then found herself unable to speak.

"My lady?" Walters said from behind the largest armload of pink, purple, and blue asters that Blessing had ever seen. "Where would you like them? They were delivered in quite a nice vase, but Mrs. Flackney said we should add water to it once we place them where you wish them to be. A scroll is tied to the neck of the vase with a ribbon. Along the edge of the scroll is written, *Read first.*"

"Read first?" As if she wouldn't notice the massive bouquet that usually didn't bloom until Michaelmas? These hothouse lovelies, forced to bloom early, must have been quite dear indeed. Blessing realized that the vase of flowers was probably growing quite heavy in their poor butler's grasp. "Forgive me, Walters. Do come in and place them on the center table there. That will do nicely."

"Thank you, Lady Blessing." The man's relief was unmistakable. He placed the arrangement on the table, then bent and pointed at the beribboned scroll hanging from the neck of the loveliest vase. Its background glaze was the deepest blue of a midnight sky and pinpricks of gold were scattered across it like stars.

Without straightening, the butler asked, "Shall I remove the scroll so you might read it, my lady?"

"That would be wonderful, Walters. Thank you."

With the greatest of care, the man untied the ribbon and slipped it out from around the vase. As he presented it to her, he offered a slight bow. "If that will be all, my lady, I shall advise Mrs. Flackney to send in a maid with more water for the flowers."

"Thank you, Walters. That will do nicely." Blessing waited until he'd left the room before moving to the window for better light to read the scroll.

Fortuity joined her, nudging in close and almost bouncing with curiosity. "Hurry and unroll it."

Blessing didn't mind Fortuity nosing in to see what the scroll said. With six sisters, there was no such thing as privacy unless one fought for it, and Blessing preferred to choose her battles with care. She unrolled the scroll and smiled at the familiar name that caught her eye.

My dearest Lady Blessing,

The legends say that the goddess Astraea lived alongside man-kind the longest of all the immortals. But she was forced to abandon her precious humans when mighty Zeus sent a great flood to rid the world of man's evil. As she fled to the sky, her tears for the terrible loss of life became stardust that spread across the earth, creating the first aster flowers. Once she reached the heavens, her sorrow was so unbearable that Zeus allowed her to become the constellation Virgo and find her peace among the other stars. It is said that when Astraea finally returns to the mortal world, she will bring with her a new Golden Age.

You are that Golden Age, Lady Blessing. A stunning ray of hope in an otherwise cynical world.

Ever your faithful and devoted servant,

Thorne

"Oh my," Fortuity said in a breathless whisper.

"Oh my, indeed," Blessing agreed, reading the scroll a second time while pressing a hand to her pounding heart. He had done this for her. Because of her love of the stars. His thoughtfulness, his attention to what she was truly interested in, touched her so much. Only Papa had ever done such things before, saying it was his job to treat all his daughters special until they found a man worthy of them, one willing to treat them with the loving care they deserved.

"What are you going to do?" Fortuity asked, still speaking in a whisper as if the scroll were a living thing that might be offended if it was not treated with the proper reverence.

Blessing pulled in a deep breath, then let it ease out, the thrilled pattering of her heart still echoing in her ears. "I honestly do not know what to do. None of this makes sense." She carefully rerolled the scroll and secured it with the ribbon, knowing she would keep this precious memento always.

"The man does not marry," she said more to herself than to

her sister. "Seri and Chance both said so, and Seri said it was well known among the *ton* that he prefers other men's wives and widows who are not interested in marriage." Her cheeks burned with a furious blush at the thought of what the widows were interested in when it came to Lord Knightwood. "He is not old, but he is old enough that he should have found a wife years ago and already have an heir or two to take over the barony when he leaves this world. Obviously, he does not wish to ever marry."

"Or perhaps he simply has not found the woman he wishes to marry."

Blessing couldn't keep from rolling her eyes. "This is not one of your happily-ever-after love tales, Tutie."

Fortuity twitched another shrug, her smug demeanor saying exactly what she thought about that.

Blessing placed the scroll in the drawer of the table beside her telescope, alongside her journals and charts. It should be safe enough from nosy siblings there, since she kept her observatory locked. After closing the drawer, she threatened her sister with a shake of her finger. "Not one word about the scroll to anyone or I will tell Chance where you hide all your finished stories."

"You wouldn't."

"Are you brave enough to try me?"

"Walters knows about the scroll," Fortuity said, "and I am sure Mrs. Flackney and *all* the maids already know it exists too. One of them will surely say something about it to Seri or Chance." She gave a temperamental jerk of her head. "If they find out about that scroll, it will not be my fault."

Blessing eked out a frustrated groan. "Gads, you are right. They are sure to come knocking at any moment, and then Chance is going to be as unstable as a tailless kite in a high wind."

"You might as well tell them the man is courting you."

"But what if he is not? What if he is merely trying his hand at seducing unsuspecting innocents rather than other men's wives or widows?"

Fortuity snorted. "I would hardly label you as unsuspecting

or innocent."

"And what is that supposed to mean?" Blessing did not have time to spar with her sister—not when the rest of her siblings could descend upon her at any moment. "I am a virgin, have never courted anyone, and you know as well as I that none of us have ever experienced what one might call a Season at the mercy of the Marriage Mart."

"What I meant was that out of all of us, you are the boldest and most likely to tell the man to go straight to the devil if he does anything you do not wish him to do." Fortuity returned to the writing table, gathered up her notes, and tucked them into the crook of her arm.

"Where are you going?" A disturbing sense of rising panic curdled in Blessing's middle. "You cannot desert me in my hour of need."

Fortuity stared at her as if she didn't know who she was. "This is not like you at all. Why would you say this is your *hour of need?*"

"You know either Seri or Chance—and possibly the others—are going to come through that door at any moment."

"You threatened my stories." Fortuity hiked her chin higher. "I am going upstairs to move them."

"Tutie...please?" Blessing hated to beg, but the thought of becoming Chance's primary focus unsettled her as much or more than the disturbing realization that she rather liked Lord Knightwood's attention a great deal more than she should.

A light rapping on the door made her jump.

"Essie—may I enter? Walters said you received a lovely bouquet," Serendipity called from the other side.

"I am here too," Chance said, his deep voice entirely too excited.

"And so it begins," Blessing muttered.

Fortuity gave her a sympathetic pat on the shoulder, then took a seat back at the writing table. "I shall be right here."

After a resigned sigh, Blessing told them, "You may come in

and see them."

The door swung open, and her siblings rushed into the room like a pair of children invited into a sweet shop.

"Oh my," Serendipity exclaimed, "asters? How stunning and unexpected this time of year."

Chance circled the table, bending, straightening, and then bending again as he examined the flowers and the exquisite vase from every possible angle. "And to whom do you owe thanks for this thoughtful gesture, dear Essie?"

"Do not play the innocent or the obtuse, brother. It does not suit you." Blessing resettled her stance, readying for the battle of wills. "You know the identity of the sender as well as I do. Of that, I am sure."

"I am crushed you would speak to me in such a way. Why would you say such a thing?" Chance assumed a hurt look that didn't fool Blessing for a moment.

"Because Walters gossips worse than the tittle-tattle sheets, and I am quite certain he sorted out who the sender was before he even brought the flowers to me." It had not escaped Blessing's notice that the ribbon securing the scroll to the vase appeared to have been untied and retied before the butler retrieved it and handed it to her. The creases in the strip of blue satin gave the servant's actions away. In Walters's defense, none of their servants would be able to resist the temptation of at least peeking to see who had sent the gift. They kept up with everything in the household.

"Lord Knightwood seems to be playing some sort of game," she announced with unhappy conviction.

"Game?" her older siblings repeated in unison.

"What game?" Serendipity stepped forward, concern tightening her features as she took hold of both of Blessing's hands. She glanced at Fortuity where she sat at the writing table. "Was his behavior unseemly? Were unsavory advances made? I will not have any of my sisters treated in such a manner." She turned and fixed a hard stare on Chance. "Will we?"

"Absolutely not," Chance said. He strode forward, took Blessing's hands away from Serendipity, and peered into her eyes. "No matter how badly I wish to see each of you married, I will not tolerate any man mistreating or maligning you. Do I need to pay Lord Knightwood a visit?"

"He was a complete gentleman, and his visit was brief," Blessing said. She turned to Fortuity. "What did it last, Tutie? Perhaps a quarter of an hour?"

"If that," Fortuity said. "He invited us to join him on a ride to the park in his landau, but Essie refused."

Blessing cringed. Fortuity would have to volunteer that tidbit.

"Why did you refuse?" Chase dropped her hands as if they burned him. "With Tutie as your chaperone, it would have been completely proper."

"It did not *feel* proper," Blessing said. "Besides, you and Seri said the man is a rake who beds rather than weds. If that is the case, what possible interest could he have in me? Perhaps his attentions are actually an insult. Did either of you happen to think about that?" It pained her to malign the man, but she couldn't ignore her fears. Why would a confirmed bachelor who had no interest in marriage waste not only his time—her gaze returned to the extraordinary flowers—but also his money on her?

"That is not a baseless question," Serendipity noted with a worried tone. "What did the scroll say?"

"And how did you know about the scroll?" Blessing arched a brow and decided to have a very stern word with Walters at her next opportunity.

"I… Uhm…" Serendipity threw up both hands. "You know very well how I knew about the scroll. What did it say?"

Rather than argue or huff about, Blessing snatched it out of the drawer and handed it to her sister. "Since privacy does not exist in this household, here. Read it for yourself."

After extending her the courtesy of looking somewhat ashamed, Serendipity unrolled the parchment, read it, then released a heartfelt sigh.

"Well?" Chance stepped closer and peered over her shoulder. "Is it insulting?"

"Not in the least," Fortuity volunteered from her perch at the writing table.

"These are not the words of a rake," Serendipity said as she handed the scroll back to Blessing.

"How would you know?" Blessing demanded. "Exactly how many rakes have sent you messages?" She returned the scroll to the safety of the drawer and then glared at her siblings.

"I shall speak with the man and ask him his intentions," Chance said.

"You will not." The mere thought of her brother doing such a thing horrified Blessing. Wasn't this entire situation humiliating enough? She hadn't a clue how to handle it, nor had she completely decided if she wished Lord Knightwood's attentions to come to an end. "Leave it alone, Chance. This is my situation to handle."

"It is not," her brother argued. "I am not only protecting your honor but keeping your best interests at heart."

"You are not. You are trying to hurry and marry me off so you can put the next sister on the auction block."

"Essie." The dismay in her brother's eyes filled her with guilt. She truly had hurt his feelings with that remark.

"Forgive me, Chance." Blessing tried to restore a modicum of control with a deep breath. "Might we simply see how things go along? Surely, if I keep a tight hold on my virtue, if that truly is Lord Knightwood's goal, he shall soon grow bored and move on to someone else."

"Not necessarily," Chance said with a dubious frown. "A man always wants what he cannot have, and when it is kept from him, his resolve often strengthens."

"That sounds like the voice of experience." Blessing folded her arms across her chest and silently dared her brother to say more.

"Lady Burrastone's party is tomorrow evening," Serendipity

interrupted. "You know how she is about including the most interesting and lively persons at her gatherings. Lord Knightwood is sure to be invited. If he is, flirt with the others in attendance and see how he reacts."

"Flirt? I have no idea how to *flirt*." Had Serendipity gone mad with the stress of life without Mama and Papa and dealing with Chance? Blessing glared at her.

Chance rubbed his eyes as if getting another of the headaches he always felt whenever dealing with his sisters. "Pay attention to other men. Talk to them. Smile at them. Laugh at whatever insipid foolishness they happen to spout in your presence."

Insulted at their suggestion that she should behave like an affectionate puppy, Blessing jutted her chin higher. "I refuse to dance upon a string like a lovesick puppet. The man I marry will love and cherish me without all those foolish parlor games."

"So you do intend to marry?" Chance said, grinning like a hunter who had just felled the plumpest partridge.

"Eventually, if—and that is a very large *if*, mind you—I love the man, and he loves me more than he loves my dowry." She nodded at the door. "You have seen the flowers and read the scroll. You may now go. Both of you." She turned and gave Fortuity an apologetic smile. "You may go now as well, Tutie, and do not worry. My lips are sealed."

"Your lips are sealed about what?" Chance eyed them both, glancing back and forth as if trying to catch them passing secret messages by blinking in a certain sequence.

"If I told you, then they wouldn't be sealed, now would they?" Blessing caught hold of his arm and then Serendipity's and tugged them both toward the door. "Out. Now. I shall see you again at teatime. Agreed?"

When finally alone, she contemplated locking herself inside but decided against it. One of the maids would soon be coming with water for the flowers. She touched the velvety softness of the aster's delicate petals, hitching in a deep breath at the memory of Lord Knightwood's sentiments on the scroll. A scroll—not the usual folded note with a wax seal, but a scroll befitting the goddess Astraea herself.

Serendipity had said a rake would not write such things, but Blessing feared her sister might be wrong. Wouldn't a man desiring to debauch a woman write exactly those sorts of things to catch the lady's heart and make her an easier conquest? And that question made Blessing sad, because even though she knew the sort of man Lord Knightwood was, she rather liked him. He was inventive—and interesting. He was also the first man who had ever taken an interest in what interested her. Of course, to be fair, he was the first man she had allowed close enough to even discover what interested her.

Her gaze lowered to the exquisite vase that held the flowers—such a gorgeous and unique depiction of a starry night. How had he possibly found it so quickly when he had only just visited today?

"What are Lord Knightwood's intentions?"

Unfortunately, the midnight-blue urn with the golden stars remained silent, as did the asters.

She turned away from the flowers and made her way to the wall of windows overlooking the gardens and the mews. From this vantage point, and with the clearness of the balmy spring day, she could see across the way to forever. Unfortunately, *forever* wasn't what she was looking for—answers were.

Then Lord Knightwood stepped out of the shelter of the ancient oak Mama had insisted they leave growing beside the stable. He smiled up at her, almost as if he had known she would come to the window and look for him as she had done the other day. After a polite nod, he touched his lips, then his heart, then extended his hand as though handing her the possession of both.

Without thinking, she touched her heart at his gesture, then hurried to drop her hand to her side when she realized what she had done.

His smile went as broad as could be, his straight white teeth gleaming. Then he laughed, swept off his hat, and bowed.

She touched the window, flattening her hand on the cool pane.

He reached for her again and held his hand the same way, as though pressing his palm to hers.

"What do you want with me, Lord Knightwood?" she whispered.

Almost as though he heard her, he touched his chest again, then offered his heart to her with another flourish of his hand.

She backed away from the window, her own heart pounding. She already liked him very much. Too much, truth be told. But was it safe to do so? No matter how lovely he made her feel, no matter how badly she wanted his attentions to continue, she would not be toyed with, nor played for a fool. Not only would that ruin her life, but also ruin her sisters. It only took one wayward daughter to bring down an entire family in the eyes of the *ton*.

With her bottom lip caught between her teeth, she eased forward once more and peered out the window. Her heart fell with the saddest thump, like a stone dropped into a pond. He was gone. As she stared at the spot where he had stood, she wished she could just race after him and demand to know what he was trying to do. What were his intentions? But then, what would she do when he told her?

"I have to know." She whirled about, went to the writing table, and took a seat. Selecting a sheet of her best stationery, she held the inked quill above it and stared at the creamy expanse of emptiness waiting to be filled with her thoughts. Yes. She would do this. She would write to him, ask him his intentions, and then act accordingly.

A huffing snort escaped her. Whatever *act accordingly* meant.

Chapter Six

THORNE RECOGNIZED HIS mother's light yet rapid tapping on his study door. Rather than bellow to make himself heard, he rose from behind his desk and crossed the room to open it. "Mother—you know you may always enter unless I am with someone." Her woeful expression sent a surge of concern through him.

Tears welled in her worried eyes, and she clasped her fisted hands to her bosom. "I cannot find Hera," she said. "Not anywhere. And neither Cook nor Mrs. Hartcastle has seen her either. I fear it may be her time."

"It will be all right, Mother. We shall find her." Business could wait. Thorne could not bear seeing his mother so upset. "Where have you not yet searched?"

"Only the library and here, in your office."

Thorne nodded, knowing his mother's precious cat delighted in sneaking into his study whenever she discovered the door left ajar. "I'll wager the minx is in her favorite hiding spot. Come, let us have a look."

Lady Roslynn clasped her hands tighter to her chest and hitched in a cautious breath. "Oh, I do hope so. I just know it is her time."

"If it is, she will know what to do, Mother. Animals have instincts about these things."

"Do not speak of her as if she has no heart or soul. Hera—nor any animal—is not some mindless beast, as some would have us believe. They need our help and understanding."

Hence, the only meat Lady Roslynn ever tolerated on their table was fish or shellfish. At one time she had allowed fowl, but that was before she befriended a chicken at their estate in the country. When Thorne craved mutton, pork, or beef, he had to find it elsewhere. Thank heavens Mother still permitted eggs, but he felt sure that once she decided eating them would upset the chickens, those would be banned as well.

Accepting his mother's unusual snappishness as a result of her overwrought state, he gently led her to the cushioned bench built into the bay window that overlooked their garden. "See that panel in the shadow of the bookcase? It's pushed in again. Let me fetch the lamp, and then I shall pry open the bench so we might see if she has snuck in there like she did the last time."

He retrieved the smaller of the two oil lamps from his desk and handed it to her. After discovering the wily Hera hiding inside the built-in bench before, he felt sure the cat would be there again. With a mighty upward yank, he separated the seat from the base and raised it enough so he and his mother could peer inside.

The enormous black and white feline, beloved Hera in all her glory, lay snuggled in the folds of an old blanket. Three tiny kittens, one solid black, one solid white, and the other colored like its mother, were tucked against her belly like tiny, furry potatoes. Hera looked up at them with her great golden eyes and unleashed a haughty *meow*, as if to tell them to get that light out of her eyes and leave her alone.

"Three babies," his mother whispered, delight dancing in her voice. She peered closer. "How did that blanket come to be in there?"

He carefully lowered the seat without so much as a thump, took the lamp from his mother, and returned it to his desk. "Hera has always liked that spot, and I suspected she might choose to have her kittens there."

"You are such a thoughtful boy."

"I try."

"I must find Zeus now and tell him he is a father."

Thorne doubted very much if the tattered old tomcat who had shown up in their garden with a pronounced limp would care that his amorous activities had been fruitful, but he decided not to mention that to Mother. "Why not give him a saucer of cream to celebrate his new status?"

"An excellent idea." She peered up at him and arched a hopeful brow but remained silent.

Surrendering without a fight, he nodded. "Yes, Mother. Bring a saucer for Hera as well. I shall place it inside her den so she doesn't feel inclined to leave her children."

A knock at the door followed by a quiet "Lord Knightwood?" interrupted them.

"Come in, Cadwick. The feline goddess is a proud mother of three and has graced my office with her presence. The household may stop searching now."

Lady Roslynn swatted his arm. "Do not tease. As a new mother, I am sure our Hera is very sensitive."

Cadwick stood there eyeing them both as if afraid to speak.

Thorne noticed the note the man held in his hand. "You wished to deliver that, I presume?"

The butler dipped a curt bow and handed it over. "Yes, my lord. It just came. No messenger waits for a reply. Shall I wait in case you wish to post one anyway?"

"That won't be necessary. Thank you, Cadwick. That will be all—Oh, wait. Would you be good enough to send in a saucer of cream for the new mother?" Thorne smiled to himself. The butler hated the cat, because if she wasn't tripping him by darting between his feet when he walked on the stairs, she was leaping down from her secret perches to startle him.

Cadwick's expression never changed. He knew better than to say or do anything against Lady Roslynn's beloved cat. "I shall see to it immediately, my lord."

As soon as the door closed behind him, Lady Roslynn giggled. "You know how he feels about Hera."

"Yes." Thorne grinned. "I am well aware."

She got on tiptoes to kiss his cheek. "I shall leave you to your correspondence." But she failed to hide her angling to peek at the seal on the letter in his hand. "That is the Broadmere crest."

"So it is." He didn't volunteer any information, curious to see if any of her spies had informed her of his recent visit to the Broadmere townhouse.

She arched a brow and waited, her dark eyes not only the mirror image of his but also quite revealing. She did, in fact, know of his calling on the lovely Broadmere daughter who adored the stars.

"Lady Blessing received me, but you will be pleased to know that she declined my invitation for a ride in the park."

"I assume there was a chaperone during your call upon her?" His mother's glare sharpened.

"But of course. I am dismayed you would even suggest such an insult to Lady Blessing's character. Her sister, Lady Fortuity, joined us in the observatory, where we studied the moon in such detail that it was quite amazing."

"Studied the moon," Lady Roslynn repeated in a dubious tone. "During the daytime?"

"Yes."

"In detail."

"Yes."

"Even though you have reached the ripe old age of four and thirty, lying to your mother is still quite unacceptable and will not be tolerated."

"I am not lying, and if you doubt me, speak with Thompson, who will tell you that my time at the Broadmere residence could not have possibly been longer than a quarter of an hour." He struggled not to smile, waiting to see if her inquisitiveness about the note would get the better of her.

"Are you not going to open your letter?" She folded her hands and propped them atop the plumpness of her stomach—a sure sign that she was not about to leave the room until she discovered what the note contained.

He snapped the wax seal, then slid his finger under the flap and removed the letter from its envelope. The flowing script on the expensive notepaper was as delicate and beautiful as a piece of art:

My dear Lord Knightwood,

I wish to thank you for the lovely bouquet that arrived in the even lovelier vase. The depiction of a midnight sky filled with stars was most pleasing both in appearance and its symbolism for my love of astronomy. Perhaps even more treasured was the scroll that related one of the many legends of the goddess Astraea. While I found it truly touching, I should warn you that your reputation is not unknown to me.

I am sure you will find this note unusually blunt and perhaps not one Society would deem fitting for a young lady to send to a gentleman, but I am the sort who considers honesty to be of the utmost importance. Since I am an honorable and virtuous type, I am in a quandary as to what you hope to accomplish in an acquaintance with me. I pray you do not take insult at such a statement, but you must admit your reputation begs the question be asked: since you do not wish to marry— what do you want with me?

While I enjoy your company very much, I would rather not become accustomed to your presence if your intentions are nefarious. Alas, as I warned, I am blunt and honest to a fault. Please accept this letter of thanks in the genuine spirit of friendship and inquiry that is intended.

Yours in kindness,
Lady Blessing Abarough

Indeed, what did he want from dear Lady Blessing? Thorne stared down at the letter, reading it a second time, slower, savoring her turn of phrase. He could hear her saying the words inside his head and took no insult at her question. After all, the lady spoke the truth. He had a reputation. But what hit him the hardest, charging him full of anticipation and hope, was that she had said she enjoyed his company. *Very much,* she'd said. A dangerous warmth surged through him as his heart lurched with the thrill of an almost successful chase. But was it a successful chase? And what did he intend to do if he caught her?

"Well?" his mother prompted him.

Thorne lifted his gaze from the letter and blinked. He had been so enraptured by Lady Blessing's voice in his mind, and the intent behind her words, that he had as good as forgotten his mother was there.

Rather than try to explain the contents, he held it out to her. "You are welcome to read it."

She snatched it from him and read it, her lips moving in silence as her gaze swept back and forth across the page. Her smile slowly stretched wider. By the time she looked up at him, she was fairly beaming.

"Well?" she asked again.

"Well, what?"

"What answer do you have for the lady's very warranted question?" She handed the letter back to him and primly folded her hands onto the shelf of her middle once again. "At least she extended you the courtesy of asking rather than trying to piece together everything through gossip." She eyed him as if daring him to answer incorrectly. "What *are* your intentions as far as Lady Blessing is concerned?"

"I fear I do not know," he admitted quietly, noting a disturbing heaviness in his chest. "She is—" He deflated with a groaning sigh, then frowned when his mother's expression brightened. "And what, pray tell, does that look mean?"

Lady Roslynn lightly touched his arm. "I find promise in your response."

"How so? I admitted that I didn't know and could not find the words to describe her."

"Exactly." She turned and wrinkled her nose at the door. "Cadwick has either forgotten or chosen not to fetch Hera's cream. I must see to it now. Mothering is thirsty work." Before exiting the room, she turned back and shook a finger at him. "Two things, my son."

"Yes?"

"Go carefully with Lady Blessing."

"And the other?"

"Help Cadwick understand that if he wishes to remain employed in this household, he would do well to remember my love of cats and dislike of people who treat any animal poorly— including ignoring a request to fetch them a special treat."

"I shall give proper attention to the matter, Mother." He returned to his desk and sank into the leather sumptuousness of his chair.

He stared at the door for a long while after his mother left. Warning Cadwick about his treatment of the cats was most definitely the easier of the two, because he had no idea what to do about Lady Blessing. As he saw it, he had three choices. Cut off all association with the lady? That would be a *no*. The mere thought of never speaking with her, dancing with her, or enjoying another visit with her made his chest tighten. Seduce her? Another no. While *parts* of him would heartily enjoy the pleasure, neither his heart nor his conscience would allow him to debauch her. And not simply because of the rage his mother would rain down upon him if he did such a thing. No. He couldn't do it because he honestly didn't think he could bear being responsible for putting hurt and disappointment in Lady Blessing's lovely blue eyes. The final choice, the only choice he had yet to *yay* or *nay*, was to court her in earnest. Seek her hand in marriage. He swallowed hard at the thought, nearly choking on the unspoken words.

Another knock on the door spared him from having to answer.

"What is it?" he asked a bit more sharply than he intended.

The door opened, and Cadwick stepped inside and said in a lowered voice, "Lady Myrtlebourne wishes to see you, my lord. I took the liberty of placing her in the smaller parlor."

"Lady Myrtlebourne?" Thorne repeated. "With her husband, I presume?" Although surely Cadwick would have announced the earl rather than his wife.

"No, my lord," Cadwick said just as quietly. "She is quite alone. Shall I inform the lady you are not in?"

"No, she must be dealt with." Thorne pushed himself up from his desk and moved to the door. "I shall join her in the small parlor, but the doors will remain open as wide as I can push them. I also wish to be interrupted at five-minute intervals. By you, the maids, the footmen, whoever. Just see that someone comes to that parlor every five minutes during this unwanted visit. Understood?"

"Yes, my lord." Cadwick stepped back into the hall.

"And Cadwick—"

"Yes, my lord?" The butler watched him as though ready to spring into action.

"If you do not treat the cats like the gods and goddesses my mother believes them to be, you value your position here very little. Am I understood?"

The man's mouth tightened before he had the good sense to bow his head and lock his gaze on his shoes. "Understood quite clearly, my lord. I shall see to it that the new mother is provided with a saucer of kippers to go along with her cream."

"A fine idea, Cadwick. Make certain Mother knows that it was yours."

"Thank you, my lord."

As the butler headed toward the kitchens, Thorne braced himself as if he were going to battle. Which, in essence, he was. It was unheard of for a married woman, a countess, no less, to call upon a man at his residence without a companion in tow. This visit smacked of danger, deceit, and quite possibly a prelude to blackmail.

He opened the sliding doors to the small parlor as wide as possible and left them that way. "Lady Myrtlebourne. What an unexpected visit."

"I notice you did not say *what a pleasant surprise*," the countess retorted as she turned from the window and glared at him. Her gaze slid past him to the open doors, and her mouth tightened into a moue of distaste. "I never thought you the heartless sort, Thorne. Nor so obtuse. Does nothing about my appearance seem different to you?"

It was then he realized she was enrobed in layers of black bombazine and crepe. Even the black ostrich plumes sprouting up from her ridiculous hat with its black veil streaming down her back shouted that the woman was in deep mourning. He promptly bowed. "My condolences, Lady Myrtlebourne. Forgive me for not noticing sooner. Whom, might I ask, have you lost? A parent or sibling, perhaps?"

Her glare turned even icier. "Do not play the innocent, Thorne. It does not suit you. My husband is dead. A mere three days ago. Did you not see the announcement in today's paper?"

"I have yet to get to it." He angled his head to one side, unable to fathom why she stood in his parlor when she should be sequestered in her home. "Your husband, you say? The man was a picture of good health but a week ago. Was there a tragic accident of which I am unaware?"

She twitched an uncaring shrug. "His valet found him dead when he went in to dress him. Apparently he died in his sleep."

While he knew the lady's marriage had never been anything more than a union to a man she despised, Thorne still found her cold disregard for the earl's death disturbing. "Should you not be at home, Lady Myrtlebourne? In the comforting care of friends and family?"

The woman laughed, shocking him even more. "Surely you jest? If not for my husband's brother, Lord Agnew Montagne, threatening to turn me out even before the proper mourning period was up, I'd be wearing my brightest red dress and dancing at Vauxhall Gardens in celebration of Arthur's death." Her eyes narrowed as she pointed at him. "That is why I am here, *my love*. I need to get with child—male issue, of course—but also have a husband-to-be waiting in the wings in case a daughter is born. You owe me."

"I owe you?" The woman was mad. Neither of them owed the other a thing. "And why, my lady, would I *owe* you?"

"Because I made it known to Lord Montagne that the earl had sought your advice about several business schemes and benefited from them greatly. Our *tête-à-têtes* were meetings to forward financial information to my husband while he was abroad."

"And why did you feel the need to invent such a lie?" Thorne had a pretty good idea but needed the time to get a handle on the outrageousness of what she had suggested.

She twitched another snappish shrug but turned aside to avoid looking him in the eye. "Arthur was aware you cuckolded him."

"How?"

Plucking at the black glass beads dangling from her reticule, she edged away, increasing the distance between them. "I might have told him."

Thorne strode forward, took her by the shoulders, and forced her to face him. "Why the devil would you do such a foolish thing?"

"I hated him," she growled through her bared teeth. "Tell me you have never spoken out of turn when infuriated beyond belief."

He set her aside and moved as far from her as the room allowed. "And I assume the earl told Montagne?"

"And his solicitor. He intended to bring a criminal conversation against you in a civil trial, then planned to request a legal separation that would leave me with nothing while he divorced me." She sneered at him while tipping her head from side to side like a taunting child. "So, you see? You owe me. Montagne intended to carry on the suit against you in the name of his

8888888

888

brother and possibly even insinuate you caused Arthur's death by making his temper flare too hot. My lie has caused him to at least pause and think about what the suit would do to his brother's memory. I told him I had lied to Arthur about the nature of our acquaintance because Arthur threw his indiscretions in my face."

"You forget, Lady Myrtlebourne, that I am not the only man you invited to your bed while your husband was away." Thorne raked a hand through his hair, wondering when the devil his servants would interrupt him as instructed. "At least three others found their names linked to yours in several of the gossip sheets. Is Montagne aware of them? Was the earl?"

"You cannot abandon me in this." She rushed toward him but halted when he dodged her. "How could you be so cruel?"

"We ended our affair months ago. Mutually agreed on it. You had already taken up another entanglement by the time your husband returned." He edged closer to the open doors until he stood partway in the hall. "Why the blazes did you give your husband *my* name?"

"Because I love you."

"You do not, my lady," Thorne snapped, suddenly realizing how he had left himself vulnerable to the calculating Lady Myrtlebourne. "You used my name because I am the only fool you took to your bed that didn't already have a wife. Admit it. I am the *easiest* solution to your predicament because I fit the requirement of a husband-to-be waiting in the wings."

Her expression hardened with an ugliness he had never seen in her before. She raised her voice to a shrill, shrewish pitch. "A bit late for you to realize the dangers of your nasty little game. Is it not, my lord?"

Cadwick appeared at his side as if stepping out of the shadows. "My lord—an urgent matter of utmost importance requires your presence."

"Thank you, Cadwick." Thorne forced a stiff bow in Lady Myrtlebourne's direction. "Good day, Lady Myrtlebourne, and again, my condolences."

"I will not be dismissed," she said, drawing herself up as though ready to scream.

"Yes, my lady, you are most certainly dismissed," Thorne said, allowing every ounce of revulsion he felt for the woman to seep into his tone. "There is nothing more to say that cannot be handled through my solicitor."

"Your solicitor?" She stared at him in disbelief. "Are you saying you care nothing for your reputation?"

"If you had bothered to check, my lady," he growled, "you would have found that my reputation as a man of the town, a rake, a debauchee, is quite alive and well without further input from you. Now, good day!" He stormed away, knowing that Cadwick would assist Lady Myrtlebourne in finding the front door and making good use of it.

By the time he reached his office, the need to rage and roar had the blood pounding in his ears. If not for his mother's cat standing in the center of his desk, lapping cream from a small bowl and nibbling at the kippers on a fine china saucer beside it, he would have surely slammed the door shut and given in to the urge to bellow. But out of respect for the new feline mother, he closed the door softly, rounded his desk, and dropped into his chair.

Hera paused in her dining, gave him a disinterested stare, then flicked an ear his way as if acknowledging his presence and allowing it.

Something about the cat's reaction empowered him to pull in a deep breath and regain control.

While he understood Lady Myrtlebourne's desperation, a great many of her problems were of her own doing. Her selfish penchant for trouble had been one of the many reasons, along with her annoying clinginess, that had convinced him without a doubt that their association needed to end. The woman simply did not *do* discretion, and had a vile temper and a cruel streak toward anyone she deemed as lesser than herself. Beauty only went so far, and hers had quickly run its course. Thus, his dalliance with her hadn't lasted longer than a fortnight and ended months ago.

"Or so I thought," he said with a heavy sigh. "I should not have dabbled with that one, Hera."

The cat lifted her head from the bowl of cream, licking her chops as though thoroughly enjoying the richness of her drink. She sat there and stared at him, not blinking her large golden eyes, as if weighing the worthiness of his soul. After a large, toothy yawn, she rose onto all fours, stretched, then stuck her behind in his face as if giving him the cut direct. Then she jumped down and disappeared back into her den inside the window seat.

Thorne started to lean forward and rest his head in his hands, but a whiff of the kippers pushed him back into the depths of the wingback chair. What the devil was he going to do? He was far from innocent in this debacle, but he would be damned if he took the brunt of Lord Montagne's ire about his brother's death.

The note on the corner of his desk caught his gaze—the note from Lady Blessing. His chest tightened and a knot of dread weighed heavy in the pit of his stomach. She already knew him to be a rake. When word of the Myrtlebourne mess went public— and he had no doubt that it would—would she think even worse of him? Shun him from her presence?

"I cannot lose the opportunity to know her better," he muttered aloud.

But why? his usually dormant conscience whispered.

"I am not ready to address that as yet," he answered. But soon, very soon, after more time spent enjoying Lady Blessing's company, he most definitely would.

Chapter Seven

"**H**AVE YOU SEEN him yet?" Serendipity whispered from behind her lacy fan. She lightly fluttered the frothy pink thing that matched the delicate blush of her new gown.

"No." Blessing chewed on her bottom lip while scanning Lady Burrastone's unusually large drawing room. Its walls had been removed to enable it to flow seamlessly into the dining room and garden, turning the area into quite an impressive space for the party.

The windows, columns, and archways were festooned with sheer white draperies reminiscent of the diaphanous gowns of Greek goddesses. The breezy material was gathered up by wreaths of greenery and flowers. Chandeliers sparkled with dancing flames and golden candelabra adorned every table.

Blessing decided that Lady Burrastone was attempting to outdo Lady Atterley. What a ridiculous waste of one's time—competing to claim the title of the largest and most impressive festivity of the Season. She tightened her grip on her closed fan until the poor thing crackled.

"Have you seen him yet?" Fortuity asked as she joined them.

"You two need to stop," Blessing informed her sisters in a hissed whisper. "I am nervous enough without the two of you constantly asking if I have seen *him* yet." She snapped open her fan in a startlingly smooth move, amazed that she had accomplished it as though born to speak the language of the fans. The piece was new and matched the shimmering aquamarine silk of her gown that everyone assured her brought out her eyes. The modiste had even gone so far as to describe her as *ethereal* when she had modeled the color. Ethereal? Indeed. Blessing recognized flummery when she heard it. The modiste was trying to ensure she would be contacted to make more gowns.

"Oh dear," Serendipity said, "Lord Pellington, the malodorous Marquess of Debt, has espied us."

"How do you know these things?" Blessing stared at her sister in amazement. Serendipity knew the financial situation of most members of the *ton* better than they knew it themselves. "Do you have a spy at the bank?"

"I shall never reveal my sources," her sister said in a lofty tone. She tugged on Blessing's arm. "This way. Perhaps Lord Pellington will not give chase."

"You are not leaving me behind to deal with that man." Fortuity scurried after them.

Blessing stole a glance back. "Poor old lord. He's headed for Merry. She'll sort him."

"The minx will send him our way," Serendipity said. "Quick. Into the music room. Someone is banging on the pianoforte. We can hide among the crowd already enduring that torture."

With a grin, Blessing hurried after her sister. At least she was not alone in her feelings about the silly games of the parties. She struggled against the temptation to cover her ears as they took a seat among those gathered to witness Lady Burrastone's daughter abuse the poor musical instrument.

Much to Blessing's consternation, she had somehow allowed Fortuity and Serendipity to seat her at the end of the aisle. A most dangerous position, considering Lord Pellington could easily access her. She cringed and kept her gaze locked on her sisters to her left as the slightest breeze of movement to her right warned she was in imminent danger.

Fortuity and Serendipity glanced past her, then their wide-eyed stares fixed on something, or *someone*, to her immediate right. Even though they hid their smiles behind their fans, the laughter in their eyes mocked her. Wicked things. How dare they enjoy her becoming the prey rather than themselves? Both would find frogs in their beds before the week was out.

"Good evening, Lady Blessing. Would you mind if I joined you?"

A heady rush of excitement and relief ignited a heated blush across her cheeks and cascaded down to the tips of her toes. It made her swallow hard and struggle to calm her rapidly pounding heart. With as much grace as she could muster, she turned and smiled. "You are most welcome to join me, Lord Knightwood. I cannot tell you how happy I am to see you."

As soon as the words left her, she wished she could snatch them back. Especially when she noticed how pleasure gleamed in his dark eyes. She could drown in those glorious *come to me, my lady* eyes—curl up and lose herself in the wicked coziness of things she ought not to even think about and wouldn't even know about if not for Serendipity's scandalous books.

"Your greeting is most definitely the height of this party, my lady," he said, then settled into the chair he'd motioned for a servant to fetch and place beside her. He leaned closer until his shoulder brushed against hers. "Your note concerned me as to whether you would allow future conversations with me."

"My note did not say I would not consider further *conversations* with you." She scooted to one side to place a bit of distance between them. After all, it would hardly be proper for them to sit with their shoulders touching—even though she rather enjoyed it. She immediately missed his warmth but placated herself with a subtle deep inhale of his lovely scent. Sandalwood and citrus. She had always adored the scent of sandalwood and citrus.

"My thank-you letter merely put forth a question." She risked a look his way and discovered him staring at her as if no other person existed in the room. "You should be watching Lady Burrastone's daughter," she whispered, unable to keep from grinning.

"If Lady Burrastone wishes her daughter to make an advantageous match, she will encourage her to entertain the guests rather than torment them." He flinched as the young lady hit a particularly sour note.

Someone near them actually groaned, making Blessing hold her breath to keep from laughing.

"My sentiments exactly," Lord Knightwood grumbled under his breath.

Blessing snorted a laugh but attempted to cover it by coughing and fluttering her fan even faster.

Knightwood rose and offered her his hand. "This room has grown overly warm. Allow me to escort you to the terrace, my lady. You appear in need of air."

She stared at his hand for a long moment, weighing her choices with a puckering of her mouth until she remembered Mama's advice against puckering and smoothed her lips. Before taking his hand, she said, "Of course, my sisters shall accompany us."

"Of course," he answered without a moment's hesitation. He even bowed their way. "Lady Serendipity. Lady Fortuity. A pleasure to see you both again."

"We should exit as quietly as possible so as not to badly interrupt the recital," Blessing whispered as she took his hand.

"I think those behind us are grateful," Knightwood murmured. "This way. Shall we?"

He escorted the three of them out of the music room and along the fringes of the crowded drawing room to the open terrace. Several benches, tables, and chairs had been scattered across the large veranda, interspersed among screens of leafy potted plants and trellises of ivy to provide several perfectly private, yet not *too* private, areas for the guests.

"I believe this spot will do us nicely. Do you not agree, Tutie?" Serendipity nodded at a pair of chairs that looked out across the garden.

"It will, indeed," Fortuity replied. "I can update my notes on all I have seen so far."

Blessing allowed Lord Knightwood to lead her farther down the veranda, far enough from her sisters for a bit of privacy but close enough to still be considered properly chaperoned.

"Would you like to sit, my lady?" He motioned toward a nearby bench beside another leafy trellis.

"That would be nice." She settled down on one end of the bench and was mildly surprised when he settled on the other and left a respectable space between them. Was he about to tell her that he had deemed their association a mistake after all? That he still intended to keep to his habit of bed them but never wed them?

A ridiculous amount of disappointment filled her, making her chide herself for such unrealistic expectations of a confirmed rake. What the devil had she hoped for? Especially after writing him that note and putting him on the spot?

"Would you think me terribly rude if I offered you a bit of advice regarding Lord Pellington?"

His question surprised her. Was Pellington a friend of his? "As I wrote in my note, my lord, I prefer bold honesty in all things."

"Yes, well…"

As his words tapered off, Blessing noticed he kept glancing off into the distance, then down at his hands, much like a nervous lad caught in a lie. But oh dear heavens, those broad shoulders of his in that finely tailored jacket made up for a multitude of sins. And his hair, black as a raven's wing and perhaps a mite too long to be considered proper—what would it feel like to run her fingers through that hair?

She blinked, silently scolding herself for such unladylike thoughts. "Do go on, Lord Knightwood. Do not be afraid."

His nervousness calmed, and he pinned her with a fierce stare that touched the depths of her soul. "My only fear, dear lady, is that I shall somehow offend you and lose your friendship."

"Friendship," she softly repeated, her disappointment from earlier evolving into a heavy stone that sank to the pit of her stomach. She stiffened her back and squared her shoulders. *Fine.* Friendship was better if he only wished to dabble in the present rather than paint an entire portrait of the future and permanently hang it on the walls of his heart. "Your advice regarding Lord Pellington?"

"The man is desperate for a dowry to clear his debts." Lord Knightwood's jaw flexed as he looked aside, revealing a profile handsome enough to make any sculptor drool. "Debts he will no doubt quickly replace with new ones once he burns through all the money. He is quite taken with the gaming hells."

"I see." She shifted on the bench, trying to appear even more prim and proper. "I appreciate your warning, Lord Knightwood, and shall pass it along to my brother so he will understand why my sisters and I choose to rebuff the attentions of the Marquess of Debt." She rolled her eyes at her miserable failure at making what one would consider appropriate social conversation. "Forgive me. I should not have said that."

Knightwood's grin made him even more dashing. No wonder the man had such a devilish reputation.

"I take it you and your sisters were already well aware of Lord Pellington's need for a hefty dowry?"

Blessing gave up on attempting acceptable behavior for a young lady perusing the Marriage Mart's shelves. "Serendipity somehow has her finger on the financial pulse of Polite Society. How? I have no idea. She refuses to reveal her sources."

"Shrewd lady." He chuckled.

"One of many words I might use to describe my sister." For her own comfort and peace of mind, Blessing decided to force his hand. "Since you mentioned my note earlier, I fear I must ask whether or not you gave my question any thought and came up with an answer?" She braced herself, knowing it more than likely would not be what she wished to hear.

He frowned at her as though in pain, storm clouds filling his eyes. "I have thought about your question, my lady. Quite a long while, actually."

"I see." And she did. The man was obviously deeply vexed about how to tell her he fully intended to maintain his rakish ways. "Thank you. I asked for honesty, and I appreciate your providing it." She rose from the bench and smoothed the wrinkles and folds from the gown that had sadly failed in the game that she hadn't even realized she wanted to win. But now she did. She rather liked Lord Knightwood and couldn't easily imagine herself liking anyone else. At least, not for now.

She pulled in a deep breath and shook the disappointment away. Time would help. Mama always said time helped everything. "I should rejoin my sisters now." She curtsied. "Thank you for the pleasant conversation, Lord Knightwood."

Confusion clouded his face as he stared up at her, then belatedly jumped to his feet. "How have I offended you, Lady Blessing?"

"You have not offended me." Drat that sad hitch in her voice that made her sound like a trapped mouse. She cleared her throat and forced a laugh that sounded fake even to her. "I appreciate your honesty. After all, is that not what I asked for?"

"But I did not tell you my answer."

"Oh, but you did, good sir," she said softly. Without thinking, she reached out and smoothed the furrow between his dark brows. "With the worry in your eyes and the petulance in your frown. You most certainly gave me your answer."

He caught hold of her wrist and pressed her gloved hand to his cheek. "You misunderstand me, my lady." The deep rasp of his voice sent a shiver through her. "I said I had thought about your question. I did not, however, give you my reply."

"Knightwood!"

The harsh shout made Blessing squeak and jump aside.

The baron stepped forward and shielded her behind him. "Bad form indeed, sir, frightening the lady with such a shout. Who are you?"

Serendipity and Fortuity rushed to Blessing, one on either side of her.

"We should go," Serendipity whispered.

"I will not," Blessing said. "Not until I hear what that fool has to say."

"Which fool?" Fortuity asked.

"Shh!" Blessing hissed.

The man who had shouted charged forward with an arrogance Blessing felt she had seen before. He appeared so familiar to her, but she couldn't quite place him. Dressed entirely in black, he halted insultingly close in front of Lord Knightwood, as though determined to shove the rude snarl of his bared teeth into the baron's face.

"I am Lord Montagne," the man said. "I believe you are an acquaintance of my brother's widow, Lady Myrtlebourne."

Knightwood bowed. "My condolences on your brother's unexpected passing, my lord."

"A passing you more than likely caused!"

Blessing gasped before she could stop herself, then pulled away from her sisters and stepped up to Lord Knightwood's side. "You, my lord, should see yourself home at once," she told Montagne. "Drunkenness is most unbecoming of a gentleman."

Montagne shifted his angry glare to her. "I assure you, my lady, I am quite sober, and you would do well to take greater care in choosing the company you keep. While I have no idea which Broadmere miss you might be, I can heartily assure you that neither of your parents would approve of this man."

"You will not speak to this lady so rudely," Knightwood said with a warning growl. He firmly but gently set Blessing back behind him. "If your issue is with me, then have the courage and good manners to deal with me directly."

"Oh, I fully intend to deal with you," Montagne countered. He cut his eyes over at Blessing and snorted. "And then we shall see what your next conquest thinks about you."

Knightwood lunged for the man, caught him by the lapels, and rammed him back against the stone banister surrounding the terrace. "Choose your second, damn you. I will not have Lady

Blessing slandered in such a manner."

Blessing wanted to rush forward and stop the fools, but Serendipity and Fortuity dragged her back. "Let me go! Someone must insert a level of good sense into this ridiculousness."

"You must not." Serendipity gave her a hard shake before shoving close to Blessing's ear and whispering, "Lady Myrtlebourne was Lord Knightwood's mistress while her husband was abroad. Word has it that the shock of discovering himself cuckolded is what killed the Earl of Myrtlebourne mere days ago."

"How do you know of these things?" Blessing stared at her sister. This was not the idle gossip of the tittle-tattle sheets. No, this was seedier, by far.

"That does not matter," Serendipity whispered. She tugged Blessing deeper into the shadows. "Come away. You cannot be seen as involved in this unsavoriness." She leaned to one side and glared at their other sister, who stood there taking notes. "Fortuity! I mean, really?"

"Sorry!" Fortuity scurried back to them, latched hold of Blessing's other arm, and joined Serendipity in forcibly escorting her inside. "Essie, you know Seri is right. We must hurry away before those two draw any more attention than they already have. We— namely *you*—must not get involved in this."

"It is bad enough that you were seen escorted to the terrace by Lord Knightwood," Serendipity added.

"You were with me," Blessing said. "Everything was completely proper."

"You know the gossips, Essie." Serendipity scanned the drawing room, then hurriedly led the way along the wall toward Chance and Merry. "We must let Chance know in case he is needed to stanch any vicious rumors."

Blessing halted and yanked her arm free. "This is beyond belief. Lives could be at stake here, and all you are worried about is rumors?"

Serendipity glared at her with the same hard-jawed expression Mama had always adopted whenever her patience was at its end. *"Your* life is my concern—not a pair of men fighting over a married woman known for collecting lovers with the same enthusiasm that she uses to fill her dance card."

Blessing arched a brow. Her eldest sister rarely spoke so crudely. "I am staying right here until I see Lord Knightwood come back inside. I will not have him thinking I deserted him."

"You will not be seen with him again this evening. I forbid it." Serendipity dared to stamp her foot, before glancing around and then assuming a calmer persona. "I forbid it," she repeated quietly.

"You forget yourself, sister," Blessing warned her. "I am of age, and you are not my keeper."

Fortuity stepped between them. "You are drawing curious looks, sisters." She turned to Serendipity. "You go advise Chance of what we witnessed on the veranda, and I shall remain here with Essie—in case she chooses to risk her reputation further and speak with Lord Knightwood again this evening."

"Subtle choice of words, Tutie," Blessing drolly noted, but had to admit, the suggestion did hold merit.

"Indeed, I will." Serendipity flounced away.

"Oh dear. Now what do we do?" Fortuity took hold of Blessing's arm and turned her toward Lady Burrastone and the Marquess of Debt, who were headed their way.

"Well, isn't this just the icing on the cake?" Blessing allowed herself a well-earned, albeit soft, groan. Could anything else go wrong this evening? "We must run," she said, moving her lips as little as possible.

"It is too late." Fortuity held fast, preventing her from escaping.

"My darlings," Lady Burrastone called out in an annoyingly high voice, "pray, wait for us! Do!"

"What sin have I committed to deserve this?" Blessing asked under her breath while forcing a smile. She held tight to Fortuity's arm to keep her in place as well. By Jove, if she had to endure the nauseating Lord Pellington, then so did Fortuity.

"I hate you," Fortuity said in a low growl.

"I hate you more," Blessing said while stretching her fake smile even wider.

"Lady Blessing, Lady Fortuity," Lady Burrastone began, making the sisters flinch in unison, "allow me to introduce you to the Marquess of Pellington."

Blessing managed a deep curtsy while skittering back just a little to make Fortuity seem the more eager to greet the man. Yes, it might be cold-hearted, but it was now every sister for herself.

"Lord Pellington," Lady Burrastone continued, "here we have but two of the Duke of Broadmere's incomparable sisters."

"Indeed, they are incomparable," replied the pockmarked marquess who was in dire need of a bath. He swooped in and made a leg to Fortuity. "When I espied your beauty, I begged Lady Burrastone for an introduction. I simply could not bear another moment spent without making your acquaintance."

Fortuity cut a sideways glance at Blessing, threatening her without a word before curtly accepting Lord Pellington's sickening flummery with a tip of her head. "Thank you, my lord."

Blessing could tell her sister was doing her best to hold her breath to keep the man's fetid stench from knocking her off her feet. He turned and reached for Blessing's hand. She grudgingly allowed him to take it while doing her best to breathe through her mouth.

"Lady Blessing, you are the eldest?" Lord Pellington asked with a smile that revealed several rotting teeth.

"Why, no, Lord Pellington." Blessing aimed a smiling nod at Serendipity where she stood beside their brother across the room. "My sister, Lady Serendipity, is the eldest."

"Ah yes," the marquess said, his abhorrent breath threatening to push her back a step. He wrinkled his nose and cast a rather disgruntled glance back at Merry. "I believe your *youngest* sister did tell me that earlier." He swiped a lacy handkerchief across his perspiring forehead and faked a laugh that made Blessing ache to roll her eyes. "I blame my forgetfulness on our hostess's exemplary champagne."

"But all of the sisters are *out*," Lady Burrastone hurried to add. "It makes no difference which is the elder and which is the younger."

Blessing had never liked Lady Burrastone and, for the life of her, could not fathom what Mama had ever seen in the woman.

"Lady Blessing?"

Her heart leapt with relief at the familiar deep voice behind her. She turned and gave Lord Knightwood a genuine smile. "Yes, my lord?"

"Forgive me, my lady." He bowed as if no one else existed in the room other than the two of them. "I understand your need to return inside, but I had to see for myself that you were unscathed by the...unpleasantness. Please accept my most heartfelt apology for exposing you to such crudeness."

Her heart swelled, but before she could respond, Lord Pellington asked, "Whatever does he mean?"

Blessing was tempted to tell the fool marquess to toddle off and take his stench elsewhere, but even she knew she could never get away with that. Instead, she ignored him.

"I am well, Lord Knightwood," she said softly. "And your apology is unnecessary. My only concern was for your safety."

"What does she mean?" Lord Pellington interjected.

"I do not know," Lady Burrastone answered in a loud whisper.

Blessing so very badly wanted to tell them both to shut their gobs and go away. But for her brother's sake and that of her sisters, she bit her tongue and didn't comment. Instead, she focused on the man in front of her—*her baron*. Yes. He was hers. The thought filled her with determination to not only protect him but convince him to change his ways. "I do hope you value your health and wellbeing enough to avoid foolhardy choices that could put them both at risk."

The dashing baron gifted her with one of his seductive smiles that made her heart beat faster. "I thank you, my lady." The tenderness in the rumble of his voice was as gentle as a lover's caress—or what she had always dreamed a lover's caress might be like. "Your kindness and concern are a balm to my soul. Precious gifts I do not deserve." He kissed the back of her gloved hand, then kept a firm hold of her fingers as though loath to release her.

Not trusting her ability to speak or curtsy, Blessing managed a graceful nod and a smile.

"Lord Knightwood," Lady Burrastone said, her tone cold enough to ice the champagne. "Did something happen upon these premises of which Lord Burrastone needs to be made aware?"

"The matter has been handled," Knightwood said with a note of finality that dared the hostess to question him further. "Pray, do not trouble yourself, my lady. Instead, revel in this delightful evening you created for all of us to enjoy." He gave her a gallant bow. "I do regret that my mother was unable to attend. She so prefers the parties you arrange."

Blessing bit her tongue to keep from laughing at the hefty amount of pure, unadulterated manure Lord Knightwood spewed. However, she had to admit that the man was impressive and knew how to play to his audience.

Lady Burrastone puffed up and preened like the proudest of peahens. "Why, thank you, Lord Knightwood. Please extend my regrets to your mother. I do so love her company, and soirées always seem brighter whenever she is present."

"I will be sure to tell her. She will be delighted at such kind words."

Her mind made up, Blessing gave Fortuity a subtle nod, then stepped forward. "Lord Knightwood, I believe you were about to share something before we were so rudely interrupted." Surely he wouldn't wish to expound on his answer in present company and would suggest that she and her sister join him for a stroll to anywhere but here.

Lady Burrastone and Lord Pellington both arched their brows like a pair of hounds perking their ears. "Do tell," Lady Burrastone said. "Do I detect the scent of some delicious *on dit?*"

"I believe you do, my lady," Lord Pellington said. He wrinkled his nose and settled a malicious smirk on Lord Knightwood. "Do share, my lord. It is quite ungentlemanly to be greedy and keep such juiciness to oneself."

The baron gave Blessing a meaningful look that sent an excited fluttering through her. "Lady Blessing and I were merely discussing the old adage about *a leopard never changing its spots.*"

Blessing swallowed hard, her throat aching the way it always did right before a good cry. She blinked faster to dispel the sheen of tears she could feel welling. "Lord Knightwood did not agree with a study I had read about the leopard's spots changing from the time it was a cub to when it was fully grown and then sometimes changing yet again in its old age. The one constant in this world is change."

Appearing dutifully disappointed and suddenly quite bored, Lady Burrastone slowly nodded. "I see. Leopard's spots. Indeed." She turned to Lord Pellington. "Shall we continue with the introductions you requested, my lord?"

The marquess stared at Blessing and Lord Knightwood as if unable to fathom their existence. He bobbed his head at Lady Burrastone as he offered her his arm. "Yes, my lady." After a polite tip of his head to Blessing, Fortuity, and Knightwood, he stuck his nose in the air and escorted the hostess away as if proud of himself for saving her from the plague.

"He is most definitely going to be in one of my stories," Fortuity murmured as she furiously scribbled on a notecard, then shoved it into her reticule. She looked up and made a face at Blessing. "Chance is not going to be pleased."

"I do not care," Blessing said. She turned her back on her sister and locked eyes with Lord Knightwood. "You can change if you wish to."

"I need time, my lady," he said softly, his eyes filled with sorrow. He reached for her hand again and held it between both of his. "The last thing I would ever wish to do is hurt you."

"You already have, my lord." She pulled free and charged away, doing her best to reach the ladies' retiring room before spilling her tears.

Chapter Eight

BLESSING KEPT HER gaze locked on her folded hands where they rested in her lap. After last night's dismal outcome, she was in no mood for yet another of Chance's family meetings.

Serendipity sat on one side of her, occasionally reaching over to give her a reassuring pat. Fortuity sat on her other side, periodically doing the same. While Blessing appreciated their caring and concern, the best thing they could do for her was leave her alone and allow her to disappear into her observatory. She needed time to mend her wounded pride and bruised heart. Nurturing a growing affection, a feeling that might have possibly deepened into love was not for the weak or cowardly. It was a dangerous war. One that she had lost early on in the battle.

"Last night was little better than Lady Atterley's ball," Chance began in a firm, authoritative voice reminiscent of their father's. He paced back and forth in front of the seven seated sisters, hands clasped to the small of his back, his expression grim with disappointment. He halted in front of Merry and glared down at her. "One does not sneak upstairs to the nursery to play with the children."

Merry sat taller, squared her shoulders, and glared right back at him. "One does when the Marquess of Debt refuses to leave one alone. The man smells like an overripe chamber pot."

With a barely restrained huff, Chance shook his head and moved to stand in front of Grace. "One also does not slip out to the stables."

"There were puppies, Chance," Grace said. "You know how I feel about puppies."

"Do not even start with me," Joy said as he made his way to her. "I trounced everyone at whist, loo, and picquet last night. When the cards are in my favor, I daren't set them aside."

He arched a brow at Felicity. "Is it true that you actually went into the kitchens and asked their cook to show you how a particular dish was prepared?"

"It was so divine," Felicity countered. "I simply had to know how to make it."

"At least I'm safe this time," Fortuity whispered to Blessing. "I was a chaperone."

"You are not safe, Tutie. When Essie chose to spend the remainder of the evening in the ladies' retiring room, you failed to join Seri and me in our attempt to quell the newly sprouted rumors regarding our sister and the infamous Lord Knightwood." Chance's broad chest swelled with a deep intake of air, which he blew out in a frustrated whoosh. "Essie."

Even though he said her name with compassion, Blessing braced herself and lifted her gaze. "What, brother?"

His deep blue eyes darkened to the almost violet hue they always took on whenever he felt something deeply. "I am sorry. I know your evening was upsetting."

"But?"

He shook his head. "*But* nothing. I do not wish you upset in any way and wish I could have prevented your witnessing that unpleasantness on the terrace."

"It was not Lord Knightwood's confrontation with Lord Montagne that upset me." She might as well set the record straight for all and sundry. "It was his avowal that his ways could not be changed—or at least that he was unsure *if* they could be changed. That is what upset me. Apparently, I am not enough to make him aspire to do better."

"His poor character has nothing to do with you, dear sister."

Chance's eyes flashed an even darker, angrier purple. "His weaknesses are his own. Not yours. The Almighty gave each of us free will, the ability to choose between right and wrong. Knightwood appears to be a damned fool controlled by his baser instincts."

"He thinks with the part of his anatomy below his waist rather than his brain," Serendipity snapped.

"Sister!" Chance stared at her in shock. "What would Mama say about such a statement?"

"I daresay she would agree," Serendipity countered.

"Be that as it may," Blessing interrupted, "I shall be forgoing any future engagements for a time."

"Nay, Essie, you must not cower." Chance moved toward her, eyeing her with consternation. "That would only inflame the tittle-tattle sheets. I fear Seri and I failed at squelching all of last night's whispers."

"What whispers? The man escorted me to the terrace, and we were accompanied by two of my sisters. Hang the *ton* and their intrusiveness." She closed her eyes and rubbed the spot above the bridge of her nose. A pounding headache had taken root and refused to give over, no matter how many cups of Cook's herbals she downed. "There are six other Broadmere sisters. I daresay I shall not be missed for the remainder of the Season."

"Yes, but none of the other sisters had their honor defended quite so loudly with the threat of a duel," Serendipity gently reminded her.

Blessing threw up her hands. "What would you have me do? I cannot control the chattering of fools."

"We shall start a rumor of our own." Chance stared at her with a thoughtful squint. He snapped his fingers. "Your dowry is the heftiest of the seven because you were Papa's favorite. That is what we shall leak to the tongue waggers."

"You wish to use me as bait to silence the gossips?" Her brother had surely lost what little sense he ever had to begin with. "To what end, Chance? So that every dowry-hungry wolf of the *ton* comes howling at our door? Might I remind you that the will states we must marry for happiness and love? Your *tongue waggers* know that as well. I overheard Lady Westerbin relay that to her dinner partner when she thought I wasn't listening."

"The wolves would still try to win your heart. Would that be so terrible?"

Only the concern in his eyes kept Blessing from throwing her shoe at him. She rose from her chair and gave him a dismissive flip of her hand as she turned to leave. As far as she was concerned, this meeting was over. "Do what you will, as you always do, since you are a man—a duke, no less. I care not anymore."

Walters appeared at the parlor door and cleared his throat with a loud *harrumph.*

"Yes?" Chance said with a weariness that almost made Blessing feel sorry for him. Almost.

The butler lifted the small silver tray a little higher. "A message, Your Grace. Delivered just now."

"To whom?"

"The young man delivering it instructed that it was intended for the Broadmere *family.*" Walters puckered a disgruntled scowl as he hitched his way across the room to Chance and held out the tray. "Quite the rude young man, Your Grace, if I do say so myself."

"Thank you, Walters. That will be all." Chance flipped open the envelope and frowned. "Closed with a plain bit of wax. No seal. Nothing to identify the sender."

An ominous sense of something very dark about to happen curdled in Blessing's middle. Rather than escaping to her observatory as she had planned, she hovered near the door and waited to discover what the mysterious message held.

"*The following is scheduled for tomorrow's edition of* On Dit – What a Treat," Chance read aloud, his scowl growing more pronounced with every word. "*Is it not strange that the seven diamonds of Broadmere, the beauties claiming to be in search of husbands, do not give so much as a passing glance to those who would gladly take them to the altar? Perhaps these glittering seven are not diamonds after all—but faux gemstones. Dare we say possibly even 'used' bits of colored glass? At least one of them appears to be in the market for a benefactor rather than a husband."* Chance's mouth hardened into a fierce line as he slowly refolded the paper.

"Who would write such a thing?" Serendipity snatched it from him, opened it again, and stared down at it.

"My guess would be the odious Lord Pellington." Blessing moved closer, sniffing loudly as she walked. "Smell the paper. I'm certain the man's stench seeps into everything he touches."

Both Serendipity and Chance fixed her with dubious looks.

"I am quite serious." Blessing took the paper, wafted it under her nose, then frowned. With some disappointment, she announced, "I was wrong. It smells like parchment. But I still say it was him."

"What would he hope to gain by doing such a thing?" Serendipity asked. "We all talked with the man. What more does he want?"

"Our dowries." Blessing passed the note to Fortuity. "Whoever wrote that hopes to have us throwing ourselves at any man who happens to walk in front of us." She allowed herself a weary sigh. "Especially me, it would seem." The fact that her reputation teetered in the balance didn't bother her in the least. Her only concern was her sisters.

Merry rolled her eyes. Grace snorted. Felicity huffed, and Joy shook her fist and growled, "What a load of rubbish! How dare that churl insinuate such rot about us—and especially about our Essie!"

Chance bowed his head while pinching the bridge of his nose. "It might not be Pellington. Although I would not put it past the foul-smelling oaf."

"We must stop this," Serendipity declared, then turned and poked Chance in his shoulder. "You must go down there immediately and demand this not be printed."

He threw back his head and laughed. "Dearest Seri—if I were

to do that, they would merely place it at the top of the page in larger print and double their production."

"We must act as though it doesn't matter." Blessing nodded at the note being passed among the sisters. "If we give it no notice and carry on as though it does not exist, the furor will die down much quicker than if we demean ourselves by responding to it. Do you not recall what Mama always said about defending yourself against gossip?"

"Hold your head high and carry on. Let the gossip hang itself," Fortuity said in a sadly reminiscent tone.

"Besides—what harm does it do?" Blessing shrugged. "If anything, I consider it a compliment that we *do not* throw ourselves at every eligible male of the peerage who happens into the same room with us. You've all seen how the marriage-minded mamas demean themselves and embarrass their daughters. The *ton* is simply not accustomed to women who know their own minds and are willing to wait for whom they feel suits them the best."

"But Essie," Serendipity said, "you could be ruined by this."

"I am only ruined when I decide I am ruined." Blessing held her head higher, determined to convince everyone, including herself, that she didn't care a whit about the cruel gossip. She clutched a fist to her chest, pressing hard to settle her heart's unhappy yet rapid thumping. "I know I am a good person. A lady. If others are unable to see that, they can happily go to the devil for all I care."

Chance groaned while covering his face with both hands. "Gads—this poor attempt at blackmail has made all of you even more determined to make my life difficult."

"You have made *our* lives difficult since we were born," Blessing shot back with a toss of her head. "Turnabout is fair play, if you ask me."

"I still say we start the rumor of your dowry being the largest. That will make those who read this vitriol quickly forget all about it." He gave her such a determined look that Blessing knew it was useless to argue. "That might also leave the impression that Knightwood was sniffing around you for the dowry rather than pursuing a dalliance or making you his next mistress."

A shocked gasp burst free of her. She whirled away and rushed for the door. This was simply too much to bear.

"Essie!" Chance caught up and barred her exit. "Please forgive me. I should not have said that."

"No, Chance, you should not have." She stared at him, willing him to feel her pain. "But one cannot un-ring a bell. Can one?"

He had the decency to bow his head and unleash a sigh of regret. "No. One cannot."

"Excuse me, Your Grace?" Walters said from just outside the doorway.

"Yes?"

He lifted the silver letter tray once more, revealing another lone envelope waiting to be opened. "For Lady Blessing."

"If it does not bear an identifying seal, I will not waste my time on it," Blessing snapped. She was thoroughly finished with this nonsense and seriously contemplating the benefits of a spinsterhood spent abroad.

"There is a crest, my lady. A familiar one, I believe." He offered her the tray, his lined face and saggy jowls reminding her of their elderly hounds that Grace tended to as though they were her children.

She glanced down at the letter and immediately recognized the script. "Take it away, Walters. I do not wish to read it." Lord Knightwood had made his position very clear last night. Whatever that letter held would only make matters worse by splitting the wound wider and causing it to bleed even more. "Thank you, that will be all."

"And the messenger?" the old butler asked with a quirk of a bushy gray eyebrow.

She held her breath and counted to ten—a habit Mama had instilled in her at a young age as a means of controlling not only her temper but whatever questionable words were at risk of rolling off her tongue. "Return the letter to the messenger and have him tell his master I refused it."

"Essie? Are you sure?" Fortuity asked. "He told you he needed time and did not wish to hurt you. Perhaps he has had a change of heart."

"And perhaps the moon is made of cheese and the stars lemon drops!" A heady mix of anger, humiliation, and heartbreak made Blessing tremble. She fixed a stern glare on Walters and pointed at the letter. "Please do as I asked. That will be all."

The butler dismissed himself with a tip of his head. As he slowly ambled away, she panicked and dashed after him. "Walters!"

He turned and waited, his face devoid of emotion.

"Give me the wretched thing." Ashamed of her inability to remain steadfast, she hung her head and waited in the hallway. A distinct shuffling behind her betrayed that her overly inquisitive siblings were watching from the parlor doorway.

After dismissing Walters with a look, she gave her family her back, started to break the seal, and then stopped. *No.* She would read this in private—in her observatory—then ring for the butler to carry a reply when she finished. She turned and charged down the hall.

"Where are you going?" Serendipity called after her.

"Privacy." A rare thing in the Broadmere household, but if they valued their lives at all, they would grant her the solitude she required. Using the key tied to the ribbon pinned to the band around the empire waist of her muslin gown, she unlocked the door to her observatory, stepped inside, then locked it once again.

With her gaze fixed on the letter, she made her way to the bench in front of the wall of windows overlooking the garden. Sunshine streamed in, flooding the room with light. But it did little to belie the bleak darkness that threatened to swallow her. If only she had not allowed herself to entertain the thought of becoming attached to this man. She snorted at that. *If only.*

Another dangerous game.

She laid the letter on the bench beside her, wishing she could know its contents without breaking the seal and revealing her inability to resist temptation. "Oh, to the devil with it!" She snatched it up, snapped the circle of blood red wax in two, and unfolded the parchment.

My dearest Lady Blessing,

I am sorry. More so than you will ever know, and I beg your forgiveness. There are so many things I wish to say, but now that I take quill in hand, the words escape me. Nothing could begin to describe the depth of my remorse as I watched you dash away from me last evening. You are a rare and precious jewel, a lady who deserves only the very best—and I fear that I am not it.

She closed her eyes and bowed her head, refusing to give way to tears as she had last night. The cur had made his intentions known then. Why did he feel the need to rub salt in her wounds today? She had not pursued him nor tried to change his mind. No—she had accepted his answer and considered the matter settled. After a hard swallow, she opened her eyes and braced herself for the remainder of his cruel note.

Yet I am a selfish man.

"That is quite apparent, my lord," she grumbled, half tempted to crumple the paper and toss it into the grate.

I can think of nothing other than you. Your eyes. Your smile. Your cutting wit. I find myself loath to forgo the delight of your company.

She frowned, refusing to let the slightest flicker of hope burst into flame and burn brighter. "The man appears unable to make up his mind," she said, forcing a nonchalant tone she in no way felt.

Once more I beg for your patience—for time to see if I can overcome my immoral history.

She growled in disbelief. "I have read enough. This man is a spoiled child, and I shall take no part in teaching him the concept of free will or developing a conscience based on decency." She crumpled the letter, hopped up from the bench, and lobbed it into the fire. "What a load of nonsense! What woman in her right mind would tolerate such a fool?"

You almost did, her inner voice accused. "Oh, be quiet—do!" she snapped. She leaned against the hearth, watching the flames lick their way across the paper and curl it into oblivion. As the letter twisted and turned into a wide black ribbon of ash, a line jumped out at her: ...*have already captured my heart, my dear lady, and I beg...*

"Damn you, Lord Knightwood," she told the ashes. Both regret and thankfulness about not reading the letter in its entirety churned through her, and she hated that feeling, the not knowing all that he had said.

"It is time to clear the air once and for all!" She stormed over to her writing desk, laid out a sheet of her finest notepaper, and inked her quill.

To Lord Knightwood,

It would be a cold day in the devil's waistcoat pocket before she addressed this letter with something as kindly as *My dear Lord Knightwood.* She stared down at the sheet, sorting her thoughts and choosing her words carefully.

You are a conundrum, my lord. A riddle that has become quite tiring. Even with six sisters and a most fractious brother, I have yet to meet someone as unable to know their own mind as yourself. I would welcome an open and honest conversation with you, but only if it ended in a clear, logical course of action rather than all this waffling about and begging for an undeter-

*mined amount of time. I will not be suspended from a shelf like
a bundle of herbs set aside to cure. I have a life, sir. One of
which I intend to enjoy and make the most of. If my beloved
parents taught me anything, it was that one must not wait for
one's happiness. One must seize it with both hands and make it
happen with every expediency because, sadly, life can end at a
moment's notice.*

    Do with this response what you will.

Cordially,
Lady Blessing Abarough

She sprinkled pounce across the wet ink to dry it more quickly, then curled the paper and tapped the powder back into its
container. After folding and sealing it with her personal stamp of
a crescent moon and several stars, she went to the door and
yanked on the bellpull for Walters. With the door ajar, she waited
for the elderly servant to appear in the hallway. Under no
circumstances would she emerge from her observatory until she
absolutely had to. She had neither the energy nor the temperament at the moment to deal with her siblings and knew they
would be champing at the bit to know what the letter from Lord
Knightwood had said.

"Yes, my lady?" Walters called out as he came into sight.

"Please give this to the messenger." She handed him the note,
then lowered her voice while warring with indecision. "And
please have the messenger inform his master that I did not read
Lord Knightwood's letter in its entirety. Halfway through the
paragraphs of indecision, I found myself compelled to toss it into
the fire."

Walters remained stoic except for the slightest upward twitch
of his brows. "Yes, my lady. I shall stress the importance of your
message to the young man waiting at the door. Will that be all?"

"Yes, Walters. That will be all—at least for now."

Chapter Nine

"**Y**OU MUST LEARN to rein in that temper, old man," Ravenglass told Thorne. "You are bloody well fortunate I was able to negotiate a ceasefire with Montagne's second. However, after speaking with the man, I concluded that the calculating lord would much rather ruin you in court than shoot you. Thankfully, he seemed sorely disinclined to accept your challenge."

"I am sure he would rather deal with me in court instead of on the dueling field." Thorne paced back and forth in front of the parlor window, watching for the messenger he had sent to the Broadmere residence. "A civil suit would also drag Lady Myrtlebourne through the mud—thereby allowing the man to kill two birds with one stone."

"What the devil has you so agitated? You are watching the street as if expecting an attack at any moment."

Thorne halted his pacing and fixed a bleak stare on his friend. "I sent her a letter."

"And who, may I ask, is *her*?"

"Who do you think?"

The viscount angled both his dark brows higher. "Surely not Lady Blessing? Not after last night."

"The only thing I did last night was defend the lady's honor." Although, if Thorne were honest about it, he had probably done the sweet lady's reputation more harm than good. There had been a great many whisperings after she fled his presence in the crowded drawing room.

Ravenglass didn't comment, just stared at him with a damning look that demanded honesty.

"Fine," Thorne ceded while raking both hands through his hair. "The woman haunts me—my dreams and every waking hour as well. I can think of nothing but her."

"We always want that which we cannot have."

"But I *could* have her," Thorne said softly. "If I knew for certain I would not become my father."

"All you must do is decide not to be your father," Ravenglass said. "The man's cruelty toward your mother was not some disease or malformity passed from father to son like some unholy birthmark. You have never been cruel by nature. All you need do is set your mind to controlling that temper of yours and give up your dabbling with other men's wives. It is a matter of will—not an inherited curse."

"But that is where you are wrong, old friend." With his gaze still locked on the street in front of the townhouse, Thorne slowly shook his head. "It would appear my grandsire was the same sort of ruthless churl—as was his father before him." A throat-tightening surge of anticipation shot through him as his footman rounded the corner and approached the house at a hurried stride. "Yon comes Donnelly—I told him to wait for an answer from Lady Blessing."

Ravenglass joined him at the window and frowned. "If his expression is any indication, your letter was not well received."

Thorne feared that as well. Unlike most servants, Donnelly's face betrayed all his thoughts and feelings. He was a good man and trustworthy, but one always knew, or at least had a fair idea of, what the lad was about to say.

Donnelly rushed into the parlor, his light blue eyes downcast and his freckled face filled with worry. He tipped a quick nod as he held out a tightly folded letter bearing a wax seal as dark blue as a midnight sky. "The lady's response, my lord—and there is more."

"More?" Thorne braced himself.

Donnelly bobbed his head and kept his gaze locked on the floor. "Yes, my lord. Their butler said it was very important I relay the rest of her ladyship's message word for word and get it right."

"I see." Thorne resettled his stance. "And the rest of the lady's message is?"

The footman nodded and cleared his throat. "Her ladyship did not read your letter in its entirety. Halfway through the paragraphs of indecision, she found herself compelled to toss it into the fire. Her words, my lord. Not mine."

Thorne stared at the footman while slowly rubbing his thumb along the hard edge of Lady Blessing's response. "Was that all, Donnelly?"

"Yes, my lord."

"Thank you. You may go and see to your tea now. I am sure Cook has it waiting."

"Thank you, my lord." The lad bowed his way out of the parlor, his relief palpable.

"Paragraphs of indecision?" Ravenglass repeated with a dubious look. "What the devil did you put in that letter?"

"Never mind." Thorne slid his finger under the seal and unfolded the reply. As he read through it, one sentence stood out; one string of words gave him the encouragement he had both hoped and feared she would offer him: *I would welcome an open and honest conversation with you, but only if it ended in a clear, logical course of action rather than all this waffling about and begging for an undetermined amount of time.* The lady was well within her rights to demand such. As she had said, she was not some bundle of herbs to be hung from a shelf until cured.

He handed it over to Ravenglass and strode across the parlor to the liquor cabinet to pour them both a drink. As he returned and handed the glass of port to his friend, he said, "I must have her."

"You understand that to have her, you must have her as your wife and nothing less?" The viscount handed back the note, glaring at Thorne with an intensity that spoke volumes.

"Yes," Thorne said, then lifted his glass. "From now on, the only begging I shall do will be for her hand in marriage." He prayed he was doing the right thing—following his heart rather than fearing his ancestry. And if he couldn't control himself, if against every precaution he became the next Knightwood monster…

He set his glass aside. "I have an oath to ask of you," he told Ravenglass.

His old friend scowled at him as if already knowing what he was about to say. "Do not do this. I am not that strong of a man."

Thorne shook his head. "I know better. You are the most honorable man I have ever known. That is why I ask that you end me if I become my father."

"I cannot." Ravenglass downed his drink, then strode over to the cabinet and poured himself another. "Do not ask it of me. You are the brother I never had."

"If you feel you cannot end my life, then turn me over to the press gangs. Impressment would be just as effective."

Ravenglass glared at him. "You are not your father."

"Promise me." Thorne needed to hear the words that would reassure him Lady Blessing would never know the misery his mother had endured.

"Will it give you peace if I agree to this ridiculous request?"

"It will."

Ravenglass heaved a defeated sigh and bowed his head. "If you become the next Knightwood monster, I will turn you over to the press gangs myself."

Thorne clapped a hand onto his old friend's shoulder. "Thank you."

"You can thank me by never making me keep this promise."

"I will do my best," Thorne said quietly.

"See that you do." Ravenglass thumped his empty glass down

onto a table and charged out of the room.

❧

THORNE NERVOUSLY PATTED the pristine white folds of his cravat as he eyed the front door of the Broadmere residence. Three days ago, Lady Blessing had said she would be open to an honest, forthright, and *productive* conversation. So be it. By the time they finished speaking today, there would be no doubt in the dear lady's mind that she had stolen his heart, and he wished her to be his wife.

It had taken every ounce of patience and control he possessed to grant her three days to somewhat cool down from his earlier indecisive behavior that had, admittedly, been rude and selfish. But now he was determined to be the man she deserved, and he hoped she would be receptive. He strode up the front steps and used the brass door knocker to request admittance to the impressive townhouse that held his priceless treasure.

The Broadmeres' ancient butler opened the door the slightest bit and eyed him with an almost insulting scrutiny before swinging the barrier open wide. With a less-than-enthusiastic bow and wave of his hand, he invited Thorne inside. "Do come in, Lord Knightwood, and join the others. I believe there might be a seat available. If not, I shall see that one is fetched for you."

"The others?"

The servant inclined his head toward the hallway lined with chairs filled with enough members of the peerage to hold a session in the House of Lords. "Yes, my lord," the butler said. "I shall inform His Grace that you are here."

"But I am here to see Lady Blessing," Thorne said. "Not His Grace."

The butler slowly blinked like a great horned owl just waking for its nightly hunt. "His Grace has chosen to receive all gentleman callers before the ladies select who they wish to see. Do be seated, my lord." After a pointed nod at the last empty chair, the servant slowly ambled down the hallway and disappeared through a set of double doors that Thorne remembered led to the parlor.

"Here for Lady Blessing, I presume?" asked the rat-faced Earl of Alcester—a man Thorne had never liked.

"I am," Thorne replied, and left it at that. Instinct warned him to weigh every word, because it would no doubt be twisted and used against him in what looked to be a robust competition to win his lady fair.

"Yes, well—from the look of this hall, that particular Broadmere lady appears to have her choice of husbands," said the Earl of Cedarswik—a man rumored to have a cruel streak worse than that of Thorne's ancestors. "However, I daresay I would settle for one of the other sisters as well. Lady Blessing's dowry might be the largest of the seven, but all are quite amply funded, I am sure." He kicked back in his chair and snorted. "I would prefer to avoid the rather large sister, though. Fatness is for dowries, not women." His haughty smile became more of a malicious sneer. "Of course, I could take the fat one and cure her of that repugnance. I feel sure it would make her more docile."

"Keep her fat, old man. More to hang on to while begetting an heir." Viscount Rampisham snickered like a hissing teakettle. "I much prefer fat over plain. Did you see the one constantly scribbling notes and stuffing them into her reticule? What a drab little thing that one is!"

"Yes," Alcester said, wrinkling his nose as though finding the memory distasteful. He twitched an arrogant shrug. "Two culls out of seven is not bad odds, though. That still leaves five acceptable pets from which to choose."

Thorne had held his tongue as long as he could. A relentless, pounding outrage forced him to his feet. To hell with controlling his temper. How dare these men speak about Lady Blessing's sisters in such a manner—and in the hall of the ladies' home, no less! He grabbed Alcester by the lapels, yanked the sputtering man to the door, and shoved him outside. "Do not return or I shall see that His Grace discovers you are a man who does not pay his vowels!"

He charged back and snatched Rampisham up out of his seat. "Out with you as well, you vile bastard. How dare you insult these fine ladies! I shall advise His Grace of your black-hearted ways."

After sending the viscount stumbling down the front steps, he headed back for Cedarswik.

The shocked earl threw his hands in the air and ran for the door. "Have you no decency?"

"You have the gall to ask for decency? Bah!" Thorne strode after him, chasing the man down the steps to ensure he carried himself away from the Broadmere residence. "I know all about you, Cedarswik, and His Grace soon shall too!"

He went back inside to find Lord Pellington and the Duke of Hethersby staring at him with their jaws dropped. However, neither they nor the other four men, whose names Thorne couldn't recall, had insulted the Broadmere ladies, so he chose to leave them alone.

"I refuse to tolerate such crude behavior," he said, daring any one of them to disagree.

The six murmured their like-mindedness while watching him with a healthy share of leeriness.

As Thorne straightened his waistcoat and yanked his jacket properly back in place, the slightest movement to his left and the click of a closing door made him turn. He stared at it, wondering which room it was, because someone had used it as a sly place to hide and observe the gentlemen waiting to be seen.

A sense of doom about his outburst of temper filled him— even though he would do it again if given the choice. If observed without benefit of the entire situation, his ousting of those three could be mistaken for something other than defending the ladies. He raked a hand back through his hair that he had meant to have trimmed to a more respectable length before today. But the thought had slipped his mind—as many thoughts had. All that remained firmly in his awareness was the delightful Lady Blessing.

With a heavy sigh, he sank back into his seat and waited for one or more of the Broadmere servants to appear to show him out as he had so unceremoniously shown out the others. At the sound of footsteps, he stared straight ahead and waited.

A rumbling *harrumph* revealed the owner of the slow, steady footsteps was none other than the aged butler. "Lord Knightwood," the man said in a deep, raspy voice one might imagine hearing in a graveyard at midnight.

Thorne stood and faced the butler, ready to accept the result of his actions. The old codger would no doubt be pleased, since he had always left Thorne with the distinct impression that he did not approve of his calling upon Lady Blessing.

The servant's mouth twitched at the corners as if he struggled to keep from smiling. He lifted his hand and pointed at the parlor doors. "This way, my lord. His Grace will receive you now."

"But I was here well before Lord Knightwood," Lord Pellington whined.

"Quite right, Lord Pellington." The butler tipped the subtlest of nods. "And His Grace thanks you for calling but finds his schedule quite full for the remainder of the afternoon." He turned to the Duke of Hethersby and bowed. "However, Your Grace, His Grace would be delighted if you would join him and his sisters for tea—along with Lord Knightwood. All others here are heartily thanked for calling and are more than welcome to leave their cards and perhaps call another day."

After a great deal of huffing, puffing, and grumbling, the hallway cleared except for the duke. The gentleman smiled as he rose from his seat and fell in step beside Thorne. "It would appear that today is our day, Knightwood," he said in a lowered voice. "By the way, well done earlier. I should have stepped in and helped, and now I regret I was not bold enough to do so."

"It is indeed our day," Thorne answered somewhat stiffly,

unsure what else to say. He knew very little about Hethersby other than the man was rumored to keep to himself and was extraordinarily quiet for an unmarried duke. "I am sure you would have eventually risen to the occasion had I not beaten you to it. We must consider ourselves fortunate, Your Grace."

"Indeed, we should."

The duke hesitated and, surprisingly, seemed somewhat embarrassed as Thorne slowed to allow the man to enter the parlor first. After all, it was only proper. A duke was highest in the pecking order—well above a baron. It appeared the rumors about Hethersby might be true. The man did indeed appear to be a quiet, almost humble sort.

Damn him. Thorne flexed his fingers and forced himself to remain calm. Of those who'd gathered to vie for Lady Blessing's hand, this gentleman unsettled him the most. He prayed one of the other ladies would catch Hethersby's eye and steer the man's attention away from Lady Blessing.

As they entered the parlor, all seven Broadmere sisters gracefully rose to greet them.

A heady rush of longing hit Thorne square in his chest, almost knocking the wind from him. Lady Blessing was a vision in a pale blue gown that matched her eyes. He clenched his teeth to keep his demeanor from betraying her effect on him.

The Duke of Broadmere stepped forward, directing Hethersby to each of the ladies in turn. "Your Grace—allow me to present my sisters. Ladies Serendipity, Blessing, Fortuity, Grace, Joy, Felicity, and Merry. Sisters..." Broadmere paused as his lovely siblings finished their curtsies that rippled down their line like a wave. Broadmere fixed them with what Thorne would describe as a warning look. "Allow me to introduce His Grace, Duke of Hethersby."

"It is my pleasure and honor to meet each of you." Hethersby smiled and gave a tip of his head to them all. "I pray you will forgive me if I do not remember your names straightaway." He twitched the slightest shrug, his expression one of sheepish embarrassment. "I fear I am terrible with names. Please do not hesitate to correct me." He gestured to Thorne. "I hope Lord Knightwood will not mind my thanking you for selecting the two of us to join you for tea. We consider ourselves most fortunate. Do we not, my lord?"

"Indeed, we do, Your Grace." Thorne tried to keep the jealousy out of his tone. That was all he needed to do, make himself appear petty beside a man who didn't hesitate to admit to a weakness. He watched Lady Blessing, wishing she would meet his gaze and toss him a crumb of hope that this visit was not in vain.

"Lord Knightwood," Broadmere said in a tone that stirred Thorne's misgivings even more. "I do not believe introductions to my sisters are necessary for you. Have you not already met them?"

"I had the pleasure of meeting Lady Serendipity and Lady Blessing at Lady Atterley's ball," Thorne said. He offered the remaining sisters his most charming smile. "I met Lady Fortuity during a prior visit here, but I have so far missed meeting the Ladies Grace, Joy, Felicity, and Merry."

"You must tell me how you do that," Hethersby said to Thorne, his voice aglow with genuine admiration.

"Do what?"

"Remember so many names so easily." The duke gave the ladies an apologetic tip of his head. "Please do not misunderstand me. You are all quite stunning and each of you unique. But so many names..."

"Have no worry," Broadmere told him. "I am sure as you get to know them, their names will come to you quite easily."

"Yes," Thorne agreed, wishing he hadn't botched his earlier interactions with Lady Blessing. If he hadn't, they could have been well and truly betrothed by now, with no danger of him losing her to the entirely too amiable duke. The unbelievably genial man should have been a vicar with a temperament like that.

After the ladies seated themselves, Thorne waited a moment

longer before settling onto the golden damask settee across from them. Hethersby sat on the other end of it while the Duke of Broadmere returned to the chair placed between the sisters and their guests, much like a host's seat at the head of the table.

"Our tea will be here shortly," Broadmere said, directing his announcement to Hethersby. He made no effort to disguise his preference for the duke as a potential suitor for one of his sisters. So much so that Thorne began to wonder why he had even been allowed to stay.

"Lord Knightwood," Lady Blessing said with a smile that threatened to bring him to his knees at her feet. "Thank you."

Thorne stared at her, unable to form a coherent thought for the longest moment because of the unmistakable affection in her eyes—affection directed at him. "Forgive me, my lady. I fear you have the advantage—for what are you thanking me?"

"Blessing," Broadmere said in a warning tone that sounded as if he meant to control his sister.

Thorne almost laughed when she gave her brother a cutting glare before turning back to him.

"I overheard everything said in the hallway, my lord—the insults, the slurs—and saw what happened afterward." Her voice softened. "I thank you because when you defend my sisters, you defend me."

"He handled those sorry types with admirable chivalry, my lady," Hethersby told her while leaning forward with the excitement of a young lad who had just witnessed an impressive fight. Then he ducked his head. "Forgive me, ladies, for sitting there and doing nothing."

Thorne wished the guilt-ridden duke would quiet himself, but rather than elbow the man out of the way, he kept his gaze locked with Lady Blessing's. "You are more than welcome, my lady. I could not allow such disturbing conversations to go unaddressed."

"Yes, well..." Broadmere shifted in his chair and looked back at the doors. "Where the devil is our tea?"

"Shall I see to it, brother?" Lady Merry leaned forward in her chair as if ready to charge away.

"No, thank you, Merry," he answered with a tight-lipped scowl.

"How are your constellations, Lady Blessing?" Thorne asked, choosing to bolster any advantage he might possess with the lovely lady. While it would be preferable to have her brother's approval and blessing, if he recalled the gossips rightly, the lady was of age and did not need the duke's permission to marry.

"They are hardly *my* constellations, my lord." Her teasing grin made the plump bow of her pink lips appear even more kissable. "They are there for all to enjoy."

"You are an admirer of the stars?" the Duke of Hethersby asked her.

Much to Thorne's relief, Lady Blessing shifted her demeanor to the polite yet detached friendliness of a hostess not particularly excited about her guest. "Yes, Your Grace. My father allowed my studies to include astronomy. We shared a love for the stars."

Hethersby shifted in his seat, fidgeting from side to side. "I often admire the stars from my country estate where the skies are not distorted by the city's lights and smoke. Do you like the country, Lady Blessing? Or do you prefer living in the city?"

"Lady Blessing is happy wherever her family is—and when she marries and has children, she will be happy wherever they are," Broadmere said with a quelling look at his sister.

Lady Blessing's eyes flared wide, and she opened her mouth to respond, but Lady Serendipity leaned forward and inserted herself into the conversation. "Have you studied astronomy, Your Grace?"

Thorne bit the inside of his cheek to keep from smiling at the fury flashing in Lady Blessing's eyes.

"Oh no, Lady...uhm, my lady," Hethersby said, as if completely unaware of the war between the siblings. "I merely enjoy looking up at the night sky and wondering at the vastness of it all."

"Indeed," Thorne couldn't resist saying.

Broadmere shot a narrow-eyed glare at him.

Thorne returned fire with a glare of its own. He might be a mere baron, but he had several years on the new duke, and not a doubt existed in his mind that he could navigate the *ton* with more agility and finesse than the young cub.

Lady Blessing rose from her seat with a suddenness that caused all three gentlemen to scramble to their feet. Ignoring her brother and Thorne, she stepped forward and offered a polite curtsy to the gangly Duke of Hethersby. "Do forgive me, Your Grace, but my sister Fortuity and I must excuse ourselves to discuss a *private* topic of the utmost urgency with Lord Knightwood. Please do not think us rude. I know this is quite unconventional, but we invited him to call today regarding our urgent topic before we became aware so many callers might visit today. I am sure you understand."

Hethersby responded with a gallant bow. "But of course, Lady Blessing. Do not trouble yourself with worry. I am grateful to have met you today and shared what time you could spare. I do hope you will consider granting me the pleasure of your company again sometime?"

With a graceful tip of her head, she offered her hand. "I will indeed, Your Grace. It has been a pleasure meeting you. Thank you so much for understanding."

He took her hand, bowed his tall frame over it, then turned to Thorne and smiled. "Good day to you, Lord Knightwood. I am sure we shall cross paths again."

"Good day to you, Your Grace." Thorne felt quite wicked about taking advantage of such a guileless man. But Lady Blessing was at stake. He would do whatever it took to win her.

"My sister sometimes confuses dates and appointments, Your Grace," Broadmere said, his tone strained and simmering with frustration. "Blessing, perhaps you might check your diary. I am quite sure you will find this afternoon was open for callers."

"No thank you, brother." Lady Blessing's smile didn't fool

anyone but the unsuspecting Hethersby. "I am quite certain about the day's appointments. If you wish, we may speak about this later."

"We most certainly will," Broadmere growled, his eyes darkening to an almost purple hue that made him appear quite sinister.

Thorne wondered if the man had trouble winning at cards with eyes like that. Many a hand could be lost by revealing one's emotions. He strode forward, held the door for the ladies, then followed them out while fighting the urge to shoot a victorious smirk back at Broadmere. The pair of dukes could enjoy their tea with the remaining sisters. Thorne couldn't help but smile. Now poor Hethersby had two fewer names to remember.

Chapter Ten

THORNE LENGTHENED HIS stride to catch up with Lady Blessing as she flew down the hallway with her sister scurrying along beside her. But after a few steps, he slowed, reveling in the vision of the lady as she moved with the grace of a sleek ship with the wind in its sails. Her ethereal blonde curls fluttered with her hurried steps, and the airy muslin of her pale blue gown flowed around her as if adoring the opportunity to caress her curves.

When they reached the observatory door with its sign that still made him smile, she unlocked it with a key tied to a ribbon that was pinned to her gown. Without a glance back, she led the way into the room, waving for him to follow.

"Do come in, Lord Knightwood. You remember the way."

"Indeed I do, my lady."

"I shall take myself to the balcony," Lady Fortuity told them as she headed for the set of doors centered in the wall of windows.

"Be sure to stay on the balcony," Lady Blessing told her while pointing at the windows. "If you risk slipping down the trellis to the garden, Chance is sure to see you and fly into one of his tantrums. He is already as fractious as can be because I defied him. I would not put it past him to interrupt us at his first opportunity."

"His Grace did seem rather nice, though," Lady Fortuity said.

She offered Thorne a mischievous smile. "Did you not think so, Lord Knightwood?"

"I am sure the Duke of Hethersby would be a perfect husband for any of the Broadmere sisters *other than* Lady Blessing."

Lady Fortuity laughed, then hurried out onto the balcony and closed the doors behind her.

Lady Blessing turned and studied him for a brief moment before meandering over to the telescope and peering into the eyepiece as if he wasn't there. Thorne remained silent. Watchful. Something made him feel that this was a test. When she straightened and faced him once more, it bothered him no small amount that she was not smiling.

"I beg your forgiveness, Lady Blessing." The apology sprang from his lips before he realized what he was saying.

Her eyes narrowed as she eyed him with the watchfulness of a hawk about to pounce on its prey. "Forgive you for what, my lord? Sullying my reputation or forcing my brother to make everyone ignore that tasty morsel of *on dit* by spreading the rumor that my dowry was largest of all?"

The range and severity of her question left him speechless. Before he could form a coherent answer, she snorted a huffing laugh. "You appear confounded, Lord Knightwood."

He lifted both hands in surrender. "That is because I am, my lady. I recall a regrettable stir after we parted at Lady Burrastone's party, but I was unaware I had damaged your reputation. Pray, enlighten me so I might beg your forgiveness more genuinely."

She crossed the room to the desk, picked up what appeared to be one of the more popular gossip rags that his mother always read, and brought it to him. "Front page. Bold type. Right below the banner."

Thorne stared down at it and read:

Is it not strange that the seven diamonds of Broadmere, the beauties claiming to be in search of husbands, do not give so much as a passing glance to those who would gladly take them to the altar? Perhaps these glittering seven are not diamonds after all—but faux gemstones. Dare we say possibly even "used" bits of colored glass? At least one of them appears to be in the market for a benefactor rather than a husband.

Raging fury threatened to consume him and turn him to ash where he stood, making it impossible to speak until he regained control—for the sake of the precious lady's sensibilities. He read the damnable thing a second time. What cruel, unfeeling blackguard would have such a thing printed?

He slowly lifted his head. "Shall we have the first of the banns read this Sunday, or do you prefer a special license? Tell me what you wish, Lady Blessing, and I shall make it so."

She blinked as though waking from a deep sleep. "I did not show that to you to force an offer of marriage." She snatched it back from him and shut it away in a desk drawer. "Were you not aware of it?"

"I was not." He scrubbed a hand across his mouth, damning himself for hurting her. He had meant to defend her honor at that ridiculous party—not destroy it. With a slow shake of his head, he glared at the drawer where she had stowed the horrid thing. "I do not make it a habit of reading such trash." However, he was surprised that his mother had not brought it to his attention—not to besmirch Lady Blessing in his eyes, but to discover whether it was he who had soiled one of the Broadmere ladies' reputations. Mother would be infuriated at such an attack on an innocent young woman.

"Having our banns read this Sunday might repair some of the damage," he said, "whereas a special license could ruin you even more."

Her thunderous expression was not that of a tearful, overset woman but of a lady frustrated beyond belief. "Did you not hear me clearly, my lord? I did not show you that bit of ridiculousness to secure an offer of marriage. When I marry"—she thumped her fist to her chest and jutted her chin higher—"I will do so for love—not because I fear the tongue waggers."

Perhaps now was the time to bare his soul and learn his fate with this priceless treasure who was about to slip through his fingers. He slowly moved closer. "When I received your response to that pathetic excuse of a letter I wrote, I realized something."

"And what was that, Lord Knightwood?" she asked, her demeanor shifting from a warrior goddess to an uncertain doe about to take flight.

"I beg you—call me Thorne."

She stared at him for a long moment, puckering those lips of hers that he hungered to taste. "You realized that you wished me to call you Thorne?"

"Actually, I realized that I wished you to call me husband."

"Husband?" Her nervous squeak as she uttered the word endeared her to him even more.

He nodded, wondering at the range of emotions flitting across her countenance in rapid succession. The aquamarine of her eyes brightened as if she might be on the verge of tears. He prayed they were happy ones.

"Yes, my precious Lady Blessing." He closed the remaining distance between them and gently took her hands in his. "Would you do me the honor of becoming my wife?"

She nervously ran the pink tip of her tongue across her lips, wetting them to an irresistible shine. "It is a rumor, you know," she whispered.

He tipped his head forward not only to better hear her but to breathe in the sweetness of her warmth. "What is a rumor?" he whispered back.

"My dowry is not larger than the dowries of my sisters." Her pained expression and the hurt in her eyes were a dagger to his heart.

"Your dowry has nothing to do with my proposal."

"Does it not?" she asked with a coldness as harsh as a slap in the face.

"No. It does not."

"What about needing time to decide if you are able to develop the self-control to leave other men's wives alone?"

He released her hand with a heavy sigh and bowed his head. "I was a fool to word my indecisiveness in such a way, and that is one of the things for which I beg forgiveness."

"And the other things?"

With a step back, he lowered his gaze to the floor, finding himself too ashamed to look her in the eye. Inwardly, he berated himself. No. Lady Blessing deserved better. He lifted his head, locked his eyes with hers, and lifted both his hands in supplication. "I beg forgiveness for expecting you to wait for me to overcome my fears." He offered her a rueful smile. "For expecting you to wait like a bundle of herbs curing on a shelf, as you so succinctly put it. I beg your forgiveness for expecting you to understand and accept my reservations even though I had yet to find the courage to explain why I felt the way I did."

"And why did you feel that way…Thorne?" An encouraging hint of compassion warmed her tone.

Her use of his name thrilled him, making him swallow hard. "I thought to prevent the continuation of my line's cruelty."

Her fair brows drew together, making her frown lovelier than a frown should be. "Your line's cruelty? I am afraid I do not understand."

"Do you know anything of my family, Lady Blessing?"

"You may call me Blessing—for now, at least. And the only thing I know of your family is that you are a man who prefers to bed them rather than wed them." Her blush belied the boldness of her words.

To hear the truth of his reputation come from such an innocent source shamed him even more. He almost cringed. "Yes… Well, that is part of my story. Thankfully, the other chapters appear to be fading in everyone's memory as time passes."

"What other chapters?"

"My father's humiliation of my mother by openly parading his mistresses for all to see. His belittling of her in public and even worse in private. While he never struck her physically, he battered her with words that left her with scars she still struggles to hide to this day."

"Those are the worst sorts of wounds," Blessing said softly as she clutched a hand to her throat. "I am so sorry. Witnessing such behavior must have made it almost impossible for you to believe that a man and a woman could have a happy, loving marriage."

"I wish it were that simple." Thorne dreaded saying his fears aloud, but she had the right to know before she seriously considered his proposal. "My father's father treated my grandmother just as horridly. It appears that all the men in my line were malicious, hot-tempered bas—" He clenched his teeth and bowed his head. "Forgive me, my lady. Suffice it to say that I fear becoming the next Knightwood monster."

Ever so slowly, she circled him, studying him as though he were one of her constellations. "You do not seem the cruel sort. According to my servants—who know everything there is to know, by the way—your immoral pastimes are your only character flaw."

"I do have a temper," he sadly admitted to her. "But to the best of my knowledge, I have never exhibited the loathsome traits of my ancestors. But then—I have never been married, either."

"You believe marriage is the impetus?"

"I fear it may be."

"Then why risk awakening the beast now?"

"Because, my precious lady, I fear you have made me come to love you."

Without taking her gaze from his, she increased the distance between them, backing away and finding her path by nervously patting the furniture she passed. "But you hardly know me," she said so quietly that he almost didn't hear her.

"What I know, I already love. I cannot help but think that the better I come to know you, the more I shall love you."

She wet her lips again.

He struggled not to groan. "What say you, my lovely Blessing?" He couldn't help but huff a quiet laugh.

She arched a brow.

"Forgive me, dear one—if I may call you *dear one*. But when I said your name, I realized that if you agree to be my wife, it will indeed be a *blessing* to me."

"You sound like my parents," she said softly, her eyes shining brighter with a renewed sheen of tears. Then she laughed. "Of course, when I was little, they sometimes teased that I could either be a *blessing* or a *curse*, depending on my temperament."

Thorne risked moving toward her, reaching for her with both hands. "Will you be my blessing?"

Tipping her head to one side, she slid her hands into his. "I will...consider it."

"Consider it?" His heart stuttered, but he refused to admit defeat. He tugged her closer, rubbing his thumbs across the silkiness of her bare fingers. Thank heavens she had removed her gloves for the tea that never came.

"I will not be propelled by the gossips, my lord." Her heady scent of sweet lilacs and warm, desirable woman swept across him, making him ache to take her into his arms. "When I agree to marry, it will be because I wish to marry the one I love—not because I wish to silence the *ton*."

"Would you grant me the honor of announcing our engagement, at least?"

Her delicate brow rose again to that same judgmental angle that indicated she was weighing his soul. Unfortunately, he felt that this time, she found him lacking.

"And what displeases you about announcing our engagement?" he asked.

"It does not necessarily displease me..."

"Yet...?"

She huffed like an adorably petite bull about to charge. "Society will think I have bowed to them—or that the only reason you, the infamous rake, have finally agreed to a proper leg-shackling is because of that ridiculous rumor about my dowry that Chance stirred into the tittle-tattle swill."

"When we are seen enjoying each other's company at the last of this Season's parties, seen riding in the park, and strolling wherever we decide to meander, the *ton* will consider us engaged whether you do or not. I do not wish to sound harsh, but the only way it will appear that you are going *against* the gossips is if you are courted by another gentleman." As soon as the words left his mouth, he wished he could snatch them back. He did not want her to even consider such a thing.

"That would be a cruel game unless all participants knew the rules."

Thorne had a fair idea as to what the calculating lady was thinking. "I doubt the Duke of Hethersby would be capable of such a farce. Remember his difficulty in remembering names?"

With a wrinkle of her nose, she fluttered her fingers as if shooing the idea away. "I daresay he is also too kind to be a part of such a masquerade. It would be unfair to even ask him." She caught her bottom lip between her teeth and eyed him as though wondering if he would bite. "You truly think you might love me?"

"I do not think it, my lady—I feel it." He kissed her hand, then pressed it to his cheek while keeping his gaze fixed on hers. "Might you feel at least a little twinge of affection for me?"

"Perhaps a twinge," she whispered.

"But you are not certain?" he said softly as he leaned in and brushed the tenderest of kisses across the sweetness of her supple mouth.

"I... Uhm..." She lifted her face and stretched on tiptoe to strengthen their gentle bond.

He deepened the kiss, savoring her with a slow tasting that was both pure pleasure and delicious torture. Never in his life had he wished for a simple kiss to go on forever. But nay, this was no simple kiss—this was a pledge, an oath from his heart to hers. He cradled the soft curve of her cheek, then slid his fingers into the silkiness of her hair.

She ran her hands up his chest, wrapped her arms around his

neck, and pressed closer. Her slight trembling reminded him of her innocence and demanded he maintain control rather than allow the joining to go any further. She deserved the utmost care and respect he could give her.

He lifted his head, his heart soaring at the high color of her cheeks and the yearning in her eyes. "It would be best if I took my leave now, my lady."

Disappointment filled her face, but she nodded. "I suppose so." With a reluctance that thrilled him, she slid her arms out from around him and eased back a step. She ducked her head, then teased him with a glance and a shy smile. "We might announce we are officially courting."

While he wasn't quite sure what the difference was between *officially* courting and being engaged, he was not about to argue with her. "That would be a wonderful start. Shall we christen our announcement with an evening ride in the park to enjoy the stars? A fitting way to celebrate, do you not think so?"

"I do think so, and I shall see if Fortuity and Serendipity might accompany us."

"I shall speak with your brother on my way out."

Her beaming happiness dimmed slightly. "I prefer to speak with him first. It would be best."

While he wanted to abide by her wishes, he was not about to allow her to face what might be her brother's wrath. "That is not the way this is done, my lady."

"How would you know? Have you courted or been engaged before?"

"Blessing—"

"Do not say my name in that tone, my lord. You will find it most unwise." She jutted her chin to the defiant angle that warned him she was digging in and was not prepared to yield. "I am of age. I do not need his permission to marry. As a matter of fact, my parents' will clearly stated that the only requirement for my union was true love—not my brother's approval."

"It is a matter of respect I should extend to the duke. From what I have seen, your family cares for each other. You are close. I do not wish to be responsible for ruining that."

She glared at him, clearly not pleased.

"I will not mention the word *engagement*. You have my word I will merely say we are seriously courting, but I owe him the courtesy of speaking to him man to man."

"Gads! *Man to man*. A more pompous term I have yet to hear!" She hissed like a boiling teakettle as she stormed over to the balcony doors, yanked them open, and shouted, "Fortuity! You may come in now."

Thorne resettled his stance, unsure whether he had emerged victorious in the discussion or lost. "Blessing?"

She turned and stared at him, her face becoming redder by the minute.

"Are you holding your breath?" Was this some sort of feminine tantrum of which he was unaware?

She exhaled with a loud whoosh. "It is sometimes safer for all concerned that I hold my breath and count to ten before I speak."

"I see." He bit the inside of his cheek, knowing that if he laughed at her now, he might not live to tell about it. Instead, he proffered an understanding nod. "I shall take my leave now and return this evening for our ride in the park."

Fortuity popped back inside, looking first at her sister, then at him. "We are going for a ride in the park this evening?"

This time it was Thorne who held his breath, fearing that Blessing had changed her mind. Relief filled him as she nodded and said, "Yes. A ride to announce our official courting. I thought it might be proper if Serendipity joined us as well."

Fortuity grinned. "May I be there when you tell Chance?"

"You may not," Blessing snapped, then jerked her head at Thorne. "Lord Knightwood insists on telling him on his way out."

"Blessing," Thorne said quietly.

"What?"

"You own my heart even more than you did before."

She gathered herself up as though fighting to remain irritated about his meeting with her brother—but failed miserably. "Perhaps my twinge regarding you is somewhat stronger, as well."

"It thrills my soul to hear that."

She marched past him to the door, unlocked it, and set it ajar. After a hard yank on the bellpull, she turned back to him, her face wreathed in the loveliest pout of frustration he had ever witnessed. "I shall ask Walters to ensure that Chance will see you—if you insist."

He joined her at the doorway and, once again, took her hands in his. "I want to do right by you...and by your family."

After a quick glance out into the hall, she upturned her face to his. "Another kiss might convince me to forgive you."

"Essie!" Fortuity gasped.

"Quiet!" Blessing told her, then lifted her face to him again, a sense of daring flashing in her eyes.

"As you wish, my lady." He cradled her cheeks in his hands and returned to the sweetness of her barely parted lips. Then he brushed a kiss across each of her closed eyes and on her forehead. "I look forward to when I may kiss you from the tips of your toes to the top of your crown," he said in a husky whisper.

"Oh my," she replied with a shuddering breath.

"Till this evening, my lady." Reluctantly, he stepped back from her as Walters appeared at the end of the hallway and slowly ambled toward them.

"Yes...till this evening, my lord."

⚭

"IF YOU WOULD kindly wait here, my lord," Walters said, "I shall inform His Grace that you wish to see him."

"Thank you." Thorne stepped into the parlor but didn't sit. The sense of foreboding within him was too great for sitting. He needed to pace, needed to compose himself, since he was well aware that Blessing's brother did not consider him a proper match for any of the sisters. And truth be told, Thorne didn't blame the man. After all, his reputation as a confirmed rakeshame had preceded him.

Within moments, the butler reappeared. "His Grace will see you now, my lord. But he asked that I inform you it must be quite brief, for he has other engagements this afternoon."

"I understand." And Thorne did. Broadmere intended to be rid of him as quickly as possible and hoped to make it a permanent dismissal. He strode into the library determined to change the man's mind as amicably as he could. He didn't wish to fracture relationships within the family, but neither would he relinquish the chance of enjoying a life with the witty, beautiful, and wonderfully unpredictable Lady Blessing.

At his desk with quill in hand, Broadmere spared Thorne a quick glance but didn't move to rise and offer a proper greeting. "Knightwood. I would have thought you'd be long gone by now. The Duke of Hethersby departed shortly after my sister chose to make a fool of herself."

Thorne took a stance in front of the man's desk, clasped his hands behind his back, and waited. It was just the two of them now. Time to speak plainly—and he would not have Blessing besmirched. "Your sister did not make a fool of herself. She should be admired for speaking her mind and making her own way as she sees fit."

After scratching another line or two on the foolscap in front of him, Broadmere set down his quill and aimed a fierce scowl at Thorne. "All the dowries are the same."

"That is not why I am here, and I believe you know that."

"Your behavior at Lady Burrastone's affair caused irreparable damage to Blessing's reputation."

"Our eventual marriage will repair that."

Broadmere's eyes widened. "Marriage?" He bared his teeth like a cornered animal. "None of my sisters will marry the likes of you, sir. I shall withhold my approval."

"According to Lady Blessing's age and your parents' will, your approval is unnecessary." Thorne didn't wish to antagonize the man, but he would not be deterred. "She did not wish me to speak with you today, but I told her I owed it to you and the closeness of your family. As of today, we are officially courting."

Broadmere snorted. "Officially courting? Ridiculous. If you were in earnest, you would at least call it an engagement."

"I wished to, however, your sister did not, and I promised to abide by her wish on that matter."

"Well, you are too late. The Duke of Hethersby has asked for her hand, and I have granted it. Good day to you, Lord Knightwood. Take yourself elsewhere, and I wish you good hunting."

Struggling to control the possessive fury pounding within him, Thorne leaned forward and propped both hands on the man's desk. "Blessing is mine—soon to be my wife."

"Blessing is not yours. She is my sister, and I do not give a damn what that will says—she will not marry the likes of you when a duke is willing to make her his wife." He pushed up from his chair and pointed at the door. "Good day, Lord Knightwood. See yourself out."

"I love her and will not relinquish her."

"If you loved her, why did you hurt her?" Broadmere rounded the desk. He jabbed a finger at Thorne, coming just short of stabbing him in the chest with it. "You made my sister cry."

Thorne admitted he deserved the man's fury on that count. He hardened his jaw but kept his head held high. "I did at that. I also begged her forgiveness for being such a fool."

His expression filled with loathing, Broadmere pointed at the door again. "She is promised to the duke and will soon be known as the Duchess of Hethersby. Now, get out."

Struggling to remain calm and reason with the man, Thorne remained rooted to the spot. "You wish to alienate your sister's affections for you? Permanently damage the closeness you share with her?" Before the duke could answer, he added, "Take care what you do, Your Grace. A family with the closeness I have seen among you and your sisters is a rare thing that should be cherished and protected at all costs."

Broadmere glared at him, pacing back and forth as if aching to either slam his fist into Thorne's jaw or challenge him to a duel. "Essie will forgive me once she realizes I have acted in her best interest."

"By handing her over to a man she does not love, as if she were one of your hound pups in need of a new home? From what she has told me about your parents, I daresay they would not approve."

"Do not presume to tell me what my parents would or would not approve of." Broadmere jabbed a finger at him again. "Blessing might not be old enough to remember your father, but I am. Well, somewhat. My father used your esteemed sire as an example of what I should never become. How do I know you will not become the man your malicious father was?"

Thorne resettled his stance and chose his next words with the greatest of care. "I understand your concerns and once shared them. But I have taken precautions."

"Precautions?"

"If ever I happen to become the next Knightwood monster, my life is forfeit. I will not share any further details on the agreement I have secured. Suffice it to say, I have ensured that an honorable man will step in and end my ways should my behavior ever warrant it." It shamed Thorne to no end to have to admit he had made such an arrangement, but he truly felt that Blessing's brother had the right to know.

The duke's eyes narrowed, and he stopped pacing. "An honorable man," he repeated in a dubious tone. "Forgive me if I take issue with your revelation, my lord. How could someone like you possibly know *any* honorable men—much less share the close friendship that such an oath would require?"

Thorne refused to reveal that Ravenglass was the friend who had reluctantly agreed to hand him over to the press gangs because he refused to go so far as to take Thorne's life. But perhaps there was another way to convince the duke of his determination to protect Blessing. "Then you do it."

"What?"

"You do it." Thorne noticed the man's fists slowly relaxing. "If ever I become the cruel tyrant my father was, end my life to save your sister from the fate my mother endured for far too long."

"End your life," Broadmere repeated slowly as if attempting to pronounce the words of a foreign tongue. "You cannot be serious."

Thorne shrugged. "I assure you, I am quite serious." He nodded at the man's desk and the wooden tray of fresh, clean writing paper waiting to be used. "Draw up the agreement this very moment, or have your solicitor do it."

"I daresay my solicitor would advise against such a questionable agreement," Broadmere said. "He would probably refuse because it would make him an accessory to murder."

"Then you write it out, and I shall sign." Thorne held up his right hand and extended the finger bearing his gold signet ring. "I am in earnest here. Your sister is to be my wife, and I shall spend the rest of my days making her happy. If it takes an additional oath to convince you that my treatment of her will never waver, then so be it." He stepped forward, selected a fresh sheet of writing paper, and thumped it down onto the center of the desk. "Why do you hesitate, Your Grace?"

"You do not fear I might abuse the agreement by claiming you an ogre just so I might end you and have you out of the way so my sister might marry better?"

"Would you?" Thorne considered himself a good judge of character. The talent had served him well whenever he'd chosen to make wagers. He read people as easily as books. Well—most people. He was still learning to read Blessing, and that was but one of the many reasons he found her so enchanting. The duke might be young, impetuous, and—from what Thorne had heard—a bit foolhardy with money. But the man was honest to a fault, and not a bad sort when he wasn't trying to be unpleasant for the sake of his sister. Thorne tried not to smile. "Would you abuse the agreement, Your Grace?"

The man turned away and stared out the window, letting an uncomfortable silence settle between them. "No. I would not." He barely turned back and glared at Thorne. "And I daresay you already knew that."

"Then write it out." Thorne settled into the lush leather wingback chair near the desk. "I shall wait so we might have this resolved between us this afternoon."

Broadmere returned to the chair behind the desk, sagged down into it, and scrubbed his face with both hands. "All I want for my sisters is…" His voice trailed off as he dropped his hands to the chair's armrests and leaned back into it. He shifted with a slight shrug. "Happiness. Security. The best in all things."

"I notice you did not mention love." Thorne eyed the young man, seeing a great deal of himself in the impetuous duke.

"I find it hard to believe that another love as strong as the one my parents shared could ever be re-created."

Thorne pondered on that for a moment, then slowly nodded. "I do not think love is a thing to be created. I believe it just exists—like an elusive jewel or a precious secret waiting for us to discover it. It lurks and teases, patiently waiting for those who dare to take hold of it."

"I have as much as promised her to the Duke of Hethersby." Broadmere propped his head in his hand and wearily rubbed his eyes. "Gads, my bed will be full of frogs from now to eternity."

Bewilderment tempered Thorne's jealousy, and Broadmere's resigned tone also gave him enough hope to keep his possessive fury in check. He had to ask, "Your bed full of frogs?"

The young duke lifted his head from his hand. "Essie's weapon of choice, you might say. Ever since she was old enough and agile enough to catch the infernal things, whenever one of us crossed her, we would find our bedsheets writhing with the croaking little bug eaters."

Laughter snorted free of Thorne. He couldn't hold it back. "And what did your parents think about that?"

Broadmere smiled, but only sadness filled his face. "Mama and Papa never interceded in our battles unless one of us picked up a weapon that might truly do the other bodily harm. They wanted us to learn to work out our differences. Negotiate our peace and find a resolution that would work for both sides."

"You were very fortunate to have such parents."

"Yes," Broadmere softly agreed before scrubbing a hand across his eyes again. Sucking in a deep breath and whooshing it out, he frowned at Thorne. "I wish my father was here. He would know what to do about Hethersby."

"What did you say to the man? You noticed that he is not exactly..." Thorne didn't wish to speak ill of the gentleman, but Hethersby was not the average duke. "The man seemed extraordinarily kind, but not always aware of other's behavior or motives."

Broadmere leaned forward and rested his folded hands on his desk. "William—as he asked me to call him—never thought he would be the duke, since he was the youngest of four brothers. He loves the countryside, reading, animals, and, most of all, the Lord God Almighty. He was a vicar until his father and three brothers died. The father succumbed to apoplexy, two of the brothers were killed early on in the war, and the last died of a terrible fever after losing his legs at Waterloo."

Thorne cringed and shifted uncomfortably in the chair. "Poor man. So much loss. And what a shock it must have been to find himself suddenly thrust into the leadership of his family."

"As you said, he is a kind man." With his elbow on the desk, Broadmere propped his chin in his hand. "Truth be told, though, I am not sure he would even remember which one Essie is."

"How could the man be a vicar and not remember names?"

Broadmere shrugged. "Perhaps his flock loved him so much for his amiable ways that they forgave his absent-mindedness."

He frowned. "I would let Essie talk to him, but that somehow seems cruel—like placing the lamb in the jaws of the lioness."

"Your sister is not that fierce."

Broadmere snorted. "You have no idea, Knightwood. Just remember—you asked for her of your own free will."

Chapter Eleven

"**Y**OU DID WHAT?" Blessing circled Chance, contemplating how to make him pay for handing her over to a man as if she were bartered goods. This overstepping of his bounds warranted something much worse than frogs in his bed. "How could you? How *dare* you?"

Her brother lifted both hands and backed away in clear surrender. "Hethersby is a good and kind man—as well as a duke with a modest approach to life, even though he is plump in the pockets. He would be a perfect husband for you, Essie."

"I think he could be a good friend," she said, "but not a husband. Especially not for me." She threw up her hands. "Does the silly man even know which one I am?"

"Eventually, he would know you for who you are."

"Eventually? Have you anything between your ears to stop the wind from whistling through your head? That must be what happened to any sense you ever hoped to have. A stout breeze blew it away."

"There is no need to be insulting."

"Yes indeed, there is." Blessing paced around the chairs and small tables cluttering the library, trying to curb the desire to rip off her slipper and beat him over the head with it. She hadn't done that since she was ten and three, when Chance had stolen her journal and tossed it into the pond to keep anyone else from discovering how infatuated he was with the newest kitchen maid.

She turned and shook a finger at him. "You will speak with him at once and retract whatever you told him."

Chance stared at her for entirely too long with a grim look that annoyed her to no end.

"Well, say something, damn you!"

"Essie! Such language does not befit a lady."

"It befits my mood," she said, striding toward him. "Whatever silly thing you are thinking—out with it now."

"If you truly think yourself enamored of Lord Knightwood, smitten with him enough to cast away any and all other suitors, why do you insist on referring to your arrangement as *courting* rather than an engagement?" He folded his arms across his chest, emitting an air of smug superiority that angered her even more.

"Because, unlike you, dear brother, I prefer to tread carefully rather than jump in over my head and flounder until I drown." She stormed closer and poked him in the shoulder. "If you had been more circumspect, rather than greedy to have one of us married off, you would not find yourself in such a quandary now."

"Find *myself* in a quandary? Do you not mean find *us* in a quandary?"

"I am not the one who agreed to marry the Duke of Hethersby." She poked him again, harder this time. "This is your problem. Not mine."

Chance rubbed his shoulder. "Stop poking—that is hardly ladylike behavior either. Have you forgotten everything Mama taught you?"

"Mama is the one who advised me to tread carefully when it came to choosing a husband." Blessing turned away, unwilling for Chance to see the frustrated tears at risk of overflowing. She headed for the door and refused to look back at him. "Repair your error, brother. Lord Knightwood is taking me for a carriage ride to admire the stars this evening. Tutie and Seri are coming along." Before stepping out into the hall, she relented and turned back to aim a cutting glare at him. "Undo what you have done.

You knew it was wrong when you did it. Did you not hear Papa's voice in your head telling you to stop?"

Chance stared at the floor. "I did, Essie—but I ignored it."

"Next time, listen to Papa and make him proud." She exited the library and slammed the door behind her before he could reply. Partway down the hall, she paused and bowed her head, a twinge of regret filling her as she remembered one of her last conversations with Mama. *Your brother has a good heart. Help him do his best. He will need all of you to help him once Papa and I are gone.* It was as if Mama had known Papa would soon follow her to the grave.

"Help must sometimes come with a tough sternness that Chance cannot ignore," she told the memory as she continued down the hall and climbed the stairs.

"Who are you talking to?" Serendipity watched her from atop the staircase, peering over the banister with Fortuity at her side. She wrinkled her nose and cringed. "Did it not go well? You didn't hurt him, did you? He is our only brother."

"And the duke," Fortuity reminded her with a sympathetic tip of her head.

Blessing rolled her eyes as she flounced past them and charged into their suite of rooms. "I am sure I did him very little damage when I advised him he would do well to remember all that Papa taught him."

"So, he attempted to thwart your courting of Lord Knightwood?" Fortuity asked.

Blessing flopped onto the fainting couch in the sitting room shared by all the sisters, since it was situated between the bedroom suites. "The fool promised me to the Duke of Hethersby!"

"What?" Fortuity nudged her over to sit beside her. "He did not."

"He did," Serendipity said. "I overheard the conversation."

"And you did nothing to stop him?" Blessing glared at her older sister. "How could you, Seri? How could you not intercede on my behalf? I trusted you."

"Because in all honesty, I feel the duke is a better match for you." Serendipity perched on the other side of the couch, her expression one of worry and regret. "Lord Knightwood has such a terrible reputation." She squeezed Blessing's arm. "I fear he will hurt you, Essie."

"That is something I must discover for myself." Admittedly, Blessing shared Serendipity's fear, but how would she know if she didn't give Thorne a chance? "I twinge for him," she admitted with a heartfelt sigh.

"You what?" Serendipity frowned at her.

Blessing patted her chest. "I have…stirrings, and I most definitely like him much more than any other man I have ever known."

"You already love him," Fortuity proclaimed with a knowing nod. "Whenever I write my characters, they always feel twingy like that right before they realize they cannot live without whomever they are twinging for."

"*Twingy* is not a word," Serendipity said.

"It is in my stories." Fortuity stood and held out a hand to Blessing. "Come—we shall write a letter to the Duke of Hethersby. He seemed the kind sort. I am sure he will understand." She grinned. "At least, he will whenever he figures out which one of us you are."

"Do not mock the man," Serendipity said. "He is kind and gentle."

"Then you marry him," Blessing said.

"I will not marry until everyone else has." Serendipity lifted her chin as if proud of her persona as some type of marriage martyr. "Mama entrusted me with the care of all of you."

Blessing was tempted to tell her she had done a poor job of keeping that promise but held her tongue. There was no need to be cruel.

Well…maybe just a little cruelty was needed. "In future, you would do well to remember that Mama and Papa wanted us to marry for love—not for status or because a man was *kind.*"

Serendipity glared at her. "I was trying to protect you. And it never hurts to have more than one gentleman interested in you." Her sly grin became a balm that eased the sting of her treachery. "After all, you want Lord Knightwood to appreciate you, before you decide to make things permanent. I think it very wise that you insisted on calling it *courting* rather than an official engagement. But you know what the *ton* will decide once they see you together more than once."

"I have no time to worry about the *ton.*" Blessing eyed them both. "My family and the ways they choose to *help* me take quite enough of my time and attention, thank you very much."

"What did I do?" Fortuity asked in a hurt tone.

"Nothing. Yet." Blessing glared at Serendipity. "Do we have an understanding? Will you act in my favor should the need arise again?"

"I will do my best to follow your wishes," Serendipity said. "But that does not mean I will agree to anything I fear might hurt you." She held out her hand like they used to do when they were children trying to resolve a spat. "Truce?"

Blessing knew Serendipity meant well and had never been able to stay angry with her for long. She took her sister's hand. "Truce—for now."

"Did you tell Chance you decided to send a letter to the duke after all?" Fortuity asked.

"I did not." Blessing swept aside the sheer panel of delicate lace hanging between the heavy draperies of the parlor's front window. The lamplighters had already done their job, lending a warm, safe glow to the ever-increasing darkness descending upon the homes of the aristocracy of St. James's Street. Lord Knightwood—no, *Thorne,* as he wished her to call him—would arrive soon for their nighttime outing to the park.

A shiver of excitement raced through her. This would be their first official *courting*. The thought made her smile, considering it hadn't been so long ago that she had sworn she would never interrupt her study of the stars with something as trivial as finding a husband.

"It was my understanding that you expected Chance to speak with Hethersby. What exactly did you put in your letter?" Serendipity's hesitant tone betrayed her dread of an answer she didn't really wish to hear. "Essie? Are you listening?"

Blessing rolled her eyes before turning from the window to face her sisters. "Do not worry. I merely told His Grace that while I considered his offer a very nice compliment, I wished to marry for love—not convenience or a social transaction to gain a title."

"He seemed very kind," Fortuity said, then held up a hand and turned aside as if knowing what Blessing was about to say. "And no, I do not wish to marry him either."

"I am sure His Grace will find a suitable wife." Blessing turned back to the window for another peek. She wished Thorne would hurry and arrive. "Hopefully, the future Duchess of Hethersby will be a kind lady who will give him many children and years of happiness."

"Do come away from the window, Essie." Serendipity tugged on her sleeve. "He will see you watching for him, and that simply will not do. Lord Knightwood needs to prove himself, and he will not do so if he believes you are longing for his company." She brushed the velvet of the dark blue spencer Blessing had donned to set off her white gown embroidered with a sprinkling of flowers in the same rich shade. "You must keep this jacket, sister. The color suits you so much better than it suits me."

Blessing laughed. "Our coloring is the same, except your eyes are vibrant like priceless sapphires whereas mine are pale like blue glass. How could this jacket suit me better than you?"

She knew the answer. Serendipity was attempting to strengthen the fragile truce between them. Blessing's dear sister felt guilty about not stepping in to keep Chance from giving her away as if she were the pick of the litter.

Serendipity smiled, then bowed her head. "You read me too easily." She lifted her gaze, her fair brows knotted. "I only want you safe and happy. Please know that is what always controls my choices."

Blessing hugged her. "Stop fretting. Remember what Mama always said about worry wrinkles?"

As Serendipity laughed and smoothed a finger between her brows, Walters stepped into the parlor and intoned, "Lord Knightwood."

Resisting the urge to press a hand to her chest to calm her suddenly pounding heart, Blessing managed a serene smile and a curtsy as Thorne joined them. "Just in time," she told him.

He bowed to her sisters, then turned to her and quirked a brow. "Just in time?" he repeated. His dark eyes danced with amusement, making it difficult for her not to drown in them and completely forget to speak.

She cast a glance at her siblings. "We tend to get a bit fractious with each other when waiting. That is one thing none of us does well."

He moved toward her with a devilish smile and offered his arm. "Then, by all means, let us be on our way. The stars await." After a subtle tip of his head for Serendipity and Fortuity to take the lead, he followed with Blessing on his arm to where Walters waited with their cloaks to shield them from the cool, damp air of the early spring evening. Then they continued outside to his impressive landau. The glossy black finish of the carriage perfectly matched the shining, dark coats of the four horses harnessed to it. The driver beside the vehicle hurried to open its door as they approached.

Thorne assisted Blessing's sisters into the conveyance first, then turned to her with a sultry look that made her so warm she wished she had carried her cloak rather than worn it.

"And so," he said in a low tone meant only for her, "our

official courting begins." He took her hand and pressed a kiss to her gloved fingers. "My treasure," he whispered.

"Are you quite certain?" she couldn't resist asking. After all, it was well known by everyone that the man enjoyed his freedom—as much as she enjoyed hers.

He tilted his jaw to a stern angle, but his teasing tone belied his feigned displeasure. "I am not certain about the official courting, my lady. If you will recall, I wanted an *engagement*, but you refused an announcement of our banns or a special license, and I can only assume you would have also refused a rousing trip to Gretna Green."

"You make it quite difficult to draw a breath when you speak like that, my lord." She swallowed hard before allowing him to steady her as she stepped up into the carriage. She settled in the seat and tried to compose herself as he took his place beside her.

"Good—I intend to keep you breathless," he whispered before casting a smile at Fortuity and Serendipity, who sat across from them. "Shall we, ladies?"

Much to Blessing's surprise, her sisters remained quiet, responding to Thorne's inquiry with nothing more than a gracious dip of their chins. She narrowed her eyes at them, letting them know she was watching them just as closely as they watched her. *Sly minxes.* She loved them dearly but knew this trick of theirs. It was the age-old *give him enough rope to hang himself* ploy. In other words, if they remained silent, they hoped Thorne would nervously fill the void with an accidental confession and convict himself of whatever nefarious ploy they thought he was attempting.

"To the park, Thompson," Thorne called out as he settled more comfortably back into the seat.

The fine landau shifted into motion with hardly a lurch, and the horses' hooves treated them to a pleasantly rhythmic clippity-clopping as they rolled down the street. As Thorne subtly pressed the hard, muscular length of his leg against Blessing, another shiver rippled through her—one that had nothing to do with the crisp breeze failing to cool her burning cheeks.

"Is the night too chilly for stargazing?" he asked her with genuine concern.

"No, my lord." She shifted and pulled her cloak closer around her while primly placing what little space she could between them. This was not a game of which she had any experience, but she needed to learn to play it well—and needed to learn its intricacies with haste. Her future and her heart depended on it. She must not allow him to know that with every meeting, the effect he had on her was more powerful. At least, she must not allow him to know it—yet. "It is the perfect night for a ride in the park to enjoy the beauty of the stars."

"It is indeed a night for beauty." He stared at her, looking into her soul, willing her to understand the true meaning behind his words.

She found herself trapped in his gaze and not minding if she remained there forever.

"How is your mother, Lord Knightwood?" Serendipity asked, raising her voice to break the moment's lovely spell.

The slightest hint of a frown creased his brow as he pulled his focus from Blessing and looked to her sister. "She is well, my lady. Thank you for asking. Forgive me, but I did not realize you were an acquaintance of my mother."

Blessing glared hard at her sister, silently warning her that if she didn't want a bed full of frogs, she had better play nice.

Serendipity retreated with a sheepish twitch of her shoulder. "I have not had the pleasure of meeting her, but a dear friend of mine, the daughter of Lady Kettering, told me how your mother so valiantly championed another of my friends when a few among the *ton* took it upon themselves to try to ruin the lady in question when she was quite innocent of any wrongdoing or impropriety."

Blessing breathed easier as she noted the tension melt out of Thorne, from the hardened line of his jaw to his wonderfully broad shoulders. It was more than a little obvious that he was quite protective of his mother. And no wonder, considering what he had shared about his father.

"At our next opportunity, I would be delighted to introduce you to my mother, Lady Serendipity. I know she would enjoy meeting you." He cast a meaningful look at Blessing. "After all, if my intentions are well met, our families will soon be joined by a blissful union."

"We shall see," Blessing managed to say with a coyness that she hoped disguised her pounding heart. "For now, we are merely courting. Remember?"

"*Seriously* courting," he stressed with a pointed look. "Official-ly."

"Seriously courting," she repeated, suddenly finding herself somewhat breathless yet again.

"Essie, look!" Fortuity pointed upward. "A prosperous sign for certain. I must use this in a story."

Blessing looked up just in time to see a series of shooting stars streaming across the dark velvet of the sky, their silvery tails sparkling like magical fairy dust.

"Make a wish, my lord," she said while smiling up at the celestial show.

"You already know my wish," he said softly. "What is yours, my treasure?"

She pulled her gaze away from the stars and allowed herself to float into his eyes again. "To find the love and happiness my parents knew," she whispered ever so quietly, fearing if she said the words aloud, somehow, the darkness of the world would destroy any chance she had for seeing the wish fulfilled.

He didn't speak, nor did he look away. Instead, he took both her hands and hugged them to his chest while leaning forward as if intent on sealing their wishes with a kiss.

Serendipity cleared her throat. Loudly.

Blessing shot a glare at her. "Really?"

"We are the chaperones, dear sister, and this fine coach makes quite the stage for all around us to see your performance."

"Your sister is correct." Thorne released her with a heavy sigh and resettled himself in the seat. "Thank you, Lady Serendipity." He glanced around as if suddenly realizing they were anything but alone. "There do indeed appear to be quite a few enjoying this balmy evening in the park." He reached over and thumped the side of the coach. "Thompson—take us to the highest and clearest point so we might enjoy more of the stars. You know this area better than most. I trust your judgment."

"Will do, my lord." The man headed the carriage to the left with such a deft touch that the passengers barely felt the turn.

"Hyde Park is fairly level. I fear you have given your man an unfair challenge," Blessing said.

"Thompson will find us the perfect spot." Thorne glanced upward. "Our show of shooting stars may have ended, but we still have that gorgeous moon."

"You were enamored of the moon in my observatory." She couldn't resist teasing him. "Just because it is easiest to see without the aid of a telescope merely means it is closer—not larger."

"Well, I like it." He gave her a dashing grin. "And, after all, the moon is for lovers."

"Ahem." Serendipity cleared her throat again, and Fortuity snorted.

Blessing scowled at her eldest sister. "Seri—if you keep clearing your throat to censor us, you will surely be hoarse by the end of the evening."

"Not if you behave," Serendipity retorted, then idly glanced to the right before turning in that direction and openly staring at an approaching phaeton. "Did you invite others to join our enjoyment of the stars, Lord Knightwood?"

Thorne scowled at the vehicle headed their way. "I did not, my lady." He inched forward until he was perched on the edge of the amply padded seat. "Thompson—stop and stay at the ready."

"Yes, my lord."

The carriage slowed to a smooth stop, then the coachman

bent and recovered something from the box beneath his seat. Blessing couldn't determine what it was but assumed it was a firearm.

Thorne disembarked and stood before the carriage door as though defending a castle.

As the light, high-perched phaeton with its pair of dapple grays drew close enough to reveal the driver in the soft lighting provided by the moon and what few street lamps dotted the park, Blessing gasped. The Duke of Hethersby was the lone occupant of the carriage, and he did not seem pleased. She cringed, knowing she had mentioned her evening plans in her letter. If anything terrible happened, it would be her fault for telling the duke where they would be.

"Lord Knightwood," the duke called out with a curt nod.

"Hethersby," Thorne replied as he resettled his stance.

"You have my betrothed in your carriage, sir." The duke shifted while resettling his reins, then turned his attention to Blessing.

She braced herself but did not correct the man about his poor choice of words. There was no need for this foolishness. Her letter to him had been quite clear. They were not betrothed.

"Lady Blessing—are you aware of Lord Knightwood's reputation?"

"I would ask you to answer a question of mine before I respond to that, Your Grace." She wet her lips, praying for eloquence. At the duke's slight nod, she continued. "Did you receive my letter this afternoon?" Of course he had. How else would he have found them? But she needed him to admit it and open the necessary discussion properly.

His gaze dropped, and his shoulders slumped, revealing he had indeed read her letter. "Your brother, the Duke of Broadmere, accepted my request for your hand in marriage. We are betrothed, my lady."

"I am of age, Your Grace, and quite capable of confirming the legalities of this situation with our family's solicitor if forced to do so. However, it is my hope that will not be necessary." She softened her tone, trying to be gentle yet remain firm. "I fear you have been misled. My brother had no right promising me to you." Blessing didn't wish to upset the man, but it wasn't as if anything had been announced. He could easily continue his search for a wife without anyone being the wiser. "As I said in my letter, you are a kind man and your offer of marriage is an honor—but I will not marry a man I do not love."

Hethersby lifted his head and gave her a forlorn look that nipped at her conscience. "You might come to love me if you'd but give me a chance."

"You can have your pick of the *ton*, Your Grace," she said. "And no one but us knows of your offer. Your pride and reputation are intact."

He frowned and shifted in his seat again, frustration shouting from him. "I do not like the marriage hunt and would have it over and done with." He jerked a shoulder as if trying to rid himself of the entire mess. "I had hoped offering for you would end my misery."

Something her mother had once told her came to mind as if Mama whispered in her ear. "You are trying too hard, Your Grace. Sometimes it is best to let go and let things happen as they are meant to happen. When you search too hard for something you cannot find, if you stop and turn your thoughts to something else, what you seek often reveals itself. You discover that what you sought was right in front of you all along—waiting for you to realize it."

He stared at her, but it felt as though he was looking within himself rather than at her. "There was a lady once," he said so quietly that she almost didn't hear him. With a sad shake of his head, he stared down at his hands. "Father did not approve of her, though."

"Your father is dead, Your Grace." Blessing shot a silencing glare at her sisters' shocked gasps before turning back to him. "You are the duke now and can do anything you want."

He looked up and locked eyes with her. "The *ton* would not approve of her either."

"You are a duke, Your Grace. Hang the *ton*. They need you more than you need them."

He smiled. "I like you, Lady Blessing."

"I like you as well, Your Grace, and would be proud to call you friend—but not husband." She hoped she had made that quite clear.

"I consider myself fortunate to have a friend like you, Lady Blessing." He gave her a gracious nod, then turned to Thorne. "Do not do ill by her, Knightwood, for if you do, I shall stand alongside her family in seeing that you regret the day you were born."

"I will not do ill by her, Your Grace." Thorne offered a polite bow but remained in front of the carriage, his determination to guard his lady unmistakable.

Without another word, the duke turned his rig and drove away.

"I must put this in a book," Fortuity said. "That was so…"

"Tutie?" Blessing arched a brow at her dreamy-eyed sister. "Must you think aloud?"

"Sorry."

"You are a wonder, my treasure." Thorne reached into the carriage and took Blessing's hand. "And I consider myself blessed above all men that you chose me rather than the duke."

Rendered speechless, Blessing pulled in a deep breath to slow the rapid pounding of her heart. Surely to goodness, this falling-in-love business was a most difficult thing to manage.

An insistent series of *meows* from the hedgerow bordering the carriage path interrupted the moment.

Blessing blinked and strained to hear the sound again. She turned to her sisters. "Did you hear kitties?"

Both of them cringed, then Fortuity shook her head. "It will not work, Essie. Grace's hounds would torment them, and you know it."

"We must find them." Blessing hopped up and struggled to untangle the folds of her cloak and gown so she might manage a respectable dismount.

"Let me help you before you tumble to the ground." Rather than offer his hand, Thorne took hold of her by the waist and swept her down to stand in front of him. He held her close for longer than necessary, the burning hunger in his eyes threatening to weaken her knees.

"My treasure," he rasped while tenderly cupping her cheek. "If I had known cats would bring you into my arms, I would have brought my mother's with me."

"I adore kitties but could never have one because of Grace's puppies." It sounded so childish to admit to such a thing. Especially at a moment like this. She ducked her head. "Sorry to be so silly and petty."

He laughed and tucked a finger under her chin, lifting her face to his. "My mother adores cats as well. You are neither silly nor petty."

"That is debatable," Serendipity called to them from the carriage. "Do stay where we can see the two of you. Please?" She turned to Fortuity. "Go with them."

"I will not." Instead, Fortuity drew her paper and pencil out of her reticule and angled herself to catch as much light as possible. "I have notes to make lest I forget. Essie will be fine."

Blessing smiled up at Thorne. "Hurry. Before they change their minds."

Chapter Twelve

"HERE, KITTY KITTY," Blessing called soft and low while quietly moving around to the side of the bushes opposite of Thorne. "We shan't hurt you. Come out so we can see you."

Thorne crouched and squinted into the shadows beneath the gently shifting branches. He needed a torch, but that would surely scare the feline…or felines. After dealing with Mother's precocious cat, Hera, who had chosen his office as the birthplace for her offspring, he had become remarkably adept at isolating, identifying, and categorizing *meows*. Not a talent he would ever boast about, but from what he had learned, it sounded as if they sought a fully grown cat and one or more kittens.

"Do you see any movement on your side?" he asked Blessing.

"I thought I did, but when I crept closer, nothing was there. I fear our hunt may be in vain."

He was tempted to join her on the far side of the dense barrier of evergreen yews, but if he did, her sisters would surely cry foul. Then a breeze ran through the branches to his left, making them waft up and down and separate enough for the moonlight to slip deeper into the shadows and illuminate a pair of golden eyes staring back at him. "Aha—there you are."

"Do you see them?"

The excitement in Blessing's voice as she rushed around to join him made Thorne smile as he got down on his hands and knees, ignoring the cool dampness of the ground. If catching this elusive cat made his precious treasure happy, his clothes could just be damned. "I see a pair of eyes watching me," he told her. "This spirit of the night is very cautious."

"People can sometimes be cruel to animals. It pays to be cautious." She crouched beside him, steadying herself by resting a hand on his shoulder. "Where did you see the eyes?"

The lovely lady's nearness made it difficult to concentrate, but he persevered for the sake of making their *official courting* bond even stronger. "Just there." He eased one of the branches higher to let the moonlight shine deeper into the shadows once again. "There. See?"

"I see her," Blessing said in a breathless whisper.

"And how do you know it is a *her*?"

"Because of the tiny meows we heard along with the big one. I may never have had a cat of my own, but I know it is the females who watch over their little ones."

"Very true, my lady." He stretched out a hand and wiggled his fingers, trying to entice the cat to come forward. "Zeus couldn't care less about his offspring."

"Zeus?"

He glanced at her and laughed. "Forgive me. Zeus is Mother's stray tom who fathered Hera's kittens."

"Here she comes." Blessing squeezed his shoulder. "No sudden moves—oh my goodness. She is carrying a kitten."

The sleek black cat, moving with the silent grace of a rippling shadow, eased out from under the branches, carrying a tiny gray and white tabby in its mouth.

"Oh no. I fear it is dead."

"No, my lady, not dead." The tears in her voice nearly made Thorne turn and gather her into his arms. "Watch when she sets it down," he whispered.

The mother cat deposited the kitten in front of him, then turned and disappeared back under the bushes. As soon as the little one was free of its mother's jaws, it came to life, crawling in a circle and mewing pitifully.

"Here she comes with another." Blessing squeezed his shoulder again.

The ginger kitten meowed in rage as soon as the mother cat placed it beside its sibling and disappeared again.

"Mother's cat had three kittens. I wonder how many this one has?" Thorne sank closer to the ground, trying to see farther under the bush with no success. It was simply too dark.

"A black one this time," Blessing whispered.

The feline mother disappeared twice more to retrieve what appeared to be the final two—a pair of solid gray tabbies almost identical to the first offspring she had laid at their feet, except these had no white spots on their coats. The cat rolled back on her haunches and twitched her tail, staring up at them as if waiting.

"Oh, how I wish I could take them home. Especially since she trusts us so." Blessing sadly shook her head. "But Gracie's hounds not only have free run of the house but also the stables, and these babies are too little to flee from them. They would never survive."

Thorne was not about to leave the cat and kittens in the park to fend for themselves. His heart, his mother, and Blessing would never forgive him for such an abandonment. He sat back on his heels, removed his greatcoat, and spread it on the ground. "Mother will take them in and act as peacemaker until Zeus and Hera learn to accept them." He carefully placed the kittens on his outspread coat while keeping an eye on the mother cat in case she changed her mind.

"She appears to be taking it well." Blessing graced him with a look that threatened to keep him on his knees in front of her. "She trusts you." She reached out and touched his cheek with a tenderness that made his heart clench. "Animals always know a person's true character."

Thorne had never been so grateful to come across a homeless cat in his life. "I hope you will always trust me as well, my treasure." He gathered up the bundle of kittens, knowing if he didn't, he would pull Blessing into a kiss, and instinct told him that now was not the time. No—now was the time to fully win her heart and mind. "Come. Let us get these felines to Mother so she might add them to her pantheon."

Blessing laughed, thrilling him with her high spirits as she hopped to her feet and stood close, holding to his arm as she peered into the bundle of kittens. "You make it sound as if she is amassing a cat army to overthrow the *ton*."

"I could think of worse things."

"I could too." She turned back to the mother cat and held out a hand. "Might I carry you to the carriage, my lady?" The feline sniffed her fingers, flicked her ears as if processing the smell, but then shied away when Blessing tried to pick her up. "Oh dear. That appears to be a solid *no* on that count. But how will she ever make it through the streets safely?"

"Perhaps we can convince her to ride in the carriage." Thorne doubted it, but the hopelessness in Blessing's voice made him ache to find a solution to make her happy once again.

"All we can do is try, I suppose." She caught her bottom lip between her teeth and kept glancing back at the mother cat as they slowly made their way to the carriage.

"Essie—we cannot take them home," Serendipity said. "You know Gracie's hounds wouldn't give them a moment's peace."

"Remember what happened to Merry's rabbit?" Fortuity said with a grimness that left no doubt about the poor rabbit's fate.

"If it ever comes up," Blessing told Thorne, "the rabbit escaped and is alive and well at our country home in the Lake District. Mr. Warren, our overseer, sees it often."

"Understood." Thorne settled the bundle of kittens on the floor inside the carriage, then turned and eyed the mother cat that was standing nearby, stretching up and balancing on her haunches to see her babies. "It would be safer if you rode with us, madame. The streets are filled with dangerous wheels and horses' hooves." To his surprise, she twitched an ear, then gracefully leapt up into the carriage, nosed open the coat to touch each of her kittens, and curled up beside them.

"Wonders never cease." He helped Blessing up into the landau, then took his place beside her. "Home, Thompson, but go slowly and with the greatest care in case our newest passenger changes her mind."

"Lord Knightwood." Serendipity leaned forward, appearing somewhat distraught. "We cannot possibly go to your home. It simply is not done."

Surely Blessing's sister did not think him that great of a cad? He eyed the woman, wishing she would calm down and not fret so much about her role as a proper chaperone. "My mother will not have retired for the evening, my lady. If it makes you feel any better, consider this as a visit for you to meet her—rather than a visit to a bachelor's home."

Serendipity folded her hands in her lap but kept passing nervous glances between Blessing and Fortuity, leaving Thorne with the distinct impression that the sisters were communicating without speaking.

Blessing rolled her eyes. "Seri! Do stop being such a ninny."

After making a frustrated moue at Blessing, Serendipity centered her aggravated scowl on Thorne. "I know nothing about being a proper chaperone, and do not wish my sisters' reputations to suffer because of it. Especially with *things* the way they currently stand."

He knew exactly which *things* she referenced. "Blessing showed me that horrid gossip rag," he told her. "Please know I would do anything to counter that abomination, and I am sure Mother will help." Guilt about the sordid thing still tormented him. His reputation as a rakehell had given whoever had written such a thing all the ammunition they needed.

"He feels responsible," Blessing told her sister. She turned to him and rested a hand on his arm. "But you should not, Thorne. People can be such fools sometimes."

"But it is my fault, my treasure. My past behavior enabled the gossips to fabricate a tale that delights those who have nothing better to do with their time. I am truly sorry." He bowed his head.

"It will give their other targets a rest from being chattered about for a while." Blessing leaned over to peer down at the cats, then turned and smiled up at him. "You treated me to a show of stars and rescued a mother cat and her kittens. There may be hope for your soul yet, my lord."

"It is not my soul that worries me," he said softly. "It is my heart." Even by the pale light of the moon and the golden glow of the street lamps, he made out the most delightful blush rushing across her cheeks. "You are the most beautiful woman I have ever known."

She ducked her head and returned to trying to convince the mother cat to allow her to stroke her head. While the feline remained close to her kittens, she leaned away from Blessing's hand each time. "She doesn't seem to mind being near us but does not wish to be touched."

"Perhaps she simply needs more time to trust us even more than she already does." Thorne appreciated the lesson the cat and her attitude offered him. Even though Blessing had warmed to him considerably, she still needed more time to fully trust him because of his past behavior with other women. That was fine by him. He would gladly spend the rest of his life proving he was a changed man, not only because of her but *for* her.

As they neared his home in Mayfair, he decided, for his mother's sake, to warn the ladies about her difficulty in hearing clearly. He didn't wish his mother pitied, but nor did he wish her embarrassed or caught off guard.

"Ladies…" He stopped himself, uncertain what to say. The three Broadmere sisters eyed him expectantly. He rolled his shoulders, then scrubbed a hand across his mouth. "I need your assistance in a very delicate matter."

Fortuity leaned forward, curious as the cat riding between their feet. Blessing tipped her head, her lovely lips barely parted as she waited for him to continue. But the ever-dubious Serendipity narrowed her eyes.

There was naught to be done but to say it. "I fear my mother's hearing has started to fail, and this malady of age wounds her pride immeasurably. Whenever you speak around her, please ensure she can see your face because she has become quite adept at reading lips. If you could do that for her, it would spare her feelings so very much."

"How terrible for her," Blessing said. "Would it help if we spoke louder?"

He hurried to shake his head. "No. Then she would know I said something to you and would be most embarrassed. It's not so much that she cannot hear but more that what she hears is garbled. She describes higher-pitched voices, such as women's voices, as somehow tangled and unclear. But if you take care to face her whenever speaking, she will follow the conversation with ease and be none the wiser that I revealed the weakness over which she has no control."

"You have our word that she will never know we know," Blessing assured him before turning to her sisters. "Agreed?"

"Agreed," Serendipity and Fortuity echoed in unison.

"Thank you, ladies. That means a great deal to me. There are some in Society who have not been so kind to her."

Filled with more optimism and hope than he had felt in a very long time, Thorne hurried to descend from the carriage as soon they rolled to a stop. He helped the ladies down, Serendipity and Fortuity first, then took his time and savored helping Blessing step down to the walkway beside him.

She glanced back into the carriage, fixing a worried look on the cat. "What about madame?"

"Surely if I carry the kittens, she will follow us as before." But when he reached for the litter nested in his greatcoat, the mother cat hissed and laid back her ears.

"It appears her opinion of you has changed." Blessing offered her hand to the cat, and the feline hissed again. "And she tolerates me even less than before."

"If I might make a suggestion, my lord," Thompson said from his perch. "Once I unhitch in the stables and leave her be, she'll more than likely move her wee ones into one of the empty stalls in the back. I'll send Donnelly to fetch her some scraps for her supper. Cook knows Lady Knightwood would want the sleek little lady fed."

"That would do nicely, except at some point, we shall need to see these lovely ladies' home," Thorne said with a glance at the Broadmere sisters.

Thompson frowned for a brief moment, then said, "I can switch the team to the barouche. Would that do, my lord?"

"Indeed, it will. Thank you, Thompson." Thorne offered his arm to Blessing, then motioned for Fortuity and Serendipity to lead the way to the door. "Now that we have the feline issue settled, come, dear ladies. I know Mother will be delighted to receive you."

Cadwick swung the front door open wide before they even reached it. Reticent as ever, he waited until all had entered, then quietly closed the door and held out his hand. "Might I relieve you of your cloaks, ladies?"

"Why yes, thank you." Blessing swept hers from her shoulders, and her sisters followed suit.

The butler gave Thorne a cursory glance, then twitched a brow. "Shall I have your greatcoat fetched from the landau, my lord?"

"Not yet, Cadwick." Thorne grinned, knowing the butler's dislike of cats. "It currently serves as a bed for five kittens, and we must wait for the mother cat to move them into a more suitable home within the stable."

The servant stared at him for a long moment but revealed no opinion or change in expression whatsoever. "Very good, my lord. Her ladyship is currently visiting with her charges in your office."

"Excellent!" Thorne turned to Blessing and her sisters. "Not only will you get to meet Mother, but it appears that Hera and her offspring are holding court as well."

"Hera had her kittens in your office?" Amused disbelief danced in Blessing's lovely eyes as she took his arm.

"She did. Pushed aside one of the bottom panels of the window seat and made herself quite at home." He couldn't resist a sheepish grin. "Once I realized she was in search of a place to bring forth her little ones, I had to add a blanket or two." He cleared his throat. "Of course, I did it for Mother's sake."

"Of course," Blessing said with a soft laugh.

"You are quite the riddle, Lord Knightwood," Fortuity said as she and Serendipity followed along behind them.

"How so?" Thorne tossed a grin back at the two ladies, thrilled with the turn the evening had taken.

"You are a renowned rake, appear to possess quite a fierce temper, from what we witnessed at Lady Burrastone's affair, and yet you rescue strays, allow cats to take over your office, and are devoted to your mother." Serendipity narrowed her eyes at him yet again, but this time, her glare seemed more impressed than filled with suspicion. She turned to Fortuity. "Is that what you were about to say, Tutie?"

"You stole the words from my tongue."

"Forgive me," Serendipity said without sounding the least bit sorry.

"And here we are." Thorne eased open his office door, a warm, happy glow filling him as he revealed his mother sitting on a low footstool in front of the window box murmuring to the furry occupants within. With his next step, he purposely landed hard on his bootheel, knowing if she didn't hear the loud thump on the hardwood floor, she would at least feel the vibration.

Already smiling when she turned his way, her face lit up with delight when she saw their guests. "My goodness, dear ladies!" she said as she sprang up from the stool. "What must you think, finding me whispering into a window seat?"

"That you are a delightful lady who adores her kitties," Blessing told her as she swept forward without waiting for Thorne's introduction. "I am Blessing Abarough, one of the Duke of Broadmere's sisters, and I have always longed for a kitten of my own but could never have one because of my sister's hounds."

"Oh, my dear, come closer." Lady Roslynn excitedly motioned her forward as if they were the only two in the room. "You must meet Hera and her darlings."

"Apparently we do not exist," Thorne told the other two Broadmere sisters. "Mother?" he said somewhat louder and in a deeper voice.

"Forgive me." His mother dipped a hurried curtsy their way. "Of course, you know that I am Lady Knightwood—but do call me Lady Roslynn. Which of the duke's sisters are the two of you? We met in passing at Lady Atterley's ball, but I fear I have forgotten all the names."

"Well, there are quite of few of us to remember," Serendipity said with a laugh before curtsying. "I am Serendipity, the eldest daughter, and this is Fortuity—she is next in line after Blessing."

Lady Roslynn waved for them both to come closer as she turned and beamed at Blessing peering down at the cats. "Come meet Hera. She adores guests and is quite proud of her little ones."

"They are so very precious," Blessing said, almost squeaking with happiness. "Oh my goodness, how do you not spend every waking moment in here watching these sweet babies?"

"Thorne indulges me, my dear, but I daresay he would draw the line at that." Lady Roslynn chortled like a happily nesting hen. "And Hera needs privacy now and then—to get her rest and offer the very best of care to her children."

Blessing looked to him with such a thrilled expression that Thorne couldn't help but laugh. "Tell Lady Roslynn of *our* evening, my lord."

"*Your* evening?" Mother arched a brow, but Thorne knew what those shadows in her eyes truly meant. She feared he had done something improper regarding Lady Blessing. The look hurt his heart, but he did not resent it. After all, his past behavior—and that of his father—had rooted those fears in his mother's mind.

"While in the park, a mother cat chose us to rescue her and her five kittens," he told her.

When his mother visibly exhaled in relief, he bowed his head, silently damning himself for putting so much doubt into the minds of the women who mattered most to him.

"I am proud of you, my son," she said ever so softly, then coughed as though struggling to clear her throat. "And where are these new guests of ours?"

"Currently bedded down in my greatcoat on the floor of the landau."

She hurried to him and stretched on tiptoe while pulling him down to kiss his cheek. Tears gleamed in her eyes. Patting his face with both hands, she gave him a happy shake of her head. "You are such a good boy."

"Mother." Even though his heart soared at her praise, he was a man in the presence of his future wife. *Future wife.* Gads, if anyone had told him he would ever love the sound of those two words in regard to himself, he would have told them they were mad.

Lady Roslynn laughed. "Oh dear. I know that tone. Forgive me for embarrassing you, dear boy." She hurried back to the opened window seat and started pointing out the kittens. "Hera and I haven't chosen names yet," she told the sisters. "We are waiting to learn everyone's personality."

"Wise decision." Blessing crouched closer and smiled down at the mother cat and her brood.

"My lord," Cadwick intoned quietly from the doorway.

Something in the butler's voice made the hairs on Thorne's nape stand on end. He turned and arched a brow at the butler so as not to alert the ladies.

Cadwick retreated a step into the hallway. A sure sign that he wished to speak in private.

Thorne followed. "What is it?"

MAEVE GREYSON

"Two gentlemen from Bow Street, my lord. I placed them in the smaller parlor."

"Did they say what they wanted?" Thorne had an inkling of what it was probably about but preferred not to be caught unaware.

Cadwick glanced up and down the hallway, then lowered his voice even more. "The investigation of Lord Myrtlebourne's death. They did not use the word *murder* but insinuated as much with their manner."

Thorne nodded. "Thank you, Cadwick. Please stay here, and if the ladies ask, tell them I shall return shortly after speaking with a messenger."

"Yes, my lord."

Thorne hurried to the smaller parlor at the front of the house, determined to deal with the Bow Street Runners and send them on their way before Blessing or her sisters were any the wiser. He strode into the room to discover both the men ambling about, examining the décor while keeping their hands shoved in their pockets. "Gentlemen?"

"Lord Knightwood." The older gentleman with a coat made of finer fabric than the other man's stepped forward. "I am Franklin Pettigrew, and this is my associate, James Rathbun. I am sure your man informed you of our business here."

"Something about a recent death?" Thorne knew better than to lie or volunteer any extra information—nor did he volunteer his cooperation. "Is this not a peculiar hour for you gentlemen to be about asking questions?"

Mr. Pettigrew nodded. "At times, we must make our inquiries in haste, my lord—no matter the hour. You are aware the Earl of Myrtlebourne died not long ago after returning from his travels?"

"I am aware of the man's passing."

"Are you also aware, my lord, of the rumors circulating that it was your liaison with the Lady Myrtlebourne that caused the earl to expire?"

"The *ton* is rife with rumor and innuendo." Thorne resettled his stance. "Do the Bow Street Runners make it a habit of considering such things as fact to solve their cases more expeditiously?"

The already ruddy-faced Mr. Rathbun gave a disgruntled huff. "We consider everything pertinent to the case, my lord. Very often, a kernel of truth hides within a lie."

"What do you require of me, gentlemen?" It was time for the runners to get to the point and leave before Blessing and her sisters realized they were there.

"We are also aware that your *association* with Lady Myrtlebourne ended several months ago—well before the earl's return to London. In fact, we have it on good authority from several reliable sources that it was you who ended the affair at that time. Would you care to comment?" Mr. Pettigrew flared his broad nostrils like an old bull trying to decide whether or not to charge.

"Your sources are indeed correct on that count." Thorne would confirm that much but no more, unless forced to step into the witness box in court. "Will there be anything else, gentlemen? As I am sure you are aware, I have guests and do not wish to keep them waiting."

Pettigrew frowned at him for a long moment before eventually nodding. "Yes, my lord. That will be all for now. Thank you for your time."

"Then I bid you good evening, gentlemen. My man will see you out."

Each of the runners gave him a curt tip of their head before allowing Cadwick to usher them to the door. Thorne stared at the parlor doorway long after the men had left. A sense of doom settled in the pit of his stomach and soured in his mouth. Why would the Bow Street Runners waste their time investigating a man found dead of a presumed heart attack? Unless there was reasonable evidence to suggest otherwise?

Thorne admitted that he had found the explanation of the earl's passing a bit hard to believe. Even though Myrtlebourne was getting on in years, the old bull had always seemed quite fit and struck Thorne as the sort of man who would delight in pummeling the daylights out of his wife's illicit lovers rather than keel over from the shock of it. Perhaps that was Myrtlebourne's brother's feeling as well.

Whatever the reason, Thorne should be safe from any accusations of murder. He hadn't returned to the Myrtlebourne residence since he had ended it with Constance—a solid three or four months before Lord Bull returned home.

Laughter echoing from his office and spilling down the hallway eased the turmoil in his heart and relaxed the tensed muscles of his shoulders. Apparently, all the ladies were getting along well. Thank heavens for that. One less worry. He shoved the gnawing uncertainty of the investigators' visit to the back of his mind and hurried to resume one of the most pleasant evenings he had enjoyed in quite a while.

Chapter Thirteen

"**I** DO NOT like the idea of us giving a ball," Blessing said to her six sisters as they idly strolled along Wigmore Street near Cavendish Square in the heart of Mayfair. Good heavens, with all of them walking together, they looked like a skirted battalion marching off to war.

"It is nearly the end of the Season," Serendipity said. "Chance knows as soon as Parliament recesses everyone will leave for the country to escape the stench of London in the heat of summer."

"It is still too soon." Blessing allowed herself a heavy sigh even though the lovely day was so warm and bright that they all sought the shade of their parasols. "Papa not even gone a year and Mama just six months before him. It just feels wrong."

"Life goes on, Essie," Serendipity gently reminded her. "Mama and Papa would not wish us to mourn them forever."

"And Chance is less than thrilled that you are the only one among us remotely considering the altar," Fortuity said, then whirled about and glared behind her. "Gracie! If you would stop treading on my heels and place a bit of space between us, our parasols would stop tangling. You are ruining their lace edging."

"You are the one who said we all had to come," Grace snapped. "I had better things to do but was informed I had no choice in the matter. Remind me again why each of us had to choose new fabrics for yet another ball gown?" She jerked her parasol shut and swung it at her side like a weapon. "The vastness of our wardrobes is already ridiculous. How can we possibly need more frippery?"

Serendipity glanced back, then abruptly turned and stamped her foot to bring the entire Broadmere herd to a halt. "Open that parasol this very minute, young lady. Do you wish to ruin your complexion? And we are getting new ball gowns because the others have already been seen in the short time since our return to Society. Chance wants us to stun everyone at our own ball."

"You recall how the butcher hangs his prize fowls in the front window to entice customers?" Blessing couldn't resist a wicked grin as she nodded at her sisters. "Chance has seven plump little geese to be rid of. He's ensuring we look our best when he hangs us in the window."

"Six little geese." Fortuity wagged a finger at her. "I know one plump little goose that will soon be fitted for her wedding gown."

A shiver ran through Blessing. An excited, tingly feeling that both thrilled and terrified her. "We are not engaged yet. Only officially courting. Remember? I need to be certain he can leave his old ways behind."

At least five of her sisters rolled their eyes, and it was quite impressive how they executed the gesture as one.

"Have you even kissed the man yet?" Grace huffed a wayward curl out of her face, then tucked it back up into her bonnet. "You should, you know. What if he is horrid at it? You need to discover if he is bearable before you allow your situation to progress."

"As a girl of naught but ten and nine," Serendipity told Grace, "you speak with a remarkable amount of certainty. Is it truly the horses and the hounds that draw you to the stables, or something else?"

"Must we have this conversation in the middle of the street?" Blessing silently lauded herself for being the voice of reason for a change rather than the antagonist. She switched her parasol to the other shoulder and took off at a determined pace. "I am in the mood for a visit to Gunter's Tea Shop. Last one to Berkley Square must treat us all to an ice of our choosing."

Fortuity fell in step beside her. The others hurried to catch up, leaving Serendipity hissing in their wake. "Sisters! It is most unseemly to be seen racing to see who gets the first treat. We are no longer children!"

"We are not racing, per se," Blessing called back to her. She flashed a smile at a trio of older ladies who obviously thought otherwise, if their shocked expressions were any indication. Humoring Serendipity, she slowed her pace. "I shall treat everyone to an ice. Come on, Seri. Don't be fractious."

"You never answered my question," Grace called out, her tone teasing. "Have you kissed the man yet?"

"Gracie!" Serendipity scolded. "Mind your voice—it carries much farther than you realize."

"I will tell you when we get to Gunter's, have our treats in hand, and find a lovely place to enjoy them on the square." Blessing flashed a wink at her younger sister, assuming the rare role of peacemaker. "Seri is right. Some things must not be shouted on the streets."

"Thank you, Essie." Serendipity glowered at her sisters, shooing them along like a mother hen herding her wayward chicks. "We do not wish another mention of our family in the tittle-tattle sheets."

Fortuity caught hold of Blessing's arm and tugged her to a full stop, making the rest of the sisters almost collide with them. "Is that not your Lord Knightwood?" She turned so her parasol shielded their faces. "To the right of Gunter's. On the bench. With a lady."

"With a lady?" Blessing barely shifted her parasol and peeked past its lacy edge. There he was, just as Fortuity had said, laughing and chatting with a young woman whose exquisite ensemble clearly labeled her as a lady of taste and breeding, a member of the aristocracy—a peer. Blessing swallowed hard, her stomach knotting so tightly it was hard to breathe. "Who is she?"

After shuffling the entirety of the Broadmere herd to a more concealed area behind an arrangement of potted trees, tables, and a waiting carriage with a team of four, Fortuity waved Serendipity forward. "Over there, Seri. Who is she?"

Serendipity squinted, then crept as close as she dared before darting back to their hiding place. "I have no idea."

"Let me go and find out," Merry volunteered, anger flashing in her eyes. "No one makes a fool of our Essie!"

"No." Sick with jealousy over how happy the pair on the bench looked, Blessing just wanted to go home and hide in her observatory but was too infuriated to do so. "We are all going to Gunter's for our treats just as we planned. I refuse to cower and pretend I have seen nothing while my sisters behave like spies for the Crown."

"Essie." Serendipity rested a hand on her arm. "We are with you on whatever you decide, but are you quite certain?"

"I am." Blessing turned, resettled her parasol on her shoulder, and strode forward as if she owned Berkley Square, keeping her gaze locked on Thorne and his lovely, dark-haired lady. She willed him to tear his gaze away from the beauty long enough to notice her, and when he did, she forced a lighthearted laugh as if she had nary a care in the world.

Thorne abruptly took to his feet, shot a nervous glance back at his companion, then resettled his stance as if preparing for battle.

And battle they would. His actions as much as shouted his guilt. Blessing set her jaw and gave him a polite nod. "Enjoying your day, Lord Knightwood?"

"Blessing—" He stopped himself, cleared his throat, and reached for her, his eyes imploring her to take his hand.

She ignored it and gripped the handle of her parasol tighter.

"Allow me to introduce you," he forced through clenched teeth. With a resigned tip of his head, he let his hand drop to his side. "Lady Blessing Abarough, this is Miss Eleanor Sykesbury. Cousin to my closest friend, Viscount Ravenglass."

Miss Sykesbury set aside her dish of molded ices and rose

with such grace that Blessing wanted to spit. "A pleasure to meet you, Lady Blessing." She smiled and offered a perfect curtsy. "Do join us." She leaned a bit to one side. "With such a resemblance among you all, you surely must be family. Sisters?"

"Yes. My sisters." Before Blessing could name them, the bell on the door of Gunter's jangled.

"Ravenglass!" Thorne called out, his voice steady but strained. "I had begun to fear that you and Mrs. Sykesbury had deserted us and escaped through Gunter's kitchens."

"Mama, come meet Lord Knightwood's acquaintances." Miss Sykesbury brought the older yet still quite beautiful woman closer. "Lady Blessing, this is my mother, Mrs. Agnus Sykesbury."

Blessing tried not to frown but couldn't help herself. Mrs. Sykesbury wore the solemn garb of deep mourning, and yet here they were, at Gunter's, enjoying sweets. And Miss Sykesbury's attire hinted at no such loss. It made no sense.

She offered the widow a curtsy and said, "A pleasure to meet you, Mrs. Sykesbury, and may I offer my condolences?"

The sad shadows filling Widow Sykesbury's kind eyes tempered the jealousy simmering in Blessing's core. "Thank you, my lady." The woman turned and started to rest a hand on Viscount Ravenglass's arm, but then stopped as though suddenly deciding it wouldn't be proper. She turned back to Blessing and bowed her head. "Pray, do not think ill of my daughter. It has been well over two years since my husband's passing, but I still cannot bring myself to dress with the colors of happiness or gaiety."

"We are in London now, cousin," the viscount told her with a gentle smile. "It is my hope that will help you move past your sorrow." He turned his attention to Blessing and offered her a proper bow. "Viscount Matthew Ravenglass at your service, my lady." He angled a sardonic brow at Thorne as though scolding him for bumbling the introductions. "My cousins here have just arrived from India and will be residing in London now—at my home. I am thankful for their company. The townhouse always seemed quite empty at times."

"How very nice." Blessing directed her response more to the viscount and the widow rather than Miss Sykesbury, then immediately felt guilty about doing so. She should not be so petty. After all, the girl had lost her father. They shared that terrible misfortune. "My brother has decided to hold a ball to celebrate our return to Society. I shall see that an invitation is sent to your home. I do hope all of you will consider joining us for an evening of festivities." She continued ignoring Thorne, still annoyed at finding him sharing quite the cozy treat with the beautiful Miss Sykesbury and then obviously feeling guilt about it when he was caught doing so.

Thorne took a step closer, his jaw set at a hard, determined angle. "Pray, forgive my ineptitude at the introductions. But I quite lose my head when in the presence of my precious Lady Blessing. She and I are officially courting." He kept his gaze locked with hers as though daring her to deny it.

"Officially courting," Miss Sykesbury repeated, then pressed her gloved fingers to her mouth as though attempting to hide a snicker. She softly cleared her throat, dropped her hand, and smiled. "How lovely." She gave Blessing a tip of her head, which came across as a bit insulting. "Congratulations on *courting*, my lady."

"Thank you," Blessing said, barely resisting the urge to growl at the chit's faintly mocking tone. She turned to her sisters and urged them toward the shop. "Since there are so many of us, perhaps you should all go ahead and order your treats. After all, we wouldn't wish to overwhelm Mr. Gunter." As they reluctantly filed past her and went inside, she handed her reticule to Serendipity. "I mean to keep my word even though my taste for an ice has left me. Do not place an order for me."

Serendipity scowled at Thorne, then gave Blessing a gracious nod. "Thank you, Essie, and I am sure the girls will thank you as well."

With a tight-lipped glare, Thorne watched the ladies disappear into the shop. "It would be my honor to take care of their treats," he informed Blessing in a wounded tone, then charged inside before she could stop him.

Ravenglass and Widow Sykesbury looked away and shifted uncomfortably, but Miss Sykesbury made no effort to hide her amusement.

I do not like her, Blessing decided with no further qualms about the woman's loss of a parent. Miss Eleanor Sykesbury warranted watching—not only because of her obvious interest in Thorne but for whatever other mischief she might decide to stir that might affect Blessing's sisters. After all, the last thing the *ton* needed right now was yet another beauty willing to snare a husband and using any method necessary to successfully leg-shackle him.

✥

"For someone who complained as loudly as Gracie about not needing a new ball gown, you look stunning in Madame Couire's latest creation for you."

Blessing fluttered her hands through the delicate layer of gossamer that gleamed with iridescent beading and silvery threads. The pristine white silk beneath the filmy material reflected the light with an even richer shimmer. It was almost as though she was lit from within. She arched a brow at Serendipity's reflection in the mirror. "Do not be waspish. It does not suit you." She turned and faced her. "You are just as stunning, if not more so, in that golden confection. You could be queen of the fae or a goddess descended from Mount Olympus."

Serendipity eyed her, her brow puckered in a worried frown. "Have you spoken to him since Gunter's? Cleared the air between you?"

"I have not."

"Then have you decided to withdraw from your *official court-ing*?"

"I have not done that either—yet." Blessing turned away, wishing her middle would cease its churning. Her insides had been a storm of emotions for the past two weeks. Why in heaven's name could she not decide what to do? Ever since she had seen Thorne laughing with the lovely Miss Sykesbury, she had lost all faith in his word—a faith that she could not possibly be without when it came to marrying. She would rather spend the rest of her life alone than marry an unfaithful man.

"Did you read any of the letters he sent?" Serendipity picked up a white fan off the dressing table. It was shot through with silver and bits of feathers. "Walters informed me you received two a day for the past fortnight."

"I burned them—and you need to cease spying on me." Blessing attempted to calm herself with a deep breath as she pulled on the white, elbow-length gloves that perfectly set off the puffiness of her short, lacy sleeves that gave the impression of bare shoulders but kept them modestly covered. "Viscount Ravenglass and the Sykesburys confirmed their attendance this evening. We shall see what comes of that if Thorne chooses to come as well."

"He and his mother confirmed," Serendipity said as she set the fan back down on the table. "He was not there alone with Miss Sykesbury, Essie." She shook her head, then stared upward as though seeking divine guidance. "I cannot believe I am defending the man, but he is quite besotted with you and determined to make a good husband. Inside Gunter's, he begged me to intercede on his behalf and swore that the entire situation was an innocent misunderstanding."

"Then why did he twitch with such nervousness and guilt as soon as he set eyes on me?" Blessing fiddled with the delicate necklace of pearls at her throat that had been one of Mama's favorites. It perfectly matched the intricate band of pearls and silver woven through her upswept curls, then wound atop them like a fragile crown. "You saw how he jumped up and kept glancing back at Miss Sykesbury. The man was as shamefaced as one of Gracie's hounds caught piddling in the parlor."

Her sister made a moue of frustration. "From all I have been able to discover, the viscount is Lord Knightwood's oldest and dearest friend. The Sykesburys are Ravenglass's desperate cousins from his mother's side who have taken refuge with him after losing everything to the late Mr. Sykesbury's relatives in India." Serendipity shrugged. "They had no money and nowhere else to go. I can only assume the viscount wished to make them feel truly welcome, so he took them on an outing, and Knightwood came along."

"Assumptions are for fools," Blessing said, then pressed a hand to her middle and willed the weak tea she'd forced down earlier to stay put. "If Thorne truly was concerned about our situation, he would have shown up here to explain himself rather than send notes."

And that was what bothered Blessing most. Thorne had not tried to smooth things over at Gunter's, nor had he followed her home to attempt to have a word in private. No. He had done nothing, simply stood there and stared at her until she and her sisters left. Then he started sending notes. So many notes over the past fortnight.

She didn't need notes. A written lie was too easily crafted and passed off as the truth because she couldn't look him in the eye and see what his heart and soul told her. So she had burned every last one of them without reading them. She swallowed hard and blinked back the tears she refused to cry. "When do we make our grand entrance that Chance insisted on?"

"As soon as the clock strikes nine, he wants us to descend the stairs—in birth order, of course." Serendipity shifted with a resigned sigh. "The proverbial geese taking their place in the butcher's window." She moved closer and adjusted Blessing's curls that were allowed to drape down from the upswept bundle and teasingly rest beside her throat. "I just want us all happy, Essie. It seems ages since we were all happy."

"We will be, Seri," Blessing promised her, even though she didn't believe it herself. She had never handled change well, and now, just as she had believed herself ready to risk her heart, she'd been rudely made aware that perhaps Thorne's past could not be so easily forgotten after all.

She swallowed hard, her throat aching with the need to weep. Time to turn her mind to something else before she dissolved into a puddle of frustrated tears and made her face all red and blotchy. "Are the other girls ready?"

Serendipity laughed. "Somewhat. Tutie is excited to observe and take notes. Gracie has her hounds settled in her room with scraps from the kitchen. Joy has ensured the tables are set and ready for cards. Felicity is excited about the menu that Cook helped her plan, and Merry is as happy as Merry always is unless someone she loves is upset—because she is concerned about you."

Blessing lifted her chin, determined to make the best of things no matter how the evening turned out. "I am fine—and will remain fine, because no matter what, I have the love of my family."

"Yes." The tension appeared to melt from Serendipity. "We always have the love of our family—even Chance, when he is not being such a *brother*."

"Indeed." Blessing grinned. She and Serendipity had long ago decided that the word *brother* should be considered an insult rather than a mere description of a male sibling.

The white clock with gold edging on the sitting room mantel chimed the nine o'clock hour.

"Lead the way, sister," Blessing told Serendipity, then sent up a silent prayer that the evening would go well, and that her poor heart could find the strength to survive it.

As BLESSING GRACEFULLY descended the curved staircase into the ballroom, Thorne lost the ability to breathe. He stood there staring, every sense focused on her. The way her hand lightly trailed along the banister. Her subtle smile—shy, yet somehow still confident. Those eyes of hers, sparkling and bright like the finest of gemstones.

She was an exquisite vision. A goddess. A priceless treasure he could not bear to lose.

Ravenglass nudged him and whispered, "Close your mouth."

Thorne snapped his mouth shut, swallowed hard, and fought the urge to rush to her and drop to his knees. She had answered none of his letters that had started out as explanations, then gradually turned into entreaties for forgiveness. He had a fair idea that they had all been tossed into the fire unopened. Mother had told him to call on Blessing in person, but he had truly felt she needed distance from him, that she needed time to calm herself and realize what she had seen was not what she feared. But in all truth, that had only been cowardice on his part, dread that she would send him away—permanently—over something that had not happened as she perceived it, because she had looked at it through the dark lens of his history. Her eyes had shouted the betrayal she felt that day, and he understood why. With his reputation, why *wouldn't* she think the worst and leap to the wrong conclusion when presented with such a scene?

Something bumped into his other side, knocking him out of his tortured musings. He looked to his left.

Mother glared up at him. "Go to her. Or do you intend to let that delightful young woman end up in the arms of a lesser man?"

The words inflamed him. "Blessing is mine." He pushed through the crowd, shoving aside any who dared stand between him and his treasure. When he reached her, he bowed, then caught her up and swept her out onto the floor without even asking her consent to the first waltz of the evening.

"I am dying without you," he whispered against her ear, not giving a damn that everyone stared at how close he held her.

"My lord—" She pushed against him, but he only tightened his arm around her and kept her close as they whirled across the floor. "You are causing a scene," she said, hissing like an infuriated kitten.

Unwilling to anger her any more than he already had, he relented and placed a more respectable distance between them. "I am dying without you," he repeated, locking his gaze with hers. Her eyes were as stormy as an untamable sea. "What you thought you saw the other day was a cruel illusion created by my reputation."

"It was not an illusion, my lord," she said coldly, shifting her glare to some vague point off in the distance. "You were quite enjoying your visit with Miss Sykesbury. I heard your laughter."

"Blessing—please." He gently squeezed her hand, willing her to *feel* how much he needed her. "I was not unfaithful to you. Nor would I ever be. I know that now."

She didn't answer, just held herself stiffly in his arms as they moved across the dance floor.

He couldn't bear her silence, nor the cruelty of her aloofness. His past would rule them no longer. He refused to allow it. Since she needed proof that he meant what he said, he would give it to her. "We are no longer *officially courting*, my love. We are engaged and will marry with the greatest of haste. Special license. Gretna Green. I care not. As long as you are my wife before this week is out."

"I cannot marry a man I do not trust." The quiver of her lips as she spoke, the unshed tears welling in her eyes, the way she trembled in his arms—everything knifed through him and twisted, rebuking him for hurting her. "I thought I could ignore your past." She clamped her mouth tightly shut and jerked with a rapid shake of her head. "I was wrong. I cannot put it out of my mind." She wrenched herself free and fled the room.

He stared after her, unable to bear the reality of what she had just told him. "I do not accept your refusal," he bellowed, triggering a wave of shocked gasps through the crowded room.

Broadmere charged toward him with a pair of footmen flanking him. "Escort Lord Knightwood out," he ordered his men.

"This way, my lord," one of them said as he hooked an arm through Thorne's. The second man grabbed his other arm in the same manner and started pulling.

"I must speak with her." Thorne yanked free, then halted as he saw his mother turn away and melt into the shadows with her head bowed. Damn everything to hell and back. He had shamed her as well.

Ravenglass rushed over, shoved one of the footmen aside, then took hold of Thorne's arm. "Lord Knightwood and I shall step outside peaceably. Such mauling is quite unnecessary."

"Let them go," Broadmere said to his men, but remained watchful.

The servants hovered close, following them out of the room and down the hall.

As soon as the front door closed behind them, Ravenglass caught hold of Thorne by the lapels of his coat and shook him. "What the devil is wrong with you, causing such a scene? Neither the duke nor the lady will allow you across that threshold ever again. Are you mad?"

"She refused to marry me." Nothing mattered other than that. Thorne raked a hand through his hair. "She said she could not marry a man she could not trust." He stared at the Broadmere front door, then tore his gaze away and fixed it on his friend. "My past." He slowly shook his head. "She cannot forget or set aside my past."

The viscount stepped back, his grim look extinguishing any remaining flicker of hope Thorne possessed. "There is naught to be done, then, but collect your mother and leave. I shall fetch her along with my cousins."

As he started for the door, Thorne stopped him. "No! I will not relinquish her. Blessing is mine."

Ravenglass slowly shook his head. "She is not yours, old friend, because you cannot erase that which you have already done. And forgive me for saying so, but perhaps the lady is right. If she cannot forget your reputation, how could the two of you ever be happy? Even I noticed how overset she became when she discovered you and my cousin outside of Gunter's." His expression soured even more. "That said, I will admit that Eleanor did not help matters. That minx would trap you in a marriage of convenience at the drop of a hat. But rest assured, her mother and I spoke to her at great length about her behavior. She may have been subtle that day, but her wicked game did not go unnoticed."

"I will not relinquish Blessing." Thorne stormed up and down the walkway in front of the townhouse. "I will find a way to convince her that we can overcome my past. I will spend every day of the rest of my life proving my faithfulness to her."

"And just how do you intend to do that?"

Thorne stared at the Broadmere house yet again, squinting up at the second-floor windows, praying that Blessing would appear in one of them. "I do not know how I will do it, but I will do it." He thumped his fist to his chest. "She possesses my heart. I belong to her. She and I belong together."

"Give me your word that you will wait here while I go back inside and fetch the ladies."

Thorne turned away and bowed his head, his heart crumbling with a pain that threatened to suffocate him. "I will not follow. To do so would only cause my precious Blessing more pain." He lifted his head and fixed a hard glare back on the house. "But this is not the end. I refuse to give her up without a fight."

Chapter Fourteen

Blessing adjusted the focus of the telescope to bring the constellation *Canes Venatici*, Latin for *hunting dogs*, into sharper detail, but it did no good. The two dogs, Asterion and Chara, remained blurry. She straightened from the eyepiece and rubbed her eyes that burned with the grit of weariness and too many tears. The problem was not the telescope. It was her.

She lowered herself to the fainting couch beside the wall of windows and stared out at the night sky that had always brought her solace—at least, until now. Now, all she saw when she looked into the darkness was the horrible mess of her life staring back at her. At times, she thought herself ridiculous and petty for taking issue with being able to trust Thorne and ignore the gossip that would surely follow them for quite a while if she married him. After all, he hadn't really *done* anything wrong. It had just *felt* wrong—and most definitely *looked* wrong. Then she remembered his laughing with Miss Sykesbury, remembered how guilty he had behaved when he realized she was there, as if he had perhaps *toyed* with the idea of dabbling with Ravenglass's cousin. Then the sickening churn of renewed jealousy and anger convinced her she deserved better. The stinging outrage and humiliation promised she would find a way to forget him and fall in love with a man she would never doubt.

A sad, huffing laugh escaped her. Papa would tell her she was caught in *analysis paralysis*—too much thinking and not enough forging ahead and taking action. How she wished Papa and Mama were here to tell her what to do. Because if she chose poorly, it would tarnish the rest of her life.

The faintest lightening across the horizon, a glowing blush of pinks and yellows kissing the rooftops, made her realize that dawn was upon her, and she had spent yet another night wrestling with her demons of heartache and indecision. She reclined on her side on the fainting couch, propping her head on her arms so she could watch her precious stars fade into the brilliance of morning's light.

Serendipity and Fortuity would come in search of her soon, when they awakened and discovered her bed empty. They would beat on the door until she unlocked it and showed them she was still alive and well. That was...not exactly well, but she was alive and truly befuddled.

The knock on the door came earlier than she expected, and it wasn't a pounding, but a reserved tap. She pushed herself up to a sitting position and frowned at the door. Why on earth would Walters disturb her at such a peculiar hour? Another rap on the door was followed by a hesitant "My lady?"

Poor man. At his age, he should still be abed, should have been pensioned off years ago but refused to accept it. "I'm coming, Walters," she wearily called out as she crossed the room. He had probably brought her a tea tray. Serendipity and Mrs. Flackney, the housekeeper, had been trying to feed her at every opportunity since the upsetting encounter at Gunter's, and then the embarrassment of the ball.

She unlocked the door and swung it open wide but was surprised to find Walters standing there with nothing but the small letter salver in his hand. At this hour? "Dear Walters—you should have saved yourself the worry and simply tossed it into the fire like I did all the others."

The butler stood there blinking at her like a great sleepy owl. "It is not from Lord Knightwood, my lady." He lifted the tray higher and waggled a bushy gray brow at the seal. "A messenger brought it before first light."

"That's rather curious, don't you think?" Blessing took the note and studied the flowery script, not recognizing the hand.

"Indeed, my lady." He tucked the small silver dish against his side. "Shall I bring you a tray? Tea or chocolate, perhaps, and one of Cook's scones fresh from the oven?"

The concern in the old man's eyes touched her. Walters rarely exhibited any emotions. "Thank you, Walters, but no. Do not trouble yourself. I'll come to the dining room and eat from the buffet along with the others. That will be all for now."

"Very good, my lady." He gave her a weary bow and shuffled away, his bent form a sad reminder that he would not be with them forever.

She closed the door but didn't lock it, then meandered back to the fainting couch, studying the sealed letter all the while. Something about the thing filled her with a sense of leeriness, as if a rabid animal hid inside the folded paper, waiting to lunge out and clamp its jaws around her throat as soon as she opened it.

She forced a weary laugh. What a ridiculous vision.

"I must try to get some sleep," she told the room at large. "I am becoming sillier by the day." As she lowered herself to the couch, she broke the seal and unfolded the expensively heavy paper someone had used for the one-page missive.

Lord Knightwood is under investigation for assisting in the murder of the Earl of Myrtlebourne. As the illicit lover of Lady Myrtlebourne, it is believed he aided her in disposing of the earl because she carries Knightwood's child. It would be in your family's best interest to stay as far away from Lord Knightwood as possible.

Regards,
The Rt. Hon. Agnew Montagne
Earl of Myrtlebourne

"Carries his child," Blessing repeated in a horrified whisper. That part bothered her more than Thorne being under investigation for the murder of the earl. She stared down at the letter, reading it a second, then a third time as her mind raced to recall everything she had heard about Myrtlebourne.

The earl had been found expired in his dressing room by his valet. The rumor mill blamed a failure of the man's heart when he flew into a rage after finding out about his wife's affair. Perhaps she had told him about the unborn child? But how in the world could that be deemed murder? If the earl had a weak heart, it would have eventually taken his life regardless of his wife's escapades. Or had they decided it was some sort of poison? Why would they decide such a thing now, rather than at the time the man died?

She frowned, clenching her teeth until her jaws ached. Something about this did not make sense. If the note had mentioned a court case regarding adultery, she would have believed that easily. But this? Murder? And Thorne might be many things, but he was not a coward who would do such a thing so quietly. The man reacted with passion and temper. Heavens to mercy, she easily recalled two instances where he had caused public scenes— once at Lady Burrastone's party when he had challenged Montagne to a duel, and then just days ago at their very own ball when he had refused to accept her rejection. The memory of it still thrilled and saddened her.

No. If Thorne ever resorted to murdering someone, it would not be something as sneaky as poisoning a man and leaving him to die in his dressing gown. Subtlety was not a trait Lord Knightwood had mastered.

Snatching up the letter, she charged from the room. She needed more information. Information that Serendipity would either possess or know how to obtain. By the time she reached their rooms upstairs, she was nearly out of breath but kept running. She raced through the sitting room and burst into the bedroom. "Seri! Wake up!"

All she could see of her sister was the top of her head. Serendipity burrowed like a hedgehog when she slept. The mound of bedcovers barely shifted, and a muffled groan rose from their depths. "Go away, Essie."

Blessing rounded the bed, lit the lamp on the bedside table, then gave her sister a hard shake. "I need you to read this note and tell me what you know about Lord Myrtlebourne and his wife." She gave her another shake. "Seri, please! This note came just this morning. Right at dawn. Supposedly from Myrtlebourne's brother."

Serendipity rolled to her back and groaned again while scrubbing her face with both hands. "What? What did you say about the Myrtlebournes?"

"Read this." Blessing shoved the letter into her sister's hands, then brought the lamp closer. "They think the earl was murdered, and they suspect Thorne and the earl's wife."

"Murdered?" Serendipity forced herself up to a sitting position against the headboard, then gave a great yawn followed by a sleepy scowl. "The man's valet found him collapsed in his dressing room. A physician was called, and last I heard, they said his temper killed him. Made his heart blow out his ears or something." She yawned again, then brought the paper closer to her face and squinted down at it. Both her brows rose, and she stared at Blessing. "Carries his child?" she whispered.

"I know." Blessing pulled in a deep breath and struggled to compose herself. "But was it not you who told me that Thorne had not *been* with Lady Myrtlebourne for quite some time before her husband returned? Several months, even?"

"I overheard Lord Ravenglass say that very thing in defense of Lord Knightwood at Lady Atterley's ball—and that was well over a month ago."

"Did the lady not appear quite thin just three weeks ago? Remember, we saw her entering her home when we were headed to the modiste to see about our ball gowns?" Blessing watched Serendipity closely, silently urging her to wake up enough to sort through the facts and come up with the same theory she had.

Serendipity frowned as she let the hand holding the letter drop into her lap. "If she is with child, she cannot be very far into her confinement at all. She is thinner than we are." Her frown deepened. "And if that is the case, Thorne would not be the father—unless he went to her for comfort after losing you. But that would have been after the earl had already died." She flinched. "Sorry."

There was that. Blessing couldn't deny it, but for now, she chose to ignore it. Instead, she tapped on the letter. "But the way this reads, she was supposedly with child *when* the earl died."

Serendipity shook her head. "Why do they suddenly think it is murder? What changed?"

Blessing shrugged. "Either they discovered a clue that made them change their minds or Montagne paid someone to fabricate evidence pointing to murder."

Appearing fully alert now, Serendipity fixed Blessing with a suspicious scowl. "Why would Montagne send this to you? Why tell you when all the *ton* knows you rejected Thorne, and Chance had him thrown out and told never to return? It makes no sense for this information to come to *you* in particular." She fluttered the letter. "I do not believe Lord Montagne sent this. And look how he signed it. Very peculiar."

"Who else would send it?" Blessing hadn't considered that angle, but now that she thought about it, it was indeed strange.

"Someone who fears a reconciliation between you and Lord Knightwood." Serendipity stared at her with such a solemn look it struck Blessing square in the conscience. "Is there to be a reconciliation after all? Have you reached an accord with your fears and inability to forget his past?"

"I do not know." Blessing looked away.

"How long will you not know, Essie?" Serendipity softly asked. "Do you mean to suspend living your life indefinitely?" She reached out and rested her hand on top of Blessing's. "Remember what Papa always said?"

"There is no greater waste of a life than one that is lived in the throes of analysis paralysis. Make a decision. Even if it is wrong, at least you made a choice and gave it your best. Mistakes are the best opportunity for learning." Blessing stared down at their joined hands. "I wish Papa was here to help me decide."

"You know better than that. Papa would never decide for you." Serendipity laughed. "He and Mama would turn red-faced with the strain, but they would leave the choice up to you and pray you chose what they secretly wanted you to choose."

"I hope I am someday as wise a parent as they were." Blessing picked up the letter and read it with fresh eyes. "The only possible authors I can think of are Lady Myrtlebourne herself, Miss Eleanor Sykesbury, and Thorne."

Serendipity nodded. "Interesting deduction. The women want him, and he wants you."

"And Montagne wants his brother avenged. Does he have enough blunt to purchase a murder conviction for Thorne?"

"Who's to say?" Serendipity threw back the covers, climbed out of bed, and stretched. "And maybe the man *was* murdered. Perhaps the valet found something while the physician was there, and they kept it quiet until Montagne decided what he wished to do." She let her arms drop, went to the window, and pulled back the draperies. "Lady Myrtlebourne hated her husband. According to the gossips, the man was a monster and deserved every ounce of her scorn." She turned and faced Blessing. "But the question is, what are you going to do about it, dear sister?"

"Do about it?"

Serendipity nodded at the letter. "Whoever decided to involve you in this, if they were wise, would have ensured there was some truth in the information they gave you. Chance could ask Mr. Sutherland to make a few discreet inquiries to either confirm or debunk the investigation."

"Would the Bow Street Runners tell our solicitor about something that had nothing to do with our family?"

"They will tell Mr. Sutherland." Serendipity grinned. "Remember how he and Papa used to argue until late into the night?

The man is tenacious."

"True—but that still leaves the question of Lady Myrtle-bourne's condition." *And what, if anything, I should do about this information at all,* Blessing silently added.

"Leave that to me to discover," Serendipity said with a mysterious air. "But as I said before, what do you intend to do?"

"There is nothing I *can* do."

"Liar." Serendipity arched a brow. "As Mama would say, *state your choices aloud, young lady.*"

Blessing rolled her eyes, wishing Fortuity would chime in and side with her rather than pretend to still be asleep with her head under the covers. "What do you think, Tutie?"

A very unconvincing snore rose from Fortuity's bed.

"Tutie!" Blessing ripped the covers off her sister. "Eavesdropping is very rude."

"It is not eavesdropping if you are standing beside my bed shouting!" Fortuity scooted back against the headboard, hugged her knees, and tucked her night rail around her feet. "I know what your choices are—but do you?"

They were determined to make her say them first, just like Mama would have done. Blessing counted off on her fingers: "Confront Thorne about the note and either help him in any way I can or damn him."

Serendipity stamped her foot. "Essie! Language!"

"Sorry," Blessing lied, then took hold of her next finger. "Speak with Viscount Ravenglass to gauge his reaction and see whether or not he suspects his lovely cousin is playing foul, and if she is, spit in her eye."

Serendipity groaned and dropped her head into her hands.

"And lastly"—Blessing gripped her third finger—"ignore it and refuse to dance on a string for whoever believes I am their puppet."

"Why am I thinking that will be the one you choose?" Fortuity asked.

"Because you know me well, dear sister." Blessing slowly

refolded the letter. "I am not prepared to speak with Thorne. Not yet."

"Analysis paralysis," Fortuity droned under her breath.

"Oh, hush!" Blessing was beginning to question the wisdom of sharing this information with her sisters. "What would the two of you do?"

"Discover who is behind the note, what their motive is, then deal with them accordingly," Serendipity said.

"You make it sound so simple when, in reality, it is not, and you know it." Blessing tossed the note into Fortuity's out-stretched hands, hoping her younger sister might provide some insight that neither she nor Serendipity had thought of.

"You know I love you and would never wish you hurt," Fortuity said while staring down at the letter.

"But?"

Fortuity looked up. "You really did overreact about seeing him with Miss Sykesbury at Gunter's."

"I know he did nothing wrong, but—" Blessing cut herself off, at a loss as to how to explain her inability to get past the immediate suspicion that sprang to mind when she saw him with another woman. Did she truly wish to spend the rest of her life jumping to those conclusions and then trying to talk herself out of them?

"Do you want him hanged for a murder he didn't commit?" Serendipity's tone was as cold and heartless as the question.

"As opposed to hanging for a murder he *did* commit?" Blessing asked, trying to make light of the subject and failing.

Serendipity and Fortuity glared at her, clearly unimpressed with her humor.

Blessing pinched the bridge of her nose and rubbed the inner corners of her eyes, remembering how weary she truly was before letting her hand drop away. "Fine. I shall call on Lord Ravenglass and go from there. That is all I am willing to do at this time. All right?"

Both sisters nodded, then Serendipity folded back the covers on Blessing's bed. "However, I do feel you should get some sleep before calling on anyone. Those shadows under your eyes are not becoming at all."

Blessing plopped onto the foot of her bed and started unlacing her boots. "Both of you are coming with me. Just so you know."

"Of course we are," Fortuity said as she burrowed back under the covers and hugged her pillow under her head. "We wouldn't miss it for the world."

WHILE THEY WAITED for Lord Ravenglass, Blessing took in the modest yet comfortable parlor she never would have envisioned belonging to a man rumored to travel more than he stayed in London. The room was done in feminine shades of delicate rose and soft blue, but rather than the usual clutter of porcelain vases, miniature statues, and various other dust-collecting baubles, books were piled everywhere—even on the floor. Stacks of them adorned the tables and the mantelpiece. The built-in shelves on either side of the fireplace groaned with the largest collection of tomes she had ever seen stored outside of a library or office. She glanced at Fortuity and struggled not to smile. Her dear sister was in literary heaven, her head slightly tilted to one side as she scanned the titles gracing the shelves.

When the viscount entered the room, his harried look gave Blessing the distinct impression that they were the last people he had either wanted or expected to receive today.

"Good day, ladies." He bowed first to Serendipity, then Fortuity, then Blessing. "Forgive me for making you wait, but it has been a rather eventful day."

Blessing eyed the man, wondering if the *eventfulness* of his day had anything to do with Thorne and the matter she was about to bring to his attention. At his rather uncomfortable gesture toward their chairs, she and her sisters reseated themselves, and she decided to get directly to the point. "It is I who must beg your forgiveness, my lord, for I fear our visit will not improve or calm your day."

"I see." He shifted in his seat as though bracing himself for the worst. "How so, may I ask?"

"It is my understanding that you are Lord Knightwood's oldest and dearest friend."

He slowly nodded, leaving her with the unmistakable feeling that he was reluctant to admit the association to her, considering the state of her relationship with the rogue baron.

Rather than attempt to explain, she drew the letter in question out of her reticule and handed it to him. "This arrived for me yesterday morning—before dawn, in fact."

The viscount's expression hardened as he slowly unfolded it and read its contents. With a resigned sigh, he lifted his gaze to hers. "And how may I help with this, my lady?"

"Reveal the truth, expose the lies, and identify the true author."

With slow deliberation, he refolded the letter and gave it back to her, but didn't speak until after she had stuffed it back inside her reticule and cinched the drawstrings shut.

"Well?" She arched a brow and waited impatiently for some sort of answer.

"There was an investigation into the earl's death, but the Bow Street Runners reported a lack of evidence regarding Lord Knightwood's part in the poisoning of Lord Myrtlebourne." He shifted with a heavy sigh. "They did, however, find sufficient evidence against persons in the Myrtlebourne household to confirm their suspicions. It is my understanding that portion of their investigation is ongoing."

A sense of relief filled Blessing. "So, Lord Knightwood has been cleared of any wrongdoing and has no charges to worry about?"

"He was cleared of the murder," Ravenglass said in a tone that worried her. "However, he is still at risk. The earl's brother,

Lord Montagne—whom I believe you met earlier in the Season—has decided not to pursue an adultery suit against Knightwood, since Lady Myrtlebourne will more than likely be charged with her husband's murder. I will not be so coarse as to mention what that means for her."

"Then how is Lord Knightwood still at risk?"

"Montagne decided to accept Knightwood's challenge from Lady Burrastone's party after all, and the two intend to meet at dawn tomorrow. A duel, my lady. I am sure you understand the dangers of such an action."

A panic so strong she wanted to scream shot through her. She fisted her hands so tightly that her nails nearly cut through her gloves and dug into her palms. "He must not. You must stop him."

"As his second, I have tried, my lady. I also attempted to reason with Montagne's man and with Montagne himself. I succeeded in averting this disaster the first time it reared its monstrous head, but I fear I failed this time." The viscount suddenly looked much wearier than when he first entered the room. "Knightwood and Montagne are well matched in their stubbornness. They are indeed a pair of fools intent on not only killing each other but ensuring they die in the process."

"Why in heaven's name would Lord Knightwood wish to die?" Blessing pushed up from the chair, too distraught to sit. "He adores his dear mother. How could he consider abandoning her and cursing her with the fate of outliving her child?"

Ravenglass slowly rose from his seat and fixed her with an almost accusatory glare. "A man cannot live for the sake of his mother. He has made arrangements so she will want for nothing after he is gone, but do not doubt me when I tell you—he plans to die."

"You are blaming me." She wanted to fall to her knees and weep, but held her head high, determined to see this visit through and remedy this deadly route that her life and the lives of those interwoven with hers had foolishly taken. "His choices are his own. Not mine." As soon as the words left her mouth, she wished she could snatch them back because of their heartlessness.

"I agree his choices are his own, but you asked for the truth, my lady." Ravenglass jutted his chin at her. "I do not believe Knightwood ever experienced love before he met you. He is unfamiliar with the power of the feeling and is unable to manage it when that love is not accepted or returned."

She covered her face with both hands, unable to bear the harshness of the viscount's judgment. Because judgment it was—he had as much as damned her for Thorne's impending death. "I do not want him to die," she whispered. "I could not bear it."

"I cannot stop them," Ravenglass said, his words dripping with despair. "I have tried, my lady. I swear to you, I have tried."

Blessing sagged to the floor, her staunch fortitude no longer able to force her legs to support her in this misery. She hugged herself, rocking while beseeching her sisters for help. "He cannot die, Seri. Tutie, you are a writer. How can we save him from this foolish waste of his life?"

Serendipity and Fortuity rushed over, crouched beside Blessing, and held her tight.

"Where is this duel taking place?" Serendipity scowled up at Ravenglass. "And you said at dawn tomorrow? Is that correct?"

"A field north of Camden," the viscount said. "And yes. At dawn."

"We must go there, Essie," Fortuity said, giving Blessing a gentle shake. "Only you can stop him. You can do this, Essie. You are the strongest of us all."

Hope and determination sparked within Blessing, then burst into a raging inferno of sheer single-mindedness to set things right once and for all. "I will stop him," she said. "If I have to stand in front of him and shield him with my body, I will stop him from this foolishness so that he can live long enough for me to box his ears." Hot, angry tears streamed down her face, strengthening her resolve. "Stupid, stupid man. How dare he put me through this worry! How dare he do this to his mother as well!"

Ravenglass smiled for the first time since he had entered the room. "You are the only one who can save him, my lady. He says he is nothing without his treasure, and that treasure is you. I will help you in any way I can, and with any luck, we can convince Montagne that more deaths will not bring his brother back, nor erase the poor choices made while the earl lived."

With the help of her sisters, Blessing forced herself up from the floor. "Montagne will listen to reason or I will shoot him myself. In the knees, so he has to lie there and listen to what I have to say."

Chapter Fifteen

T HE SOFT GRAY morning mist floated across the meadow and
puddled at the base of the hill like a down blanket meant to
protect the wildflowers as they slept. The entire world was absent
of color, caught in that time between night and day where the
dark reluctantly let go and the light just as reluctantly crept from
its bed to illuminate creation. And it was raining. Not a hard
shower that would wash away the fog but an airy drizzling that
merely fed it and made it all the more cloying.

Thorne sat in the carriage at the crest of the hill and pulled in
a deep breath of the damp dreariness. Quite fitting, actually. It
was a good morning to die, to be shot down by his past choices
that had already killed whatever hope he had for his future. His
main regret—for he had many—was not knowing the joy of
seeing his precious Blessing one last time. But that would be
selfish, and selfishness was what had brought him to this
damnation he so rightly deserved.

"Montagne has been rumored to cheat," Ravenglass said,
breaking the dismal silence of the carriage.

"I would expect no less of the brother of Myrtlebourne."
Thorne squinted down at the long stretch of empty road winding
below them, the only route to the hilltop. Where was the devil,
anyway? "The grayness of the morning is growing lighter. I
would have thought he would be here by now to prepare."

"As did I." Ravenglass twisted and peered out the window.

"The physician is here, but still no sign of Montagne. Perhaps he has reconsidered and will send his second to inform us he realizes he spoke rashly, and formally apologizes to Lady Blessing for speaking so coarsely in front of her at Lady Burrastone's party."

"Surely not. The man would be deemed a coward if he backed out now."

"Not if we accepted his decision with grace and discretion." Ravenglass scowled at him. "Are you so determined to die?"

"At least I will die defending my lady love's honor. 'Tis a far cry from the way I lived."

Ravenglass snorted.

"What?" Thorne tore his gaze from the road below and glared at his friend.

"I never would have believed you capable of such nauseating depths of self-pity. You think yourself the only man in creation to be rejected by the woman he loves?" Ravenglass snorted again, louder this time. "You have become a pathetic shadow of the man I once called friend."

"Insulting me will not make me change my mind." Off in the distance, muffled by the weather, the faint crunch of carriage wheels and the steady thudding of hooves drew Thorne's attention back down to the roadway. After what felt like forever, a black brougham pulled by a pair of bays seemed to solidify out of the mist. "I believe Lord Montagne will soon be here," Thorne said, then rose and pushed open the carriage door. "Shall we?"

Without waiting for Ravenglass's response, he stepped down, then wondered at the fog still swirling in the wake of Montagne's carriage. Another pair of horses burst into view, pulling a middle-sized phaeton. He squinted harder at the driver, disbelief making his jaw drop.

Almost standing and leaning forward with racing intent, Blessing flipped the reins to urge her team to move faster and pass Montagne's rig in their climb up the hill.

An overwhelming surge of alarm and fear crackled through Thorne like lightning. "Gads! She's going to kill herself." He charged toward them, waving his arms to slow her. He bellowed, "Blessing, you must stop at once!"

Her two sisters, Serendipity and Fortuity, were seated behind her, holding on to the sides of the phaeton as it rocked from side to side. They squinted into the wind, shouting, "Faster, Essie! Faster!"

"Stop at once!" he roared as they careened into the lead and tore up the hillside.

"*You* will stop at once!" Blessing shouted at him as she pulled back on the reins and brought the team to a halt. Hair wild and tumbling down her back, cheeks red, and breathing hard, she gathered up her skirts in a most unladylike fashion and leapt down from the rig. She stabbed the air with her finger as she marched toward him, pointing at his carriage. "Get back in there and sit yourself down. There will be no dueling this day. I forbid it!"

"I am not a child, and you have no right to forbid me anything! Remember? You rejected me." Fighting the urge to yank her into his arms and kiss her until she realized she belonged with no one other than him, he strode toward her and pointed at her vehicle. "Go home, Blessing. This is no place for a lady."

"This *is* my place, you stubborn fool." She closed the distance between them and thumped him in the chest. "You will not do this. What about your mother?" She thumped him again, harder this time. "You cannot risk your life and toss it aside like a worn pair of shoes ready to be discarded. What about your friends? What about those who love you?"

The emotions storming in the blue of her eyes gave him pause and the merest sliver of hope. "Who loves me, Blessing? There is only one whose love I cannot live without. Only one whose love would make my life worth living."

She narrowed her eyes at him, threatening him with that look of hers that only made him love her all the more. "I am quite sure you are loved by many," she said. "Family. Dearest friends. I have no doubt you even have some servants who are quite fond of you."

"There is only one whose love I need like the air that I breathe." He stepped closer, clenching his fists to keep from taking hold of her and pulling her against him. "Only one." He adored the way her petite nostrils flared when she snorted, like the loveliest little disgruntled calf that thought itself grown into a bull.

"You are going to make me say it. Aren't you?" She glared at him harder.

"I am, my lady."

"Fine," she spat like she were ridding herself of a bad bite of food. "I love you, you fool. Are you happy now?"

"Somewhat."

"Somewhat?" she squeaked. "What the bloody hell is wrong with you?"

"Essie!" Serendipity scolded from the carriage.

Blessing turned and shook her fist at her. "Not now, Seri." She turned back to him, her eyes flashing. "I repeat, sir. What the bloody hell is wrong with you? I told you I loved you. What more do you want?"

"There is the matter of your becoming my wife—preferably as quickly as possible. Either as soon as I can obtain a special license, or we can reach Gretna Green." He would not consider anything less, because as much as he wanted to believe her, what if she was purely driven by the intent to stop the duel and, once that was achieved, would refuse him yet again? Women could be sly, wicked beasties when they set their minds to something.

"Are we dueling or not?" Montagne called out from where he and his second stood beside his carriage.

Blessing jabbed a finger at him. "Silence, you! I will deal with you in a moment, and if you move, one of my sisters will shoot you."

Thorne jerked his attention back to Serendipity and Fortuity and was shocked to discover each lady holding a rifle steadied on the back of the driver's seat, aimed at Montagne.

"Papa taught us all how to shoot quite well," Serendipity said as she resettled her cheek against her firearm. "Fortuity here is the best of the six of us, but I have been known to bring down a pheasant or two."

"This is quite irregular," the physician said from where he stood beside Ravenglass.

Ravenglass grinned like a fool, his shoulders trembling with silent laughter.

Montagne, his mouth ajar, shifted his weight from one foot to the other, then turned to his second, who shrugged and backed up a step to keep himself out of the line of fire.

"It appears the Broadmere family is overflowing with untold talents," Thorne said to Blessing. "But that still leaves the matter of our marriage, my treasure. Will it be Gretna Green, or special license so we might marry here with our families and friends?"

"I did not say I would marry you," she said, her pert chin jutting higher. "I said I loved you and did not want you to throw your life away in some ridiculous, and illegal, way."

His heart fell, and he blew out a heavy sigh. "Then the duel is on, my lady. To not only defend your honor but to also put me out of my misery." He took her hand, kissed it, then stared down at it. "I think I fell in love with you that first night we met, when you were spatting with your sister about having to put yourself on display for the Marriage Mart." He rubbed his thumb across the silk of her fingers, a sad smile coming to him as he realized it was more than a little scandalous for her to be out without her gloves. "I have never felt this way about anyone, Blessing. Not ever. And it both thrills and terrifies me." He lifted his gaze to hers, finding her eyes wide and gleaming with unshed tears. "How does one live a life with such powerful feelings?" he whispered. "Especially when those powerful feelings end in a hopelessness that aches and burns as though my heart has been rent from my chest." He swallowed hard and tugged her to him. "My past is just that—the past. I cannot change it, but I can swear that I will never repeat it. Please, Blessing—please give me a chance."

"Essie," she whispered, leaning in to rest a hand on his chest.

"What?"

"Since we are to be married, you may call me Essie."

Before she could change her mind and take it all back, he took her mouth with his and crushed her against him, pouring every ounce of relief, joy, and yearning that he felt into her. She tasted of hope and happiness and kissed him back with just as much hunger.

When he touched her cheek, he discovered it wet with tears. He pulled back with dread clenching his chest. "Why do you weep, my treasure? Pray, tell me it is from happiness."

"It is," she said with a shy smile, but then caught her bottom lip between her teeth. "And perhaps a little fear. I swore I would never marry."

"So did I, and yet here we are."

"And yet here we are," Montagne repeated in a rude, sing-song voice. "I assumed we would duel with pistols, not witness the nauseating spectacle of you begging the woman to accept you."

"May I shoot him now, Essie?" Fortuity asked. "Not to kill him, mind you. Just to give him something else to think about."

"You wouldn't dare!" Montagne growled.

Serendipity rose to her feet and aimed. "If she wouldn't, I would."

"You will leave from here and forget this ridiculous duel," Blessing told him. "Or I shall file a report with the Bow Street Runners that you colluded with your sister-in-law to kill your brother so you could have not only her but the title as well."

"That is ridiculous," Montagne said. "I am the one who urged them to investigate my brother's murder and pointed them to my brother's wife."

"What better way to make yourself look innocent?" Blessing winked at Thorne, then turned to her sisters. "Tell him what you found out, Seri."

"Several of your brother's servants are now in our employ," Serendipity said while keeping the rifle aimed at the man and ready to fire. "And they are willing to sign affidavits regarding your regular *visits* to Lady Myrtlebourne that made the term *looking after your brother's wife* take on an extremely immoral meaning."

Even though Montagne huffed and rolled his eyes as if he couldn't care less, his face flashed to a deeper red and sweat peppered his forehead. "I daresay the Bow Street Runners will be more likely to accept my word over that of a few servants. After all, the title is mine now."

The longer Thorne studied the man, the more certain he was that the greedy cove had rid himself of his brother to get the title. Montagne had also probably decided that Constance could not be trusted, and the attending physician could not be silenced, so he had artfully accused her of the murder.

Montagne sneered at the rifle-bearing sisters. "An earl always trumps a commoner."

Serendipity gave Montagne a condescending smile. "Beg your pardon, my lord, but our solicitor, Mr. Sutherland, has also obtained signed statements from two ladies—not commoners—who shall remain anonymous until their statements are needed, but I believe you know them. In the biblical sense, in fact—as in the story of Sodom and Gomorrah. You and Lady Myrtlebourne often invited them to join you in your...uhm...*visits*, shall we say?"

"They would not dare," Montagne sputtered.

"They already have dared, my lord," Serendipity replied. "After all, they do not wish to be considered accessories in the murder."

Thorne lifted both his brows at Blessing. "How does she discover these things?" he whispered.

Blessing shrugged. "I have often wondered the same, but she refuses to reveal her sources."

Montagne glared at Serendipity, then shifted his scowl to

Blessing. "What do you intend to do?"

"I have yet to decide." Blessing tipped her head to one side, eyeing him thoughtfully. "All I know for certain is that you will cease any and all hostilities against Lord Knightwood. After all, our solicitor has this information. So if anything happens to him or ourselves, you will be the prime suspect."

"You intend to hold this over my head—blackmail me with this information?"

Blessing nodded. "Exactly. For as long as necessary." Her smile turned wicked, sending a surge of pure, unadulterated lust burning through Thorne. "You might consider leaving London, Lord Montagne. Permanently. Settle yourself on the Continent and start over. Small price to pay for murdering your brother. Wouldn't you say?"

Sweat streamed down the sides of Montagne's face. He fisted his hands, bared his teeth, and trembled as though stricken with the beginnings of apoplexy. "Leave London?"

"Did I not speak clearly?" Blessing asked Thorne with a feigned expression of befuddlement.

"Quite clearly, my love." He kissed her hand and kept her tucked against his side, reveling in her closeness. "Leave London, Montagne, and never return, or go to the gallows with Constance. Your choice. I feel certain the Broadmere solicitor will be happy to keep the evidence safe and locked away should you ever attempt to return—and surely you cannot expect Constance to go to her death quietly."

"She has already leveled accusations against me," Montagne said, looking defeated and miserable. "Repeatedly and in writing. It has taken a great deal of blunt to have those accusations ignored."

"Apparently not enough blunt," Serendipity told him. "Our Mr. Sutherland obtained a copy of her confession and her accusations. He will safeguard those for us as well."

"Well, isn't that just bloody wonderful?" Montagne sent a malicious sneer Thorne's way. "You win, you rutting bastard. I shall be gone from London by nightfall."

Thorne accepted the coarse announcement with a curt nod. "I would wish you Godspeed, but, somehow, that seems inappropriate."

"To the devil with you." Montagne launched himself up into his carriage. His second joined him, then the door slammed shut, and a hard thump from inside signaled the driver to take them away.

"Now I wonder if we should not have turned him over to the authorities." Her expression one of concern, Blessing squeezed Thorne's arm. "Should we have? Was it wrong to let him go?"

"If we knew for certain he would hang, there would be no question about giving him over to the gallows." Thorne hated discussing such unpleasantness with her. She should not have to worry about such things. "But many a peer has escaped justice with the aid of contacts and a fat purse, and then he would be our problem all over again, and with all our ammunition spent." He smoothed the furrow of worry creasing her brow. "You and your sisters made the wisest choice in this game of risk, I think."

Ravenglass approached them, grinning like a fool. He bowed to Blessing, then clapped Thorne on the back. "Let me be the first to congratulate you, old friend, and also the first to remind you that if you do not keep this wonderful lady happy, I shall make you regret it more than you have ever regretted anything in your life."

Thorne gazed into Blessing's eyes, his chest about to burst with everything he felt for her. "Fear not—this lady's happiness shall be my utmost priority from this day forward."

Leaning into him, she laughed—a joyous, effervescent sound of which he would never tire. "You may regret saying that, my lord. I can sometimes be quite fractious."

"Indeed, she can," Serendipity and Fortuity said in unison as they alit from the phaeton and hurried over to join everyone.

"So, what shall it be, my darling?" he asked Blessing after kissing her hand again. "Gretna Green or special license?"

"Gretna Green is an average of four days from London," she said with a smugness that made her smile quite teasing.

"Special license it is, then, my treasure." He cupped her face between his hands and sealed the promise with a heated kiss that had Serendipity clearing her throat more than once, and Fortuity telling her sister to hush it. He smiled against Blessing's mouth as she pressed tighter to him with even more ardor and made him wish everyone would go away so he could lower her onto the soft, grassy hillside and consummate their union in advance.

With a great deal of reluctance, he broke their bond and lifted his head. "I shall have the special license before the day is out. We shall marry tomorrow—agreed?"

She smiled up at him and touched his cheek with such tenderness that he wanted to roar to the world that this incomparable woman was his. "Tomorrow," she said softly, "In my observatory."

"The perfect place. Your stars and my moon can bless our union, because as you taught me, just because it is daytime, it does not mean they are not there."

"You remembered." She rewarded him with another of her teasing smiles, then saddened him by stepping away. He missed her warmth immediately.

"I should go," she said. "There is much to be done if I am to become a married woman tomorrow."

"Indeed," Serendipity echoed while holding up her fingers to count off the tasks. "Cook must be alerted to plan a wedding luncheon. Mrs. Flackney must give the staff their instructions. You must decide which gown to wear, and everything else must be packed. And—"

Fortuity grabbed hold of her hand and tugged her toward the carriage. "Come along, Seri. Leave them to another proper kiss, and then I am sure Essie will join us."

Thorne almost groaned as Blessing stepped back into his embrace, slid her hands up his chest, and hugged her arms around his neck. He caught hold of her and pulled her tight against him.

"Until tomorrow, my treasure."

She tortured him with a slow kiss and a teasing flick of her tongue to his. "Until tomorrow," she whispered, then tore away, ran to the carriage, and hopped into it with such grace and agility that he drowned in admiration of her.

"Until tomorrow," he repeated under his breath, knowing he would count the hours until he held her as his wife.

Chapter Sixteen

E VEN THOUGH SHE was all warm and fluttery about becoming Thorne's wife, a part of her mourned what she would soon leave behind. Blessing trailed her fingers along the cool smoothness of the brass tube of her telescope, sadly smiling at her blurry reflection on it. This was her last private time in her precious observatory, the most priceless and thoughtful gift she had ever received from Papa.

She swallowed hard against the risk of tears and reminded herself that if she indulged in a weeping spell now, her nose would still be red as a raspberry at half past eleven, when she and Thorne exchanged their vows.

"Exchange our vows," she repeated aloud, making that delightfully fluttery feeling shift to a feverish pounding that sent her in search of a sheet of notepaper to use as a fan. She wanted... *Oh my*, what *did* she want? She tried to remember everything she'd read in Serendipity's scandalous books, but they had been heavy on innuendo and light on intricate details that would have been extremely helpful right now. Mama had always promised to have the *wedding night talk* with her daughters whenever such a talk would be relevant. Sadly, consumption had denied her the ability to keep that promise.

"Essie—what are you doing in here? It's not even dawn," Serendipity called from the doorway. "And in your nightdress and dressing gown, no less? You should still be abed. Today is a big day."

Blessing shrugged, not quite sure how to make her sister understand. "Saying goodbye, I suppose."

"Goodbye? To whom?"

"Memories. Ghosts. Things that will never be the same after today." She moved to the wall of windows and stared out at the fading stars and the hint of a pale glow creeping across the horizon.

The light scuffle of footsteps across the worn Persian rug warned her that Serendipity was joining her. She soon found herself enveloped in a sisterly hug from behind.

"You will always have your memories," Serendipity whispered as she tightened her arms around Blessing's shoulders. "And the ghosts, too. Mama and Papa will always be with us."

"But it will never be the same."

Serendipity shifted with a heavy sigh. "No. It will not." She stepped back and turned Blessing to face her. "But then, life never is. The one constant in this world is change, remember?"

"You sound like Mama."

"Thank you." Serendipity gave her a sad smile. "Someday, I hope to be just as wise and kind and able to see the good in things as her."

Blessing returned her sad smile. "I would say you have quite a good start on those things, sister. Better than the rest of us, in fact."

"Oh, I am not so certain about that." Serendipity turned toward the door and firmly steered them across the room. "I am proud of you, by the way."

"Thank you. But what for?" Blessing knew her sister was trying to distract her from realizing they were headed back upstairs to their beds.

"For being brave enough to trust your heart and give your Lord Knightwood a chance. I do believe he loves you."

"Bravery had nothing to do with it. It was fear."

"Fear?"

"Fear of hearing about his death because of some ridiculous duel. Fear of never seeing him again. Fear of discovering what the world would be like without him in it." Blessing slowly shook her head as they climbed the stairs. "It almost suffocated me—that fear."

"And yet you faced it and overcame it."

"I suppose."

"You suppose?" Serendipity gave her a teasing shake. "You should be impressed when I impart such words of wisdom."

"Oh, I am, dear sister. Trust me. I am."

They laughed together as they crossed the sitting room and tiptoed into the bedchamber.

"I am not asleep, and what have you two been into without me?" Fortuity sat up in her bed, her hair a laughable mop of tangles that made her scowl less effective. "Out with it. I want to know everything."

Blessing went to her and tugged on her knotted curls. "How many times must we remind you to braid your hair and wear a cap to keep it from becoming a ratty bird's nest?"

Fortuity pushed her hand away. "I fell asleep whilst writing." She twisted around, searching the bedclothes until she came up with several sheets of parchment and her pencil. "Thank goodness the graphite didn't mark the sheets again. Mrs. Flackney's looks are most scathing when the laundress tattles on me." She squinted at the window. "Now, what is going on? Is something amiss? First light is barely upon us."

"I couldn't sleep," Blessing said as she perched on the end of the bed. She tapped her temple. "Too much going on in here for me to close my eyes." She allowed herself a heavy sigh. "So, I went to my observatory, and Seri came down to drag me back up here."

"I hardly dragged you," Serendipity said as she made herself comfortable on the other side of the bed. "She said she was saying goodbye," she told Fortuity.

"Goodbye to whom?" Fortuity asked.

"To everything I have known up to this point in my life." Blessing turned so she could gaze out the window as the sun slowly rose. The sky and all it held always helped her center herself and find a bit of peace. "You know I do not handle change well, and that is all that we have had for over a year now."

"The one constant in life is—"

Blessing stopped Fortuity before she could finish. "Yes, yes. I know. Serendipity already quoted Mama quite effectively, thank you."

"You sound as though you are having second thoughts about marrying." Fortuity nudged her shoulder. "Are you?"

"No. I want to marry Thorne, and I am most excited to start that chapter of my life. But..." Blessing didn't know how to explain the churning mess of contradictory emotions knotted in the center of her chest. "It is complicated."

"It is normal," Serendipity said. "Or, at least, I think it is. I am sure all brides go through this." She fetched a comb from the night table and set to untangling Fortuity's hair. "At least you know your husband and agreed to marry him because you love him," she told Blessing. "Imagine all those poor girls bargained off to marry someone they have never even met."

"And think of the ones promised to men old enough to be their grandfathers." Fortuity flinched and snatched the comb away from Serendipity.

"Yes, I am well aware of my good fortune," Blessing told them both. "And I do indeed love Thorne—but so many things will change."

"Indeed, they will." Fortuity nodded. "You will not have to wonder which sister stole your best stockings, ruined your favorite reticule, or lost your place in the book you were reading."

"Nor will you have to hurry to the breakfast buffet out of fear that your brother and sisters have snatched up all the warmest scones and hot chocolate, and left the cover off the coddled eggs, and allowed them to grow cold." Serendipity unbraided her hair and combed her fingers through the curly tresses. "You also will not have to wait for more water to be brought up because your sisters beat you to it and used it all."

"What else?" Fortuity frowned and tapped her chin. "Oh yes! And never again will you ruin your fresh stockings when you step in a warm, wet spot on the rug where one of Gracie's pups has piddled because she failed to get the poor thing to the door fast enough." She leaned closer to Blessing. "Unless you have dogs in the house. Then you might still have that particular problem."

Blessing laughed, the knot of nervousness in her middle loosening tremendously. "Cats. Remember Lady Roslynn's cats?"

Fortuity nodded. "Ah, that's right. Cats." She shrugged. "You should be fine, then." As she continued combing out her snarled hair, she glanced at the wardrobe. "Why is your gown not hanging at the ready? Have you still not decided?"

Blessing stared at the wardrobe, wishing the thing would come to life and say, *Here. Wear this.* "I am not wearing Madame Couire's silvery-white creation that I wore to our ball. It would be awful of me to remind Thorne of the evening that I refused him."

Serendipity nodded her agreement, but Fortuity narrowed her eyes. "But if you wore it, it would negate that refusal as you became his wife. It might remedy that bad memory for him and replace it with a joyful one."

"No." Blessing frowned at the wardrobe, then smiled as the solution came to her. "I shall wear the gown I wore the first night we met. The pale blue satin with the sheer overlay of deep blue flowers."

"A lovely choice." Serendipity rose from the bed and stretched while gazing out the window. "Since it appears there shall be no more sleeping, shall I ring for Meggie and ask her to draw you a bath?"

"I suppose so." Blessing drew up her feet and hugged her knees, rocking herself like she used to do as a child. She wanted to marry Thorne, really, she did, but she was so afraid. She knew nothing about running a household. When Mama had passed,

Serendipity had taken up that task. What if she was a disappointment to him? What if she disappointed him in her *wifely*
responsibilities? "Do none of your books go into detail about
what is expected of me tonight when we…?"

Serendipity paused on her way to the bellpull and stared at
her. "When you…" She fluttered a hand as if trying to help
Blessing finish her sentence.

"Good heavens, Seri." Fortuity rolled off the bed, yanked
open the bottom drawer of her night table, and started rummag-
ing through it. "Sometimes the thickness of your head utterly
amazes me. Essie's worried about what to do tonight." She
glanced over her shoulder at their eldest sister. "In *bed*."

"Exactly." Relief that at least Fortuity understood her nervousness somewhat eased the tension in Blessing's shoulders. "I
know about the kisses. Those are divine and so…so…"

"So *easy* to naturally manage?" Fortuity finished for her. She
straightened from the drawer while paging through the book in
her hands.

"Yes." Blessing squinted at the title but couldn't make it out.
"Which one is that, and does it go into detail?"

"That is not one of mine," Serendipity said as she rejoined
them on the bed.

"No," Fortuity said. "It is one of mine. Mrs. Mortimore highly
recommended it."

"That book shop is most questionable, and you know it."
Serendipity scowled at her, then glanced at the bedroom door.
"But hurry. Meggie will come to fetch Essie for her bath any
minute. You know how efficient she is."

Blessing scooted closer, leaning forward and hugging her
knees even tighter. "Read it, Tutie. Do not leave out a single
word."

Fortuity came to a certain page and sat straighter as though
surprised. She turned the book and showed it to Blessing. "Here is
a picture entitled *most common copulation*."

Blessing squinted at the drawing of a nude woman spread-eagled on a bed with a nude man jammed between her thighs. The woman had her head turned as if staring off into the distance, and the man was arched back as though stricken with some sort of spasm that affected his entire body. "She looks bored, and he appears to be in pain."

Serendipity turned the book so she could study it. "That does not look very pleasurable at all, does it?"

Blessing pulled the book closer and peered at the paragraph beneath the illustration. "What does it say? Is the woman just supposed to lie there and not move? It looks as though she is bearing it until the man has finished with whatever he's doing, I suppose?"

Serendipity sat back as though dubious about the whole thing. "That cannot be accurate."

"How would you know?" Blessing asked, wondering what erotic secrets her eldest sister had kept from her.

Serendipity clamped her mouth tightly shut and looked away.

"Out with it, Seri." Blessing poked her shoulder. "What have you done?"

"I have not *done* anything." Serendipity jutted her chin higher, then cleared her throat and rolled her shoulders as if ridding herself of a weighty burden. "I sort of...came upon something. Quite by accident."

"And you didn't tell us?" Blessing said with a gasp before poking her sister again. "You secretive little minx. Share! Right now. Especially if it is something I need to know in order to keep from disappointing my future husband!"

Serendipity resettled herself and primly clasped her hands in her lap. "It was before Mama died. At our country house. I had gone to the stables to saddle Locket for our morning ride, and I heard what I thought was someone in sheer agony." She cleared her throat again and stared down at her hands. "It turned out to be Tom—the one who always helped Papa choose and train the new horses—and Alice the milkmaid."

"And?" Blessing wished her sister would get on with it. This information could prove to be crucial to her and Thorne's happiness. "What do you mean, *it turned out to be* them?" She shook her head. "They're married now and still work at our estate. Surely it was not anything dire?"

Serendipity fixed her with a stern glare. "That depends on your definition of 'dire.'"

"Well, get on with it, then." Blessing poked her again.

"Stop poking and I will."

"Fine." Blessing sat on her hands to keep from nettling her sister into spewing the rest of her tale rather than eking the story out one painfully slow dribble at a time.

"I followed the…uhm…sounds of anguish to one of the stalls at the far corner of the stable." Serendipity clutched her throat and wet her lips as if suddenly growing quite disturbed. "They were both in a state of undress." She paused and blinked hard. "Complete undress, actually. In an impassioned embrace. Up against the back of the stall with Alice's legs wrapped around Tom's waist, him holding her wrists against the wall over her head and rutting into her with thrusts so hard that I thought the boards behind them would surely snap in two." She visibly swallowed hard. "Alice did not in any way appear to be bored. Her expression conveyed a state of extreme bliss, as did her shouts to Almighty God."

"And what about Tom?" Fortuity asked in a rapt whisper.

"Growled and roared like a wild beast." Serendipity pressed her hands to her flaming cheeks. "His words were not intelligible, but he seemed most pleased as well."

"So, we should do the act standing up, pressed against a wall?" Blessing said as she snatched up Fortuity's book and fanned herself with it. The room had become unbearably warm. "That would ensure us both the greatest amount of pleasure?"

"It would seem so," Serendipity answered.

Blessing nodded and fanned herself faster. "Thank you, sister. That was most helpful." She glanced at the bedroom door and frowned. "I think I shall tell Meggie to let the bathwater cool some before I enjoy it. Heated water presently holds no attraction."

"I understand completely," Serendipity said. "I believe I shall enjoy a cooler bath this morning as well."

"Me too," Fortuity agreed.

<hr/>

"LORD RAVENGLASS AWAITS in the parlor, my lord," Cadwick announced from the doorway. "Shall I see that he is served a refreshment while you finish dressing?"

Thorne tilted his chin higher to aid his valet in tying his cravat. "Send him up, Cadwick. Lyles is nearly done with me."

"Very good, my lord."

The butler disappeared, and soon thereafter, Viscount Ravenglass stepped into the dressing room with a wide grin and a wicked gleam in his eyes. "Ready to be leg-shackled, old boy?"

"More than you will ever know." Thorne turned from eyeing himself in the mahogany cheval mirror. He straightened his white waistcoat as his valet brushed even the slightest evidence of lint from his best black tailcoat. He winked at his friend. "Come to make sure I am not late?"

"Come to make sure you do not miss the appointment completely."

Thorne found himself suddenly filled with a somberness beyond measure. "Trust me, old friend, if the past few days without my precious treasure have taught me anything, it is that I cannot imagine a life without her. I would not miss our vows for anything in the world."

Ravenglass shifted to one side, attempting to dodge the fluffy white feline entranced with the buckle on his polished black shoe. "Does your lady love enjoy the company of cats as much as your mother?"

"Gads, I hope so. The place is overrun with them." Thorne

tugged on the pristine white cuffs of his shirt to pull them out past the sleeves of his black coat. "I have yet to convince Mother they would all be much happier in the stable, where they could spend their days chasing mice rather than tripping the servants."

"Indeed." Ravenglass frowned down at his pant leg, then bent to pick off several strands of cat hair before shooing the kitten away. "Why is it the white felines always rub on the black trousers and the black felines shed their fur on the light pantaloons?"

"The sly things conspire against us, old boy." Thorne shook his head. "They can be most endearing but never make the mistake of presuming you can control the wily little furies."

"Sounds like women." Ravenglass chuckled.

With a laugh, Thorne motioned for his friend to precede him out into the hallway. "I shan't agree or disagree on that count. Someone might overhear and report me either to my wife or my mother—both of which could prove disastrous." *His wife.* Gads, he liked the sound of that.

As they reached the main floor, he turned into the parlor. Ravenglass followed, watching the floor as he walked and deftly sidestepped a pair of kittens intent on tripping him. "Where is your mother, by the way? I thought to give you both a ride to the Broadmere residence."

"Already there." Thorne headed to the liquor cabinet. While he was anxious to make Blessing his wife, a drink to settle his nerves would not go unappreciated. "She wanted to help with whatever might be needed, since it has not been all that long since the Broadmeres lost their parents." He held up a bottle of port and waited for Ravenglass's nod before pouring them both a generous glass.

As he passed the front window, he paused and frowned. "That hackney, there. Pulled extremely close to yours, did it not?"

Ravenglass joined him at the window. "How odd. I believe that to be the same one that was parked on the other side of the street when I arrived. That is most definitely the same driver, without a doubt. Rather strange for one to tarry so long in this part of Mayfair, wouldn't you say? I know they come and go, but how often do they come and sit?"

"Probably a physician attending to one of my neighbors." Thorne sipped his drink while noting that every window of the hired carriage had its black shades drawn and tightly fastened down even though the day was bright and clear. Not a rain cloud as far as the eye could see. He shrugged away the observation and turned from the window. "As much as I hate to sully this day with mention of the man's name, do we yet have confirmation that Lord Montagne—pardon me, the *new* Earl of Myrtlebourne—has, in fact, taken our advice and left London?"

"According to my contacts, the man is crossing the channel as we speak." Ravenglass meandered around the parlor as he sipped his port. "Lady Myrtlebourne has been sentenced to hang with the next lot due to the gallows." He snorted out a hearty burst of air as though trying to clear his nostrils of a terrible stench. "I find it most disturbing that Montagne does not face a similar fate. Why did the Broadmeres not unleash their solicitor and have the man hauled away?"

"While I cannot say for certain, I believe they feared Montagne would bribe his way to freedom, and then become even more of a problem when they no longer had anything to hold over him. Theirs was a well-played bluff, and thankfully, it worked." Thorne hated that Constance, Lady Myrtlebourne, would pay the ultimate price whereas Montagne had gone free. But the memory of her cruel haughtiness to anyone she deemed *beneath* her assuaged his conscience somewhat. He rolled his shoulders to rid himself of the dark subject. "I never should have brought up the unpleasantness on this glorious day. Nothing but joyful topics from this moment on—agreed?"

"Most definitely." Ravenglass set his empty glass aside and pulled his watch from his waistcoat pocket. "We best be off, old friend. Better to arrive early than late."

Cadwick appeared with Thorne's hat and gloves as if he had

stood in the hallway with his ear pressed to the parlor door. "Mrs. Hartcastle asked me to assure you that the new lady of the house shall find her rooms in good order, and that Lady Roslynn herself inspected them and approved."

"Good." Thorne tugged on his gloves. "And is my mother happy with her new rooms adjacent to the gardens?"

"Yes, my lord." The butler's expressionless face somehow became stonier. "Lady Roslynn is quite overjoyed, and informed me that her cats are pleased as well."

"Well, we would never want the cats unhappy, now would we, Cadwick?" Thorne couldn't resist goading the man, knowing he despised the felines.

"No, my lord," the butler replied with a dullness in his tone that made his feelings quite clear. "We would not."

Thorne struggled not to laugh as he headed down the hallway and out the front door. As he stepped outside, he donned his hat before skipping down the steps. "A glorious day," he told Ravenglass while casting a smile at all creation.

"Indeed, it is, old friend. Indeed, it is."

"Knightwood!" someone bellowed in an oddly deep voice that sounded almost contrived.

Thorne turned toward the shout. Gunfire exploded, and he found himself knocked back off his feet with his left shoulder ablaze with excruciating fire. His hand clutched to it, blood streaming through his fingers, he tried to roll and stand as the street in front of his home erupted into chaos. Horses screamed. Carriages rattled and people shouted. Another shot went off, hitting him in the back of his right leg, high in the thigh. It knocked him forward, enraging him even more.

The hackney driver split the air with a sharp whistle then slapped the reins, and the vehicle careened out of sight.

Deafened by an unholy roaring that he came to realize was the sound of his own blood pounding through his body, Thorne fought Ravenglass as his friend tried to help him. "Get me in your carriage. We have to catch that bastard!" he growled. "It has to be

Montagne. We cannot let him near Blessing."

"You are in no condition to catch anyone." Ravenglass caught hold of him by the front of his jacket and dragged him up the steps and into his home. "Fetch the physician! At once!" he shouted as he continued dragging Thorne down the hallway toward the kitchens. "The constable, the watchman—and fetch the runners as well! This is bloody Mayfair, for heaven's sake, not Seven Dials."

Through all of this, Thorne fought to free himself, grappling with his friend. The physical agony ripping through him was nothing compared to the terror in his heart. He had to get to Blessing, had to protect her—or if he could not, then Ravenglass should. "Leave me and get to the Broadmeres! They must be warned."

"I shall send word to them as soon as we get you on the table. We must slow the bleeding until the physician arrives."

Thorne clenched his teeth and pushed up with his good leg, groaning from deep in his gut, both from frustration and pain. "Now, send word. Now! It could already be too late."

"I can go, my lord." Donnelly, the footman and messenger Thorne had sent to the Broadmere residence once before, stepped up to the kitchen worktable, tensed as though ready to take off like a shot.

"Yes. Go." Thorne gripped the edges of the table as Ravenglass tightened a rag around his upper thigh in a makeshift tourniquet, and Cook pressed more rags against his bloody shoulder. "Run, man!" he roared after the footman, fighting to lift his head and watch the lad shoot out the door. "Run like you have never run before."

Chapter Seventeen

BLESSING HELD TIGHTLY to Lady Roslynn's hand as their carriage rattled through the streets. A queasy lightheadedness had her gulping for air to keep from casting up her accounts. This could not be happening. Today was her wedding day, her and Thorne's. She swallowed hard and gasped, drowning in her fears. They should have gone to Gretna Green, should have left London, then Thorne would be at her side, safe, charming, and as frustrating as ever—instead of shot while standing in front of his home.

Serendipity reached across and tapped her knee. "I know it must be an almost insurmountable task, but you must try to calm yourself, Essie. Breathe slowly, else you may swoon again."

Swoon. Blessing had always scoffed at females who succumbed to such dramatic silliness, but never again. Not after her world had spun into darkness and tossed her into a bottomless pit when she heard Thorne had been shot not once, but twice.

She closed her eyes and forced herself to ease the air deeply into her lungs, held it for a count of five, then released it once again. She needed to be strong. For Thorne. No more fainting.

Lady Roslynn squeezed her hand tighter.

Blessing opened her eyes and met the poor woman's teary-eyed gaze. "He will be all right," she said as much to herself as to the dear lady. "We must not consider otherwise."

"He has to be," Thorne's mother whispered. "I cannot bear it if he is not."

Neither can I, Blessing thought as she looked away, unable to endure the terror on the woman's face.

"Will we never arrive?" Fortuity asked while leaning out the window in a very unladylike manner.

Blessing wondered the same, but knew that a large part of the problem was because Chance and six armed footmen surrounded the carriage on horseback as they made their way to the Knightwood townhouse in the heart of Mayfair. Her brother could be an irritating fool at times, but he would protect his sisters as long as he drew breath. He had left an additional line of defense at Broadmere House to ensure the rest of their sisters remained just as safely guarded.

"We should not have bargained with that devil," Blessing told Serendipity.

"We feared he would bribe his way to freedom, remember?"

"You and Tutie should have shot him when you had the chance."

"That particular thought has crossed my mind," Serendipity said while scowling out the window.

"Are we certain it was Montagne?" Lady Roslynn asked while clutching a lacy handkerchief to her chest.

Blessing cast a pained glance at Thorne's mother, unsure exactly how much Lady Roslynn knew about her son's rather indelicate notoriety. After all, the woman's hearing loss was quite pronounced. Perhaps that had proven to be a blessing for her, rather than a curse, and protected her son's image in her eyes.

Lady Roslynn gave her a quivering smile and patted her hand. "I know what my son was," she admitted softly. "That is why I asked. Are we certain it was not another enraged husband seeking revenge?"

With a defeated shrug, Blessing shook her head. "I do not know, my lady. All I know for certain is that he *must* be all right— and hopefully, quite angry about having our wedding day ruined." She needed lightheartedness right now. They all did. But she found it impossible to hold a smile for long. She would do better once she saw Thorne and knew him to be safe.

As the carriage stopped, she found herself on the edge of the seat, ready to bolt out the door, but forced herself to wait until Chance offered to help them all out.

"Well done, Essie," he told her as he held tightly to her hand while she stepped down to the walkway. "Take heart now. You are not alone."

Not trusting herself to answer, she ran up the steps and burst inside. "Take me to him," she told the wide-eyed butler. "Now!" she added when the man failed to move.

"Lord Knightwood needs his rest," said a short, barrel-shaped man with wild white hair as he ambled down the stairs with a black leather satchel in one hand and a glass of some golden beverage in the other. "I do not recommend disturbing him at this time."

"I do not recommend your standing in my way, sir." Blessing charged past him, then paused at the top of the stairs. "Which room?" she shouted down to the butler staring up at her in even wider-eyed wonder. "And if you do not see fit to answer me, I shall search every one of them until I find him."

The white-haired man pointed his drink at her and puffed like an insulted toad. "Who is that young woman?"

"Lady Blessing Abarough, Lord Knightwood's betrothed," Chance answered tersely. "My sister—and I am the Duke of Broadmere. Who the devil are you?"

The gentleman backed up a step and offered a proper bow. "Dr. Sebastian Tattersol." He lowered his voice. "Lord Knightwood suffered two very severe wounds, Your Grace. It is imperative that he rest."

Blessing descended a few steps, jabbing the air and shaking her finger at the irritating little man. She halted midway down the staircase. "Do not whisper your information to my brother as if I am some sort of ninny incapable of understanding you. Lord Knightwood and I were to be married today until this…this…hell storm. I demand to know his condition before I go to his bedside and see to his care. You will speak to me directly, sir. Now!"

The physician glanced at her brother.

"Tell her," Chance ordered the man.

Dr. Tattersol nodded, then turned and gave Blessing a conciliatory bow. "His lordship was shot in the left shoulder and quite high in the back of his right leg." He paused and made a face as if finding it extremely distasteful to speak to a lady in such insensitive detail. "I repaired the damaged tissue as much as possible. He was very fortunate in that the bullets passed through with no damage to nearby bones. His extreme loss of blood, while quite concerning, will, hopefully, have flushed out the wounds properly and prevent infection from setting in. Therefore, I did not bleed him further. All we can do now is keep the wounds clean, change the dressings as necessary, and see that he rests." He glanced at Blessing's brother again, then turned back to her and dipped another nod. "Whisky and laudanum are at his bedside. Administer as needed for his pain."

"Thank you," she forced out even though she'd had to wring the information out of the man. She shifted her glare back to the butler. "Take me to him. Now."

The servant bowed, then hurried up the stairs. "This way, my lady."

Blessing followed, finding herself almost breathless with worry, fear, and dread. "Calm down," she told herself. She had to be the strong one now. Thorne was alive. That irritating doctor had seen to him. Now she would nurse him back to health. Serendipity and Fortuity could help her. Between the two of them, they had taken care of Mama—the very best of care, their dear mother had often said. They would do the same for Thorne.

The butler opened the door to a darkened room that reeked of an almost choking smokiness that Blessing immediately recognized. She wrinkled her nose and pointed at a table bearing a brazier of smoldering coals ruining the air. "Get that mess out of here," she said. "Burning wet herbs and whatever else is mixed in there to create that stench will only cause him to choke and breathe shallower." She hurried to the window, yanked open the curtains, and pushed up the sash as far as it would go.

"But Dr. Tattersol insisted it would help his lordship balance his humors," the butler said.

Blessing turned from the window and advanced upon the man. "What is your name?"

"Cadwick, my lady."

She pointed at the brazier again. "I know of what I speak. My mother suffered with consumption, and one of those braziers nearly took her from us sooner rather than later." She took another step closer, not allowing herself to look at Thorne until she had the air of his room cleared and put in order. "I am the lady of this house now. Or soon will be. I suggest you decide at this very moment if you wish to remain in my employ. Understood?"

The butler hurried to do her bidding.

Only then did Blessing allow herself to look at Thorne. The unnatural frailty of his appearance made her head swim and threatened to throw her to the floor. She steadied herself by grabbing hold of the bedpost, breathing deeply, and holding the breaths to a count of five. Scolding herself for such weakness, she forced herself to stand straighter and made her way to his side.

He lay too still among those pillows, looking as though his wounds had drained him of every last drop of his blood. His left shoulder bulged with layers of dressings secured by bandages wrapped around his bare chest. Unable to resist, she combed her fingers through his dark hair, raking it back from his face. Angry red scrapes on his chin and cheek made her bite her lip. Had he done that when he fell to the ground after the bullets cut through him? She kissed his forehead, pressing her lips against his skin and staying there, not only because the touch of him brought her comfort but because Mama had always said that was the best way to check for fever. Praise God Almighty there was none. "Thank you, Lord," she whispered against the coolness of his flesh. She prayed it stayed that way.

She pulled a chair closer and settled down beside the bed with her gaze fixed on his slow, steady breathing. After checking the bandages to ensure that fool doctor had not wrapped them too tight, she sat back in the seat and folded her hands in her lap. She scowled at the residual smoke still hanging in the air. Burning herbs and what had smelled like horse dung for gunshot wounds? "I mean, really," she muttered. If Thorne had suffered from an ailment of the lungs, burning sage to create a cloud of smoke to ease him would have made sense. She blinked hard and fast against the sting of tears as she remembered reading an herbal aloud to Mama, and how they had worked their way through the many remedies to try to find her any relief possible.

"Put in a good word for him, Mama," she whispered. "He is much too young to die—and…and I love him."

The draperies fluttered as a stronger breeze shushed its way into the room. Blessing smiled. "You put in a good word for him too, Papa. Please?" Her parents had always lovingly vied for their children's attention—each wanting to be their offspring's favorite.

She leaned forward and rested her hand on Thorn's forearm. His muscles flexed and rippled beneath her fingers as if sleepily recognizing her touch. He was so nicely made. She let her gaze travel across him and suddenly wished for her fan.

The bedclothes had been folded back and allowed to rest across his stomach, revealing his broad chest and abdomen covered with dark hair that seemed to sweep into a ridge down his center and point lower like an arrow guiding her to…

She rose, wrung out the cloth in the bowl of cool water, and pressed it to her throat before dabbing it across his forehead and cheeks.

"Oh dear heavens," his mother said from the doorway. "Has fever already set in?"

Blessing turned to Lady Roslynn so the matron could read her lips. "No. I just thought it might let him know I was here while he slept."

Thorne's mother moved to the end of the bed and fixed a worried frown on her son. "He seems so…vulnerable."

On impulse, Blessing gently raked her fingers through his hair again, then paused and pressed her palm to his cheek. Without removing her hand, she turned her head and faced Lady Roslynn. "We will be strong for him. Protect him. As he would do for us if the situation were reversed."

Lady Roslynn studied her for a long moment, then wiped her eyes and sniffed, fighting against tears. "He told you."

Blessing had a fair idea of what the lady meant but didn't wish to betray Thorne sharing his mother's hearing difficulties unnecessarily. "He loves you very much, Lady Roslynn. Your happiness and comfort mean the world to him."

"You are a kind girl," the lady said, her sad smile returning. "I am grateful my prayers for my son were answered."

Blessing couldn't help but smile back at her. "Mind you, my papa always teased I was sometimes a curse rather than the blessing I was named for." She twitched a little shrug. "Something about my obstinance."

Lady Roslynn laughed softly. "I am sure I have no idea what he meant by that."

"Neither do I." Blessing settled back down into her chair. She fixed her gaze on Thorne's sooty lashes resting on his pale cheeks, willing him to heal quickly so they could hunt down Montagne and give the evil cove a proper thrashing.

Lady Roslynn drew another chair over to the other side of the bed and lowered herself into it. "I shall help you keep watch—if you do not mind?"

"You are his mother. You have every right to keep watch over your son."

With a nod of thanks, Lady Roslynn shifted her focus back to her son's face. "He is nothing like his father," she said as if speaking more to herself than Blessing. "That is his greatest fear." She huffed a silent laugh. "Or it was until he thought he had lost you." She tore her gaze from Thorne and locked eyes with

Blessing. "Please be kind to my boy. I beg you."

Blessing rested her hand over her heart. "I will, my lady. I promise."

Someone lightly tapped on the bedroom door. Knowing Lady Roslynn hadn't heard it, Blessing told her, "I thought I heard someone at the door," then went to answer it.

Serendipity, Fortuity, Chance, and Ravenglass stood in the hallway, their expressions varying between enraged and worried.

"I wanted to check on you before I returned home." Chance took hold of both her hands and leaned in close as if determined to read the secrets of her soul by looking into her eyes. "Seri and Tutie wish to stay here and help however they can, but I dare not leave the others to themselves until the reprehensible devil responsible for this has been captured." He flinched with frustration. "I shan't attempt to get you to come home, because I know you too well. But please take every precaution, Essie. I beg you. Seven sisters can be a chore, but I cannot imagine my life without each and every one of you nettling me to the ends of the earth." He pecked her cheek. "I love you, Essie. Send for me immediately if—"

"I will." She couldn't bear for him to finish that sentence. It held too much darkness and pain. "And thank you, brother. I would never say this in front of the others, but I do not know what I would do without you."

Chance grinned, then turned and shot Serendipity and Fortuity a smug look. "You heard her."

Both sisters feigned wide-eyed innocence.

"I heard nothing," Serendipity said, before turning to Fortuity. "Did you hear anything?"

Fortuity shook her head. "Not a thing."

Chance turned to Ravenglass, who lifted both hands and backed away while shaking his head.

Surprising herself, Blessing laughed. "Hug the precious ones for me," she told her brother. "And apologize to Felicity for all the wasted treats, and ask if she will help Cook with another wedding luncheon once Thorne heals enough for us to say our vows."

"I am certain she will not mind." Chance gave her an up-and-down scowl. "I do not like leaving you here unprotected."

"I am staying here, Your Grace," Ravenglass told him. "And I have already sent word to those I trust the most to assist me in guarding the premises."

"Good man." Chance gave the viscount a grateful bow, then nodded to his three sisters. "I pity the unsuspecting oaf who believes he can outwit these three." He shook his head and blew out a disgruntled huff. "And there are four more at home who are just as cunning."

"Be safe, Chance," Blessing called out as her brother turned to leave. "You are the only brother I have."

He winked and shook a finger at her. "Remember that the next time I vex you."

She blew him a kiss, then turned back toward the bedroom, but paused with her hand on the door. "I should tell Lady Roslynn that her household has increased."

"Before you do," Ravenglass said, "you should know that we are almost positive it was Montagne. My contacts who watched to ensure he left England confirmed that the man never showed to board the ship crossing the channel."

"I knew Seri and Tutie should have shot the devil when they had the chance." She barely opened the door and peered inside. "Forgive me, but I must get back to his side. I know his mother is there, but I want him to know I am as well."

Ravenglass bowed. "I understand, my lady, and rest assured, you shall be informed of any new developments."

Blessing looked to Serendipity and Fortuity, who both gave her reassuring smiles and nodded.

"Pray for his recovery," she told the three of them, "or all the protection in the world is for naught."

❧

HE HAD TO get to her, but he couldn't move. Darkness swirled around him. Muddled images, faces blurred by he knew not what, danced around him, taunting that his darling Blessing was about to die. He heard them chanting it in their deadly song.

Thorne thrashed, or tried to, fought to push himself to his knees so he might escape the strange place, but his limbs didn't respond. Something had bolted his arms and legs to the earth with the heaviest of iron shackles.

"Blessing!" he roared. "Blessing, I am coming!"

A gentle coolness pressed against his burning flesh, dabbing as though attempting to ease him. "Free me," he begged the tender touch. "Release my bonds. I must save her."

"She is safe," an angelic voice told him. An angel. It had to be an angel that had somehow found him in this hellish place. For only an angel could be heard above the din of the demonic furor howling for Blessing to die.

"Go to her," he begged the angel. "Please—keep her safe until I can get to her."

"Blessing is safe," the angel said as the cool wetness touched his forehead again.

"Swear it," he demanded. If an angel swore something to be true, then it had to be, or the Almighty Himself would cast it out of heaven. Or so he thought. That had to be right. Surely God would not allow them to speak falsehoods. "Swear my precious Blessing is safe."

"I swear on everything I have ever loved that your Blessing is safe."

Thorne found it easier to breathe now, but it troubled him that the angel sounded sad—even tearful. "Why do you weep?"

"I weep to make you stronger," the angel said, "to heal you with my tears. Your Blessing waits for you. She needs you to return and hold her in your arms."

Thorne wasn't sure, but it felt as though a smile pulled at his mouth. "I will return to her," he promised softly. "Tell her so—and tell her that I love her."

"I will tell her," the angel whispered close to his ear, then pressed a kiss to his temple. "And she loves you too."

"You promise?"

"I promise."

⚈⚈⚈

IN A DRESS splattered with whisky, bone broth, and a dose of laudanum Thorne had thrashed out of her hand, Blessing sagged back into the chair beside the bed. She prayed that he fought the fever as hard as he fought her whenever she tried to minister to him. She rested her hand on his arm, his flesh so hot it was a wonder he didn't burn her. She had finally managed to get a little willow bark tea down him, but who could say if it was enough to break the fever? At least, it hadn't yet.

Ravenglass, Lady Roslynn, and that useless physician assured her his wounds had not turned putrid, nor appeared inflamed. She had shocked them all by getting Serendipity and Fortuity to help her change his bandages so she could see for herself. The wounds did look to be healing with an acceptable level of redness and bruising, but if that was the case, what was the root of this terrible fever? It had to be something to do with the bullets. She had read somewhere how the metal of the projectiles, even once they were removed, could still taint the flesh and cause sickness.

And poor Thorne most assuredly had sickness. Moaning. Shouting. Thrashing and cursing.

She raised a shaking hand to her head and massaged her throbbing temple. Her poor sisters. A silent yet almost hysterical laugh shook her. They could now say they had seen a man fully naked. And so could she—but somehow, it hadn't mattered because all she cared about was getting him well. She reached out and gently stroked his forearm, hoping that the violence of what had to be horrible dreams had passed. Laudanum could be a curse that way. It helped him escape the pain but tormented his mind. Mama had hated it and refused to take it until her suffering became more than she could bear.

Blessing sagged forward and rested her cheek on his arm, soaking in the feel of him and willing him to heal. Bone-deep weariness nagged at her, but she refused to leave his side. She closed her eyes and sent up yet another silent prayer. *Heal him. Save him. Make him all right.* Disjointed words, but Mama had always told her it was the heart behind the prayer that mattered.

She vaguely heard a light tapping on the door but ignored it. Thorne was finally still and seemed to be resting peacefully for a change. She refused to move or speak out of fear that it might jostle him back into the terrors of one of his inner battles.

"My lady?" Meggie called out softly. Chance had sent the girl over from Broadmere to help his sisters and, if Blessing wished, to stay on as her lady's maid. "I brought some tea—for you, my lady. To keep up your strength."

Blessing forced herself to sit up and wearily motioned her into the room. She tried to smile but failed. "Thank you, Meggie."

The maid hurried in, set down the tray, poured a steaming cup, and brought it to Blessing. "Extra sugar and cream, my lady. I know you rarely take it that way, but, begging your pardon, you look as though you need it." The girl twitched her small, upturned nose, making Blessing envision her as a thoughtful rabbit. "I can have you a bath drawn right quick, if you like. Lady Serendipity said she would sit with Lord Knightwood so you could have a nice, hot soak and rest for a little while."

Blessing sipped the sweet concoction that resembled treacle and tried not to gag at the cloying sweetness. "I do not wish to leave him that long." She turned and stared at Thorne. With each passing day, the sickly, dark circles under his eyes became worse.

"His breathing is easier than yesterday," Meggie said. "That right there is a grand sign, I tell you."

"He does seem more at peace, but that fever..." Blessing shook her head. "Nothing we do seems to break it."

"Mam always used feverfew or willow bark."

Blessing forced down another sip of the syrupy tea, then rubbed her gritty, burning eyes. "Seri and I tried both, but with him like this, it is difficult to get enough down him to do any good. If only he could become lucid enough to drink without us having to pour it down his throat."

"Shall I at least help you change into a fresh gown for when he wakes?"

Blessing knew the girl was only trying to help and lift her hopes, but she merely wished to be left alone with Thorne until he opened his eyes and recognized her through his feverish haze. "Perhaps later, Meggie. Thank you, that will be all."

"Yes, my lady." Meggie dipped a nod and left the room.

Blessing slid the teacup onto the bedside table, then combed her fingers back through Thorne's hair. Some of the unruly strands insisted on sticking to his damp forehead, so she wet a cloth and washed them aside. "You need a hair trim, my lord." She tipped her head to one side and smiled at him. "Although I must admit you cut quite the dashing figure with your long black hair and chest only covered with bandages." She washed his face, then ran the damp cloth down his arms, praying the stubborn fever would loosen its hold. "You could be a pirate. All you need is a cutlass and a black beard."

"And a ship," came his weak, breathy reply, even though his eyes were still closed.

She stared at him, wondering if she had wanted so badly for him to speak that she had imagined it. "And lots of rum," she said quietly. "Pirates are reported to love rum."

He twitched his upper lip into a sneer. "I would rather have port, my lady." Then he slowly forced his eyes open as though the effort cost him everything. "And your kisses," he said in a raspy whisper. "I would give my soul for your kisses."

A cry burst from her as she cradled his face between her

hands and obliged him, tenderly pressing her mouth to his poor lips, all dried and cracked from the high fever no matter how many salves she had applied to them. Hot tears coursed down her cheeks, and she sobbed unashamedly as she touched her forehead to his. "Praise God Almighty—you have come back to me."

"I missed you," he said softly with the barest touch of her cheek. "So very much."

"And I you." She hugged him to her breast, then released him. "Forgive me! Did I hurt your shoulder?"

With a sleepy-eyed look, he slowly shook his head. "No, my treasure. The joy of seeing you makes all else disappear." Then a sternness came across him. "Has that bastard been captured yet? No one else has been hurt, have they?"

"No one else has been hurt," she told him, then debated on sharing the latest news they had received that very day.

"Tell me, Essie. I see trouble brewing in your eyes."

"Lady Myrtlebourne has escaped. It is thought that Montagne aided her."

To her immense relief, Thorne reacted with a lopsided smile. "They deserve each other. Any word on whether they left London?"

"None as yet." She supported his head and held a cup of water to his mouth. "We need to get this and plenty of broth into you to help you fight the return of the fever." As she eased his head back down onto the pillow, she noticed how he flinched. "More laudanum. You are hurting."

He barely shook his head. "No more laudanum. I do not wish to return to that hell." He shifted his head on the pillow and stared at her with so much love in his eyes that it made her catch her breath. "The pain is not so bad," he said. "I can bear anything now that I know you are safe and here with me."

She hugged his hand to her chest, a joyous storm of renewed hope surging through her. "I am here, and here I shall stay."

Chapter Eighteen

"LET YOUR MAID tend to you while Lyles tends to me." Thorne held both of Blessing's hands in his, rubbing the heels of his thumbs back and forth across the silkiness of her skin. She had lost weight while watching over him, and the shadows under her eyes worried him. Ravenglass had told him she had refused to leave his bedside and barely eaten during the days he had battled with the fever. "Please, Essie. A hot, leisurely bath and a decent nap in a bed rather than dozing in that chair is what you need. I cannot have you falling ill from exhaustion."

She looked at the valet patiently standing in the dressing room doorway with a bundle of linens folded across his arm. "You are not to get his wounds wet," she told the man. "They were cleaned just this morning, and we mustn't irritate the flesh further. Is that understood?"

Lyles gave her a respectful bow. "Yes, my lady."

"Lyles knows his duties," Thorne told her, his heart swelling with her protectiveness of him. "He is a good man."

She frowned at him, clearly unhappy about handing over his care to someone other than herself. "I suppose it is just as well. Viscount Ravenglass wishes to speak with you and refuses to tell me what it is about without talking to you first." She snorted. "Infuriating man."

Thorne kissed each of her hands to keep from smiling. "Go and rest. Please?"

The flintiness of her eyes softened as she touched his cheek. "Only because you appear to be doing so well. But at the first hint of trouble—"

"I will send for you," he said, hoping she wouldn't see through the false promise.

Blessing narrowed her eyes at him. "You are lying."

A hearty laugh burst free of him, making him clutch his aching shoulder. "Not even officially my wife and already you read me with as much accuracy as you name off your constellations." He caught her by the skirt and tugged her closer. "I promise I will send for you, but I cannot imagine anything going wrong. I grow stronger each day. Even Dr. Tattersol said so." He lifted his face to hers and pulled her down for a kiss. "It is my hope that within days, rather than weeks, we may marry."

"Mine too," she said softly, then gave him a nervous smile that made him frown. Before he could ask her about it, she turned away. "I shall go now, my lord, and leave you to the care of your fine manservant." Then she hurried out of the room.

"Now, what on earth do you make of that?" he asked Lyles.

"I am sure I do not know, my lord," the man said. "But one must remember the lady has been through a great deal over the past several days and allowed no one other than herself to see to your care."

"You like her even though she spoke sternly to you." Thorne was impressed. Lyles kept to himself and liked very few people. Even Cadwick had admitted as much when pressed for an answer about the valet's terseness one day.

"It is not my place to like or dislike her ladyship," the man said. He pushed Thorne's bath chair closer to the dressing room door, placed a small table beside it, and fetched the articles needed for a shave and further refreshing ablutions. "Lady Blessing and her sisters have maintained a calm throughout the household during a very turbulent time. All the servants find it quite admirable and are more than a little pleased at the respect and care they extend to Lady Roslynn." He carefully leaned

Thorne back and placed a warm, wet towel on his face.

"As I live and breathe," Ravenglass said as he entered the bedroom, "it does my heart good to see you well enough for a shave."

"It does my heart good to get out of that bed." Thorne patted the arms of the bath chair. "Well done on finding this. I know those of this quality can sometimes be hard to come by here in London."

"It was not any trouble at all. I merely sent a man to fetch one from Bath. Everyone knows the best ones are there where the *ton* takes the waters." The viscount leaned against the door and frowned down at him. "I do have some rather serious news, though, old man."

Thorne studied his friend, then braced himself for the worst. He nodded for the viscount to continue.

"I intercepted a letter meant for Lady Blessing."

"Intercepted?" Thorne thought it a bit strange that his trusted friend had taken up the habit of prying into someone else's post. "How did you know to intercept it?"

"Montagne is not the creative sort," Ravenglass said. "I recognized the man delivering the message as the hackney driver from the day you were shot."

Wishing he could spring up from the chair and track the fiend down, Thorne held out his hand. "I would see this message."

Ravenglass drew the folded bit of paper from inside his waistcoat and placed it in Thorne's palm. "The man is deranged—as you will surmise upon reading that."

Thorne opened the paper and read it aloud. "*Lady Blessing—I meant to be rid of him and still will, so my Constance will stop loving him and love me instead. I relieved the world of my brother to have her for myself. Now only the bastard Knightwood stands in my way. Help me end him, and you shall be rewarded handsomely.*" Thorne looked up at his friend. "So, he murdered his brother as a way to get Constance—and not the title?"

"I am sure he wanted the title as well." Ravenglass shrugged.

"Who knows what sort of arrangement Montagne and Lady Myrtlebourne shared? After all, they invited others to join their *visits* on several occasions. We have witnesses who attested to such."

"I do not suppose you had the hackney driver followed when he left here?"

Ravenglass tipped his head and gave a smug grin. "You know me too well."

"Where are they?"

"Covent Gardens' worst. Seven Dials, in fact."

Thorne found that difficult to believe. "Constance? In that area? Are you certain?"

"Your man Donnelly confirmed it, and she might be more accepting of that rough neighborhood now that she is an escaped murderess intended for the gallows."

"True." Thorne scratched the stubble of his yet-to-be-shaved face, still struggling to believe that all of this had come about because the lust-crazed Montagne had become obsessed with Lady Myrtlebourne, and Thorne had foolishly bumbled into the middle of it.

"What do you wish done?" Ravenglass glanced at Lyles. "And can everyone in your household be trusted?"

The valet hardened his ever-sour expression and gave a curt nod. "My loyalty to Lord Knightwood is unquestionable."

"I trust Lyles." Thorne leaned back again and motioned for the valet to begin. "After all, not once has he slipped while putting that blade to my throat."

Lyles applied a liberal froth of shaving soap and, with his usual efficiency and care, gave Thorne a perfect shave without so much as a single nick.

"You did not answer," Ravenglass said. "What do you wish to do to resolve the Montagne Myrtlebourne issue once and for all?"

Thorne waved away the hand mirror Lyles held in front of him for inspection of his handiwork. "If I could get there without aid of a crutch or a bath chair, I would confront the man and give him a taste of the lead he gave me." He accepted a toothbrush coated in tooth powder from Lyles, then scrubbed his teeth and tongue, ridding himself of the foul aftertaste of the laudanum concoction he hoped never to use again. After rinsing his mouth with water, he rinsed it a second time with a hearty mouthful of *Eau de Bouche Botot*, welcoming the refreshing taste of gillyflower, cinnamon, ginger, and anise. As he wiped his mouth, he fixed a hard stare on his friend. "You know there is only one way we will truly be rid of the man and his madness."

Ravenglass's expression hardened, his distaste for the matter clear. "We are not murderers, Knightwood. Neither of us."

"No, we are not," Thorne agreed. "But neither are we cowards afraid to protect those we love. I will not have Blessing or her family harmed because I allowed the wants of my cock to lead me where I should never have gone." He gripped the arms of the bath chair, shame and frustration threatening to overwhelm him. His precious Blessing was paying for *his* sins, and he refused to allow it to continue. Making up his mind, he shifted his weight to his good leg and scooted forward. "Help me stand."

"But your leg…" Ravenglass nervously opened and closed his mouth, greatly resembling a fish out of water. "The doctor said you would be weak for quite some time because of the fever. You should not try to stand."

"I know my body better than he does." Thorne rocked closer to the edge of the seat, doing his best not to put too much strain on his left shoulder, which burned and ached like a raging inferno. "Give me a hand, Ravenglass. Lyles! You help too."

"Is this wise, my lord?" the valet asked with a rare expression of doubt.

"I have never been accused of being wise, Lyles. Now do as I ask."

"We better help him," Ravenglass said, "or his arse will land on the floor, and then there will be hell to pay with Lady Blessing."

"Yes, my lord." Lyles took a position on Thorne's left, and

Ravenglass stood on his right.

"Whatever you do, Lyles, do not pull hard on my left arm and stir my shoulder even worse than it is. Hold me about the ribs, if you can." Thorne leaned forward, rocking all his weight to his uninjured left leg as Ravenglass held tightly to his right arm. "On the count of three, gentlemen. One…two…three."

With a mighty groan to fuel the effort, Thorne shoved upward and stood. Lyles slid underneath his left arm without yanking on it and held tight to his middle, while Ravenglass pushed up under his other arm and supported him on his right.

Head swimming and a cold sweat peppering his flesh, Thorne sucked in great, deep breaths and kept his gaze locked on the wall in front of him. He could do this. He would not retch, nor would he collapse. For Blessing's sake and the sake of their future, he would do this, and do it well.

"You have gone a bit green around the gills, old boy," Ravenglass said. "Shall we sit you back down?"

"No," Thorne said, forcing the words through clenched teeth. Ignoring the angry churning in his gut, he shifted and put some weight on his injured leg. "Bloody hell!"

Ravenglass and Lyles kept him from dropping, then eased him back down into the bath chair.

"That is plenty for today. Now leave off with your stubbornness and see sense, or I shall inform Lady Blessing." Ravenglass glared at him, then looked to Lyles. "A glass of water for him would not go amiss. I doubt he can stomach anything stronger at the moment."

"Do not talk around me as if I am too incapacitated to speak for myself." Agonizing pain shot through Thorne's leg as he shifted in the chair. "Bloody hell, I have rightly stirred the demons now."

Lyles handed him a glass of water, then placed a cool, damp cloth across the back of his neck. "To curb the need to retch, my lord."

After taking a sip, Thorne handed the glass back to the valet, then held the wet linen tighter against his nape. It did help ease the queasiness. "I cannot give in to the pain or the weakness." He sucked in a deep breath, held it, then blew it back out. "I must get back on my feet with the greatest of haste."

"And do what?" Ravenglass took to pacing, his curt stride shouting his frustration. "We can send someone to the Dials to deal with Montagne and his doxy. It does not have to be you."

"It has to be me." Thorne twisted in the chair to defend his argument eye to eye but wrenched his injured shoulder. The agony sent a swirling mass of black spots blinking through his vision, and an ominous roar thundered in his ears. His stomach clenched with a warning gurgle, and he clapped a hand across his mouth.

Lyles leapt toward him with an empty basin and held it as he spewed out the contents of his boiling innards.

Ravenglass descended upon him. "You are much better than you were but are still quite unwell. By the time you gain the strength to throttle the man with your own two hands, who knows what evil the devil will have stirred?"

Thorne sagged back into the chair. "Bloody hell." He needed to rant, needed to rage, and all he had the strength to do was sit in a damnable bath chair and vomit into a basin. "Not a word of this to Blessing. Understood?" When the viscount didn't answer, he thumped his fist on the arm of the chair. "Understood, Ravenglass?"

"Forewarned is prepared." Ravenglass puckered with a particularly stubborn scowl. "She should be informed, as should her brother, the duke. The Broadmere family is large. Who is to say that if she does not respond to this letter or at least acknowledge it, Montagne may decide to attack one of her sisters to convince her to help him?"

"How is she supposed to respond if the messenger did not wait for said response?"

"The man informed Cadwick that he would return on the morrow for the lady's answer. I overheard him say so myself, and that helped to convince me to intercept the letter and bring it to your attention rather than Lady Blessing's."

Thorne scrubbed a hand across his mouth, relieved that his stomach was settling now that his wounds had returned to the bearable ache he could manage. "Did you make Cadwick aware that he was not to speak of this to my mother either?"

"I did." Ravenglass handed Thorne the glass of water and nodded for him to drink. "Your staff's loyalty to your mother and her felines has not gone unnoticed."

"Good." Thorne narrowed his eyes. "We shall draft a reply for the messenger to carry back to Montagne so the man believes his threats have been acknowledged. I believe our first response in this game of cat and mouse should be one beseeching him for mercy—just to see how he reacts. What say you?"

"Providing you agree to warn Lady Blessing and the rest of the family?" Ravenglass arched a brow at him.

As much as he hated involving Blessing any more than she already was, Thorne grudgingly admitted that his friend was correct. "Fine. But not until she has enjoyed her bath and a refreshing nap free of the worrisome burden this will surely add to her."

Ravenglass nodded. "Agreed." He caught hold of the back of the bath chair and wheeled Thorne over to the side of his bed. "You should rest as well. She will accept this news much better if you appear stronger and well rested when it comes time for tea."

"You are well on your way to becoming an annoying nurse-maid," Thorne told his friend.

"Good." Ravenglass offered his hand to help Thorne back into the bed. "Annoying you is one of the few delights of my life."

⋘⋙

THORNE LOOKED SO hale and hearty with his white shirt of the finest lawn stretched across his broad chest and open at the throat. His loose trousers of the softest buckskin, held up by braces, and paired with stockings and shoes, made it seem as though he could jump to his feet at any moment. Even with him temporarily confined to the bath chair, his handsome strength threatened to melt Blessing into a puddle of breathless fluttering. This man would be her husband. Quite soon, in fact.

Refreshed from her bath and a luxurious nap in a bed overflowing with pillows, she seated herself in a chair beside him and reached over to squeeze his hand. "I feared this day would never come," she whispered, almost choking on the words. She blinked hard and fast, trying to stop the happy tears and failing. She swiped them away, embarrassed at being so emotional. "Goodness me. What a silly ninny I am."

Thorne kissed her hand and clasped it to his heart. "Not a silly ninny at all. You are my precious treasure, and I am more thankful for you than you will ever know."

But something in his eyes gave her pause. "What is wrong?"

He bowed his head and kissed her hand again before lifting his gaze to hers. "I fear our game with Montagne and Lady Myrtlebourne is not yet finished."

A heady mix of rage, hatred, and the unfairness of it all crackled through her like a windswept blaze. "What now?" She braced herself, clenching her teeth until her jaws ached.

Thorne tipped the slightest nod at Ravenglass, who sat across the sitting room from them. "Show her."

The viscount's troubled look filled Blessing with the unreasonable urge to fly out of the room and never look back. But she had never been a coward and was not about to start now. She lifted her chin, squared her shoulders, and sat taller as he crossed to her and held out a note.

"This arrived for you earlier today," he said, his manner wary.

"For me?" She took the message, noticed the broken seal, then looked back up at him while fighting to control both her tone and the feeling of being intruded upon. "And how did you come to have it in your possession, my lord?"

"I intercepted it when I recognized the messenger as the same man who drove the hackney carrying Montagne on the day he shot your betrothed."

"I see." She would accept that answer for now even though she resented the invasion of her privacy. Determined to stop her hands from shaking, she slowly unfolded the dreaded thing and read it.

"The man is mad." She reread the disturbing message, then turned to Thorne. "How could that fool even begin to think I would help him do you in? I love you."

Serendipity, Fortuity, and Lady Roslynn beamed at her from the settee on the other side of Thorne. She rose and handed them the letter so they could read it too.

"We must hunt him down and shoot him." She turned to Ravenglass. "Since you have yet to act upon this disturbing matter, I must assume you cannot stomach the challenge, so I shall do it myself."

"Essie!" Thorne shook his head at her. "Ravenglass has yet to address this for several reasons—he thought you and your family should first be informed, and I told him that I wished to handle it myself."

Contrition pricked her conscience. Lord Ravenglass had been nothing but kind and helpful. "Forgive me, my lord. You have been most protective of all of us since this mess began. I should not have slandered you so." Then she turned and shook a finger at Thorne. "You are in no condition to *handle* anything and will not be so silly as to attempt to do so."

"Essie—"

"Do not *Essie* me, or I shall retract the permission I gave you to use my pet name." She was in no mood to be reasonable. Not when an insane devil threatened everyone she loved. "Now, what is our plan to end this worrisome business?"

"Your betrothed wishes to stall the demented cove until he is strong enough to take control of the matter himself." Ravenglass shot a smug look at Thorne.

Blessing held her breath and counted to ten to keep from giving a most inappropriate response to such a ridiculous notion. Instead, she clasped her hands in front of her waist and asked, "Stall him how?"

"I suggest you think long and hard before answering," Fortuity warned Ravenglass and Thorne. "She has already held her breath once. That indicates she has reached a most dangerous level."

"Held her breath?" Ravenglass asked.

"An exercise her mother taught her," Thorne said. "Now is not the time to discuss it."

"As I asked," Blessing said in a much louder manner that they would do well to heed, "stall him how? And are you *stalling* Lady Myrtlebourne as well?"

"The messenger said he would return tomorrow to pick up your response and deliver it," Ravenglass told her.

"My response." Blessing narrowed her eyes and took to pacing around the room. "So, we plan to follow the man, find the self-proclaimed earl, and offer him the same treatment he gave to Thorne—yes?"

"There is no *we* in this matter," Thorne said with a fierce scowl. "I will not have you endangered any more than you have already been."

"Says the man sitting in the bath chair because he is so weak from a raging fever caused by two gunshot wounds."

"Essie!" Serendipity hurried over, took hold of Blessing's hand, and escorted her back to her chair. "*You* cannot be the one to finish this. I know Mama and Papa taught us independence, courage, and the belief that we can do anything we set our minds to—but *this* is not one of those occasions. I beg you to see sense. This matter is better left to the men. Please be reasonable. Look into your heart and mind and heed the advice Mama and Papa would surely give us all at a time like this."

Blessing caught her bottom lip between her teeth and bowed her head. She wanted to shriek with rage and charge off to punish the devil who had caused Thorne so much pain and suffering. But as much as she hungered for revenge, a small part of her knew Serendipity was right, and that her wisdom should be noted.

She pulled in a deep breath but no longer felt the need to hold it. Lifting her head, she arched a brow first at Ravenglass, then angled it at Thorne. "So, tell me, my lords, what are your plans to end this torture for us all?"

Thorne reached over and gently took her hand. "I need to do this, Essie. Handle this in my own way. I have seen what this has done to you, and it grieves me because it is my fault. I deserve to suffer for my past. You do not."

"You make my heart hurt when you say things like that."

"It is my love for you that makes me say them." He pressed a kiss to the backs of her fingers so tender that she almost wept. "Ravenglass and I intend to compose a letter that will properly start this evil game of cat and mouse. I will keep you informed, but I forbid you to get any closer than that." He leaned toward her and tugged her in so he could brush the sweetest of kisses across her lips. "You are my heart, Essie. I cannot bear to lose you."

On the verge of tears, she touched his cheek, then smiled at the smoothness of his jawline in an attempt to distract herself from crying. "You have had a shave, my lord."

"I wondered if you would notice." He turned his head and kissed her palm, sending a warm fluttering through her.

Snuffling across the room pulled Blessing's attention to her sisters and Thorne's mother. All three openly wept as if someone had just died.

"Heaven help us," she whispered more to herself than Thorne.

He grinned and kissed her again. "Heaven already has, my love. We shall win this battle. I swear it."

Every possible thing that could go wrong churned through Blessing's mind like a storm at sea. But she forced a calm façade. After all, if she was to be a wife, did they not always have to appear to trust their husband's judgment? She hoped not, because she would not be good at pretending he was right when he was so plainly wrong. Faking an agreeable smile, she nodded. "I know we will win. We have to."

While she grudgingly admitted that Serendipity was right about a woman's limitations in this world, there was no reason why Blessing couldn't help in this situation—just a little. And no matter what Serendipity said, Blessing could never imagine Mama standing idly by and letting Papa rush into a dangerous situation that could have been better managed. And manage this situation she would. She would keep Thorne safe, since he obviously had no intention of looking after himself.

"Shall I write tomorrow's letter?" she volunteered to him. "That way he will see it written in a feminine style."

Thorne frowned, but then his furrowed brow gradually smoothed. "I suppose you could. We thought the first letter should be quite beseeching. A plea for mercy and compassion."

"Beseeching?" she repeated, almost gagging on the word.

"Yes." He nodded. "That will provide us with a modicum of time while waiting for his response. I am certain it will be a coarse one."

"Indeed." Blessing rose, crossed the room to the writing table, and seated herself, all the while silently chanting, *This will buy me time to think of something as well.* She selected a sheet of their best stationery, inked her quill, then stared down at the blank page, completely incapable of coming up with anything remotely *beseeching*. Curses, threats, and general ranting came to mind, but nothing meek and pleading. She turned to Fortuity. "You are going to have to do this. All I can think of are the multitude of ways I wish for the man to suffer and die."

"Essie!" Serendipity subtly tipped her head in Lady Roslynn's direction as if warning Blessing to mind her tongue around her future mother-in-law.

Thorne's mother offered Blessing a curt nod. "I understand completely. If it were me writing that letter, I would only be able to threaten the bastard—not placate him with mewling."

Thorne choked on his tea, and Ravenglass barked out a laugh.

Fortuity shooed Blessing away from the writing table, took up the quill, and immediately scratched out a message while reading it aloud. *"Lord Myrtlebourne."* She paused and looked at each of them. "I would assume the mad devil would take offense if I addressed him as *Montagne."*

"Quite right." Thorne held out his cup to Cadwick. "No more tea—brandy, if you please."

"Very good, my lord." The butler fetched the decanter and made the rounds of the room, topping off everyone's cups.

"Carry on," Blessing urged Fortuity, knowing her imaginative sister would never fail her.

Fortuity inked the quill again, scribbled several lines, then wafted the paper to dry the ink. "I do not like sanding. The wicked stuff ends up on everything."

"Oh, do read it to us, Tutie. Do not keep us on tenterhooks." Blessing chewed on her bottom lip, hating Montagne for monopolizing time that would be better spent helping Thorne grow stronger.

"I kept it brief." Fortuity gently blew on the paper, then squared her shoulders and read, *"Lord Myrtlebourne—I beg that you set aside your unholy plan of murder and sorrow. Escape London with your lady love and start anew. Please. I beseech you to leave us in peace, as my beloved Thorne may yet die from your earlier attack. Again, I most humbly beg you to leave us be. Lady Blessing Abarough."*

Blessing wrinkled her nose at the message's weak, sniveling tone, but she supposed that was the *feel* that Thorne wished to achieve. She sidled a glance at him, then rolled her eyes at his broad smile. "And shall I know the pleasure of putting that letter into the messenger's hand?"

Thorne's smile disappeared. "Absolutely not. No one is to go near the front door when that man arrives, and Cadwick?"

"Yes, my lord?"

"He is not to be granted admittance to this house. You will

pass the message outside to him."

The butler nodded and accepted the folded note from Fortui-ty. "Fear not, my lord. It will be handled exactly as you wish."

Blessing bit her tongue at the annoying level of difficulty added to the plan, but she kept her irritation to herself. She sipped her brandy and muddled over the options left for her to discover Montagne's location. While she wanted with all her heart to serve the man the retribution he deserved, this was one of those rare occasions where she grudgingly agreed with her sister—she should not do this herself. Even Mama and Papa would agree that their daughters should never take on a deranged murderer themselves. So she wouldn't. But that didn't mean she couldn't hire it done. She wasn't quite sure how to go about hiring someone to do such an odious task, but she would figure it out. Thorne's life depended on it.

Chapter Nineteen

B LESSING STARED DOWN at the open book in her hands, oblivious to its contents. It was a sham to keep others from interrupting her thoughts. Particularly Thorne, who had grown more fractious with each passing moment as the entire household waited for Montagne's messenger to appear at the front door.

After much wheedling, cajoling, and unabashed begging to her maid to help her find out as much as possible from the other servants, Blessing had discovered that Thorne's favorite footman, the young Mr. Donnelly, had discovered Montagne's whereabouts and reported it to Ravenglass. She struggled with her resentment about not being given that information. Crafty devils—Thorne and his dear old friend had better realize she never gave up that easily.

She'd had a word with Mr. Donnelly and felt a tad guilty about tricking him into revealing everything by having him relay his observations to Thorne while she eavesdropped on the other side of the sitting room door. The footman hadn't seemed to think it odd that Ravenglass might not have adequately informed the master of the house. Perhaps Donnelly felt Thorne preferred to hear the details from the horse's mouth.

It didn't matter. All that mattered was that it had worked, and she now knew that Montagne held Lady Myrtlebourne prisoner in Seven Dials—a place so rough and dangerous that even Blessing dared not go there. The footman reported that the murderous countess had shrieked obscenities from the depths of a squalid room above a gin palace. He had only known it to be Lady Myrtlebourne because Montagne had shouted back at her from the door, calling her by name when he told her he'd silence her by hanging her from the window if she didn't quiet herself.

"Essie?"

"Sorry?" Blessing jerked her focus back to the present and looked over at Thorne. "Forgive me. I was so engrossed in my book, I failed to hear what you said. Are you ready to return to bed? You have been in your chair for quite a while."

He arched a brow at her. "Why did you insist Donnelly speak with me?"

"Donnelly?" she repeated, scrambling to think of a convincing lie even though she hated telling Thorne an untruth.

"Essie."

"I do not like it when you say my name that way."

"That is because you know you are caught." He flinched as he shifted in the seat, then deepened his scowl. "I forbid you to go to Seven Dials."

"I would never."

"Oh, no?" His brows knotted over his narrowed eyes. "Then why were you listening at the door the entire time Donnelly spoke with me?"

"How dare you ask me such a thing!"

"The hem of your skirt was caught in the door. I saw it." He pointed at her. "What are you up to?"

She hiked her chin higher. "I am merely enjoying my book of poetry."

"You are not."

"What?"

He scrubbed his hand over his eyes, then let it drop to his lap and nodded at her book. "Do you make it a habit of reading your poetry while holding the book upside down?"

Bloody hell. She was well and truly caught, but that did not mean she would surrender and confess her plans. Thorne needed a distraction. "Send for the vicar."

He stared at her as though she had sprouted horns. "Beg pardon?"

"Send for the vicar." She dropped the infernal book into her lap and folded her hands atop it. "We have the special license. Send for the vicar so we can marry within the hour."

His dubious scowl conveyed a firm disbelief in her anxiousness to marry. "Marry within the hour without your entire family in attendance?"

"Do you wish to marry me or my family?"

"Fine." His smugness shouted his decision to call her bluff. He rang the bell from the table beside him. When Cadwick appeared at the sitting room door, Thorne never took his eyes from hers. "Fetch the vicar with the greatest of haste. My lady love wishes for us to marry before the hour is out."

Blessing swallowed hard. Perhaps she had gotten a bit carried away, but there was no going back now. Besides, they had planned to marry anyway. In fact, would have already *been* married if Thorne hadn't been shot. She stiffened her spine and nodded. "Yes, Cadwick," she said, "do hurry."

The butler pondered them both for a long moment, then bowed and disappeared.

Thorne's self-satisfied grin made her yearn to growl at him, but instead she returned his smile. "You might as well speak your mind," she told him. "Your eyes are dancing with accusations."

"Accusations of what, my treasure?"

"Accusations that my wish to marry you this very day is false."

"Do you not wish to marry me before the hour is out, as you so strongly asserted?"

"Of course I wish to marry you, or I would not have said it." Much to her dismay, her voice appeared to be getting squeakier with the strain of concealing her plotting. "I also wish to protect you from that bloody fool!"

"We agreed that I would handle the bloody fool, and you

would handle remaining safe." He reached for the bell. "I shall inform Cadwick we no longer need the vicar."

She chucked her book at the bell and knocked it out of his reach. "We are marrying as soon as the vicar arrives."

He threw back his head and laughed, then held out both hands. "Come here, my lovely—yet stubborn—treasure. Tell me what you planned to do with whatever information you discovered about Montagne."

After recovering the book and the bell and returning them to the table, she took his hands and squeezed them. "I intended to hire a person."

"Hire a person?" He tugged her closer, guiding her to his good leg. "Since we are marrying today, I think it quite appropriate for you to sit on my lap."

She snatched her hands away and pulled up a chair beside him. "I do not wish to reopen the wound on your leg—and it would not be appropriate for me to sit on your lap until we *are* married."

"Then tell me about this person you intended to hire while we wait for the vicar."

"Montagne must be stopped, and if we are honest, I believe we both know there is only one way to do that." She stared down at her hands, ashamed for even thinking of such a horrible thing. That madman had corrupted her, dragged her down to his level by making her consider murder as the only possible solution. She bit her lip and lifted her gaze to Thorne's. "But now that I ponder my plan a bit more, I realize that the likelihood of my carrying it through is very low." She sadly shook her head and whispered, "I would protect you with my life, but I do not think I can take the life of another." She gave an awkward shrug. "Unless, of course, I was cornered and forced to fight my way out to save us."

He took her hand and pressed tender kisses across her knuckles. "Let us hope it never comes to that, my love—and that is why I shall remedy the situation with Montagne. Agreed?"

"Agreed…I suppose."

"So, no more schemes, plots, or sneaking about?"

She couldn't help but scowl at him. "You ask a great deal of me, my lord."

He lifted a brow, his amused yet stern sincerity disarming. "Please?"

"Fine," she agreed with a resigned sigh. "I shall strive to behave, but I want it duly noted that I do so under protest."

"Duly noted, my love." He tugged her closer and kissed her cheek, then held her there and breathed into her ear, "Tonight, you will join me in my bed—never to leave it again."

That familiar hot fluttering that took her over whenever they kissed came to life and raged through her. Their *marriage bed*. The thought of what that meant made her wet her lips and try to breathe through the rapid pounding of her heart. "Uhm...but your injuries." She caught her bottom lip between her teeth and almost cringed while eyeing him. "We will not be able to...uhm... Will we?" She knew so little and hadn't had the time nor the courage to ask Lady Roslynn for any motherly guidance on the delicate subject.

He grew quite serious, staring into her eyes with such intensity that she found herself delightfully trapped in his gaze. "We will do what we can...as we can, my treasure. At least we will be together—as we should be."

"The vicar, my lord. Mr. Darbley," Cadwick announced from the doorway.

"My goodness." Blessing hurried to stand and put a more appropriate bit of space between herself and Thorne. She nodded at the doddering old man while trying to put all his laughable eccentricities from the pulpit out of her mind. He should have employed a curate years ago to take over his parish but insisted that his work for the Almighty was far from finished. "How kind of you to come so quickly, Mr. Darbley."

"I happened to be at the next house over offering the dowager countess words of comfort in her mourning. I had just stepped outside when your footman informed me the matter here was quite urgent." The vicar squinted around the room, nudged his smudged spectacles higher upon his nose, and then peered around again. "I am not too late, am I? Where is the ailing babe?" He patted his waistcoat pocket and gave them all a compassionate shake of his head. "I always carry a vial of holy water in case none has been obtained for the christening."

Blessing glanced at Thorne, who appeared to be holding his breath to keep from laughing. "There is no christening, Mr. Darbley," she said. "We wish for you to marry us." She motioned at Thorne. "We have the special license." A horrifying thought occurred to her. "Were you supposed to christen an unwell child today? Did someone speak to you about coming to their home to minister to them?"

The absent-minded gentleman frowned while thoughtfully wringing his hands. "Oh dear." He slowly shook his head. "No. No… Come to think of it, the hasty christening was days ago." He tapped his chin and nodded faster. "Yes. Days ago, and the little mite is much better now. I am certain of it." He toddled toward her, wobbling back and forth as if one of his legs was shorter than the other. He took her hand and patted it. "I get a bit confused when rushed, you see." He tapped his temple. "Or when I am thirsty. Might there be time for tea before the ceremony? I fear the dowager was too overset to order refreshments."

"Of course," Thorne said, before jangling the bell from the table beside him.

Cadwick appeared at the door so quickly that Blessing felt certain the butler had been standing in the hall.

"Yes, my lord?"

"A proper tea, Cadwick," Thorne said. "And do be good enough to fetch Ladies Serendipity and Fortuity along with my mother. After all, we shall need witnesses." He motioned to a nearby settee. "Have a seat, Mr. Darbley. Our tea shall arrive presently."

"Thank you, my lord." The vicar bowed and availed himself

of the seat, then cocked his head to one side while staring at Thorne's bath chair.

"I was shot in the leg," Thorne told the man, the humor in his tone unmistakable. "But I am completely on the mend."

Mr. Darbley leaned toward him and cocked his head to a more pronounced angle. "Did you say *shot*, my lord?"

"I did."

The vicar shook his head. "I thought the war had ended."

Blessing looked away so the man couldn't see her close her eyes in disbelief.

"You are marrying today?" Serendipity exploded into the room with Fortuity close behind her.

"This very hour?" Fortuity said, hurrying around her to reach Blessing first.

Blessing lifted her chin and smiled. "Yes."

"What about Chance?" Serendipity asked.

"And the rest of the flock?" Fortuity added.

"The entire church does not need to witness the ceremony," Mr. Darbley said. He held up two fingers. "We merely need two witnesses."

"I meant..." Fortuity shot Blessing an exasperated look. "I meant the rest of our sisters. Mama and Papa always referred to us as the flock."

"Ahh..." Mr. Darbley acted as if he understood, but it was clear by his strained smile that he had not. The vicar had obviously forgotten about the size of the Broadmere family even though they had always filled two entire pews whenever Mama and Papa herded them all to church. In fact, the forgetful vicar had christened each and every one of them.

Serendipity seated herself beside Blessing and scooped up her hand. "Why the hurry to marry without the entire family here?" she whispered. After leaning forward and stealing a glance at Thorne, she lowered her voice even more. "Did something...*inappropriate* happen?"

Blessing glared at her, wondering if Serendipity had misplaced her good sense somewhere in her dressing room. "Thorne and I would already be married if not for the accident. I am tired of waiting," she lied. "I thought it best to merely get on with it."

"None will care except Felicity," Fortuity said. "You know she had her heart set on helping Cook with your wedding luncheon."

"Felicity can feed us all at a later date." Blessing turned to Thorne. "Should I check on that tea? It should be here by now."

"That is probably why Mother is not here," he said, just as Lady Roslynn charged through the door with her large black and white cat cradled in her arms.

"Hera wished to attend." She settled in on the settee beside the vicar and politely nodded. "Good afternoon, Mr. Darbley."

The vicar eyed the cat while edging farther away. "Good afternoon, Lady Roslynn."

Cadwick and Donnelly the footman appeared bearing trays filled with a proper tea.

"Do serve Mr. Darbley first," Thorne told them. "Extreme thirst troubles the poor man and affects his memory."

Blessing held her breath to keep from hissing with a very unladylike snicker. Both servants remained expressionless as they poured the man a cup of tea and served it to him with a small plate filled with a sampling of cakes and delicate sandwiches.

The vicar took a sip, then frowned down into the teacup. "No brandy?"

Thorne arched a brow but, admirably, did not snort with laughter. "Cadwick—get the man some brandy. By the way, where has Ravenglass got to?"

"While waiting for…" Cadwick trailed off. He glanced at the vicar, then cleared his throat. "While watching for the *post*, Lord Ravenglass became tired of waiting and decided to go in search of it."

Blessing locked eyes with Thorne. Ravenglass had gone to Seven Dials? Alone? "Should we not wait for his return?" she asked Thorne. "After all, he is your closest friend."

"Bloody hell," Thorne growled under his breath.

"Beg pardon?" The vicar leaned forward while balancing his brandy-laced tea in his hands.

Thorne ignored the man and blew out a frustrated snort. "No. There is no certainty as to how long he might be gone. If he has not returned by the time the vicar has finished enjoying his tea, we will marry without him." He cast a grim glance around the room. "We have plenty of witnesses."

A great deal more contented than when he arrived, the vicar smacked his lips and held out his cup. "Perhaps just a few drops more, if you do not mind?"

The butler looked to Thorne, who nodded at the brandy bottle on the table among the platters of teacakes.

"Ah yes," the vicar purred as the servant filled his cup. "Nothing warms the soul quite as nicely as a good blackcurrant brandy."

"Indeed," Blessing said. She bit her tongue to keep from reminding Mr. Darbley about a cleric's more usual enthusiasm for God's word over the benefits of brandy. Now she understood the probable origin of the vicar's forgetfulness.

The man drained his cup, set it aside, then pushed up from his seat. He steadied himself after stumbling sideways before chuckling and pulling his prayer book and holy water from inside his coat. "Are we ready for the christening now?"

"Wedding," Blessing snapped.

"Essie!" Serendipity hissed.

"Ah, yes." With trembling hands, Mr. Darbley paged through this small book. "Wedding—not christening." He hiccupped. "My goodness, do forgive me."

"Might we get on with it, man?" Thorne reached over and took hold of Blessing's hand.

Mr. Darbley frowned down at his book while slowly flipping through the pages. "We could, my lord, but I cannot seem to locate the proper text."

"I, Blessing Isolde Iris Abarough, do hereby take Thorne

Knightwood to be my lawful husband," Blessing said in a loud voice that caused the vicar to jump. "I shall stay at his side in sickness and health, good days and bad, and will always honor this day's vows because I love him and want this union more than anything."

Before Mr. Darbley could comment, Thorne squeezed her hand and smiled. "And I, Thorne Alexander Knightwood, do hereby take Blessing Isolde Iris Abarough to be my beloved wife. Through sickness and health, good days and bad, I shall honor her body, mind, and soul and spend the rest of my days making her happy."

"Well, then." The vicar shrugged and stuffed his prayer book back inside his coat. "By the power vested in me by Almighty God and the Church of England, I hereby proclaim you man and wife, Lord and Lady Knightwood. Let no man put asunder what God Himself hath joined."

"Donnelly," Thorne said, "please escort the vicar back to the vicarage and ensure today is properly recorded. You may take whatever carriage you wish."

"Yes, my lord." The young footman moved to Mr. Darbley's side and politely turned the teetering man toward the door. "Come, vicar. Time to go."

"But I thought I might have more tea," the cleric sputtered as he toddled toward the door. "Is it all gone?"

"I am afraid so, Mr. Darbley." Blessing rose and herded the man into a faster pace. "Thank you so much for today."

He waved a shaking hand as he and the footman exited. "My pleasure, my lady," he called back. "My pleasure."

"Well, that explains a great deal about his sermon where he mentioned Jonah riding the whale like a horse because he hoped to catch up with Noah and his ark and give him the pair of unicorns he had forgotten." Lady Roslynn shook her head while idly stroking the sleeping cat on her lap. "I do hope the union is valid."

"The union is valid," Thorne assured his mother while offering Blessing a grin. "All of you witnessed it, heard our vows, and I sent Donnelly to ensure it is correctly recorded."

"It will be an amusing tale to tell our children someday," Blessing said.

"Indeed, it will, my love," Thorne agreed in a tone that made her shiver with heat rather than cold.

Lady Roslynn rocked her way to her feet, then deposited her cat in Thorne's lap. "I must tell Cook to prepare a proper celebratory dinner." Then she went still and gave him and Blessing a sad smile. "You two are even more united than before. I pray that helps with this unsavory battle in which you find yourselves."

"I pray so too, my lady," Blessing said. "And I pray Ravenglass makes it back to us safely."

Thorne reached for her. "Come to me, my wife. Let us seal this union with a kiss."

Wife. She never thought that word would thrill her as much as it did coming from Thorne's lips. Hurrying to him, she framed his face between her hands and kissed him with her heart and soul. When she lifted her mouth from his, he caught hold of her and held her there, keeping her from straightening and stepping away.

Staring up into her eyes, he whispered, "I love you, my treasure."

"I am glad, my lord, because it seems that I love you too."

PROPPED UP IN the bed in a mound of pillows piled against the headboard, Thorne watched the door that connected his bedroom to Blessing's. Not wishing to call attention to his wounds, he had lessened the bandages on his left shoulder and right thigh to the smallest wrappings possible.

A mirthless laugh huffed free of him. He really should thank

Montagne at his first opportunity. Somehow, the man had managed to shoot him with enough accuracy for the bullets to pass through his flesh without shattering any bone. Even the physician had marveled at such luck.

Everything still hurt like hell, but he was getting stronger—due in large part to his forcing himself to his feet at every opportunity. But even so, he was in no condition to make love to his beautiful new wife the way he wished to the first time she came to him.

The door slowly opened, and she peeped into the room as if fearing he might be asleep. He smiled at that notion. He had never been more alert in his life.

She slipped inside with her long blonde braid draped down the front of one shoulder, wide-eyed, and her bottom lip caught between her teeth, her appearance a breathtaking mix of inexperienced virgin and emerging seductress. Her soft white nightdress, sheer enough to tease him with tempting shadows of her alluring form, was open at the throat. She eased toward him, her bare feet soundless on the thick Turkish rug covering the floor.

Without a word, he pulled back the covers on her side of the bed and waited.

Still biting her lip, she slipped beneath them, pulled them up to her neck, and then propped her fisted hands atop her chest. "Uhm…I suppose you are quite weary. Seeing as how you stayed upright in your chair most of the day."

Mindful of his wounded leg, he slid closer to her and propped himself onto his right side. He smiled down at her as he tugged one of the ties of her neckline out from under the firmly tucked counterpane and sheets. "I am not weary in the least."

"No?"

"No."

"But you are still quite sore—and…and you are still wearing your bandages."

"Yes. I am sore, but not so sore as to be unable to enjoy our first of many nights together." He tugged the other tie of her neckline out from under the covers as well. "I do regret, however, that I am not quite able to remove your nightdress."

"Oh." She lay there for a long moment, then stole another nervous glance at him. "Shall I remove it, then?"

"That would give me a great deal of pleasure and prove most helpful. But do so only if you wish to, Blessing. The choice is always yours—I want you to know that."

"All right, then," she said with a breathlessness that made him ache for her even more. Rather than get back out of the bed as he expected her to do, she reached under the covers and wriggled and squirmed until she had her nightwear bunched up around her neck and could slip it off over her head. With amazing quickness, she yanked it off, then clenched the covers up to her chin as she flung it to the floor.

"There now." She gave him a nervous smile. "That's done."

He leaned over and kissed her shoulder, smiling against the warm satin of her skin as she nervously twitched against his lips. "I know you have seen me bare as the day I was born, my lady."

"Yes. Yes, I have. I had to in order to wash all the blood away." She squeaked as he kissed her shoulder again. "And I thought you would rest easier without nightclothes bunching up around you and making uncomfortable lumps and bumps."

"Most thoughtful of you." He nibbled along her collarbone as he slid a hand underneath the covers and stroked his fingertips ever so lightly around her breast.

"That is your left hand," she said, her voice hitting a high raspiness.

"Yes."

"It does not hurt your shoulder to use it?"

"Only a little, my love, and your beauty makes it ever so easy to ignore the bothersome pain."

"Thorne?"

Her use of his name made him pause, lift his head, and look her in the eyes. "What is it, Essie?"

"I do not wish you to hurt yourself," she whispered.

He caressed her cheek. "As much as I wish to, these damnable injuries make me unable to love you tonight as I would like to." He grazed his thumb across the fullness of her bottom lip, plump and reddened from her nervous chewing of it. "But I can give you some pleasure that I believe you will enjoy—if you will allow it."

"And it will not hurt you?"

"No."

Her frown gave him pause.

"What troubles you, Essie?"

"What about you? What about your enjoyment? Do men not need to achieve their pleasure to keep them from falling ill?"

While he wanted to ask her where she had gotten such an idea, he decided not to out of fear of embarrassing her. "I will not fall ill. I promise."

From the look in her eyes, the way they gleamed in the candlelight, she appeared to make a decision. "Go ahead, then. As long as it does not hurt you and make you fall ill."

"Might I uncover you, then, my lady?"

Her eyes widened even more, and she wet her lips. "I suppose...uhm... Yes, you may."

Ever so gently, he folded back the counterpane and bedsheets and failed at stifling a groan.

"Are you all right?" She rolled toward him and touched his chest, her face filled with concern.

"I am more than all right, my love," he said, his voice now raspy with desire as he nuzzled kisses along her jaw and down the satiny curve of her neck. "Your beauty—you are indeed a blessing to me." He allowed his fingers to travel lower, stroking the wonderful softness of her dips and curves.

She thrilled him with hesitant kisses along his throat and collarbone. When he shuddered, she paused and asked, "Do you enjoy that, or should I stop?"

"I enjoy everything about you, my treasure."

She pulled back and arched a brow at him, her eyes flashing

with a teasing gleam. "What about when I am fractious?"

"I enjoy the wittiness with which you snap at those around you."

"And when I am sulky?"

He leaned in for a kiss and gently sucked on her bottom lip. "I adore the way your bottom lip pokes out like you're an adorable child denied its treats."

She huffed with a soft laugh. "You possess quite the silver tongue, my love."

"My love," he repeated, his heart swelling with an all-consuming fire he had never known before meeting her. "I believe that is the first time you have ever said that to me."

She combed her fingers into his hair and looked into his eyes with a lazy smile. "I do love you—so very much."

"Then lie back and allow me to give you as much pleasure as my broken body will allow until I have healed—because I love you very much as well."

She rolled to her back but kept her fingers laced in his hair as he lowered his head and set to the task of showing his beloved bride how much he loved her.

Her breathless squeaks as he caressed and tasted her glorious breasts made him ache to join with her, but his infernal leg would never allow it. Not yet. So he worked his way lower, determined to take her to the ecstasy she deserved.

As he eased her thighs farther apart and dipped a finger into her warm wetness, she gasped and fisted a hand in his hair. He breathed her in, reveling in her mouth-watering scent of lilacs mixed with a woman filled with desire. With the tip of his tongue, he teased her with flicking nibbles and tastes while sliding a finger in and out, then adding another as he deepened the thrusts.

"Oh my—I never dreamed of such." She moved her hips and clutched his head with both hands now, bucking and arching as he closed his mouth over the nubbin of her sex and sucked with the same rhythm of his fingers working deep inside her.

She was so close. Her louder cries and the pull of her hot sweetness around his fingers urged him for more. He laved her with his tongue, then sucked harder while pumping faster.

She jerked upward, arching her back and holding in place while clutching him against her. Her groans exploded into shrieks as she spasmed and trembled. Then she sagged and slid back down to the bed, gasping as she went limp. "I never knew," she admitted to him with a breathlessness that made him proud. "Dear heavens, I never knew."

"I am glad," he said as he kissed his way back up her wondrous body, the flush of her satisfaction shading her ivory skin with a most becoming rosiness. "It pleases me to be the one to introduce you to such pleasure."

"Pleasure?" With her eyes still closed, she huffed and flipped a hand at his silliness. "That was bliss, my love. Pure bliss."

He leaned over her and kissed both her breasts, her long, slender throat, and then savored her sweet lips. "Pure bliss indeed, my love."

She opened her eyes and treated him to another of her seductively lazy smiles. "But what about your bliss?"

"Tonight, my bliss is found in yours. When I am stronger and healed a bit more, we shall find our bliss together and never wish to emerge from this bedchamber ever again."

With a serious thoughtfulness that made him wonder what she was thinking, she touched his cheek. "I am glad I decided to marry you. But…"

His heart lurched. "But?"

Her fair brows drew together over her lovely eyes. "I still wish to be me."

"I am afraid I do not understand."

"Well…we probably should have spoken about this before we married, but the right time to broach the subject never seemed to arise. The person I was before—the one who studied the stars and avoided attending every party and ball of the Season is who I wish to be."

She curled closer and snuggled against him, resting her head on his good shoulder and making it exceedingly difficult for him to think straight. "I want to take care of you and learn from Seri and your mother about the most effective way to run a household, but I do not wish to waste our time with lavish entertainments just so those of the *ton* can gossip about us."

"What about babies?" he hazarded to ask, almost dreading the answer. As one of the older Broadmere siblings, he feared she might not wish for many—if any—children. He also wondered if he had not sated her properly. Should she not still be floating in the warm lull of physical completeness? "Blessing?"

A soft, snoring sigh answered him.

"Blessing?" he repeated quietly, then kissed the top of her head.

She barely shifted and nuzzled her head more comfortably in the dip of his shoulder.

Thorne smiled. He had indeed done proper by her. Praise God Almighty. He allowed himself a deep sigh and decided that Blessing could *be* whoever or whatever she wished, as long as she did it at his side.

Chapter Twenty

I T HAD BEEN three days since Ravenglass left to search for Montagne's messenger and, with all probability, Montagne himself, even though Thorne had told the bloody fool that he wished to be the one to deal with Montagne. Frustrated beyond measure, Thorne stared out the sitting room window from his seat at the large table and chairs that Cadwick and Mrs. Hartcastle had ordered carried up to his private suite of rooms, since he had yet to conquer the stairs and make it down to the dining room. The others, Serendipity, Fortuity, and Mother, would be up soon to join him and Blessing for breakfast.

"I am worried about him too." Blessing rested her hand on his arm. "I cannot imagine why we have not heard from him."

"Since I am managing well enough with a cane now and able to dress appropriately, I shall take to the streets and search for him myself."

"You cannot." She squeezed his arm and held it tightly as if determined to prevent him from leaving. "You walk with some difficulty, still have trouble with stairs, and tire easily. How the devil do you expect to survive a trip to Seven Dials, where they will surely club you and leave you in the gutter as soon as you figure out a way to stumble out of the carriage?"

"Ravenglass could be in the gutter as we speak."

"Then send Donnelly to find him." Eyes flashing, she hardened a fierce scowl at him. "I did not marry you just to become a widow three days later."

"Send Donnelly to find whom?" Serendipity asked as she and Fortuity entered the room.

"Ravenglass," Blessing said before Thorne could answer.

Lady Roslynn came through the door next, absent-mindedly picking cat hair off her dress as she toddled over to the table. "Still no word from him?"

"No." Thorne held up a hand as Cadwick started to pour him a cup of hot chocolate. "Coffee this morning, if you please."

"Of course, my lord." The butler nodded at the footman waiting by the trays that had been carried up and laid out to serve the elaborate breakfast. "And Lord Ravenglass took two of the men he employed as guards when he left in search of Lord Myrtlebourne's messenger."

"Then why the bloody hell have we not heard anything by now?" Thorne clenched his hands on either side of his plate, ready to roar and gnash his teeth over the current state of affairs. His best friend could very well be dead, he was trapped on the second floor of his home because those damnable stairs set his leg on fire, and he had yet to properly make love to his beautiful new wife. He hit the table with his fist. "Bloody, bloody hell!"

The room went still, and the ladies and servants alike stared at him.

He bowed his head, then scrubbed both hands down his face. "Forgive me. My patience with all the challenges of late grows quite thin."

"What is all this bellowing and cursing about?" Ravenglass asked as he strode into the room. He swept a look around and frowned. "And in front of these ladies, no less? I know your mother taught you better manners than that, Knightwood."

A surge of relief and thankfulness made Thorne shove his chair back, hoist himself to his feet, and, with his cane, unsteadily limp over to his friend. He caught hold of the viscount's shoulder and squeezed. "Where the devil have you been?"

"Sit back down, and I shall tell you." Ravenglass glanced over at the trays bearing covered dishes, teapots, and coffeepots. "And might I trouble you for a cup of tea and some breakfast?"

"That goes without saying." Thorne gave Cadwick a quick nod to fetch a chair and set another place at the table. He hobbled back to his seat and lowered himself into it with a strained grunt. "Now—as I said before, where the devil have you been? We have been worried sick."

The ladies hurried to shift and make room as a footman returned with a chair and placed it at the table.

Ravenglass seated himself and leaned back, looking a bit too dusty and worn around the edges for Thorne's liking. But at least the man was alive and appeared to be well.

"I found our man," the viscount said as he added cream and sugar to his tea and nodded for Cadwick to place a generous helping of coddled eggs, kippers, and fried bread upon his plate. He made a moue of distaste as he glanced around the table at the ladies. "However, I am none too sure I should go into the details in front of present company."

"You most certainly will go into detail here and now!" Lady Roslynn pointed at him with a knife coated in butter.

"Absolutely," Blessing echoed, and her sisters nodded their agreement as well.

"Get on with it, man." Thorne shifted in his chair, gripping its arms and bracing himself for Ravenglass's story. "They are as invested in this tale as I am, and stronger and more determined ladies do not exist in London."

"Very well, then." The viscount still did not appear comfortable about speaking about such things in front of the ladies, but he carried on nonetheless. "Montagne and the countess had moved from the room above the gin palace where Donnelly observed them after following the messenger the first time."

"Where did you find them?" Thorne leaned forward and rested his forearms on the table.

"My men and I discovered Montagne's messenger behind the gin palace." Ravenglass tightened his mouth into a flat line.

"Someone relieved him of his life in a rather brutal manner that I will not describe."

"And he was our only lead to Montagne," Thorne said.

"That is why I was gone as long as I was." Ravenglass sipped his tea, then frowned down at his plate while nudging his food around with his fork. "But I did find him. Him and Lady Myrtlebourne both."

Something about his friend's voice told Thorne that the two were no longer a problem. "Go on."

"On the far side of the Dials, I came upon a trio of ladies fighting over…" Ravenglass paused and looked around the table again. After a deep breath, he locked eyes with Thorne. "They were fighting about who was responsible for paying for the removal of a pair of bodies from their establishment."

"What happened to them?" Thorne knew Ravenglass was talking about Montagne and Lady Myrtlebourne without having to ask.

The viscount puckered another sour face as if unable to rid himself of a very bad taste. "The *ladies* of the establishment said the two constantly fought, creating quite a disturbance. After a day of the room being extremely quiet, they went up to discover Lady Myrtlebourne with her neck broken and Montagne hanged."

"How awful." Blessing pressed a napkin to her mouth and bowed her head.

"Surely you did not leave them there?" Fortuity asked as she pushed her plate away.

"No, my lady," Ravenglass said. "I notified Montagne's solicitor and the Bow Street Runners so they could close the case regarding Lady Myrtlebourne's escape from prison."

"You did well," Lady Roslynn told him. "I am sure you will struggle to forget that unpleasantness, but I thank you for protecting my son and daughter-in-law."

"Daughter-in-law?" Ravenglass arched a brow first at Blessing and then at Thorne.

"Indeed. The very day you disappeared without a word is the day we married." Thorne leveled a hard glare on his friend and took on a rebuking tone, pouring all of his frustration and worry about the man into his voice. "Had you been here, you could have been a witness. Stood at my side. An honor I would have thankfully bestowed upon you." He jutted his chin higher. "Instead, you made me worry about whether you were alive or dead."

"Well, not too worried, I wager, since you survived the day by making the lovely Lady Blessing your wife."

"Had I not been crippled—"

"Had you not been crippled by your wounds," Ravenglass interrupted, "you more than likely would have gotten yourself shot again. A risk I was not willing to take. I do not have many whom I consider close friends. Feel honored that you are one of them."

"Stop fighting!" Blessing smacked the table hard enough to make the silverware rattle. "What matters now is that Lord Ravenglass is home safe, Thorne is mending well, and we no longer have to worry about Montagne or Lady Myrtlebourne—and thank heavens none of us were forced to soil our hands with their blood. May God have mercy on their souls."

"God rest their souls," everyone at the table hurried to say.

"And as soon as my fine brother-in-law is healed enough to attend," Lady Serendipity said, "Chance insists we throw the celebration of the Season at Broadmere House."

Blessing closed her eyes and groaned. Ravenglass stared at her in bewilderment, and Thorne threw back his head and laughed, feeling happier and more contented than he had in a very long while. He reached over and took Blessing's hand. "Surely we can bear one soiree for the sake of your brother?"

"One?" She snorted. "Surely you jest. He still has six more sisters to marry off to gain his inheritance. We shall have to hide in the country to avoid all his plotting." She narrowed her eyes at Ravenglass. "You appear to be a good man, my lord, albeit a bit foolhardy. And quite single. How do you feel about marriage?"

Ravenglass jumped up from his seat and bowed. "I do beg your pardon, but I hear my horse calling. Forgive me, but I really must see to him." He darted from the room before any of them could argue.

"Essie." Thorne patted her hand. "You should not tease old Ravenglass so. Especially not when he has just returned to us."

She hiked a brow at him. "Who said I was teasing?"

❧

BLESSING ROLLED OFF Thorne, exhausted, breathless, and so limp with satisfaction she was boneless. "You were so right, my love." She draped an arm across his heaving chest, her leg across his middle, and snuggled against him. "We should never leave this bed. Stay in it always and make love forever."

Thorne rumbled against her with a low, throaty chuckle. "It is good to be right and have one's wife agree."

She tickled a finger through his chest hairs and down the dark midline where the hairs swept together and ran downward. "Did you know your hairs form a trail that points to your manly bits?"

He chuckled again. "I cannot say that I ever realized that, my love."

She ran her fingertip down the trail and took hold of his heavy member that was slowly but ever so surely reawakening. "See? Straight as an arrow—right to the pot of gold."

"The pot of gold, eh?" He rolled her over and settled between her legs.

She glared at him with a scolding look. "The last time we tried that position, you said it hurt your shoulder."

"That was yesterday. I feel the need to try again."

"Do you now?" She gently stroked his warm, muscular back, taking care to avoid his sore shoulder and the healing wound just below his right buttock. "I have often wondered if Montagne was trying to shoot you in the arse."

"That is a subject for another time, and is that the sort of word my beloved wife should use?"

"What word?"

"Arse."

"I use that word and many more." She couldn't resist a wicked grin as his rock-hard length nudging her confirmed that her wonderful rogue of a husband was fully restored and ready to go again. She rocked her hips against him. "Come inside, my love. I am where you belong."

"Indeed, you are, my treasure," he groaned as he thrust into her. "Indeed, you are."

Epilogue

Knightwood Manor
London, England
January 1821

THORNE GENTLY BUT firmly ousted three cats from the bedchamber and hurried to close the door to keep them out. "They should sleep with Mother. Not us."

Propped in bed, her hands folded atop her slightly rounding middle, Blessing tipped her head to one side and smiled. "Mother Roslynn says I put out more warmth than she does, and the kitties cannot resist it."

In her growing state of pending motherhood, Blessing did indeed put out more heat than a smithy's roaring forge, but far be it from Thorne to be foolish enough to admit it out loud. Not only did he value his life too much, but he also wished to meet his child in a few months.

He got into the bed and tugged her into his arms. "Well, you are mine, and I do not like to share."

"Then what will you do when the little one arrives?"

"That is different. The little one and I shall adore you equally."

She snorted.

"You do not believe me?" He nuzzled kisses across her collarbone and nibbled his way down to her delightful breasts, which had taken on an amazing new fullness that he thoroughly enjoyed.

"Yes, I believe you."

With a heavy sigh, he ceased reveling in her bounty and lifted his head. "What is it, my love? I can tell by your tone that something troubles you."

"I fear that Fortuity is the next in Chance's sights, since he discovered that marrying everyone off at the same time is an impossibly daunting task." She idly twiddled with the end of her braid while staring off into the distance.

Thorne rolled to his back and pulled her close to settle her with her head nestled in the dip of his shoulder. "Does she not wish to marry?"

"She wishes to write her stories and someday see that they are published."

"Can she not do both?"

Blessing snorted again. "Very few men allow their wives the liberties that you do."

"I am not certain I like the way you put that." But he knew what she meant. Blessing regularly visited her observatory and sisters at Broadmere House, and he saw no problem with that. But her thoughtful frown worried him. "What are you plotting?"

She didn't answer, simply pushed up, returned to a sitting position beside him, and cast a side-eyed glance his way.

"Essie?"

"Ravenglass loves books. I remember his parlor when Seri, Tutie, and I visited him because I was worried about you." She stared at him intently. "Tutie was enraptured with all his books."

"Ravenglass does not wish to marry."

"Neither did you when we met. You told me so yourself."

"Essie."

The intensity of her look shifted from plotting to a direct glare, with him as the target. "I find your tone most annoying," she said.

"If Ravenglass does not wish to marry, we should not pressure him. Besides—did you not tell me that all the sisters must marry for love for the terms of the will to be satisfied? Are you telling me Fortuity loves him?"

She huffed at him—a sure sign his assumption was correct.

"So, she does not love him?" he hazarded to ask.

"I guess we shall just have to wait and see, shan't we?" She huffed again, turned her back to him, and pulled the bedclothes up past her ears.

Thorne cast a glance upward, silently praying for wisdom. "I love you, my treasure," he said ever so softly.

"I love you too," came her muffled reply through the covers. "Just not so much when you are trying to prove me wrong."

"I would never try to prove you wrong." He needed to make peace with her before they slept. His heart never rested if they tried to sleep when all was not well between them. "I love you, Essie—more than anything."

She backed up and wiggled her bum against him. "I love you too, and I am not angry. You will speak to Ravenglass about Fortuity? Please?"

God in heaven help him and Ravenglass both. "Yes, my love. I will speak to Ravenglass."

"Thank you, my love."

"You are most welcome, my precious treasure."

THE END

About the Author

If you enjoyed BLESSING'S BARON, please consider leaving a review on the site where you purchased your copy, or a reader site such as Goodreads, or BookBub.

If you'd like to receive my newsletter, here's the link to sign up:
maevegreyson.com/contact.html#newsletter

I love to hear from readers! Drop me a line at
maevegreyson@gmail.com

Or visit me on Facebook:
facebook.com/AuthorMaeveGreyson

Join my Facebook Group – Maeve's Corner:
facebook.com/groups/MaevesCorner

I'm also on Instagram:
maevegreyson

My website:
https://maevegreyson.com

Feel free to ask questions or leave some Reader Buzz on
bingebooks.com/author/maeve-greyson

Goodreads:
goodreads.com/maevegreyson

Follow me on these sites to get notifications about new releases, sales, and special deals:

Amazon:
amazon.com/Maeve-Greyson/e/B004PE9T9U

BookBub:
bookbub.com/authors/maeve-greyson

Many thanks and may your life always be filled with good books!
Maeve